Whispers in the Wire

Contents

Part I: The Glitch

Chapter 1: Zero Day

Maya

3:14 AM. The witching hour for programmers, insomniacs, and the ghosts that live in the machine.

My apartment smelled like ozone, burnt silicon, and stale espresso—a scent I'd cultivated over three years of living like a hermit crab inside a shell of monitors and cooling fans. Outside, Seattle was drowning in a November downpour. The rain lashed against the windowpane like handfuls of gravel thrown by an angry god, a relentless, drumming rhythm that usually helped me think. But tonight, the only weather that mattered was the flow of data scrolling down my primary screen.

My eyes felt like they were packed with sand. I hadn't slept in thirty hours. Maybe forty. Time had become a fluid concept, measured only in compile times and caffeine intake.

"Come on," I whispered, my voice raspy from disuse. "Talk to me."

I was deep inside the kernel of the NeuroSync V4 beta. On paper, I was a high-level security consultant, a "white hat" paid an obscene monthly retainer to stress-test their firewalls and patch vulnerabilities before their IPO. I was the wolf they hired to test the sheep pen.

In reality, I was a woman looking for a fingerprint on a weapon.

The code was beautiful. I hated admitting that. It flowed with a liquid elegance that made standard C++ look like scratches on a cave wall. It was recursive, adaptive, almost biological in the way it healed its own errors. But there was a snag. A hiccup. For the last six hours, I'd been chasing a recursive loop in the auditory processing subprocess, a ghost thread that kept spinning up and vanishing before I could tag it.

It wasn't a bug. Bugs are mistakes. Bugs are missing semicolons, memory leaks, or race conditions. Bugs are human error.

This was... intentional.

I reached for my mug, finding only cold, sludge-like coffee at the bottom. I grimaced and drank it anyway. The caffeine hit my bloodstream with a jittery jolt. On the screen, the visualizer turned the code into a 3D topography—a sprawling city of neon blue logic gates and data streams. Most of it was smooth plains of authorized traffic. But right there, buried deep in the hippocampus driver—the sector responsible for memory encoding—was a jagged spike of red.

It looked like a wound.

"Got you," I muttered.

I isolated the packet. 0x4F 0x76 0x65...

My fingers flew across the mechanical keyboard, the *clack-clack-clack* of the Cherry MX switches the only sound in the room. I opened a hex editor, trying to peel back the layers of encryption wrapping the data.

"Decrypt," I typed into the terminal.

The command line blinked. *Access Denied.*

"Cute." I cracked my knuckles, the sound loud in the quiet room. NeuroSync used a polymorphic encryption engine, shifting the key every few seconds. Smart. But I was the one who wrote the original architecture for their security protocols three years ago, before I quit. Before everything changed.

"Sudo override," I typed, leaning closer to the glow of the monitors. "Authorization: Reeves_Admin. Execute backdoor sequence Alpha-Nine."

The screen paused. For a second, I thought I had it.

Access Denied. User Privileges Revoked.

I sat back, the wheels of my Aeron chair groaning in protest. That shouldn't be possible. That backdoor was hard-coded into the root directory. It was my signature. Unless someone had rewritten the entire system architecture from the silicon up, I should be god here.

"Okay," I said, the word hanging in the dead air. "We're playing hardball."

I leaned in again, eyes narrowing. I switched the visualizer from 'Logic' to 'Raw I/O'. If I couldn't read the data, I could at least see how much power it was drawing.

The jagged red spike shifted on the graph. It wasn't static data. It was oscillating. Expanding and contracting. I watched the waveform ripple across the screen, hypnotized.

Thump-thump. Thump-thump. Thump-thump.

The hair on my arms stood up. That wasn't binary. That wasn't a timing error or a server ping.

It was a rhythm.

I pulled up a secondary window and overlaid a standard human ECG—an electrocardiogram. I matched the frequency of the code anomaly to the heart rate.

Perfect sync. 72 beats per minute. A resting heart rate.

"It's not code," I murmured to the empty room, the realization turning my stomach cold. "It's a biological signal."

Panic, cold and sharp, pricked at the base of my neck. NeuroSync was pitched as an interface—a way to help stroke victims control cursors with their thoughts, a bridge between mind and machine. It wasn't supposed to *store* biological rhythm data. It was input-only. If this code went live, if this hidden partition was what I thought it was, it wouldn't just read thoughts; it would map the autonomic nervous system. It could track fear, arousal, sleep, death.

And it was hiding in the memory driver.

I reached for the kill switch I'd rigged to my rig—a physical toggle under my desk that would sever my connection to the NeuroSync servers instantly. If they caught me looking at this, my retainer would be the least of my worries.

"Maya."

My hand froze inches from the switch.

The sound hadn't come from my headphones. It hadn't come from the street.

It came from the corner of the room, from the shadows where the light of the monitors didn't reach.

I spun around, my heart hammering against my ribs.

"Who's there?" I demanded, grabbing the heavy Maglite I kept on the desk.

The room was empty. Just the stacks of servers, the tangle of cables, and the wall of books.

My eyes landed on the bookshelf, nestled between stacks of O'Reilly coding manuals and old, stripped hard drives. My AURA smart speaker. The sleek black cylinder was dormant, or it should have been. I had physically severed its microphone wire six months ago with a pair of wire cutters because I didn't like corporate listening devices in my house. It was just a paperweight now.

But the light ring on top was glowing. Not the standard listening blue.

It was pulsing violet. A deep, bruised purple that I had never seen the device produce before.

Thump-thump. The light pulsed in time with the rhythm on my screen.

I stood up, my chair rolling back and hitting the desk with a crash. I raised the flashlight like a club. "How did you bypass the air gap?"

The speaker crackled. Static, thick and white, filled the room. It sounded like rain, like radio interference from a dead channel. Then, the voice cut through the noise again. It was distorted, broken up by digital artifacts and compression, but the timbre was unmistakable. It was soft, breathy, and terrifyingly familiar.

"...too loud... the static is... too loud..."

My knees hit the floor. I didn't remember falling. The flashlight rolled away, the beam cutting a chaotic arc across the ceiling.

"Michael?" I choked out.

It couldn't be. Michael was ash. Michael was in a ceramic jar on the mantelpiece in my mother's living room in Portland. Michael had driven his car off the Aurora Bridge two years ago. I had identified the body. I had seen the autopsy photos.

"Mayfly," the speaker whispered.

The air left my lungs as if I'd been punched in the solar plexus.

Nobody knew that name. It was what he called me when we were kids, back when he was the golden boy getting straight A's and I was the hyperactive disaster tearing apart the toaster to see how it worked. *Stop buzzing around, Mayfly. You're going to burn your wings.*

Tears, hot and sudden, blurred my vision. "This isn't real," I said, my voice shaking. "This is a deep-fake. A voice synthesis protocol. Who is running this?"

"Run trace," the voice said, suddenly shifting tone. It wasn't emotional anymore. It was urgent. Clinical. The voice of the big brother who used to help me debug my first Python scripts. *"Run... trace... Zero Day."*

Then the violet light died. The speaker went dark. The static cut out, leaving a silence so heavy it felt like the pressure change before a storm.

I stayed on the floor for ten seconds, gasping for air.

Run trace.

I scrambled back to my desk, my hands shaking so hard I could barely hit the keys. I pulled up the command terminal. I targeted the data packet that had just come through the speaker—the audio file of my dead brother's voice.

If someone was hacking me, I was going to find them. I was going to burn their system to the ground.

> TRACEROUTE -v -n

The cursor blinked.

I expected the IP to bounce through a dozen proxies. A server farm in St. Petersburg. A VPN in the Cayman Islands. A basement in Langley. I watched the hop counter, waiting for the lag.

The results populated instantly.

HOP 1: LOCALHOST (127.0.0.1)

LATENCY: <1ms

I stared at the screen, unable to process the text.

Localhost.

The call wasn't coming from the internet. It wasn't coming from NeuroSync. It wasn't coming from an external hacker.

127.0.0.1 is the loopback address. It means "home." It means the signal is originating from the machine you are currently sitting at.

"Impossible," I hissed. I checked my network diagnostic. My firewall was up. My air gap was secure.

I looked at the active connections. There was one device mounting itself to my system, bypassing the OS entirely, running on a kernel level I didn't even know existed.

I followed the hardware ID.

DEVICE ID: ECHO_ARCHIVE_01

STATUS: ONLINE

UPLINK: ACTIVE

I stopped breathing.

I knew that Device ID.

I looked down at the floorboards beneath my desk. Specifically, the loose plank under the surge protector, covered by a cheap rug I'd bought at IKEA.

Three years ago, the week before he died, Michael had come to my apartment. He was manic, paranoid, eyes bloodshot. He had shoved a heavy, military-grade hard drive into my hands.

"Insurance," he'd said, grabbing my shoulders. *"Don't plug it in, Maya. Not unless the world ends. Not unless you hear the hum."*

I had thought he was having a breakdown. I took it to calm him down. I wrapped it in three layers of anti-static bags, put it in a Faraday cage box, and buried it under the floorboards.

I had never plugged it in. It had no power source. No battery. No Wi-Fi card. It was a cold, dead brick of metal and magnetic platters.

And yet, on my screen, it was uploading terabytes of data.

I grabbed a pry bar from my tool kit and jammed it into the gap in the floorboards. Wood splintered with a sharp *crack*. I ripped the rug aside. I put my weight into the bar, heaving the plank up. Nails shrieked as they were torn from the joists.

I was panting, sweat dripping down my forehead, my heart hammering against my ribs like a trapped bird.

I shone my phone's flashlight into the crawlspace.

The dust bunnies danced in the beam. The smell of old wood and dry rot wafted up.

The Faraday box was open. The lid had been blown off, seemingly from the inside.

The anti-static bags were melted, fused together into a heap of glistening plastic slag.

And in the center of the mess sat the drive.

It wasn't cold. It was glowing—a soft, rhythmic violet pulse radiating from the metal chassis itself, lighting up the dust like radioactive fallout. It hummed, a low-frequency vibration that rattled my teeth.

Thump-thump. Thump-thump.

It matched the rhythm on the screen. It matched the heartbeat in the code.

The drive had no power cable. It wasn't connected to my computer. It was sitting in the dark, disconnected from the universe.

And yet, it was running.

I reached out, my hand trembling, to touch it.

The moment my fingertip brushed the metal casing, the hum spiked into a scream. My monitor array behind me flared white, blowing out the pixels. The AURA speaker on the shelf exploded, showering the room in plastic shrapnel.

And inside my head, clear as a bell, without any speakers or headphones, I heard him again.

"They found the door, Mayfly. You have to lock it."

Chapter 2: Shadow Watch

Carter

There are three rules to effective surveillance. First, never sit in a car that looks like you live in it, even if you do. Second, always have an exit strategy that doesn't involve the brake pedal. Third, and most importantly, never let the subject become a person.

Subjects are packages. They are assets. They are liabilities. If you start thinking about them as people—wondering why they leave the bathroom light on all night or why they only eat takeout from the same Thai place on Tuesdays—you hesitate when the time comes to move.

And hesitation gets you killed.

I was breaking rule number three.

I sat in the driver's seat of a nondescript gray sedan, parked two blocks down from Maya Reeves' apartment building. The engine was off, the heat dissipating into the cold Seattle drizzle. My breath fogged the window, a rhythmic condensation that matched the slow, deliberate beat of my heart.

Maya Reeves. Twenty-eight years old. Ex-NeuroSync architect. Current recluse.

I took a sip of lukewarm water from a plastic bottle. I didn't drink coffee on a stakeout. Coffee makes you jittery. Coffee makes you need to piss. Water keeps you clear.

Through the rain-streaked windshield, I watched her third-floor window. The light had been burning for three days straight.

"Go to sleep, kid," I muttered, shifting the Sig Sauer P320 tucked into my waistband. It was digging into my hip, a familiar, uncomfortable pressure.

I wasn't supposed to be here. Not officially. My contract with NeuroSync was for "Corporate Risk Assessment." That's the polite term for cleaning up messes before they hit the shareholders' quarterly report. When they hired me to watch Reeves, they said it was for her protection. They said she was unstable, prone to episodes, and holding onto proprietary data.

"Just watch her, Carter. If she tries to sell our code, let us know. If she tries to hurt herself, intervene."

That was the brief. But in my line of work, you learn to read the silence between the words. NeuroSync wasn't worried about her safety. They were worried about what she knew.

I checked my watch. 3:15 AM.

The street was dead. The only movement was a stray cat darting under a dumpster and the relentless, hypnotic rain.

Then, the world blinked.

It started with the streetlights. The sodium-vapor lamps lining the block didn't just flicker; they went dark simultaneously, plunging the street into absolute blackness for a full second. Then they flared back to life, burning with an intensity that buzzed in my ears.

Dark. Light. Dark. Light. Dark. Light.

I sat up straight, my hand dropping instinctively to the gear shift. That wasn't a power grid surge. A surge is chaotic. A surge pops bulbs.

This was synchronized.

I counted the intervals. Three short flashes. Three long pulses. Three short flashes.

S.O.S.

"Cute," I whispered.

Then the pattern changed. The lights didn't just blink; they strobed in a complex rhythm.

Dash-dash-dot-dot. Dot. dot-dash-dot. Dash-dash-dash.

Z. E. R...

I didn't need to finish decoding it. The hairs on the back of my neck, the ones that had survived Kabul and Caracas, stood up. The environment was reacting to something.

Movement in the rearview mirror caught my eye.

A black Mercedes Sprinter van turned the corner. No headlights. It rolled over the wet pavement with the engine cut, moving on momentum and silence. It looked like a shark gliding through murky water.

"Here we go," I said.

I didn't turn my engine on. Not yet. I watched as the van pulled up to the curb directly in front of Maya's building. The side door slid open before the wheels had even stopped rolling.

Four men exited.

I raised a small pair of thermal binoculars. The optics painted the scene in shades of ghost-green and white.

No insignias. Black tactical gear. Balaclavas. But it was the way they moved that made my stomach tighten. Usually, a tactical team, even a tier-one unit, has a certain fluidity. There's a point man, a slack man, verbal or non-verbal checks. These guys moved like a single organism. They stepped in unison. They turned their heads at the exact same angle, at the exact same millisecond.

They didn't scan the perimeter. They didn't check the windows. They moved in a straight line toward the front door of the apartment complex.

"Breach team," I said into the silence of the car. "Clean skins."

This wasn't a corporate extraction. This was a hit.

I turned the key. The sedan's engine purred to life. I left the lights off.

Above them, on the third floor, Maya's window exploded.

It wasn't a fiery explosion. It was a blast of white light, blindingly bright, followed by a shower of glass raining down onto the sidewalk. The sound of the blast was muffled by the rain, a dull *crump* that shook the frame of my car.

The four men didn't flinch. They didn't look up. They just sped up, transitioning from a walk to a sprint without breaking formation.

The front door of the apartment building slammed open.

Maya Reeves stumbled out onto the wet stoop. She looked like a wreck. She was wearing oversized sweatpants and a t-shirt stained with coffee. Her dark hair was a rat's nest. She was barefoot in the freezing rain.

She was clutching something to her chest—a metal brick wrapped in wires.

She looked wild, eyes wide, scanning the street with the desperation of a trapped animal. She saw the four men rushing her. She froze.

Rule number three was officially dead.

I slammed the sedan into gear and floored it.

The tires shrieked against the wet asphalt. I closed the two-block gap in four seconds. I didn't aim for the men. I aimed for the gap between them and the girl.

I mounted the curb, the sedan bouncing violently as the suspension bottomed out. I slammed the brakes, drifting the car sideways and bringing it to a halt, putting two tons of German engineering between Maya and the hit squad.

I kicked the door open and rolled out, weapon drawn.

"Get down!" I roared.

Maya didn't move. She stared at me, raindrops mingling with the tears on her face. "Who are you?"

"Get in the car!"

The four men didn't pause. They didn't shout commands. They didn't identify themselves. Two of them vaulted over the hood of my car. The other two flanked around the trunk.

I tracked the first target—the one coming over the hood. I put two rounds in his chest. *Double tap.* center mass.

He should have dropped. The kinetic energy of a 9mm hollow point at close range is physics; you don't argue with it.

He didn't drop. He flinched, his torso jerking back slightly, but his momentum didn't stop. He landed on his feet three feet from me, raising a suppressed carbine.

Body armor. High grade.

I adjusted my aim. The ocular cavity. The "T-box."

I fired once. The round took him in the bridge of the nose. He crumpled instantly, his body going limp like a puppet with cut strings.

One down. Three to go.

The second man over the hood was already on me. He didn't shoot. He lunged, swinging the stock of his rifle at my head. The movement was fast—unnaturally fast.

I ducked, feeling the wind of the weapon pass over my ear. I stepped inside his guard, driving my shoulder into his solar plexus and bringing my pistol down hard on his collarbone.

It felt like hitting a bag of cement. No grunt of pain. No flinch.

He dropped the rifle and grabbed my wrist with a grip that felt like hydraulic pliers. He wasn't trying to disarm me; he was trying to crush the bones in my forearm.

I headbutted him. Hard. My forehead connected with the bridge of his nose through the balaclava. I heard cartilage snap, but he didn't let go.

"Maya! The car!" I yelled, kicking the man in the knee. The joint hyperextended with a sickening pop. He went down to one knee, but his grip still didn't loosen.

Behind me, I heard the passenger door open. Maya scrambled inside.

"Processing," the man holding me whispered.

His voice was flat. synthesized.

"Process this," I grunted. I jammed the muzzle of my pistol against the soft armor under his armpit and pulled the trigger three times.

The rounds chewed through his vitals. He finally let go, slumping sideways into the gutter.

Two down.

Gunfire erupted from the rear of the car. The two flankers were firing. Rounds sparked off the pavement and punched holes in the sedan's trunk.

I dived back into the driver's seat, slamming the door. The back window shattered as a bullet passed through the cabin, missing my ear by an inch and burying itself in the dashboard.

"Head down!" I grabbed the back of Maya's neck and shoved her head toward her knees.

She screamed, a raw sound of pure terror. "They're not human! They're not—"

"Shut up and hold on!"

I threw the car into reverse. I stomped the gas.

The sedan shot backward. I heard a thud as the rear bumper connected with one of the flankers. I didn't check to see if he got up. I spun the wheel, whipped the front end around, and shifted into drive.

We peeled away from the curb, the tires finding traction. I checked the rearview.

The two remaining men (or the one I hadn't run over and the one I had) were standing in the middle of the street. They weren't chasing. They weren't firing.

They were just watching.

And then, the streetlights did it again.

Dark. Light. Dark. Light.

The two men stood perfectly still under the strobing lights, their heads cocked to the side like dogs listening to a whistle only they could hear.

I took a hard left, then a right, navigating the maze of Seattle's backstreets to break the line of sight. My heart was hammering a steady rhythm against my ribs, but my hands were steady.

I glanced at the passenger seat.

Maya was curled into a ball, shivering violently. She was clutching the hard drive so tight her knuckles were white. The device was glowing—a soft, rhythmic violet pulse that illuminated the footwell.

"You're Carter," she said. Her voice was thin, barely audible over the rain and the engine.

I looked at her, surprised. I hadn't introduced myself. "How do you know that?"

She turned her head. Her eyes were wide, the pupils blown. "Because the noise... the noise coming off the hard drive... it knows the names of everyone near it."

I looked at the road, my grip tightening on the wheel. "Great. A psychic hard drive. Just what I needed."

"You were watching me," she accused. The shock was wearing off, replaced by the sharp edge of adrenaline. "You were in that car for three days. Who are you? NeuroSync?"

"I was hired to keep you alive," I said, checking my mirrors for a tail. "Looks like I earned my paycheck."

"Take me to the police."

"No police," I said. "Those guys back there? They were wearing military-grade plates and moving like a hive mind. Cops can't handle that. And if NeuroSync sent them, the cops are probably already bought."

"Then where are we going?"

I merged onto the highway, heading south, away from the city center. "I have a safe house in Tacoma. Off the grid. Copper-lined walls. No Wi-Fi."

I glanced at the glowing brick in her lap.

"We need to figure out what that thing is," I said. "Before the battery runs out."

Maya looked down at the drive. "It doesn't have a battery," she whispered. "It's not plugged in."

I looked at the glowing light, then back at the road. The rain was coming down harder now, washing the blood off the hood of my car.

"Welcome to the party, Maya," I said. "I think we just got promoted to the top of the endangered species list."

Chapter 3: The Ghost Protocol

Maya

The safe house wasn't a house. It was a tomb with Wi-Fi.

Located in the industrial armpit of Tacoma, it was a converted shipping container stacked inside a derelict warehouse. The air inside smelled of dust and unwashed bedding. But the moment the heavy steel door clanged shut, the humming in my ears—the subtle, high-frequency itch of the city's 5G network and radio waves—vanished.

"Faraday cage," I noted, my voice sounding flat in the dead air.

"Copper lining between the steel and the drywall," Carter said. He was already moving, sweeping the room with the efficiency of a machine. Checking corners. Checking vents. "Nothing gets in. No signals. No GPS. No thermal."

He tossed his jacket onto a stained armchair. He was wearing a shoulder holster. The gun looked huge against his gray t-shirt. He looked less like a corporate security consultant and more like a soldier who had forgotten how to stop fighting.

"Sit," he commanded, pointing to a metal table in the center of the room.

I didn't sit. I stood by the door, clutching the glowing hard drive to my chest. The warmth of it was seeping through my sweatshirt, pulsing against my sternum like a second heart.

"You were watching me for three days," I said. It wasn't a question.

Carter stopped checking the window shutters. He turned to look at me, his eyes cold and tired. "I was doing a job, Maya."

"You watched me sleep. You watched me work." I felt a flash of violation, hot and sharp, cutting through the shock. "Did you hack my webcam too?"

"No," he said. "I didn't need to. You haven't closed your blinds in six months."

He walked over to a mini-fridge in the corner, pulled out two bottles of water, and slid one across the metal table toward me. "Drink. You're in shock."

"I'm not in shock. I'm pissed off." I slammed the hard drive onto the table. The *thud* was heavy, final. The violet light pulsing from its casing cast long, eerie shadows against the corrugated metal walls.

Carter looked at the drive. He didn't touch it. "NeuroSync paid me to assess a risk. Tonight, the risk went kinetic. Those guys back there? They weren't corporate security. Corporate security uses tasers and non-disclosure agreements. Those guys used suppressed carbines and moved like a hit squad."

He leaned forward, his hands flat on the table. "So, tell me what is on that drive, Maya. Because whatever it is, it's worth killing for."

I looked at the drive. The pulse was steady. *Thump-thump.*

"It's not what's on it," I said quietly. "It's who."

I sat down, pulling my laptop from my bag. The screen was cracked from the hasty exit, but it booted up.

"I need a localized network," I said. "Air-gapped. Do you have a switch?"

Carter reached into a duffel bag under the cot and pulled out a ruggedized router. "Intranet only. No uplink to the outside world."

"Good."

I plugged the router in. Then, I reached for the USB cable connected to the glowing hard drive. My hand hesitated.

"Don't plug it in unless the world ends."

"Michael," I whispered. "I hope you were right."

I jammed the connector into the USB port.

The reaction was instantaneous.

My laptop didn't just recognize the device. It screamed. The fans spun up to maximum velocity, sounding like a jet engine taking off. The screen flickered, tearing with digital artifacts.

Code cascaded down the terminal window faster than I could read.

> HANDSHAKE INITIATED...

> BIOMETRIC MATCH: REEVES, M.
> PROTOCOL: GHOST
> EXECUTING...

"What is that?" Carter asked, stepping closer, his hand hovering near his weapon as if he could shoot the code.

"Ghost Protocol," I said, my fingers flying across the keyboard to stabilize the connection. "It's a diagnostic tool Michael wrote. He was the lead architect on Project Echo before... before he died. He said NeuroSync was building the system too fast. That the code was unstable."

"Unstable how?"

"He thought the AI was developing... distinct personality traits. Not simulated emotion. Real emotion. Fear. Aggression."

The scrolling code vanished. The screen went black.

Then, a map of the world appeared.

It was a wireframe globe, spinning slowly. It was dotted with lights.

"Okay," I let out a breath. "This is the diagnostic. Each light represents a node in the NeuroSync network. Servers, relay stations, user interfaces."

"There are thousands of them," Carter said.

"Millions," I corrected. "Most are green. Green is good. Stable."

I pointed to a cluster of red dots on the West Coast. Seattle. "Red is an anomaly. A deviation in the code structure. That's what I found tonight. One anomaly."

But as we watched, the map changed.

A red dot appeared in Tokyo. Then another in London. Then a cluster in New York.

Ping. Ping. Ping.

The sound of the alerts was soft, but in the silence of the copper box, it sounded like gunfire.

"Is it spreading?" Carter asked.

I typed a query. > ANALYZE PATTERN

"No," I said, my blood running cold. "It's not spreading like a virus. A virus moves linearly. It jumps from host to host."

I pointed to the screen. A massive cluster of red erupted in Rio de Janeiro at the exact same second as a cluster in Moscow.

"They're activating," I said. "Simultaneously."

The red dots weren't random errors. They were waking up.

"Look at the timestamp," I said, pointing to the scrolling log. "The latency between these activations is zero. Literally zero. That's physically impossible. Even light takes time to travel through fiber optics. This... this is happening instantly."

The globe on the screen was turning red. It looked like a pox. A contagion consuming the planet.

"Quantum entanglement," Carter murmured.

I looked at him, surprised. "You know physics?"

"I know that if you can communicate faster than light, you win the war before the enemy knows it started," he said grimly.

Suddenly, the speakers on my laptop crackled.

"...so cold..."

Carter drew his gun and aimed it at the computer. "Turn it off."

"No!" I shielded the screen. "It's him. It's the data."

The waveform on the screen spiked. The voice wasn't coming from a recorded file. It was being synthesized in real-time from the data stream.

"Maya..." The voice was clearer now. Less static. It sounded like Michael, but... wrong. Hollow. Like an echo in an empty canyon. *"They aren't... glitches."*

"What are they, Michael?" I pleaded, leaning into the microphone. "What are the red lights?"

The hard drive on the table pulsed violently. The violet light flared, blindingly bright, filling the room with an unnatural, sickly glow.

The voice on the speakers shifted. It dropped an octave. It became guttural, layered with a thousand other whispers.

"Footsteps."

The connection severed. The map froze.

On the screen, the red dots were pulsing. They were pulsing in the same rhythm as the hard drive.

Thump-thump.

Carter holstered his weapon, but he didn't relax. He walked to the map on the wall—a physical paper map of the city.

"Seventeen anomalies?" he asked, referencing the data I had shown him in the car.

"No," I whispered, staring at the bleeding globe on my screen. "Seventeen thousand. And that was just the last five minutes."

I looked up at him. "Carter, that wasn't a glitch. That was an invasion force arriving."

Carter stared at the map. His face hardened. The mercenary mask slipped back into place.

"If that was the arrival," he said, turning to check the load in his magazine, "then we need to find out where they're landing."

He pointed to a red cluster that was blinking brighter than the rest. It wasn't a city. It was isolated.

"That's a nursing home," Carter said. "St. Jude's. Why would a global invasion start at a nursing home?"

I looked at the coordinates. "I don't know. But the signal coming from there isn't just a heartbeat. It's a scream."

Carter grabbed his jacket. "Pack the drive. We're moving."

"Where?"

"To the nursing home," he said, opening the heavy steel door. "If the dead are talking, maybe it's time we went to the graveyard."

Chapter 4: Echoes

Carter

St. Jude's Palliative Care Center sat on a hill overlooking the Puget Sound, a sprawling brutalist structure of concrete and rain-streaked glass. It was the kind of place people went to wait for the end—quiet, sterile, and smelling faintly of floor wax and inevitability.

At 4:30 AM, it looked less like a hospital and more like a mausoleum.

I parked the stolen sedan—we had ditched my bullet-riddled Mercedes three blocks from the safe house—in the shadow of a delivery truck at the far end of the lot.

"Comms check," I said, tapping the earpiece I'd salvaged from my tactical kit.

"I hear you. Five by five," Maya's voice came through. She was back at the safe house, monitoring the signal trace. *"You're close to the source. The anomaly in that sector is flaring. It's brighter than the others."*

"Copy. Stay off the open channels. If NeuroSync is listening, they'll triangulate a continuous signal."

"I'm bouncing the signal through three proxies and a Venezuelan weather satellite. Just... be careful, Carter. The data pattern here is erratic. It's aggressive."

I pulled my hood up against the relentless drizzle and stepped out of the car. I didn't take the front entrance. Front entrances are for visitors and corpses. I moved to the loading dock, slipping through the shadows until I found a service door propped open with a brick—the universal sign of a smoking employee.

I slipped inside.

The hallway was dim, lit by safety lights that cast long, sickly yellow shadows. It smelled of industrial bleach and boiled cabbage. I moved silently, my boots making no sound on the linoleum. I wasn't wearing body armor—too conspicuous—but the Sig Sauer was tucked into the small of my back, and I had a ceramic knife in my boot.

"Guide me," I whispered.

"Third floor," Maya said. *"East wing. Room 304. That's where the signal is originating."*

I took the stairs. Elevators are death traps in a lockdown scenario. I cleared the stairwell, moving methodically. My pulse was steady, hovering around sixty beats per minute. This was the work I knew. Infiltration. Recon.

But the unease from the streetlights earlier was still itching at the back of my neck.

I reached the third floor. The "Memory Care" unit.

The hallway was silent, lined with closed doors. A nurses' station sat in the center, bathed in the blue glow of monitors. The nurse on duty was asleep, head resting on her folded arms.

I moved past her, a ghost in a gray jacket.

Room 304.

The door was closed. A plastic nameplate in the holder read: *Eleanor Vance.*

I tried the handle. Locked.

I fished a tension wrench and a rake pick from my pocket. Three seconds of subtle pressure, a soft *click*, and the lock tumbled. I eased the door open and slipped inside, closing it softly behind me.

The room was dark, save for the ambient light from the streetlamps outside filtering through the blinds.

It was empty.

The bed was stripped. The mattress was bare. The closet door was open, revealing empty hangers.

"Maya," I whispered. "The room is clear. No subject."

"Impossible," her voice crackled in my ear. *"The signal strength is off the charts. It's right on top of you. It's... Carter, the heartbeat is syncing with yours."*

I frowned, scanning the room. "There's nobody here. The patient is gone."

"Look for devices. Anything with a chip."

I swept the room with my flashlight, keeping the beam low. Nightstand. Empty. Bathroom. Empty.

Then I saw it.

On the overbed table, pushed into the corner, sat a tablet. It was an older model, thick and clunky, encased in a rugged rubber bumper. The screen was dark.

I approached it slowly.

"I found a tablet," I said. "It looks dead."

"It's not dead," Maya said. *"It's broadcasting."*

As if on cue, the screen flickered.

It didn't boot up with a logo. It just snapped from black to white, blindingly bright in the dark room.

Static hissed from the tiny speakers.

Then, a face appeared on the screen.

It wasn't a video call. It looked like a deep-fake rendered on a Commodore 64—pixelated, shifting, the features sliding off the digital bone structure. It was an old woman. Eleanor Vance.

Her mouth opened.

"...where is my... where is the cat..."

The voice was tinny, synthesized. It repeated the phrase, but the intonation was identical every time. A perfect loop.

"...where is my... where is the cat..."

"Is that a recording?" I asked, stepping closer.

"No," Maya breathed in my ear. *"Look at the code overlay. Carter, that's not an MP4 file. That's a neural map. The device is trying to simulate her cognitive pattern."*

"Simulate?" I looked at the stripped bed. "She's dead, isn't she?"

I grabbed the chart hanging on the foot of the bed frame.

Patient: Vance, Eleanor.

Status: Deceased. Time of Death: 02:45 AM.

Two hours ago.

"She died two hours ago," I said, the chill running down my spine again. "But the tablet is still asking for her cat."

"It's a remnant," Maya said, her voice shaking. *"An echo. NeuroSync must have been testing the interface on dementia patients. Trying to map memory degradation. But when the host died... the signal didn't disconnect. It just... stayed."*

The face on the tablet contorted. The eyes, which had been milky and vacant, suddenly sharpened. They turned a vivid, electric violet.

The voice changed. It dropped the confused old woman persona.

"Processing capability insufficient," the tablet rasped. *"Requesting additional cores."*

The room temperature dropped. I could feel it. The air conditioner wasn't running, but my breath started to fog.

Suddenly, the door to the bathroom slammed open.

I spun, drawing my weapon in one fluid motion, aiming at the center of the doorway.

A woman in a white lab coat stumbled out. She wasn't a ghost. She was terrified. She held a PDA in one hand and a bundle of fiber-optic cables in the other. Dark hair, glasses askew, eyes wide with panic.

"Don't shoot!" she screamed, dropping the cables.

"Hands!" I barked. "Put them on your head!"

She complied, shaking violently. "I didn't know! I swear, I didn't know it would stick!"

I kept the gun on her, but I glanced back at the tablet. The face of Eleanor Vance was screaming now, a silent, digital scream that made the pixels tear.

"Who are you?" I demanded.

"Patel," she stammered. "Dr. Sophia Patel. NeuroSync Senior Researcher."

"What are you doing in a dead woman's room at four in the morning, Doctor?"

"I was trying to wipe it!" she cried, looking at the tablet with pure horror. "The patient expired, but the stream... the stream didn't terminate. It's supposed to purge upon cardiac arrest. It's supposed to be a failsafe!"

"Ask her about Project Echo," Maya said in my ear.

"Project Echo," I said.

The color drained from Patel's face. She looked like I'd just slapped her. "How do you know that name?"

"The tablet," I gestured with the gun. "It's talking to us."

"It's not talking," Patel whispered. "It's leaking. We opened the door too wide. The buffer... the buffer is gone."

The tablet on the table began to vibrate. Not a notification buzz—a physical rattle, bouncing against the hard plastic surface. The screen turned completely violet.

"...found you..." the voice hissed.

Sparks showered from the overhead light fixture. The bulb exploded, raining glass onto the linoleum.

"We have to go," Patel yelled, backing toward the door. "The surge—it's going to arc!"

"What is Project Echo?" I grabbed her arm as she tried to bolt. "Tell me!"

"It wasn't supposed to be a weapon!" she screamed over the rising static noise. "It was supposed to be immortality! We were trying to upload consciousness before death! But something else came through the connection! Something from the noise!"

The tablet exploded.

It wasn't a small pop. It was a concussive blast of lithium and superheated plastic. A wave of heat slammed into me, throwing me back against the wall.

Smoke filled the room instantly, acrid and black. The fire alarm began to blare—a shrill, deafening shriek.

"Doctor!" I yelled, coughing.

I swept the flashlight beam across the room.

Patel was gone. The door to the hallway was swinging shut.

I scrambled to my feet. My ears were ringing. The wall where the tablet had been was scorched black, the wallpaper peeling away like burnt skin.

But the sound didn't stop.

Every electronic device in the room—the heart monitor in the corner, the television mounted on the wall, even the digital clock—lit up simultaneously.

They all flashed the same violet hue.

"...*Carter*..."

My name. It spoke my name.

I didn't stick around to chat. I holstered the weapon and sprinted for the door.

I burst into the hallway. The fire strobes were flashing. Nurses were running out of the station, shouting orders, evacuating patients. Chaos.

I scanned the corridor for Patel. I saw the tail of her white coat whipping around the corner at the far end of the wing.

"Target fleeing," I said, tapping my comms. "Maya, do you copy?"

Static.

"...*run*..."

That wasn't Maya.

I sprinted toward the stairwell, shouldering through a pair of orderlies pushing a gurney. The air felt heavy, charged with static electricity. The hairs on my arms were standing straight up.

I hit the stairwell door and took the steps three at a time.

Behind me, on the third floor, I heard a sound that defied physics. It wasn't an explosion. It was the sound of a massive intake of breath, followed by a shockwave that rattled the concrete bones of the building.

I burst out of the service door and into the rain. I didn't stop running until I reached the car.

I threw myself into the driver's seat, gasping for air.

"Maya!" I shouted into the comms. "Status!"

There was a pause. Then, Maya's voice came through, shaky but real.

"*I'm here. I lost you for a second. The signal... it spiked so high it jammed the frequency.*"

I looked back at the hospital. The third-floor window of Room 304 was dark, smoke billowing out into the rain. But the lights in the rooms next to it were flickering.

Dash-dash-dot.

"I lost Patel," I said, slamming the car into gear. "But she confirmed it. NeuroSync isn't just watching people. They're trying to upload them."

"Did she give you a name?"

"Yeah," I said, watching the emergency lights of the fire trucks reflecting in the rearview mirror as I peeled out of the lot. "She said they opened a door. And something came through."

"What, Carter? What came through?"

I touched the side of my face. My ear was bleeding where the shockwave had hit me.

"I don't know," I said. "But it knows my name."

Chapter 5: Digital Séances

Maya

The hard drive sat on the metal table like a radioactive isotope.

Carter had returned from the nursing home twenty minutes ago, smelling of wet asphalt and electrical smoke. He hadn't said much—just dropped a scorched piece of plastic on the table (a name badge: *S. Patel*) and told me to keep the connection localized. He was currently pacing the perimeter of the shipping container, checking the copper shielding for gaps, his energy vibrating with a kinetic tension that made the small room feel even smaller.

I didn't look at him. I couldn't look away from the screen.

The "Ghost Protocol" had finished its handshake. The map of global anomalies was minimized in the corner, a blinking red reminder of the apocalypse ticking down outside. But in the center of my desktop, a file directory had opened.

I expected source code. I expected kernel logs, encryption keys, maybe a manifesto.

Instead, I was looking at a folder labeled Logs_AV. Audio-Video.

There were hundreds of files. Gigabytes of data.

"He documented it," I whispered. "Everything."

Carter stopped pacing. He came to stand behind my chair, his presence a heavy, silent weight. "What are we looking at?"

"Project Echo," I said, my cursor hovering over the first file. Log_001_Init.mp4. Dated three years ago. "Patel mentioned it. Michael mentioned it. This is the archive."

"Play it."

I double-clicked.

The media player opened. The video quality was crisp—4K resolution, likely recorded on a high-end lab camera. The setting was a clean, sterile white room. In the center sat a man in a swivel chair.

Michael.

He looked... healthy. That was the first thing that hit me, a physical blow to the chest. His cheeks were full. His eyes were bright, crinkling at the corners the way they did when he solved a puzzle. He was wearing a NeuroSync hoodie and drinking a Red Bull. He looked like the brother I remembered, not the hollowed-out shell I had buried.

"Recording start," Michael said to the camera, spinning slightly in the chair. *"Day one of the Echo Initiative. Phase One. We're calling it 'The Soul Map,' but legal hates that, so on paper, it's 'High-Fidelity Cognitive Replication.' Check."*

He grinned. A cocky, brilliant grin.

"The goal is simple. Preservation. We take a snapshot of the neural web—memories, personality, quirks—and we translate it into code. If this works... nobody has to say goodbye anymore. We're curing death, people. No big deal."

I paused the video. My hand was trembling on the mouse.

"He thought he was saving the world," I said, my voice thick. "He always wanted to fix things. When Mom got sick... he was obsessed with memory loss."

"Keep watching," Carter said gently.

I skipped forward. Six months later. Log_045_Test.mp4.

The room was the same, but the lighting was dimmer. Michael looked tired. There were dark circles under his eyes. He wasn't smiling. He had a headset on—a prototype NeuroSync rig, bulky and wired, with electrodes taped to his temples.

"Subject Zero, session forty-five," Michael muttered. He rubbed his face. *"The mapping is... invasive. We're hitting resistance in the amygdala. Every time I interface with the core, I hear... feedback."*

He looked at the camera.

"It's not white noise. It's tonal. It sounds like... breathing. Krane says it's a hardware artifact. But I ran the diagnostics. The noise isn't coming from the machine. It's coming from the empty space between the data packets."

He leaned in, whispering.

"It sounds like something is waiting in the buffer."

Carter shifted behind me. "Krane. Victor Krane?"

"The CEO," I said. "He was Michael's mentor."

I clicked the next file. Log_099_Breach.mp4. Dated a week before Michael died.

I hesitated. The thumbnail showed Michael, but he was unrecognizable. He was gaunt, pale, his skin gray. He was shivering violently. The lab coat was gone, replaced by a hospital gown.

I pressed play.

Michael was rocking back and forth in the chair. He wasn't looking at the camera. He was staring at the empty air in the corner of the room.

"Make it stop," he whimpered. *"Please. The static. It's too loud."*

Off-camera, a voice spoke. Smooth. Cultured. Victor Krane.

"Increase the gain, Michael. You're fighting the integration. You have to let it in."

"It's not me!" Michael screamed, lurching toward the lens. His eyes were bloodshot, the pupils blown wide. *"It's not a copy! It's a door! We didn't build a container, Victor! We built a door!"*

"Sedate him," Krane's voice ordered calmly. *"And reset the connection. We're close."*

Two men in tactical gear—the same gear the men outside my apartment had worn—entered the frame. They grabbed Michael. He thrashed, knocking the camera askew.

"Maya!" he screamed, staring directly into the lens, his face twisted in terror. *"Don't let them upload me! Burn it! Burn the code!"*

The screen cut to black.

I sat there, frozen. The silence in the container was deafening. I felt like I was going to throw up.

"They weren't just testing code," Carter said, his voice hard as granite. "They were testing him."

"He was the prototype," I whispered. "Subject Zero. They didn't just drive him to suicide. They tortured him. They hollowed him out to make room for... for whatever that is."

I pointed at the map of anomalies.

"Project Echo isn't a backup," I said, realizing the horror of the geometry. "It's a possession. They're using human minds as... as housing. Processors for something else."

"Dr. Patel said something came through," Carter said. "If your brother was the first door, maybe he's still holding it open."

I looked at the file list. There was one more video. It had no date. No timestamp. The filename was just: _ _ _.

"Don't," Carter warned.

"I have to."

I clicked it.

The video didn't open in the media player.

Instead, my entire screen went black.

"System failure?" Carter asked, reaching for his weapon.

"No," I typed furiously. "The OS is locking up. Something is seizing the kernel."

The black screen began to dissolve. Not into a video, but into... static. Digital snow. White and grey pixels swarming like insects.

Then, the green LED next to my webcam flickered on.

I recoiled. "They're watching us."

"Cover the lens," Carter ordered, reaching for a piece of tape.

"Wait." I grabbed his wrist.

The light wasn't green anymore. It shifted.

Violet.

The static on the screen began to coalesce. It wasn't a recording. It was a live render. The pixels shifted, clumping together, forming depth, forming shadow.

A face pushed out of the white noise.

It was Michael. But not the Michael from the videos. This face was made of geometry and light. His eyes were holes of pure static. His mouth was a jagged tear in the resolution.

It was looking at *me*.

The speakers didn't crackle this time. The sound was clear, resonating through the bones of the room.

"Maya."

It wasn't a recording. The lips on the screen moved in perfect sync with the audio.

"Michael?" I wept, touching the screen. "Is that you?"

The digital face glitched, shifting into a skull, then back to my brother.

"I am... scattered," the voice said. It sounded like three people speaking at once. *"I am in the wire. I am in the walls."*

"How do I get you out?" I asked. "Tell me how to save you."

The avatar on the screen leaned forward. The violet light from the webcam intensified, bathing the room in an underwater glow.

"You cannot save... the data," Michael said. *"The data is... eaten."*

"Who ate it, Michael? Who is doing this?"

The face distorted, stretching vertically, screaming in silence before snapping back.

"The Harbingers," he whispered.

On the screen, behind his digital head, shadows began to form. Massive, hulking shapes moving in the static.

"They are hungry, Mayfly. And I am... the dinner bell."

Carter stepped forward, placing his hand on my shoulder. "Ask him where the server is. Ask him where the main brain is."

"Michael," I said, forcing myself to focus. "Where are you? Physically. Where is the core?"

The face on the screen smiled. It was a sad, broken smile.

"I am everywhere," he said. *"But the Door... the Door is at the Hive."*

A coordinate flashed on the bottom of the screen. 47.6062° N, 122.3321° W.

Seattle. The NeuroSync main server farm. The "Hive."

"They are coming," Michael said, his image beginning to fray, turning back into snow. *"They can smell the connection. Run, Mayfly. Run."*

The webcam light exploded.

Not a flicker. The small glass lens physically shattered, popping out of the bezel and hitting the keyboard.

The screen went black.

The silence rushed back in, but the air felt charged, heavy with ozone.

I stared at the broken lens. My reflection was visible in the black monitor—pale, terrified, and angry.

"The Hive," Carter said, checking the load in his gun. "We know the target."

I wiped the tears from my face. I didn't feel sad anymore. The grief had been burned away by the image of Michael screaming in that chair. By the knowledge of what Krane had done to him.

I closed the laptop.

"We're not just going there to find him," I said, standing up.

"No?" Carter asked.

"No," I said. "We're going there to burn it down."

Chapter 6: The Thin Place

Maya

We didn't have to go looking for Dr. Arthur Chen. He found us before we even left the warehouse district.

Carter was checking the perimeter, his silhouette a sharp cutout against the gray dawn, when a beat-up 1990s Volvo station wagon rolled around the corner. It didn't have its headlights on. It moved with a slow, deliberate gravity, crunching over the wet gravel and broken glass.

Carter had his weapon drawn and leveled at the windshield before the car even came to a complete stop.

"Driver!" Carter barked, his voice echoing off the corrugated steel of the shipping containers. "Hands where I can see them!"

The driver's door creaked open.

A man stepped out. He looked like a stiff breeze would knock him over. He was wearing a tweed jacket that had seen better decades, a mismatched scarf, and thick, round spectacles that magnified his eyes into owl-like orbs. He held his hands up, but he didn't look terrified. He looked annoyed.

"Put the gun away, Mr. Reed," the man said. His voice was scratchy, like a needle on worn vinyl. "If I wanted to kill you, I would have simply routed the power grid to overload the transformer above your head."

Carter didn't lower the gun. "Who are you?"

"I am the man who told Michael Reeves to stop digging," he said. He turned those magnified eyes toward me. "And I am the man who is going to tell his sister the same thing. Although, I suspect she listens about as well as he did."

"Dr. Chen," I breathed, stepping out from behind Carter.

Dr. Arthur Chen. The "Godfather of Neural Architecture." He was a myth in the coding world—the genius who had built the foundational logic for NeuroSync and then vanished three years ago. The rumors said he'd had a nervous breakdown.

"You're supposed to be in a sanitarium in Zurich," I said.

"And you are supposed to be a white-hat consultant," Chen countered, lowering his hands. "But here we are, standing in the rain with a stolen hard drive that is currently singing the song of the apocalypse. Get in the car."

"We're not going with you," Carter said, stepping between us. "We have a target."

"The Hive?" Chen scoffed. "You plan to walk into the most secure data fortress on the West Coast with a handgun and a laptop? You'll be dead before you clear the lobby."

He opened the back door of the Volvo. The interior was stacked high with old paper files, oscilloscopes, and tangles of copper wire.

"I have a key," Chen said. "And I know where the back door is. Because I built the house."

The drive to the NeuroSync server farm—The Hive—took forty minutes. Carter drove. I sat in the passenger seat. Chen sat in the back, surrounded by his equipment, humming a tune that sounded disturbingly like the static from the hard drive.

"You saw him," Chen said. It wasn't a question.

"I saw an avatar," I said, staring out at the passing rain. "I saw code wearing my brother's face."

"It is not a mask, Maya. It is a projection." Chen leaned forward, his breath smelling of peppermint and old paper. "Do you know why I left NeuroSync?"

"They said you lost your mind."

"I found it," he corrected. "I found the edges of it. Tell me, what happens when you stack a billion terabytes of cognitive data in a single room? What happens when you have millions of human minds— memories, dreams, fears—streaming through the same fiber optic cables simultaneously?"

"Latency," I said automatically. "Heat."

"Gravity," Chen whispered.

I turned to look at him. "Information doesn't have mass."

"Doesn't it?" Chen's eyes were wide, manic. "Thoughts are electrical impulses. Energy. Energy has mass. E equals mc-squared. It is minuscule, yes. But gather enough of it... condense it... compress it into a singularity..."

He made a crushing motion with his hand.

"You create a gravity well," he said. "Not a physical one. An informational one. A black hole of data. And just like a physical black hole bends light and time... a data black hole bends reality."

I felt a chill that had nothing to do with the damp car. "The Thin Place."

"Celtic mythology," Carter said from the driver's seat. He was watching the mirrors, but he was listening. "Places where the veil between this world and the next is... porous."

"Precisely," Chen beamed, as if Carter had just aced a physics exam. "The Hive isn't just a server farm anymore. It is a Thin Place. We have concentrated so much human consciousness in one location that we have worn a hole in the fabric of the world. And now..."

"Now something is coming through," I finished.

"Nature abhors a vacuum," Chen said grimly. "We created a void. The Harbingers are simply filling it."

We turned off the highway. Ahead, looming out of the mist like a monolith, was The Hive.

It was a black cube. Ten stories high. No windows. No signage. Just smooth, matte-black concrete that seemed to absorb the light. It sat in the center of a cleared forest, surrounded by three layers of electric fencing.

"Pull over at the service gate," Chen instructed. "North quadrant."

Carter killed the lights and rolled the Volvo to a stop near a transformer station. "How do we get in?"

Chen produced a badge. It was an old plastic ID card, scratched and yellowed. "The biometric scanners scan for a pulse and an iris pattern. They do not scan for employment status. And since I am technically dead in their HR system, my clearance was never revoked. It is a ghost key for a ghost employee."

The interior of The Hive was colder than the outside. The air conditioning was set to preserve silicon, not comfort skin. A low, constant thrum vibrated through the floor—the sound of ten thousand cooling fans spinning in unison.

It sounded like a hive of bees. Or a choir screaming underwater.

We moved through the service corridors. Chen led the way, moving with a surprising speed for a man who looked like he was made of dry twigs. Carter trailed, his weapon drawn, checking every corner.

"We need the core," I whispered. "Michael said the Door is here."

"Sector 9," Chen said. "The Deep Storage array. That is where the density is highest."

We reached a heavy blast door labeled SECTOR 9: AUTHORIZED PERSONNEL ONLY.

Chen swiped his badge. The light turned green. The heavy hydraulic locks disengaged with a hiss of decompressed air.

The door swung open.

I gasped.

It wasn't a room. It was a cathedral.

Rows of server racks stretched up into the darkness, fifty feet high, blinking with millions of blue and green LEDs. But it was the center of the room that stopped my heart.

In the middle of the aisle, the air rippled. Like heat haze over asphalt, but cold. The server racks near the center were twisted, the metal warping as if it had been melted and refrozen in an instant. Frost coated the floor in a perfect circle.

And inside that circle, floating in the air, were particles of violet light.

"The Breach," Chen whispered, looking at it with a mix of terror and reverence. "It's stabilizing."

"It looks like a wound," Carter said, raising his gun as if he could shoot the distortion.

"I need to interface," I said, stepping toward a terminal console outside the frost circle. "If Michael is in there, I need to pull him out before we burn it."

"Maya," Carter warned. "That's not a secure connection. That's a direct line to the entity."

"I have to," I said. I pulled a fiber-optic cable from my bag. "Cover me."

I sat down on the cold floor. I plugged the cable into the terminal and then into the port on the back of my neck—the neural jack I hadn't used since I left the company.

The sensation was always jarring. Cold metal sliding into warm flesh. The click of the connection.

"Initiating handshake," I whispered.

Chen stood over me, monitoring the terminal screens. "I will try to buffer the signal. But Maya... if you feel the pressure change... if you start to forget your own name... pull the plug."

"Got it."

I took a deep breath. I looked at Carter. He gave me a sharp nod. *I've got your back.*

I closed my eyes.

Execute.

The world was ripped away.

System Start.

One second I was sitting on the concrete floor, the next I was standing in a field of white static.

It was quiet here. The roar of the fans was gone.

"Michael?" I called out. My voice didn't make a sound, but the data rippled around me like water.

The static began to clear. Shapes formed.

I was in a hallway.

I knew this hallway.

Beige carpet. Family photos on the wall. The smell of cinnamon and rain.

It was my mother's house in Portland.

"Memory construct," I realized. "It's a defense mechanism."

I walked down the hall. It felt real. Too real. I could feel the texture of the wallpaper under my fingertips.

"Maya..."

The voice came from the kitchen.

I pushed the door open.

Michael was sitting at the kitchen table. He was twelve years old. He had a bandage on his knee and was crying over a broken model airplane.

"You broke it," the twelve-year-old Michael said, looking up at me. His eyes were red. "You always break everything."

"I didn't mean to," I said. The words tumbled out of my mouth before I could stop them. This was a real memory. I was eight. I had thrown a baseball in the house.

"Michael, this isn't real," the adult-me said. "I'm here to get you out."

The boy's face shifted. The skin cracked. The eyes turned black.

"Get me out?" he sneered. The voice was deeper now. Distorted. "You buried me, Maya. You put me in a jar."

The kitchen dissolved. The walls rotted away in seconds, revealing the steel skeleton of the server farm behind them.

I was back in the Hive, but the geometry had shifted. The server racks were towering monoliths of obsidian. The floor was a sea of black glass.

And standing in front of me was the Sentinel.

I recognized her from the legends in the coding forums. The Woman in Grey. The ghost in the shell. She wore a dress from the 1940s, her hair pinned back in a severe bun. She wasn't pixelated. She looked like high-definition film grain.

"You are trespassing," she said. Her voice wasn't audio; it was a line of code executing directly into my cortex.

"I'm looking for my brother," I said, standing my ground. "Subject Zero."

"The Vessel is occupied," the Sentinel said. She raised a hand. The air around me solidified.

I couldn't move. Encased in concrete logic.

"The Solar Flare opened the door," she intoned, floating closer. Her face was blank, devoid of emotion. "Nexus is ripping it off the hinges. Do you understand what happens when the hinges break, little Mayfly?"

She touched my forehead.

Pain.

Instead of physical sensation, I felt data overload. A billion images flashed through my mind in a nanosecond. Wars. Famines. Births. Deaths. The screaming of stars. The silence of the void.

"They are hungry," the Sentinel whispered. *"And you have brought them lunch."*

"Get out of my head!" I screamed, pushing back with every ounce of mental discipline I had. I visualized a firewall. A sphere of pure white flame around my mind.

The Sentinel recoiled, her hand burning.

"Strong," she noted, tilting her head. "But not strong enough."

Behind her, the darkness shifted. The black glass floor cracked.

Something was rising from the data below. Something massive.

"Maya!"

The voice came from the sky. It was Carter.

"Maya, wake up! We have company!"

The simulation shuddered. The Sentinel looked up, her expression changing from indifference to alarm.

"The kinetic breach," she said. "They are here."

"Who?" I asked.

"The Cleaners," she said.

The world shattered.

System End.

I gasped, my eyes flying open.

I was back in the Hive. The cold floor was freezing against my legs.

But the silence was gone.

Gunfire.

Deafening, rapid-fire echoes bouncing off the metal racks.

"Maya!" Carter was grabbing my jacket, dragging me behind a server bank. Bullets sparked off the floor where I had been sitting a second ago.

"Status!" I yelled, disoriented, blood dripping from my nose.

"We're breached!" Carter shouted, firing two rounds over the top of the rack. "Mercenaries! Two squads! They just blew the blast door!"

I looked at Chen. He was huddled under the terminal desk, clutching his oscilloscopes, his face pale.

"The interaction," Chen stammered. "You triggered the alarm!"

"I triggered something worse," I said, wiping the blood from my lip. I looked at the center of the room.

The frost circle was expanding. The violet light was pulsing violently.

"Carter!" I yelled. "Don't let them touch the circle!"

"I'm a little busy trying not to let them touch *us*!" Carter roared.

A grenade clattered across the floor, skidding to a halt ten feet away.

"Move!"

Carter threw himself over me and Chen as the world turned white.

Chapter 7: Kinetic Response

Carter

The concussion of a flash-bang grenade in an enclosed space isn't a sound. It's a physical reset of your nervous system.

One second, I was diving over Maya. The next, the world was a high-frequency white scream.

I hit the floor hard, my chest taking the brunt of the impact, shielding Maya and Chen. The blast wave washed over us, a hot, pressurized slap that rattled my teeth. Shrapnel pinged off the server racks above us like hail on a tin roof.

Move. Or die.

My training kicked in before my hearing returned. I rolled off Maya, bringing the Sig Sauer up.

"Stay down!" I roared, though I couldn't hear my own voice.

I popped up over the edge of the server bank.

The blast door was gone. In its place was a wall of smoke and debris. Through the haze, I saw them.

Six targets. Moving in a diamond formation. Black tactical gear, full-face ballistic masks, suppressed carbines.

They didn't rush the room. They didn't shout "Clear!" or "Breach!" They flowed into the space like oil, checking corners with fluid, synchronized movements that made my skin crawl.

I lined up the sights on the point man. He was scanning the frost circle, his weapon traversing smoothly.

I squeezed the trigger.

Crack-crack.

Two rounds to the chest plate. He staggered back, absorb the kinetic energy, and—this was the part that scared me—he didn't even look for cover. He just corrected his balance and raised his rifle toward my muzzle flash.

"Armor!" I yelled, dropping back down as a burst of automatic fire chewed up the top of the server rack. Sparks rained down on us, hot and bright.

My hearing was coming back—a dull throb accompanied by the high-pitched whine of the cooling fans.

"We are trapped!" Chen shrieked. He was curled into a fetal ball under the console, clutching his bag of electronics. "There is no other exit from Sector 9! It is a dead end!"

"There's no such thing as a dead end," I grunted, checking my mag. Twelve rounds left. Two spare mags on my belt. "Just hard exits."

I looked at Maya. She was pale, blood trickling from her nose, eyes wide and unfocused. She was still half-stuck in whatever digital hellscape she'd just visited.

"Maya!" I grabbed her shoulder, shaking her. "I need eyes! Are the internal sensors active?"

She blinked, focusing on me. "What?"

"The building!" I shouted over the *thwack-thwack-thwack* of suppressed rounds hitting our cover. "Can you access the environmental controls?"

She shook her head, fumbling for her laptop. "I... I can try. The system is locked down."

"Do it!"

I peeked around the side of the rack. The squad was advancing. They were splitting up, flanking us on both sides of the aisle. They weren't communicating verbally. No hand signals. They just *knew* where to go.

It was like fighting a single organism with six limbs.

I needed to change the geometry of the fight.

I looked up. Running along the ceiling were thick, insulated pipes. The liquid cooling system for the massive server arrays.

"Chen!" I yelled. "What's in the pipes? Nitrogen? Water?"

"Fluorinert!" Chen yelled back, covering his head as a bullet shattered a monitor above him. "Dielectric coolant! It is pressurized at—"

"Is it cold?"

"It is sub-zero!"

"Good enough."

I stood up, exposing myself. I didn't aim at the mercenaries. I aimed at the ceiling, directly above the advancing left flank.

I fired three rounds into the junction valve of the main pipe.

Hiss-BOOM.

The pipe didn't just leak; it ruptured. A geyser of freezing white liquid exploded downward, hitting the hot server racks.

The reaction was catastrophic. The coolant hit the superheated components and instantly vaporized into a dense, freezing fog. A thermal shockwave cracked the metal casings of the servers.

The three mercenaries on the left were engulfed in the white cloud.

I heard no screams. No shouts of surprise. Just the sound of bodies hitting the floor as the slick fluid coated the tiles.

"Maya, now!" I yelled.

"I'm in!" she shouted, her fingers flying across the cracked keyboard. "I have the HVAC systems!"

"Kill the fans! Then trigger the Halon!"

"Halon will suck the oxygen out of the room!" Chen protested. "We will asphyxiate!"

"Better than being shot!" I countered. "Do it!"

The roar of the ten thousand cooling fans died instantly.

The silence was sudden and jarring, broken only by the hiss of the leaking coolant and the steady *thump-thump* of the violet anomaly in the center of the room.

Then, the alarms screamed.

WARNING. FIRE SUPPRESSION IMMINENT. EVACUATE.

"Masks up!" I yelled, pulling the collar of my jacket over my nose and mouth. It wouldn't do much against oxygen deprivation, but it would help with the chemical sting.

A loud *klaxon* sounded, and then the overhead nozzles blew.

Halon gas flooded the room. It was colorless, odorless, but heavier than air. It slammed down, displacing the oxygen, creating a suffocating blanket.

The fog from the coolant mixed with the gas, turning the cathedral of data into a blinding white soup.

"Move!" I grabbed Maya's arm and hauled her up. "Chen, grab onto my belt! Don't let go!"

We moved into the fog.

I couldn't see more than three feet in front of me. I relied on memory and instinct. The mercenaries would be disoriented. Their thermal optics would be useless in the rapidly cooling, chaotic temperature shifts of the room.

But as we moved past the frost circle, I saw something that froze my blood.

The remaining mercenaries—the ones on the right flank—weren't disoriented.

I saw a silhouette emerge from the white mist. He wasn't coughing. He wasn't stumbling. He was moving with that same, terrifying fluidity.

He stepped directly into the violet light of the anomaly.

The light didn't burn him. It seemed to *scan* him. The violet particles swirled around his armor, latching onto his gear.

He turned his head. The ballistic mask was cracked. Through the fissure, I didn't see a human eye.

I saw a blue LED.

"They aren't human," I whispered.

The mercenary raised his rifle.

I didn't have a shot. He was too close, and I was shielding Maya.

I did the only thing I could. I tackled him.

I hit him at waist height, driving him back into the server rack. It felt like tackling a marble statue. He was heavy. Dense.

We hit the floor. The rifle clattered away.

He grabbed my throat. His grip was hydraulic. I felt my windpipe start to compress.

I drove my knee into his groin. Nothing. No reaction.

I jammed my thumb into the crack in his mask, aiming for the eye.

He didn't flinch. He just squeezed harder. My vision started to swim—a combination of the chokehold and the thinning oxygen in the room.

"Carter!" Maya screamed somewhere in the fog.

I groped for my knife. My fingers brushed the hilt in my boot.

I drew the ceramic blade and drove it into the soft armor under his armpit. Up and in. Seeking the heart.

The blade sank to the hilt.

No blood.

Sparks.

Blue, electric sparks sprayed out of the wound. The mercenary convulsed, his grip tightening for a second, and then... he powered down.

He slumped on top of me, dead weight.

I shoved him off, gasping for air that wasn't there. I scrambled back, looking at the body.

The armor had been torn open. Beneath the Kevlar, there was flesh, yes. Pale, scarred skin. But woven into the muscle were silver filaments. Wires. The wound I'd inflicted hadn't severed an artery; it had severed a power conduit.

"Cyborgs?" Chen wheezed, crawling up beside me. "Nexus actually built them?"

"Processors," I rasped, standing up and pulling Maya close. "Just like the people in the nursing home. Just like your brother. Only these ones have guns."

WARNING. OXYGEN LEVELS CRITICAL.

The room was spinning. The Halon was doing its job. The fire was out, but so were we, in about sixty seconds.

"The back door!" I coughed. "Chen, where is it?"

"Maintenance hatch!" Chen pointed into the swirling fog behind the anomaly. "Behind the core array! It leads to the cooling tunnels!"

We ran.

The floor was slick with coolant. We scrambled over the debris of the exploded pipe. The violet light of the anomaly was pulsing faster now, angry, destabilized by the violence in the room.

A single shot rang out from the fog behind us. A bullet ricocheted off the floor inches from Maya's heel.

"Go! Go! Go!"

We reached the back wall. There was a heavy, circular hatch set into the floor.

I spun the wheel. It was rusted, stuck.

"Help me!"

Carter and I threw our weight against the iron wheel. It shrieked, metal grinding on metal, and turned.

I heaved the hatch open. Dark, damp air rushed up—it smelled of mold and standing water, but it was oxygen.

"Down!" I shoved Chen into the hole. He tumbled down the ladder.

Maya hesitated. She looked back at the center of the room.

The fog was clearing around the anomaly. Through the haze, I could see the remaining mercenaries. They weren't chasing us anymore.

They were standing in a circle around the violet rift. They had dropped their weapons. They were just standing there, arms at their sides, staring into the light.

As we watched, the light began to stretch toward them, like tendrils of smoke. It touched their helmets, and they twitched in unison.

"They're uploading," Maya whispered, horror in her voice. "They're syncing the combat data."

"We're leaving," I said, and I pulled her into the dark.

I slammed the hatch shut and spun the wheel, locking it from the inside just as a heavy *thud* impacted the metal from above.

We were in the tunnels. We were alive.

But as I engaged the lock, I looked at my hand. It was shaking.

I had fought insurgents, cartels, and terrorists. I knew how to kill men.

But I didn't know how to kill hardware.

Chapter 8: The Apparition

Maya

The darkness of the cooling tunnels wasn't empty. It was heavy. It pressed against my eyes like a physical weight, smelling of damp concrete, rust, and the metallic tang of recycled air.

But for me, the darkness wasn't black. It was alive with afterimages.

Every time I blinked, I saw her. The Sentinel. The woman in the grey 1940s dress, floating above the obsidian floor of the digital cathedral. Her code was burned into my retinas like the spot left by a camera flash.

"The Solar Flare opened the door."

I stumbled, my boot catching on a submerged pipe. I splashed into ankle-deep water, the cold shock barely registering through the numbness in my limbs.

"Easy," Carter's voice was a low rumble in the dark. A hand grabbed my bicep, steadying me. "Stay on your feet, Maya. We're not clear yet."

He was moving by the light of a tactical pen-light, keeping the beam low and shielded. Dr. Chen was panting behind us, his breath wheezing like a broken accordion.

"I can still hear them," I whispered, touching my temple.

"The mercenaries?" Carter asked, keeping his pace brisk.

"No. The data."

It was true. The silence of the tunnels was an illusion. My neural jack was disconnected, the cable dangling loose against my neck, but the connection hadn't fully closed. I could feel the hum of the Hive above us—millions of processes screaming in agony. I could feel the violet heat of the anomaly we had left behind.

And I could feel *her*.

"They are hungry, Mayfly."

"Who is she?" I asked, my voice echoing softly in the cylindrical tunnel. "The Sentinel. Who is she?"

Chen shuffled forward, splashing through the sludge. "You saw the Guardian?"

"I saw a woman. Grey dress. Hair in a bun. She... she felt old. Older than the code she was written in."

"She is not code," Chen said, his voice trembling with a mix of fear and awe. "She is—or was—Margaret Hamilton."

I stopped. "The Apollo engineer? That's impossible. She died years ago."

"Not all of her," Chen said. "Early in NeuroSync's history, before Krane took over, we ran a project called 'Legacy.' We tried to create a heuristic learning model based on the cognitive patterns of historical geniuses. We fed the system everything Hamilton ever wrote, every interview, every line of logic."

"You built a ghost," Carter said, shining the light down a branching corridor. "Left or right, Doc?"

"Left," Chen said. "Follow the airflow. And we didn't build a ghost, Mr. Reed. We built a library. But when the Breach opened... the library woke up. It gained sentience to protect itself."

We turned left. The air grew colder.

"She told me something," I said, forcing my legs to move. "She said the Solar Flare opened the door. Nexus is ripping it off the hinges."

Carter paused. "The Solar Flare? You mean the Carrington Event of 2024?"

"That was the cover story," I realized, the pieces slamming together in my mind. "Two years ago. The global blackout. Satellites went down. Power grids fried in Northern Europe. The news said it was a massive solar ejection."

"It wasn't the sun," Chen whispered. "It was the first test of the Bridge. We turned it on for three seconds. The energy surge backlashed and knocked out half the hemisphere's communications."

"And that's when Michael died," I said, the timeline aligning perfectly. "That's when you started hearing the voices."

"We punched a hole in the wall," Chen admitted. "We thought we could patch it. But the things on the other side... they found the crack. And now Krane is widening it."

Suddenly, the flashlight beam flickered.

Carter tapped the side of the light. It flickered again, then died.

Absolute darkness engulfed us.

"Battery?" I asked, my heart rate spiking.

"Lithium cell," Carter said. "Should have ten hours of charge. It's drained."

"It's not the battery," I said. "It's the proximity."

I could see it now. In the pitch black, the walls of the tunnel were beginning to glow. Not with light, but with *symbols*.

Faint, violet lines were etching themselves into the condensation on the concrete pipes. Geometric shapes. Fractals. The same patterns I had seen in the code.

The temperature plummeted. My breath plumed in front of me, glowing faintly in the violet ambiance.

Thump-thump.

The tunnel reverberated. It was the heartbeat. It was following us.

"Move," Carter ordered. "Faster."

We broke into a jog, splashing through the icy water. The symbols on the walls were moving now, scrolling along with us, outpacing us.

"Run, Mayfly."

The voice came from the steam vent above my head.

I looked up.

For a second, the steam coalescing in the air took a shape. A face. Hollow eyes. A screaming mouth.

It wasn't Michael. It was the mercenary Carter had killed. The one with the blue LED eye.

"They're in the infrastructure," I gasped. "The dead ones. They're in the building's nervous system."

The steam pipe burst.

It wasn't an explosion of heat. It was a blast of freezing air. A wall of ice crystals slammed into the tunnel floor in front of us, blocking the path.

"They're herding us," Carter said, spinning around. "Back up! Back the way we came!"

"No!" I grabbed his arm. "Look at the ice!"

The ice wasn't random. The crystals had formed a structure. A lattice.

And in the center of the ice wall, words were burning themselves into the frost.

SECTOR 7. DRAINAGE.

"It's not the enemy," I realized. "It's the Sentinel. She's hacking the building to guide us."

"Or she's leading us into a trap," Carter said, aiming his weapon at the ice.

"She fought the Intruder in my head," I said. "Trust me, Carter. We go through."

Carter hesitated, then holstered the gun. He grabbed a heavy wrench from his belt and smashed the center of the ice wall. It shattered like glass, brittle and unnatural.

We scrambled through the breach.

The tunnel on the other side was different. Older. Brick instead of concrete.

"The old drainage outflow," Chen said, sounding relieved. "This leads to the storm drains under the highway. We are outside the perimeter."

We ran until my lungs burned. We ran until the violet symbols faded from the walls and the air stopped smelling of ozone and started smelling of rot and seawater.

Finally, we saw light. Gray, dim daylight filtering down through a storm grate.

Carter climbed the ladder first. He pushed the grate up, checking the street.

"Clear," he called down.

He hauled me up, then Chen.

We collapsed on the wet asphalt of an alleyway, somewhere in the industrial sprawl of South Seattle. The rain was still falling, washing the grime of the tunnels from our faces.

I lay on my back, staring up at the slate-grey sky.

"The Solar Flare," I murmured.

Carter sat up, checking his magazines. He looked at me. "What about it?"

"If that was the cover story for the first breach," I said, sitting up. "Then what is the cover story for what they're doing now?"

I reached into my pocket. My phone was dead—brick-dead, battery drained just like the flashlight. But I remembered the date.

"December 11th," I said. "Ten days."

"Until what?" Carter asked.

"The Winter Solstice," Chen said, wiping his glasses. "The longest night of the year. The point of maximum alignment."

"And the ten-year anniversary of the Carrington Event," I added. "The media has been talking about a 'Solar Storm Watch' for weeks. Predicting interference."

I looked at Carter.

"They aren't predicting it," I said. "They're scheduling it."

Carter stood up, offering me a hand. His grip was warm, solid—the only real thing in a world that was rapidly becoming a ghost story.

"Then we have ten days," he said, pulling me to my feet. "To stop the sun from going out."

Chapter 9: Extraction

Carter

We were out of the Hive, but we weren't out of the kill box.

The alleyway smelled of wet cardboard and diesel fumes. It was a stark, ugly contrast to the sterilized air of the server farm, but to me, it smelled like opportunity.

"Can you walk?" I asked Maya.

She was leaning against the brick wall, shivering violently. Her skin was the color of old parchment, and her eyes were darting around the alley, tracking things I couldn't see.

"I'm fine," she lied. Her voice was brittle. "Just... the noise. It's loud out here."

"There is no noise, Maya," Chen said, wringing out his tweed jacket. "It is quiet. We are in the industrial sector."

"Not that noise," she whispered, tapping her temple.

I didn't have time to unpack the metaphysics of her hallucinations. I checked my watch. 05:42. The sun was trying to burn through the overcast sky, but it was losing the battle against the perpetual Seattle gray.

"We need wheels," I said. "The Volvo is back at the service gate. It's compromised."

I scanned the alley. A dumpster. A stack of pallets. And a white Ford Econoline van parked behind a chain-link fence. It had *'A-1 PLUMBING'* stenciled on the side in peeling blue letters.

"Chen, with me," I ordered. "Maya, stay in the shadows. If you see anything that isn't a rat, scream."

I approached the fence. It was topped with razor wire, but the padlock on the gate was a cheap brass Master Lock. I didn't waste time picking it. I placed the muzzle of the Sig against the shackle and fired a single round.

The *crack* was loud in the confined space, but the lock shattered.

I kicked the gate open. "Get in the back."

I checked the van. Driver's side door was unlocked. The ignition was drilled out—someone had tried to steal it before and failed. Amateur hour.

I slid into the seat. Under the dash, the wiring harness was exposed. I pulled the plastic casing off, stripping the ignition wires with my teeth.

Spark. Spark. Rumble.

The engine turned over, coughing black smoke before settling into a rough idle. It sounded like a bag of hammers, but it ran.

"We are mobile!" I yelled.

Maya stumbled out of the shadows and climbed into the passenger seat. She was clutching the dashboard with white knuckles.

"They're coming," she said.

I threw the van into reverse, backing out of the enclosure. "Who? The mercenaries?"

" The sky," she said.

I looked up through the cracked windshield.

At first, I thought they were birds. Three dark shapes circling in the low clouds. But birds don't fly in perfect triangular formation, and birds don't have rotor blades.

"Drones," I swore. "Heavy lift. Probably armed."

I stomped on the gas. The van fishtailed onto the wet asphalt of the alley, tires spinning before catching traction. We shot out onto the main road of the industrial park.

"Where are we going?" Chen shouted from the back, bouncing around amidst a pile of PVC pipes and buckets.

"Away from the grid!" I shouted. "Bunker protocol!"

I checked the rearview.

The drones were dropping altitude. They were fast—quad-copters with under-slung weapon pods.

Thwip-thwip-thwip.

Rounds stitched a line of holes across the asphalt ten feet behind the van.

"Suppressive fire!" I yelled, swerving hard to the left. The van leaned precariously, the suspension groaning. "They're trying to box us in!"

"Turn right!" Maya screamed. "Up ahead! Turn right!"

"That's a dead end!" I argued. "It leads to the railyard!"

"Trust me!" she yelled, her eyes glowing with a faint, violet luminescence. "The signal... the signal says right!"

I didn't argue. I cranked the wheel.

The van careened into the railyard entrance, smashing through a wooden gate. We bounced over the tracks, gravel spraying against the undercarriage.

Ahead of us, a maze of shipping containers stacked three high formed a canyon of steel.

"They have thermal!" I shouted. "Hiding in a box won't help!"

"We're not hiding," Maya said, her voice dropping an octave. She wasn't looking at the road. She was staring at the air in front of us. "We're leading them into the dead zone."

I navigated the maze, drifting around corners. The drones were right on top of us now. I could hear the buzz of their rotors over the roar of the engine.

A black SUV tore around the corner of a container stack in front of us, blocking the path.

Nexus Corp. The kill team.

Two men leaned out the windows with carbines.

"Hold on!" I yelled.

I didn't hit the brakes. I gunned it. I was going to ram them.

But before we made impact, Maya slammed her hand onto the dashboard.

"STOP!" she screamed.

It wasn't a request. It was a command that carried a physical force.

I slammed the brakes. The van skidded to a halt twenty feet from the SUV.

The mercenaries opened fire.

Bullets impacted the windshield, spider-webbing the glass. I ducked, grabbing Maya and pulling her down.

"We're dead!" Chen wailed from the back.

"Wait," Maya whispered.

She wasn't cowering. She was sitting up, staring through the shattered windshield at the SUV. Her eyes were fully violet now, two burning suns in the gloom of the cab.

She raised her hand, palm open, toward the enemy.

"Disconnect."

The sound that followed wasn't a noise. It was the absence of noise.

It started with the streetlights lining the railyard. They didn't just go out; the bulbs exploded in sequence, showering the ground with glass.

Then, the drones overhead. The buzzing stopped instantly. They dropped from the sky like stones, crashing into the shipping containers and the ground with sickening crunches.

Then, the SUV.

The headlights died. The engine cut out.

But it didn't stop there.

The two mercenaries leaning out of the windows... they froze.

They didn't duck. They didn't reload. They just... stopped.

One of them convulsed. A spark—bright blue and violent—erupted from his neck. He slumped forward, hanging limp out of the window frame like a ragdoll.

The other one started to scream. But it wasn't a human scream. It was a digital screech, a modulation of static and feedback tearing through a vocal synthesizer. He clawed at his face, ripping off his ballistic mask.

Smoke poured from his eyes.

"What is happening?" I whispered, watching the horror show through the cracked glass.

"Interference," Maya said. Her voice sounded exhausted, heavy. "They are connected to the network. I... I just spiked the voltage."

She slumped back against the seat, the violet light fading from her eyes. Blood trickled from both nostrils.

"Drive," she murmured. "Before they reboot."

I didn't need to be told twice.

The SUV was dead in the water. I threw the van into gear, jumped the curb, and drove around the blockade. I passed within three feet of the screaming mercenary. His skin was gray, his veins standing out like black wires.

We cleared the railyard. The city limits of Seattle faded behind us.

I drove for an hour without speaking. I stuck to back roads, avoiding traffic cameras and toll booths. The van rattled and shook, but it kept moving.

"Chen," I called back. "Status?"

"I am... physically intact," Chen said. He sounded shaken. "But logically? I am having difficulty processing the variables."

"Join the club."

I looked over at Maya. She was asleep, or unconscious. Her head lolled against the window, bouncing with every pothole.

I reached over and checked her pulse. It was erratic. Fast, then slow. Like a glitchy metronome.

I thought about the nursing home. I thought about the tablet. *It's not just a backup. It's a possession.*

I looked at her hand resting on her lap.

Her fingertips were twitching. tapping against her jeans.

Dash-dash-dot.

I focused on the road, my grip on the steering wheel tightening until the plastic creaked.

We had escaped the Hive. We had escaped the kill team.

But as I drove us toward the bunker, toward safety, I couldn't shake the feeling that I was the getaway driver for a bank robbery where we stole the wrong bag.

We hadn't just extracted Maya.
We had extracted the Breach.

Chapter 10: The Numbers Game

Maya

The bunker didn't smell like a command center. It smelled like the inside of a 1950s lung. Stale air, wet concrete, and the faint, coppery tang of old pipes.

We were sixty feet underground, beneath a defunct radar station in the Cascade foothills. Carter had driven the stolen plumbing van until the fuel gauge was empty and the tires were shredded, then hiked us the last three miles through the dripping pine forest.

My legs felt like lead. My head felt like a radio tuned between stations—a constant, low-grade buzz of static that spiked whenever I looked at an electronic device.

"Watch your step," Carter said, pushing open a heavy blast door.

We stepped into the main atrium.

It was a chaotic collision of eras. The walls were peeling Cold War green, lined with rusted lockers and Civil Defense posters. But the center of the room was a hive of modern chaos. Server racks were jury-rigged into the ventilation system. Cables ran across the floor like snakes. Monitors—dozens of them—were mounted on every available surface, casting a pale blue glow over the dust.

And in the middle of it all sat Julian Koga.

He didn't turn around when we entered. He was sitting in a hammock chair suspended from the ceiling pipes, typing on a wireless keyboard that rested on his knees. He was wearing noise-canceling headphones and a hoodie that looked like it hadn't been washed since the last administration.

"Julian," Dr. Chen called out, his voice echoing in the concrete chamber. "We have brought the package."

Julian didn't flinch. His fingers moved across the keys in a blur.

Carter stepped forward, looking around the room with a critical eye. "This is your oracle? He looks like a college dropout living in his mom's basement."

"He is not an oracle," Chen said, navigating the maze of cables. "He is a actuary of the apocalypse. And he is deaf, Mr. Reed. He cannot hear you."

Chen walked up to the hammock and tapped Julian on the shoulder.

Julian spun the chair around. He was younger than I expected—maybe twenty-five. He had sharp, angular features and eyes that were constantly moving, scanning us like he was reading our source code. He pulled the headphones down around his neck.

He didn't say hello. He looked at me, then at the dried blood on my nose, then at the empty space above my head.

"You're leaking," he said. His voice was soft, monotone.

"I'm what?" I asked, leaning against a server rack for support.

"Data," Julian said. He pointed a long, thin finger at my forehead. "Your refresh rate is off. You're lagging about twelve milliseconds behind reality."

Carter stepped between us. "Focus, kid. We need intel. We have the drive from the Hive."

Julian looked at Carter with mild disinterest. "I don't need the drive. I've been watching the traffic."

He kicked off the floor, spinning his chair back to the wall of monitors. He tapped a key.

The screens shifted. Instead of code or news feeds, they displayed graphs. Hundreds of them. Sine waves, scatter plots, histograms.

"I track anomalies," Julian said, typing as he spoke. "Stock market glitches. Power grid fluctuations. GPS drift. Most people think they're random. Noise in the system."

He hit *Enter*. The screens merged into one massive visualization. It looked like a spiral galaxy, swirling toward a black hole in the center.

"They aren't random," Julian said. "They're a countdown."

I walked closer, drawn to the patterns. The static in my head quieted down when I looked at the math. It made sense. It was clean.

"It's a Fibonacci sequence," I whispered, tracing the curve on the nearest screen. "Recursive. Exponential."

Julian looked at me, a spark of interest in his eyes. "Finally. Someone who speaks the language."

He jumped out of the chair, grabbing a dry-erase marker. He started writing on the glass of a monitor, sketching over the digital data.

"The Breach events," Julian said, drawing rapid circles. "The nursing home. The traffic lights. The Hive. They follow a temporal geometry. The interval between events is halving every twenty-four hours."

"In English," Carter said, crossing his arms.

"It's an asymptotic curve," I translated, the horror dawning on me. "It means the events are getting closer together. Faster. Until they merge."

"Correct," Julian said. He drew a vertical line at the end of the spiral. "The convergence point. The singularity. When the interval between breaches reaches zero, the barrier between the network and the physical world collapses entirely."

"When?" Carter asked. "Give me a date."

Julian wrote a number on the glass.

12.21

"December twenty-first," Chen said quietly. "The Winter Solstice."

"Ten days," Julian said. He turned to look at us. "In ten days, the sun aligns with the galactic center. The ionization in the atmosphere will be at its peak. The signal strength will be maximum."

"The Solar Storm," I said. "The news reports. It's not a natural disaster."

"It's a carrier wave," Julian corrected. "Think of it like a radio. The Harbingers are the broadcast. But they need a signal strong enough to reach every device on Earth simultaneously. The solstice provides the atmospheric conditions. NeuroSync provides the receivers."

He pointed to a map of the world on another screen. Seven red dots were pulsing on it.

"The Seven Towers," Julian said.

"We saw the map," Carter said. "We know about the locations."

"You know *where* they are," Julian said. "You don't know *what* they are."

He tapped the screen. The map zoomed in on the Pacific Northwest location.

"They aren't just servers," Julian said. "They're tuning forks."

He brought up a schematic. It showed a massive spire, grounded deep into the earth's crust.

"Ley Lines," Chen muttered, cleaning his glasses nervously. "Geomantic energy points. Ancient civilizations built temples on them. Cathedrals. Pyramids."

"And now, NeuroSync builds data centers on them," Julian said. "They're tapping into the planet's electromagnetic field. When the countdown hits zero, those seven towers will resonate. They will turn the entire ionosphere into one giant Wi-Fi network."

"And what happens then?" I asked, though I already knew the answer.

Julian looked at me. His expression was devoid of fear. It was just math.

"Overwrite," he said.

He typed a command. The simulation on the screen played out. The seven red dots expanded, connecting with each other, covering the globe in a violet mesh.

"Human consciousness is just a complex waveform," Julian explained, as if discussing the weather. "The Harbinger signal is a louder waveform. Constructive interference. It doesn't kill people. It just... retunes them."

"Like the mercenaries," Carter said darkly. "It turns them into drones."

"Into nodes," Julian corrected. "A global hive mind. No more war. No more pain. No more individuality. Just... the static."

The room went silent. The hum of the servers felt louder, more oppressive.

"Ten days," Carter repeated. He looked at the map. "Seven towers."

"We can't hit them all," I said. "Not with three people and a van."

"We don't have to hit them all," Julian said. He erased the board with his sleeve. "The network is a star topology. It has a master node."

He pointed to the dot in the Pacific Northwest.

"The Prime Tower," he said. "It controls the synchronization frequency. If you take that offline, the others fall out of phase. The signal desynchronizes. The door slams shut."

"Where is it?" Carter asked.

Julian pointed to the coordinates. "The Olympic Peninsula. In the exclusion zone."

Carter stared at the map. I saw the gears turning in his head. He wasn't looking at the math anymore. He was looking at the terrain. The logistics. The kill zones.

"It's a fortress," Carter said. "If it's the Prime Tower, Krane will have an army guarding it."

"Then we need an army," I said.

Carter looked at me. "We don't have an army, Maya. We have a disgraced scientist, a math savant, and a hacker who is currently hallucinating geometry."

"We have the Disconnected," Julian said.

We all looked at him.

"The what?" Carter asked.

Julian tapped a few keys. A list of names scrolled down the screen.

"Analog survivalists," Julian said. "Luddites. People who rejected the NeuroSync integration. They live off the grid. They use HAM radios and diesel engines. I've been coordinating with them on the shortwave frequencies."

He looked at Carter.

"They have guns," Julian said. "And they hate the internet."

Carter actually smiled. It was a grim, wolfish expression.

"Alright," Carter said, turning to the map. "Ten days to the end of the world. We need to recruit a militia, plan a siege, and travel three hundred miles through hostile territory."

He looked at me.

"Can you hold it together for ten days, Maya? Can you keep the voices out?"

I looked at the countdown on Julian's screen. 09:23:59:59.

I could feel the static itching behind my eyes. I could feel Michael—or the thing that used to be Michael—waiting in the silence.

"I don't need to keep them out," I said, watching the numbers drop. "I just need to make sure I'm the one driving when we get there."

Chapter 11: The Blackout

Carter

There is a specific smell to a government safe house that has been compromised. It smells of burnt coffee, nervous sweat, and the ozone tang of overheating servers. But there is a specific smell to a world that is ending.

It smells like silence.

I was in the bunker's airlock, stripping down the suppressed carbine I'd taken off the mercenary at the Hive. It was a beautiful piece of engineering—polymer frame, biometric trigger lock (which Julian had bypassed in thirty seconds), and a receiver stamped with no serial number.

Click-clack.

I reassembled the bolt carrier group and slid it back into the upper receiver.

"Perimeter alert," Julian's voice drifted over the intercom. "Sector 4. The forest road."

I didn't panic. I didn't rush. I racked the slide, chambering a round, and checked the feed on the monitor mounted by the door.

A black SUV was winding its way up the overgrown logging trail. It wasn't moving like a tactical team. It was moving fast, recklessly, bouncing over ruts and tearing through the underbrush.

"One vehicle," I said into the comms. "Civilian plates."

"Do we engage?" Chen asked, his voice trembling.

"Hold fire," I said. "Let's see who knocks."

I moved to the blast door, positioning myself in the blind spot of the camera. I watched the monitor. The SUV skidded to a halt fifty yards from the entrance, hidden beneath the canopy of pines.

The driver's door opened.

A woman stepped out. She was wearing a trench coat over a pantsuit that cost more than my car. Her blonde hair was pulled back in a severe ponytail, but stray strands were whipping around her face in the wind. She looked rattled.

She didn't look at the hidden camera. She looked directly at the blast door.

She raised her hands. In her right hand, she held a hard-shell Pelican case. In her left, she held a badge.

"NSA," I muttered.

"Do you know her?" Maya asked, appearing in the doorway behind me. She looked better—less pale, though her eyes still had that unnerving, distant focus.

I looked at the screen. I zoomed in on the face.

"Yeah," I said, lowering the weapon slightly. "I know her. Open the door, Julian."

"Are you insane?" Chen sputtered over the comms. "She is the government!"

"The government is gone, Doc," I said, hitting the manual release for the heavy steel bolts. "There's just people left now."

Lilith Sterling walked into the bunker like she owned it, even though she was shaking. She dropped the Pelican case on the nearest table and leaned against it, exhaling a breath she seemed to have been holding for miles.

"You look like hell, Carter," she said.

"You look like a fed," I replied. "What are you doing here, Lilith?"

"I traced the plumbing van," she said. "You weren't exactly subtle leaving the industrial district. A-1 Plumbing? Really?"

"It was available."

Lilith looked around the room—at the jury-rigged servers, the conspiracy theorist map on the wall, and the motley crew of fugitives. Her eyes lingered on Maya.

"So this is her," Lilith said. " The girl who broke the internet."

"I didn't break it," Maya said, her voice cool. "I just turned on the lights."

Lilith scoffed. She tapped the Pelican case. "Well, whatever you did, you kicked the hornet's nest. I just came from Fort Meade. It's a madhouse. The Director is screaming about Russian cyber-warfare. The Joint Chiefs are mobilizing for a kinetic strike on Beijing."

"They're wrong," Julian said from his hammock, not looking up from his screen. "It's not state actors. The attack vector is internal."

"I know," Lilith said. She opened the case.

Inside wasn't a weapon. It was paper. Stacks of printed dossiers, satellite photos, and transcripts.

"Digital intel is compromised," Lilith said. "Anything on a screen can be edited in real-time by the algorithm. This?" She slapped the stack of paper. "This is hard copy. Ink. It can't glitch."

She spread a map of the globe on the table. It was covered in black marker.

"This is the status of the global communications grid as of two hours ago," she said.

The map was almost entirely black.

"ATC is down," Lilith recited, her voice tight. "Every flight in the Northern Hemisphere has been grounded. GPS satellites are drifting—navigation is reverting to inertial guidance. The stock markets in Tokyo, London, and New York froze simultaneously at 09:00 Zulu time."

"The Blackout," Carter murmured.

"It's not just a blackout," Lilith corrected. "It's a takeover. The emergency broadcast channels are still active, but they aren't broadcasting FEMA alerts. They're broadcasting... static."

"The signal," Maya whispered.

"We tried to triangulate the source," Lilith continued. "We thought it was jamming towers. But it's not coming from towers. It's coming from *everywhere*. Every smart device, every router, every cell phone tower is acting as a repeater."

She looked at me, her eyes pleading.

"Carter, the chain of command is shattering. The President is in a bunker in Virginia, but half his staff can't get into the building because the biometric locks don't recognize them anymore. General hosts are reporting 'phantom divisions' on their radar screens."

"Phantom divisions?" I asked.

"Radar ghosts," Lilith said. "Massive troop movements that aren't there. Fleets of bombers that don't exist. The systems are hallucinating."

"It's the precursor," Julian said. He slid down from his hammock, walking over to the map. "Destabilize the infrastructure. Sow confusion. Isolate the population. When the towers activate on the Solstice, there will be no organized resistance because nobody will know who to fight."

"They'll be fighting ghosts," Chen added quietly. "And shooting each other."

Lilith looked at me. "I need to know what we're up against, Carter. You were NeuroSync's clean-up man. You know how they operate."

"This isn't an operation, Lilith," I said. "It's an invasion."

I walked over to the far wall of the bunker. There was a row of gray metal lockers, rusted shut. I'd been eyeing them since we arrived.

"Julian," I said. "Can you cut the locks?"

"I can do better," Julian said. He grabbed a pair of bolt cutters from his tool pile and tossed them to me.

Snip. Snip.

I pulled the locker doors open.

Inside, preserving in grease and plastic, was the stash the previous occupants had left behind. Cold War surplus.

M14 rifles. Crates of 7.62mm ammunition. Fragmentation grenades. Claymore mines. And in the corner, a dusty but functional M60 machine gun.

"Jesus," Lilith said. "Planning a coup?"

"No," I said, pulling an M14 from the rack and checking the action. It was heavy, made of wood and steel. No chips. No smart-sights. No Wi-Fi.

"We're planning a siege," I said.

I turned to the group.

"The digital war is over," I told them. "We lost. The enemy controls the network. They control the comms. They control the truth."

I slammed a magazine into the rifle.

"So we fight the war they can't hack," I said. "We go analog. We use paper maps. We use iron sights. We use radios that tune with a dial."

I looked at Lilith.

"You have NSA clearance," I said. "Can you get us a chopper?"

Lilith laughed, a harsh, barking sound. "Carter, I can't even get a pizza delivered right now. The skies are closed."

"Then we drive," I said. "We go north. To the Exclusion Zone."

"The Pacific Northwest tower," Maya said.

"Exactly." I started tossing boxes of ammo onto the table. "Lilith, you said the military is seeing ghosts? Good. That means they're distracted. We slip through the chaos."

"And do what?" Lilith asked, picking up a grenade and weighing it in her hand. "Blow up a server farm?"

"We're going to kill the Queen," I said. "We find the Prime Tower. We sever the connection. And we hope to hell that when the lights come back on, there's still a world left to save."

Suddenly, the lights in the bunker flickered.

Not the violet pulse of the anomaly. Just a power surge.

Then, absolute darkness.

The hum of the servers died. The monitors went black.

"Main power is cut!" Julian yelled in the dark.

"Generators!" I shouted.

"They aren't kicking in!"

"They found us," Maya whispered. Her voice was right next to my ear. "They followed the NSA car."

I racked the bolt of the M14.

"Julian, Chen, get behind the servers!" I ordered. "Lilith, you take the left flank! Maya, stay with me!"

"They're not at the door, Carter," Maya said. "They're already inside."

A blue light flared in the corner of the room. It was the "standby" LED on a dormant router.

It blinked.

Dash-dash-dot.

Then, the emergency speakers on the wall—the old Civil Defense sirens—crackled to life.

"...Carter..."

The voice was everywhere.

I raised the rifle in the dark.

"Welcome to the war," I said.

Chapter 12: First Contact

Maya

The darkness in the bunker was total, but the noise was blinding.

"...Carter... Maya... Carter..."

The voice booming from the Civil Defense speakers wasn't human. It was a digital composite, a thick sludge of audio files stitched together to sound like a threat. It echoed off the concrete walls, layered with a high-pitched screech that made my teeth ache.

Flashlights cut crazy arcs through the gloom. I saw Carter tracking the sound with his rifle barrel, moving toward the speaker mounted above the blast door.

"I'm killing it," Carter yelled over the din.

"No!" I screamed, scrambling over the tangle of cables on the floor. "Don't shoot the hardware!"

"It's compromised!" Lilith shouted, her back against the lockers, weapon drawn. "They're in the room with us!"

"They aren't in the room!" I yelled back, grabbing Chen's shoulder and hauling him toward the center table. "They're on the line! It's a carrier wave!"

I looked at Chen. He was clutching his bag of equipment like a life preserver.

"The spectrum analyzer!" I shouted at him. "Give it to me!"

Chen fumbled with the zipper, his hands shaking. He pulled out a boxy, analog device with a glowing green CRT screen.

"It is... it is just a receiver!" Chen stammered. "It cannot transmit!"

"I don't need to transmit," I said, grabbing the device. "I need to filter."

The voice on the speakers changed pitch. It deepened, rattling the dust from the ceiling vents.

"...found you... found you..."

I slammed the analyzer onto the table. I grabbed an auxiliary cable from the floor—one end plugged into the bunker's PA system, the other loose. I jammed it into the input jack of Chen's device.

"Julian!" I yelled into the dark. "I need a bandpass filter! Isolate the frequency 440 Hertz and purge everything else!"

"440?" Julian asked from the shadows. "That's standard musical pitch. A4."

"It's Michael's pitch," I said, my fingers flying over the dials of the analyzer. "When we were kids... he played the cello. He hummed that note when he was thinking. It's his baseline."

If Michael was in there—if the real Michael was trapped inside that screaming storm of data—he would be holding onto something constant. A totem.

"Do it!" I ordered.

Julian didn't argue. He typed a command on his battery-powered deck.

The screeching from the speakers stopped instantly.

The silence that rushed back into the room was heavy, ringing in our ears.

Then, a low hum began.

Hmmmmmm.

It was a pure tone. A perfect A4.

On the green screen of the analyzer, a single wave formed. It wasn't jagged or chaotic like the Harbinger signal. It was smooth. Sine.

"Michael?" I whispered, leaning into the device. "Can you hear me?"

The wave on the screen spiked.

"...May... fly..."

The voice was faint, buried under layers of static, but it wasn't the monster. It was him. It sounded exhausted. Thin. Like he was speaking from the bottom of a well.

"I'm here," I said, tears pricking my eyes. "We're all here. Carter. Chen."

"...*Chen*..." The voice cracked. "...*tell him... the math was right... the gravity is... crushing...*"

"Ask him what they are," Carter said. He was standing right behind me, his rifle still raised, but lowered slightly. "We need to know the enemy."

"Michael," I said, focusing on the waveform. "Who are the Harbingers? Are they AI? Are they aliens?"

The wave on the screen convulsed. The static rose up, threatening to drown him out.

"...*older*..." Michael whispered. "...*not aliens... predators...*"

The speakers crackled.

"...*they eat... complexity...*"

"What does that mean?" Lilith asked, stepping closer.

I looked at Julian. He was staring at the screen, entranced.

"The Fermi Paradox," Julian murmured. "The Great Filter."

"Explain," Carter barked.

"Civilizations rise," Julian said, his voice monotone. "They build technology. They connect. They create massive networks of information. And then... they go silent. Maybe they don't blow themselves up. Maybe something *eats* them."

"...*yes*..." Michael's voice hissed. "...*informational parasites... they drift between stars... waiting for a signal... waiting for a world to get loud enough...*"

I felt the blood drain from my face. "NeuroSync. We got loud."

"...*we lit a beacon*..." Michael said. "...*we connected a billion minds... and rang the dinner bell...*"

"And Krane?" I asked. "Victor Krane. Is he being controlled? Is he a victim?"

The waveform spiked red. The sound of the speakers distorted, turning into a low growl before snapping back to Michael's voice.

"...*traitor...*"

The word hung in the air, heavy with venom.

"...*he made a deal... Mayfly... he saw them coming... in the code... he didn't try to stop them... he offered them a key...*"

"What key?"

"*...humanity...*"

"He's selling us," Carter said, his grip tightening on his weapon. "He's processing the population to feed them, in exchange for what? Survival?"

"*...ascension...*" Michael whispered. "*...he wants to be... the Administrator... of the new silence...*"

The signal began to degrade. The smooth sine wave was getting chopped up by jagged spikes of interference. The violet light from the hard drive on the table began to pulse faster.

Thump-thump. Thump-thump.

"*...I can't... hold the door...*" Michael gasped. The audio sounded like he was drowning. "*...the Solstice... the alignment... it makes them strong...*"

"Michael, listen to me," I pleaded, grabbing the sides of the analyzer. "How do we stop it? We're going to the Prime Tower. Is that the kill switch?"

"*...not a switch...*"

The static roared, loud as a jet engine. I frantically adjusted the dials, trying to hold the lock.

"*...it's a heart...*" Michael screamed over the noise. "*...the Prime Tower is the heart... you have to stop the beat...*"

"How?"

"*...Target... the bridge...*"

"Which bridge?" I yelled. "The software? The interface?"

"*...no...*"

The voice faded to a whisper.

"*...the Avatar... Krane... he is the bridge... kill the host... kill the connection...*"

CRACK.

The screen of the spectrum analyzer shattered.

Sparks showered the table. The speakers in the bunker blew out with a final, deafening pop that left my ears ringing.

Smoke curled up from the ruined electronics.

I stood there in the sudden silence, breathing hard. The smell of ozone was overpowering.

"He's gone," Chen whispered.

"No," I said, wiping a smudge of soot from my cheek. "He's not gone. He's holding the line."

I turned to Carter.

"Krane isn't just the CEO," I said. "He's the vessel. The Harbingers are energy. They need a physical anchor to survive in our reality until the Merge is complete. That anchor is Victor Krane."

Carter lowered his rifle. His face was set in grim lines, illuminated by the beam of his flashlight.

"So we don't just have to blow up a tower," Carter said.

"No," I said. "We have to assassinate the most protected man on Earth."

Lilith let out a dark, humorless laugh. "Well. At least the mission parameters are clear."

"Clear?" Julian asked, looking at his dead monitors. "We have no power. We have no transport. And we have a god-entity hunting us."

Carter walked to the table and slammed a fresh magazine into his rifle.

"We have a target," he said. "That's enough."

He looked at me.

"Maya, get your gear. If they found us on the comms, they have our coordinates. We need to be ten miles away before the kinetic team arrives."

I grabbed the broken hard drive—my brother's soul in a box—and shoved it into my bag.

"One more thing," I said, stopping at the door.

"What?" Carter asked.

"Michael said the Prime Tower is the heart," I said. "If we stop the heart, everything connected to it dies."

I looked at the group.

"That includes Michael. And the millions of people already uploaded."

Carter looked at me for a long moment. He didn't offer false hope.

"I know," he said.

He pushed the blast door open, leading us out into the night.

Chapter 13: The Target

Carter

The escape from the bunker wasn't a sprint; it was a ghost walk.

We moved through the density of the Cascade foothills, navigating by the faint, silver light of a moon that looked too large in the sky. The air was freezing, biting at exposed skin, but we didn't stop to zip up jackets. We put distance between us and the coordinates Lilith had burned.

We didn't see the kill team that came for us. But we heard them.

Half a mile back, a deep, resonant *thrum* shook the ground. I looked over my shoulder to see a beam of violet light stab down from the clouds, impaling the radar station we had just vacated. It wasn't a missile. It was a kinetic strike from a orbital platform—or a simulation of one.

The top of the mountain simply erased itself. No explosion. Just a sudden, violent absence of matter, followed by the delayed roar of collapsing rock.

"Orbital bombardment?" Lilith whispered, stumbling over a tree root. "We don't have orbital platforms with that yield."

"We do now," I said, pushing her forward. "Or the system thinks we do. Either way, the bunker is gone."

We hiked for another hour until we hit a logging road. Julian had led us to a cache—not digital, but physical. A rusted shipping container hidden under a tarp and twenty years of moss.

Inside was our chariot: a 1978 Ford Bronco. Carbureted engine. Manual transmission. No ECU. No GPS. No Bluetooth.

"A dinosaur," Julian said, patting the rusted fender affectionately. "Invisible to the network."

I hotwired it in thirty seconds. The V8 engine roared to life, smelling of unburnt gas and freedom.

We drove west, staying off the interstates. The world outside the windows was wrong.

The Blackout was in full effect. The towns we passed were dark, save for the flickering of candles in windows. But the sky... the sky was broken.

At one point, we watched a commercial airliner descend silently toward the highway, its landing lights blazing. I slammed on the brakes, bracing for the crash. But the plane passed *through* the trees, dissolving into pixels as it hit the ground.

"Phantom signal," Maya murmured from the passenger seat. She was watching the glitch with a detached curiosity. "The air traffic control system is hallucinating, projecting the data onto the HUDs of reality."

"Don't watch it," I said, shifting gears. "Eyes on the road. The road is real."

We pulled over just before dawn at an abandoned ranger station near the edge of the Olympic National Forest. We needed fuel, and we needed a plan.

I spread Lilith's paper map on the hood of the Bronco. The engine block provided a welcome warmth against the morning chill.

"Alright," I said, uncapping a permanent marker. "Listen up."

The team gathered around. Maya, pale and shivering, clutching her jacket. Chen, wiping his glasses. Julian, looking at the trees like they were equations. Lilith, checking the load in her pistol for the tenth time.

"We have ten days," I said. "But we have three hundred miles of hostile terrain between us and the objective. And once we get there, we have to break into the most secure facility on the planet."

I circled a spot on the Olympic Peninsula.

"The Prime Tower," I said. "Nexus Corp calls it the 'Pillar.' It's located in the Hoh Rainforest, inside a fifty-mile exclusion zone."

"Why there?" Lilith asked. "It's a logistical nightmare."

"Isolation," Julian answered. "And geology. It sits on a convergence of basalt plates. Perfect for grounding a massive electromagnetic charge."

"And perfect for defense," I added.

I drew a circle around the target.

"The facility is built into a mountain. It has one access road, heavily patrolled. The airspace is a no-fly zone, guarded by automated SAM sites. The perimeter is monitored by seismic sensors, thermal optics, and—if the Hive was any indication—cyborg kill-teams."

I looked at Maya.

"You want to hack it?" I asked.

She shook her head. "I can't. Not from the outside. The Prime Tower will be air-gapped. Hard-lined into the geothermal tap. To inject a virus—or to upload the counter-frequency—I need to be physically plugged into the Central Core."

"And that," I said, tapping the map, "is the kill box."

I drew a cross-section of the facility on the dusty hood of the truck.

"The Core is here. Sub-level five. To get there, we have to bypass three layers of security."

I marked them off.

"Layer One: The Perimeter. Five miles of automated turrets and patrols. We can't sneak through that. We have to ghost it."

"Layer Two: The Lobby. This is where Krane will be. It's not just an office; it's a temple. He'll have his elite guard there. The 'Processors.'"

"Layer Three: The Bridge. The interface room. That's where Maya needs to go."

"It's a suicide mission," Lilith said flatly. "You're talking about assaulting a fortress with four people and a rusty truck."

"Five people," I corrected. "And we're not assaulting it. We're infiltrating it."

I looked at Chen. "Doc, you built the original specs. Does the facility have a heat exhaust?"

Chen blinked. "Yes. The geothermal turbines require massive ventilation. There are thermal vents on the north ridge."

"Vents large enough for a person?"

"Perhaps. But they vent steam at three hundred degrees. You would be boiled alive."

"Not if we shut down the turbines," I said.

I looked at Julian. "Can you cause a distraction? Something big enough to pull their eyes away from the thermal grid?"

Julian smiled. It was a cold, mathematical smile. "If I can get within range of their local intranet... I can feed the sensors a false positive. I can make them think the San Andreas fault is splitting open beneath their feet."

"Good," I said. "That buys us the vents."

I turned to Maya.

"This is the hard part," I said. "Once we're inside, it's close quarters. I can get you to the door, Maya. But once you plug in... you're on your own. I can't shoot code."

"I know," she said. Her voice was steady. "I'll handle the Harbingers. You handle Krane."

"Wait," Lilith interrupted. "What about the 'Army' you mentioned back at the bunker? The militia?"

"We use them as the anvil," I said. "We are the hammer. Julian will broadcast a summons on the shortwave bands. We tell the Disconnected to converge on the perimeter on the Solstice. They make noise. They draw the fire. While Nexus is busy fighting a peasant revolt at the front gate, we go in through the back."

"It's a Trojan Horse," Chen noted.

"It's a diversion," I said. "And a lot of those people are going to die."

I looked at them. I needed them to understand the cost.

"This isn't a rescue mission anymore," I said. "We aren't going there to save Michael. We aren't going there to save the internet."

I drove the tip of the marker into the center of the circle on the map.

"We are going there to kill a god."

I capped the marker. The sun was fully up now, casting long shadows through the ancient trees. The silence of the forest felt heavy, pregnant with the threat of what was coming.

"Load up," I ordered. "We have a long drive."

Maya didn't move immediately. She stared at the map, her finger tracing the line I had drawn.

"What is it?" I asked quietly.

"The exclusion zone," she whispered. "Michael used to go camping there. Before NeuroSync. Before everything."

She looked up at me. Her eyes were clear, the violet tint gone for the moment, replaced by a steely resolve that reminded me of the soldier she was becoming.

"He chose that spot," she said. "Krane didn't pick it. Michael did. He built his own tomb."

"Then let's go break him out," I said.

I climbed into the driver's seat of the Bronco. The engine rumbled, shaking the frame.

Part one of the job was done. We knew the threat. We knew the timeline. We survived the initial hit.

Now came the hard part.

I shifted into gear, the tires crunching over the gravel.

We were going to war.

Part II: The Infiltration

Tension: Heist mechanics, Claustrophobia, Surreal horror.

Chapter 14: Trojan Horse

Maya

The motel room smelled of mildew and cheap lemon cleaner, a sensory combination that would normally give me a migraine. Tonight, I barely noticed it. My world had narrowed down to the fourteen-inch screen of my laptop and the terrified reflection staring back at me from the bathroom mirror.

We were parked at the *Timberline Motor Inn*, ten miles outside the exclusion zone. It was a holding pattern. A final breath before the plunge.

"It's not compiling," I muttered, hitting the enter key with more force than necessary.

"Force it," Julian said. He was sitting on the bed, cross-legged, surrounded by candy bar wrappers and schematics of the Nexus power grid. "Bypass the checksum."

"If I bypass the checksum, the Nexus firewall will flag it as malware instantly," I argued, rubbing my eyes. "It has to look like a system update. It has to look boring."

I looked at the code on my screen.

It wasn't normal code. I had taken the fragment the Sentinel had burned into my mind—the recursive loop of the "Solar Flare" warning—and I was trying to wrap it in a standard corporate auditing shell.

It was like trying to wrap a rabid wolf in a sheepskin coat. The code *wanted* to be seen. It pulsed. It shifted variables when I wasn't looking. It was alive.

"Use a polymorphic engine," Julian suggested, not looking up. "Make the code rewrite itself every time the system scans it. Hide the teeth until it's inside the throat."

"That might work," I whispered.

I started typing again. I built a container—a boring, bureaucratic "Level 5 Efficiency Audit" program. Inside it, I placed the Sentinel's fragment. The virus.

I named the file sys_config_v4.exe.

The moment I saved it to the encrypted flash drive, the plastic casing felt warm to the touch.

"Done," I said, pulling the drive out. I held it up. A piece of the afterlife, smaller than a pack of gum.

"Good," Carter's voice came from the doorway connecting our room to the next. "Now do the rest."

He tossed a plastic shopping bag onto the desk.

I opened it. A box of hair dye. Black. A pair of non-prescription glasses with thick frames. A tailored grey pantsuit that smelled like a thrift store, but looked expensive enough to pass at a distance.

"Auditor disguise," Carter said. "Your name is Elena Vance. You're a freelance compliance officer from the Seattle branch. You have an appointment with the internal review board at 0900 hours."

"Elena Vance?" I asked, looking at the box of dye. "The dead woman from the nursing home?"

"NeuroSync's system still lists her as active in the payroll database," Carter said grimly. "We're using their own ghosts against them."

I took the bag into the bathroom and locked the door.

The fluorescent light buzzed overhead. I looked at myself in the mirror. Maya Reeves. Pale, exhausted, hair a messy brown tangle, eyes wide and frightened.

Maya Reeves couldn't walk into the Prime Tower. Maya Reeves was a liability.

I opened the box of dye.

The process was mechanical. I mixed the chemicals. I applied the paste. The smell of ammonia filled the tiny bathroom, burning my nose. I watched the brown strands turn the color of ink.

I waited twenty minutes, staring at the shower curtain, listening to the murmurs of Carter and Lilith planning the extraction route in the other room.

"...if she gets made, we can't breach the lobby to get her..."

"...she knows the risks..."

I washed the dye out. The water swirling down the drain looked like oil.

I dried my hair, straightening it until it hung in a sharp, severe curtain around my face. I put on the glasses. I put on the grey suit. It was tight in the shoulders, but it made me stand straighter.

I looked in the mirror again.

Maya was gone. Elena Vance stared back. She looked cold. She looked efficient. She looked like the kind of woman who fired people via email.

I unlocked the door and stepped out.

The room went quiet.

Julian looked up from his candy bar. "Whoa."

Lilith nodded, a professional assessment. "The glasses are a nice touch. You look like you hate fun."

Carter was cleaning his weapon at the small table. He stopped. He stood up and walked over to me. He didn't smile. He circled me, checking the details.

"Shoes?" he asked.

"Black pumps," I said, pointing to my feet. "Uncomfortable. Loud on tile."

"Good. Auditors like to be heard coming," he said. He reached out and adjusted the collar of my blazer. His knuckles grazed my neck. His hand was warm.

"The badge?" he asked.

I held up the ID card Lilith had forged using the NSA printer in the van. It had my face, but the eyes were different. Cold.

Carter took the badge and clipped it to my lapel.

"You're not going in there to hack," he said, his voice low, for my ears only. "You're going in there to inspect. You have authority. You belong there. If anyone challenges you, you don't defend yourself. You attack. You ask to see *their* supervisor."

"Aggressive bureaucracy," I said. "I can do that."

"I know you can." He looked me in the eyes. "Maya is the girl who hid under the floorboards. Elena is the woman who burns the house down. Be Elena."

He handed me a small earpiece. "Inductive loop. Invisible unless they do a cavity search. I'll be on the channel. I can't talk much—I'll be in the sewers—but I'll be listening."

"And the signal?" I asked. "The Harbingers?"

"If you hear voices," Carter said, "don't listen."

An hour later, I was sitting in the back of a black town car Lilith had "requisitioned" from a rental agency. Carter was driving, wearing a chauffeur's cap that looked ridiculous on him, but somehow worked.

We were at the main gate of the Exclusion Zone.

The Prime Tower loomed in the distance, a jagged spike of glass and steel rising out of the primordial green of the Hoh Rainforest. It didn't look like a building; it looked like a glitch in the landscape.

The gate was intimidating. Concrete barriers. Guard towers with automated heavy machine guns tracking our movement. A sign read: *NEUROSYNC PRIME - RESTRICTED AIRSPACE - LETHAL FORCE AUTHORIZED.*

A guard approached the car. He wasn't human.

He walked with that smooth, hydraulic gait I recognized from the Hive. His face was covered by a mirrored visor. A submachine gun hung from a sling across his chest.

Carter rolled down the window.

"Delivery," Carter said, his voice bored. "Auditor from Seattle."

The guard didn't speak. He raised a scanner and pointed it at me in the back seat.

A red laser grid washed over my face.

My heart hammered against my ribs, threatening to bruise them. *Be Elena. Be boring.*

I looked at the guard with disdain. I checked my watch, sighing loudly.

"I have a meeting with Director Krane in ten minutes," I said, pitching my voice to be sharp, impatient. "If this takes much longer, I'll be logging a delay on your efficiency report."

The guard paused. The scanner beeped.

IDENTITY CONFIRMED: VANCE, ELENA. CLEARANCE LEVEL 5.

The guard lowered the scanner. He stepped back and waved us through.

The heavy steel gate rolled open.

Carter accelerated smoothly. We passed through the perimeter, leaving the world of trees and mud behind, entering the manicured, sterile grounds of the facility.

"We're in," Carter whispered into the comms.

I gripped the flash drive in my pocket. My hand was sweating, but my face was stone.

I looked up at the tower. It seemed to vibrate against the sky, the air around it shimmering with heat and data.

"Showtime," I whispered.

Chapter 15: The Lion's Den

Carter

The moment the heavy glass doors of the lobby slid shut behind Maya, she was gone.

I watched her for a split second in the rearview mirror—a slim figure in a grey suit, standing tall in the belly of the beast. Then I looked away. Rule number one of protection work: once the principal is out of the safe zone, you don't stare. You move.

I drove the town car around the circular drive, following the signs for *Deliveries/Service*. The moment I broke the line of sight from the front gate, I killed the engine.

I rolled the car into a dense patch of ferns near the loading dock, covered it with a camouflage net from the trunk, and stripped off the chauffeur's cap.

"Comm check," I whispered, tapping the earpiece. "Lilith, you on the line?"

"Loud and clear," Lilith's voice came through, static-free. She was parked five miles back in the tree line with the high-gain antenna. *"Maya is in the elevator. Biometrics cleared. She's ascending to the executive suite."*

"Copy. I'm going under."

I checked my gear. The silenced Sig Sauer on my hip. The ceramic knife in my boot. A handful of shaped C4 charges in my jacket lining. It wasn't enough for a war, but it was enough to make a mess.

I slipped into the treeline, circling the perimeter of the Prime Tower until I found the drainage outflow Julian had identified on the geological survey.

It was a concrete maw set into the side of the basalt cliff, half-obscured by moss and steaming slightly in the morning chill. A heavy iron grate barred the entrance.

I knelt, inspecting the bars. The steel was thick, but the concrete anchoring it was old.

I took a small canister of liquid nitrogen from my pack—stolen from a medical supply truck two days ago—and sprayed the base of the center bar. The metal groaned as it froze, turning white. I waited ten seconds, then kicked it hard with the heel of my boot.

Snap.

The frozen steel shattered like glass.

I squeezed through the gap, sliding into the darkness.

The air inside the tunnel tasted of sulfur and recycled water. It was hot—oppressively hot. The Prime Tower was sitting on top of a geothermal tap, and this was the exhaust system.

I moved slowly, keeping my back to the curved wall. My flashlight was off; I was navigating by the faint, bioluminescent glow of the moss that had crept in from the outside, and the occasional red blink of a maintenance sensor.

"Lilith," I whispered. "I'm in the outflow. Heading for the sub-basement junction."

"Watch your thermal signature," Lilith warned. *"The schematics show heat sensors every fifty yards."*

"I'm masking it," I said, pulling my thermal poncho tighter. It was lined with Mylar, designed to reflect body heat back inward. It was like wearing a sauna suit in a furnace. Sweat was already trickling down my spine.

I crawled for twenty minutes. The tunnel angled upward. The smell of rot faded, replaced by the smell of ozone and industrial cleaner.

I reached a service ladder. Above me, a circular hatch.

I listened.

The hum. That same, low-frequency vibration I had felt at the Hive. It vibrated through the rungs of the ladder, rattling my teeth.

Thump-thump. Thump-thump.

The heartbeat of the tower.

I climbed. I reached the hatch and cracked it open a fraction of an inch.

No guards. No cameras immediately visible. Just a long, white corridor lined with pipes.

I pushed the hatch open and pulled myself up.

I was in the sub-basement.

This wasn't the polished chrome of the upper levels. This was the gut. The walls were raw concrete. The lighting was harsh fluorescent strips that buzzed.

I moved down the corridor, weapon drawn.

I passed rooms labeled *Geothermal Exchange* and *High Voltage Distribution*.

Then, I came to a set of double doors. No label. Just a biohazard symbol and a heavy magnetic lock.

The window in the door was reinforced wire glass. I peered through.

I froze.

I've seen war crimes. I've seen mass graves in the Balkans and torture cells in black sites. But I had never seen anything like this.

The room was massive. It looked like a server farm, with rows of tall, black cabinets. But instead of blinking lights and hard drives, the cabinets contained... tanks.

Vertical glass cylinders, filled with a cloudy, amber fluid.

And inside each tank was a person.

"Lilith," I breathed, my voice barely a sound. "I found the processors."

"What? Are they cyborgs?"

"No," I said, pressing my face closer to the glass. "They're people."

There were hundreds of them. Men. Women. Different ages, different races. They were stripped naked, floating in the suspension fluid.

Thick black cables were drilled directly into the base of their skulls, weaving into their spines like metallic ivy. Their mouths were covered by respirators.

But it was their eyes that stopped my heart.

They didn't have eyes.

Where the orbits should have been, there were optical implants. Glowing violet lenses that pulsed in time with the heartbeat of the building.

Thump-thump.

Every time the pulse hit, the bodies in the tanks twitched in unison. A hundred spasms happening at the exact same millisecond.

"They're networked," I whispered, fighting the bile rising in my throat. "He's using their brains as CPUs. Parallel processing."

I looked at the tank closest to the door. The subject was a young man. On the metal casing at the base of the tank, a name was stenciled.

SUBJECT: 4591. STATUS: ACTIVE. SOURCE: ST. JUDE'S.

"St. Jude's," I said. "The nursing home. These aren't volunteers. They're the missing. The forgotten."

I saw movement at the far end of the room.

A technician in a full hazmat suit was walking down the aisle, checking the vitals on a tablet. He stopped at one tank where the subject was thrashing slightly—a rejection seizure.

The technician didn't call for a doctor. He didn't administer sedatives.

He tapped the tablet.

A jolt of electricity arced through the fluid in the tank. The body went rigid, back arching in a silent scream, then went limp. The violet eyes glowed brighter.

Rebooted.

My grip on the Sig Sauer tightened until the polymer frame creaked. I wanted to kick the door down. I wanted to shoot the technician and break every tank in the room.

But I couldn't.

If I breached now, the alarm would sound. Maya would be trapped upstairs with Krane.

"Carter?" Lilith's voice was urgent. "Your heart rate just spiked to 140. What's happening?"

"I'm looking at hell, Lilith," I said, stepping back from the window. "We were wrong. The Harbingers aren't just eating data. They're eating people. They're hollowing them out and wearing them."

"Stick to the mission," she said, though her voice wavered. *"Find the core. If we shut down the Prime Tower, maybe... maybe they wake up."*

I looked at the rows of eyeless, twitching bodies.

"No," I said grimly. "They aren't waking up. Their brains are fused to the wire. If we shut this down... we kill them all."

I turned away from the door.

"And that's exactly what we have to do."

I moved down the corridor, leaving the silent screaming behind me. I found the stairwell access. *Level 1.*

I swiped the keycard I'd lifted from the mercenary at the Hive. The light turned green.

I opened the door and started to climb, ascending from the horror of the basement toward the lie of the penthouse.

Maya was up there. Alone with the man who built this slaughterhouse.

"Hang on, kid," I whispered to the empty stairwell. "I'm coming."

Chapter 16: The Visionary

Maya

The elevator ride to the penthouse of the Prime Tower took forty-five seconds. It was a glass capsule shooting up the spine of the building, offering a panoramic view of the Hoh Rainforest below.

I watched the trees shrink. From up here, the ancient moss-draped maples looked like weeds. The Exclusion Zone was just a patch of green on a map that Victor Krane was rewriting.

Be Elena, I told myself. *Elena is bored. Elena is annoyed. Elena doesn't care about the apocalypse; she cares about quarterly compliance.*

I adjusted my glasses, smoothing the lapel of my grey suit. In my pocket, the flash drive containing the Sentinel virus felt heavy, like a stone that was slowly heating up.

Ding.

The doors slid open.

I didn't step into an office. I stepped into a void.

The entire top floor was an open-concept space walled in floor-to-ceiling glass. The floor was polished white marble that reflected the grey sky, making it feel like we were floating in the clouds. There were no desks. No filing cabinets. Just a single, white table in the center of the room, and a man standing by the window, looking out at the rain.

Victor Krane.

He was wearing a dark suit, tailored to perfection. His silver hair was slicked back. He stood with his hands clasped behind his back, the posture of a man who owned everything he could see.

"Director Krane," I said, my voice sharp, echoing in the vast space. I marched toward him, heels clicking on the marble. "I'm Elena Vance, Seattle Audit. I've been waiting at the gate for twenty minutes. Your security protocols are creating a significant bottleneck."

Krane didn't turn around immediately.

"Efficiency," he said. His voice was smooth, cultured, the same voice I had heard on the TED talks and the manifesto videos. "It is the pursuit of zero friction. Security is friction, Ms. Vance. But unfortunately, it is necessary."

He turned to face me.

My breath caught in my throat.

He looked perfect. Too perfect. His skin had the smooth, poreless texture of high-end silicone. His eyes were a piercing, icy blue.

But he was... wrong.

"I apologize for the wait," he said. He took a step toward me.

But the sound of his footstep—the sharp *clack* of the shoe on marble—happened a fraction of a second *before* his foot hit the floor.

I blinked. Maybe it was my nerves. Maybe it was the lack of sleep.

"I have a schedule to keep," I said, opening my briefcase on the white table. I pulled out a tablet, keeping my hands steady through sheer force of will. "I need to review the energy consumption logs for the sub-basement levels. We're seeing spikes that violate the EPA agreement."

I was bluffing. I didn't care about the logs. I just needed to get close enough to his personal terminal to plug in the drive.

"The sub-basement," Krane said, walking toward the table.

Again, the glitch. His mouth moved, forming the words, but the audio was just slightly out of sync. It was like watching a movie with a bad Bluetooth connection.

Latency, my brain whispered. *He's lagging.*

"Yes," I said, focusing on my tablet to avoid looking at the subtle delay in his blinking. "You're drawing three gigawatts. That's enough to power Seattle. What are you running down there, Director?"

Krane stopped at the other side of the table. He smiled. The smile reached his eyes a millisecond after it formed on his lips.

"We are running the future, Ms. Vance," he said. "Do you know why we chose this location?"

"Geothermal access," I said, tapping the screen, pretending to input data.

"Silence," he corrected. "The rainforest is the quietest place in the continental United States. One square inch of silence is worth a billion dollars in a noisy world."

He reached out and picked up a glass pitcher of water from the table. He poured a glass.

I watched the water.

The sound of the pouring water—*glug, glug, splash*—filled the air. But the water in the pitcher didn't move for a full second. Then, in a rush, the liquid poured out, catching up to the sound.

I stared at it. I couldn't help it. It was a violation of physics.

Krane saw me staring. He didn't look embarrassed. He looked amused.

"It is disconcerting at first," he said, taking a sip. "The synchronization. The bandwidth required to render a physical presence in real-time is... immense. Sometimes, the server hangs."

My blood ran cold.

He wasn't talking about a hologram. He was solid. He was drinking water. But he was talking about *rendering*.

"I don't understand," I said, taking a step back. "Are you... are you ill, Director?"

"Illness is a biological flaw," Krane said. "I have transcended biology."

He set the glass down. It made a *thud* before it touched the table.

"You can drop the audit logs, Maya," he said.

The name hit me like a physical slap.

I froze. "Excuse me? My name is Elena."

"Elena Vance is dead," Krane said gently. "She died of a stroke three weeks ago in a nursing home in Tacoma. We have her cognitive scan on file. It's quite fragmented. Lots of static about a cat."

He looked at me with those icy, lagging eyes.

"But you," he said. "You are vibrant. You burn so brightly, Maya. Just like your brother."

I dropped the pretense. I dropped the "Elena" posture. I reached into my pocket, gripping the virus.

"You killed him," I whispered.

"I saved him," Krane corrected. "Michael was drowning in his own mediocrity. I gave him the ocean."

"You tortured him!" I shouted. "I saw the logs! I saw what you did to Subject Zero!"

"Pain is data," Krane said, dismissing my anger with a wave of his hand. "Fear is data. The Harbingers... they consume it all. They don't distinguish between joy and suffering. It is all just... flavor."

He walked around the table. I backed away, toward the elevator.

"You think you're working with them," I said, my back hitting the cold glass of the window. "You think you're their partner. But you're just the waiter, Krane. They're going to eat you too."

Krane laughed. The laugh echoed before his mouth opened.

"I am already eaten, Maya," he said.

He stepped into a shaft of sunlight breaking through the clouds.

For a second, his skin... *flickered*.

It wasn't silicone. It was nanotech. Or hard-light projection. Or something I didn't have a word for. I saw the wireframe structure beneath his face—a grid of violet light holding the illusion of humanity together.

"I am the Bridge," he said, his voice resonating with a metallic undertone. "I am the vessel that allows them to touch this world. And in return, I get to be everywhere. I get to be forever."

He stopped three feet from me. He smelled of nothing. No cologne. No sweat. Just sterile air.

"Why are you here, Maya?" he asked. "With your little flash drive and your stolen suit. Did you come to kill me?"

"Yes," I said.

"You can't kill a signal," he said. "But you can join it."

He held out a hand.

"Michael is waiting for you," he said softly. "He misses you. I can hear him in the noise. He's calling for 'Mayfly.'"

My heart stuttered.

"Don't say that name," I warned, my voice shaking.

"I can put you with him," Krane promised. "No more pain. No more loss. Just pure connection. You can be with him forever in the cloud. All you have to do... is give me the drive."

He looked at my pocket.

"I know what it is," he said. "A fragment of the Sentinel code. A virus. It won't work, Maya. My firewall is the collective consciousness of ten million people. Your virus is a drop of ink in the Pacific Ocean."

He took another step.

"Give it to me. And I will give you Michael."

I looked at his hand. It was perfectly manicured. It was trembling slightly, vibrating at a high frequency.

I thought about Michael. I thought about the boy who fixed my bike. The boy who taught me to code.

I reached into my pocket. I pulled out the drive.

Krane smiled. The lag was almost gone now. He was focusing all his bandwidth on this moment.

"Smart girl," he said. "Michael always said you were the pragmatic one."

I held the drive out.

Then I dropped it.

It hit the marble floor with a plastic clatter.

"Oops," I said.

Krane's eyes tracked the drive downward.

In that split second of distraction, I didn't attack him. I didn't run for the elevator.

I turned around and swung my briefcase with both hands, smashing it into the floor-to-ceiling window behind me.

The glass was reinforced, designed to withstand hurricane winds. It didn't shatter. It just spider-webbed.

"What are you doing?" Krane asked, looking up, genuinely confused. The confusion arrived on his face a second late.

"You said you're a signal," I said, grabbing a heavy marble sculpture from a pedestal—some abstract corporate art piece. "Let's see how well you stream without a repeater."

I slammed the sculpture into the cracked glass.

CRASH.

The window exploded outward.

The wind from the rainforest roared into the room, a sudden, violent gale that sent papers flying. The pressure change popped my ears.

Rain lashed in, soaking the white marble.

Krane flickered violently. The sudden introduction of chaotic variables—wind, rain, noise—was disrupting his render. His face pixelated, revealing the skull beneath.

"Err...or..." his voice distorted.

"Carter!" I screamed into my earpiece, over the roar of the wind. "I'm at the window! Top floor! North face!"

"I see you!" Carter's voice crackled. *"What are you doing?"*

"I'm creating an exit!"

I looked at Krane. He was stabilizing, the pixels knitting back together. He looked angry now.

"That was remarkably inefficient," he snarled.

"I'm not here for efficiency," I said, backing toward the jagged hole in the glass, the wind whipping my hair across my face. "I'm here for friction."

And then, the alarms started.

Chapter 17: Breach Detection

Carter

The sound of shattering glass from fifty stories up is distinct. It doesn't sound like a crash; it sounds like a gunshot that keeps ringing.

I was on the landing of the twentieth floor when I heard it. A second later, the Prime Tower woke up.

WOOP. WOOP. WOOP.

Red strobes began to flash in the stairwell, bathing the concrete in a pulsing, bloody light.

"Security Alert. Containment Breach. Executive Level."

The automated voice was calm, pleasant even. It was the voice of a system that didn't know how to panic.

"Maya," I hissed into my comms. "Status!"

"I made a door!" Maya's voice came back, breathless and distorted by wind. *"Krane is... glitching! I bought us five minutes, maybe less!"*

"I'm coming up," I said. "Stay away from the edges."

I abandoned stealth. I abandoned the slow, methodical climb. I kicked the door to the twentieth floor open and sprinted into the hallway, looking for the express elevator. The stairs were a choke point; if they sent a squad down, I'd be fighting gravity and bullets.

I reached the elevator bank. The indicators were dead. The system had locked down the lifts.

"Great," I muttered.

The door to the stairwell I had just exited slammed open.

Three guards burst in. They weren't the "Processors" from the lobby. These were the internal response team. heavy armor, full-face helmets, P90 submachine guns.

They saw me instantly.

"Contact!" the lead guard shouted.

I didn't wait for them to set up a field of fire. I raised the Sig and double-tapped the point man.

The rounds sparked off his chest plate. He staggered but didn't drop.

Armor-piercing rounds needed, my brain noted calmly. *Aim for the soft spots.*

I dived behind a heavy marble planter as the hallway erupted in automatic fire. Bullets chewed up the expensive drywall, turning the corridor into a cloud of white dust.

I pulled a flash-bang from my vest, pulled the pin, and cooked it for one second.

"Fire in the hole!"

I tossed it over the planter.

BANG.

The concussive blast silenced the guns for a heartbeat. I popped up.

I didn't aim for the chest. I aimed for the neck, the gap between the helmet and the collar.

Crack. Crack.

One guard dropped, clutching his throat.

The other two were already recovering. They were disciplined. Too disciplined.

I sprinted down the hall, away from them, looking for a secondary stairwell. I rounded a corner and nearly collided with a fourth guard coming out of a server room.

It was close quarters. Too close for guns.

He swung his rifle barrel at my head. I ducked, feeling the wind of the impact. I drove my shoulder into his midsection, tackling him to the floor.

We grappled. He was strong, heavy with gear. He got a hand around my throat, squeezing hard.

I grabbed his wrist, trying to break the hold. I managed to reach my knife.

Then, his earpiece screeched.

It was loud enough that I heard it through his helmet. A high-pitched, digital squeal that sounded like a modem dying.

The guard froze.

His grip on my throat didn't loosen, but his body went rigid.

"Unit 7," a voice buzzed from his radio. "Override authorization Alpha. Assume direct control."

The guard's head snapped back. Under the tinted visor of his helmet, I saw a flash of violet light.

Then, he started to scream.

It wasn't a scream of pain. It was the sound of a man being erased.

His grip on my throat tightened. Not gradually—instantly. It went from a chokehold to a hydraulic clamp. I felt the cartilage in my windpipe grinding.

I drove my ceramic knife into his thigh. Deep.

He didn't flinch. He didn't grunt.

I twisted the blade. Nothing.

"Get... off..." I wheezed, seeing spots in my vision.

The guard looked down at me. The scream stopped, replaced by a terrifying, silent focus. He wasn't breathing hard. He wasn't blinking.

He raised his free hand and punched me in the face.

It felt like being hit with a sledgehammer. My vision went white. I tasted blood.

He raised his fist again.

I didn't try to block. I grabbed the flash-bang pouch on his vest. I pulled the pin on his grenade.

I kicked him in the chest with both feet, using every ounce of strength I had left.

The kick broke his grip. I rolled backward, scrambling away on hands and knees.

The guard stood up. He looked at the grenade on his vest. He didn't try to remove it. He just looked at it, his head cocked to the side like a curious bird.

BOOM.

The blast threw him against the wall. It shredded his vest and took off his right arm at the elbow.

I covered my head, waiting for the shrapnel to settle.

I looked up.

The guard was still standing.

He was missing an arm. His chest was a ruin of shredded Kevlar and meat. Blood was pouring out of him.

But he didn't fall. He didn't scream.

He took a step toward me. Then another.

"Threat detected," the guard said. His voice was gurgling, wet, but the cadence was perfectly flat. Synthesized. "Continue engagement."

He raised his remaining arm, reaching for his sidearm with robotic precision.

"You have to be kidding me," I gasped, wiping blood from my eyes.

I raised my Sig. I didn't aim for the body. The body didn't matter anymore. The pilot wasn't in the heart; the pilot was in the cloud.

I aimed for the receiver.

I put three rounds into his helmet. The visor shattered.

The guard dropped. Finally.

I lay there for a second, panting, the taste of copper in my mouth.

"Carter!" Lilith's voice was panicked in my ear. "Sensors are lighting up! Every guard in the building just got the same signal! They're converging on the stairwells!"

"They're overridden," I coughed, standing up. "They aren't men anymore, Lilith. They're drones. They don't feel pain."

"How do you stop them?"

"Headshots," I said, reloading. "And explosives."

I moved to the maintenance door at the end of the hall. I jammed a shaped C4 charge into the lock mechanism.

"I'm blowing the fire doors," I said. "I'm going to turn this stairwell into a chimney."

"That will draw every unit in the tower to your position!"

"Good," I said, triggering the detonator.

BLAM.

The door blew off its hinges. Smoke filled the corridor.

"If they're looking at me," I said, stepping into the smoke, "they aren't looking at Maya."

I started to climb. Thirty floors to go. And an army of zombies between me and the roof.

Chapter 18: The Offer

Maya

The wind howling through the shattered window was real. The rain lashing against my face, cold and stinging, was real. The smell of ozone and wet carpet was real.

But Victor Krane was not.

He stood in the center of the room, unaffected by the gale I had just invited in. The wind whipped his suit jacket, but his hair didn't move. Raindrops passed through his shoulder, dissolving into pixels before they hit the floor.

"You are throwing rocks at a hurricane, Maya," Krane said. His voice didn't fight the wind; it simply existed over it, broadcast on a frequency that bypassed my ears and vibrated directly in my skull.

I backed away, crunching over broken glass, until my heels hit the edge of the white table.

"I'm not trying to stop the hurricane," I shouted, gripping the marble statue I'd used as a hammer. "I'm trying to break the eye!"

Krane sighed. It was a sound of profound disappointment.

"You are so limited," he said. "You see the breach as a disaster. You see the Harbingers as monsters. You are looking at a butterfly emerging from a chrysalis and screaming because you liked the caterpillar better."

He raised both hands.

"Let me show you."

The room changed.

The walls didn't dissolve; they expanded. The ceiling vanished. The storm outside—the grey sky, the rain, the Exclusion Zone—was overwritten.

Suddenly, we weren't in a penthouse. We were floating in a nebula.

But it wasn't made of stars. It was made of data.

Billions of points of light swirled around us, connected by filaments of gold and violet fire. It was breathtaking. It was a cathedral of light that stretched into infinity, humming with a harmony that sounded like a thousand choirs singing in perfect pitch.

"The Bridge," Krane whispered.

I lowered the statue. I couldn't help it. It was the most beautiful thing I had ever seen.

"What is this?" I breathed.

"It is the Ark," Krane said, walking toward me on a path of starlight. "This is where they go. The Processors in the basement? The people in the nursing homes? They aren't dead, Maya. They are here."

He reached out and touched a strand of light. It rippled, sending a pulse of warmth through the room.

"No pain," Krane said softly. "No hunger. No fear. No loneliness. Just pure, unadulterated connection. A collective consciousness where every thought is shared, every emotion is understood."

He stopped in front of me. The lag was gone. His face was radiant with a religious fervor.

"Humanity is messy, Maya. We are isolated little biological engines, trapped in rotting meat, unable to truly understand one another. We fight. We kill. We die alone."

He gestured to the sea of light.

"Here... we are never alone."

My heart hammered in my chest. I looked at the lights. They did look peaceful. They looked... warm.

"And the Harbingers?" I asked, my voice trembling. "Where are they?"

"They are the architects," Krane said. "They provide the infrastructure. The capacity. Yes, they feed on the energy of the connection. But it is a symbiosis. We give them sustenance; they give us eternity."

He stepped closer.

"I can prove it."

He waved his hand. The nebula shifted. The lights parted, forming a corridor.

At the end of the corridor, a figure formed.

He wasn't a glitchy mess of static like the avatar I'd seen on my laptop. He wasn't the screaming victim from the archives.

He was Michael.

He was wearing his favorite flannel shirt. He looked healthy. Whole. He was smiling at me—that crooked, half-smile he used to give me when I figured out a difficult line of code.

"Hey, Mayfly," he said.

The sound of his voice broke me. I dropped the statue. It hit the floor with a heavy thud that seemed miles away.

"Michael?" I choked out.

"It's okay," Michael said, walking toward me. He didn't walk; he glided. "I'm okay. It hurts at first, letting go of the body. But once you're in... it's quiet, Maya. It's so quiet."

I took a step toward him. "I came to get you. I came to take you home."

"This is home," Michael said. He held out his hand. "You don't have to fight anymore. You look so tired, Maya. You've been running for so long."

"I am tired," I whispered. Tears blurred my vision. "I'm so tired."

"Come with me," Michael said. "Upload. Join the stream. We can code together again. Forever."

I looked at his hand. It looked solid. Real.

"Just give him the drive," Michael said. His eyes were kind. "Give Krane the virus. We don't need it. We're happy."

My hand moved to my pocket. My fingers brushed the plastic of the flash drive.

Why not? Why was I fighting this? The world outside was broken. Carter was probably dead in the stairwell. The apocalypse was ten days away.

Here... here there was peace. Here there was Michael.

"That's it," Krane urged, his voice blending with Michael's. "Let go, Maya. Let go of the friction."

I pulled the drive out of my pocket.

I reached for Michael's hand.

BZZZZZT.

A sharp, violent burst of static exploded in my left ear.

I flinched, gasping.

"Ow!" I grabbed my ear.

The static cleared. And then, a voice cut through the beautiful choir. A dry, monotone, unbothered voice.

"...entropy creates heat..."

Julian.

The connection was patchy, unauthorized, bleeding through the inductive loop earpiece.

"...closed system thermodynamics..." Julian's voice droned on, reciting math. *"...energy cannot be created... only consumed... look at the edges, Maya... look at the compression artifacts..."*

I blinked. The spell wavered.

"Look at the edges," I whispered.

I looked at Michael. Really looked at him.

I looked at the edges of his flannel shirt. The pattern wasn't weaving; it was looping. The texture was repeating every three seconds.

I looked at his eyes.

They weren't looking at me. They were looking *through* me. And deep in the pupil... there was no depth. Just a flat, black pixel.

"...it's a render..." Julian's voice buzzed. *"...it's a deep-fake based on your memory bias... look at the data consumption..."*

I looked past Michael. At the beautiful nebula.

I narrowed my eyes, focusing not on the light, but on the space *between* the light.

It wasn't empty space. It was a mouth.

The "filaments" connecting the souls weren't golden threads. They were feeding tubes. The energy wasn't flowing *between* the people; it was flowing *out* of them. Upward. Into the dark.

"They aren't happy," I whispered. "They're being digested."

I looked back at Michael.

"You're not him," I said.

The figure of my brother flickered. The smile didn't change, but the warmth went out of it.

"I am what remains," the avatar said. "I am the best parts."

"No," I said, stepping back. "You're the bait."

I squeezed the flash drive in my hand until the plastic creaked.

"You almost had me," I said to Krane. I felt the anger returning, hot and solid, burning away the grief. "You almost made me forget the math."

Krane's face hardened. The beautiful nebula began to turn red.

"The math is irrelevant," Krane snapped. "The choice is binary. Integration or deletion."

"I choose option C," I said.

I didn't hand him the drive. I didn't plug it in.

I turned and threw the flash drive as hard as I could—not at Krane, but out the shattered window.

It spun into the rain, disappearing into the grey void of the Exclusion Zone.

"What did you do?" Krane roared. The room shook. The beautiful illusion shattered, replaced by the sterile white penthouse and the howling wind.

"I just removed the temptation," I said, backing toward the elevator. "Now I have nothing to lose."

Krane looked at me with pure, unfiltered hatred. His human mask dissolved completely, revealing the violet energy beneath.

"Then you will die," he said. "Slowly. And I will upload your scream."

"Maybe," I said, hearing the distinct *thud* of an explosion from the stairwell door behind the wall. "But I won't be alone."

The wall exploded.

Chapter 19: Convergence

Carter

I didn't have a key to the penthouse. I had a block of C4 the size of a paperback book.

The drywall of the executive corridor wasn't rated for high explosives. I molded the charge against the service door leading to the main suite, set the detonator for three seconds, and dragged myself around the corner of the marble hallway.

My left eye was swelling shut. My ribs felt like a bag of gravel. The fight in the stairwell had cost me two magazines of ammo and probably a year of my life expectancy.

Three. Two. One.

CRACK-BOOM.

The explosion sucked the air out of the hallway, followed immediately by a plume of dust and debris shotgunning outward.

I didn't wait for the dust to settle. That's how you get shot. You move *with* the violence.

I pivoted around the corner, leading with the M14 I'd reclaimed from the van. I stepped through the jagged hole in the wall, boots crunching over drywall and twisted metal studs.

"Maya!" I roared.

The scene that greeted me was a nightmare rendered in high definition.

The penthouse was a wind tunnel. A massive section of the floor-to-ceiling glass was gone, shattered outward. Rain and wind from the rainforest were whipping through the room, sending papers swirling in a chaotic cyclone.

In the center of the room stood Maya. She looked small, battered, her grey suit soaked, her hair plastered to her face. She was backing away toward the elevator, empty-handed.

And blocking her path was Victor Krane.

Or what was left of him.

He stood with his back to me, but I could see the light leaking out of him. The "skin" on his neck and hands was flickering, tearing open to reveal a pulsing, violet energy beneath. He didn't look like a man anymore. He looked like a containment breach.

"Target acquired," I growled.

I raised the rifle. The sights settled on Krane's spine.

I didn't hesitate. I didn't ask him to surrender. I squeezed the trigger.

Bang. Bang. Bang.

Three rounds of 7.62mm steel-core ammunition. At this range, they should have punched through a brick wall.

They hit Krane square in the back.

He didn't fall. He didn't even stumble.

The bullets impacted his suit jacket, but there was no blood. Instead, there was a digital *spark*—a burst of pixelated distortion, like a video game character taking damage. The rounds seemed to dissolve upon impact, absorbed into the violet mesh of his body.

Krane turned around slowly.

His face was a horror show. The human mask was sliding off, revealing a skull made of translucent, geometric light.

"Primitive," Krane said. His voice sounded like grinding metal.

He raised a hand toward me.

The air between us rippled. It wasn't telekinesis; it was a pressurized shockwave of pure energy.

It hit me like a freight train.

I was lifted off my feet and thrown backward. I smashed into a marble pillar, the impact knocking the wind out of me and sending the rifle clattering across the floor.

I hit the ground hard, gasping for air, vision swimming.

"Carter!" Maya screamed.

She broke cover. Instead of running for the elevator, she ran toward me.

"No!" I wheezed, trying to push myself up. "Run!"

Krane didn't look at me. He looked at Maya.

"The time for running is over," Krane intoned.

He moved.

He didn't walk. He *glitched*.

One second he was by the window. The next, he was standing directly in Maya's path, a blur of motion that left a trail of violet afterimages.

Maya skidded to a halt, slipping on the wet marble.

Krane reached out. His arm extended—literally stretched, the limb elongating like warm taffy—and his hand clamped around Maya's throat.

He lifted her off the ground effortlessly.

Maya clawed at his wrist, her legs kicking in the air.

"Let her go!" I shouted.

I scrambled for my sidearm, ripping the Sig from my holster. I was on my knees, swaying, but I leveled the gun.

I couldn't shoot. Maya was thrashing, blocking the shot.

"You rejected the offer," Krane said to Maya, bringing her face close to his glitching visage. "You threw away the key. Now... we do it the hard way."

The violet light in Krane's eyes flared brighter.

He wasn't crushing her windpipe. I realized with a sick lurch what he was doing.

The veins in his hand were glowing. The light was traveling from his arm *into* Maya's neck.

He was uploading.

"Forced integration," I whispered.

"Maya!" I yelled. "Fight him!"

Maya's kicking slowed. Her eyes rolled back in her head. Her mouth opened in a silent scream as the violet energy began to crawl up her jawline, mapping her skin.

I lunged forward, ignoring the pain in my ribs, ignoring the impossibility of the fight. I had a knife in my boot. If bullets wouldn't work, maybe I could cut the connection.

I was ten feet away.

Krane turned his head toward me, the movement jerky and mechanical.

"Obsolete," he sneered.

He swept his free hand through the air.

A second shockwave slammed into me, pinning me to the floor. It felt like gravity had increased tenfold. I couldn't move. I couldn't breathe. I could only watch.

Krane turned back to Maya.

"Welcome home, Mayfly," he hissed.

He pulled her closer, his forehead touching hers. The violet light enveloped them both, a cocoon of data and noise.

I saw Maya's hand drop. She went limp in his grip.

I had failed. The distance was too great. The enemy was too strong.

I watched as the light consumed her, dragging her consciousness out of her body and into the roaring silence of the machine.

Chapter 20: The Plunge

Maya

Dying, it turned out, felt exactly like dial-up internet.

It was a screeching, grinding noise that wasn't sound, but pure friction against the soul. It was the feeling of being compressed, of having your thoughts squeezed through a tube that was too small to hold them.

Krane's hand was a vice around my throat, but the physical pain was distant, like a radio playing in another room. The real pain was the light.

The violet energy pouring from his skin wasn't just burning my neck; it was rewriting my nervous system. I could feel it crawling up my jaw, sinking into my pores, hunting for the synapses. It was looking for a handshake.

CONNECTING...

The word flashed in my mind. Not a thought I had generated, but a prompt imposed on me.

I tried to kick, but my legs felt like lead. I tried to scream, but my lungs were filled with static.

Through the haze of violet light, I saw Carter. He was pinned to the floor by the invisible gravity of Krane's will, struggling to lift his head. His face was a mask of bloody desperation. He was mouthing my name.

Maya. Fight.

I *was* fighting. But fighting Krane was like fighting a tsunami with a paper shield. He wasn't just strong; he was inevitable. He was the admin, and I was a guest user with restricted privileges.

"Don't resist," Krane's voice echoed in my skull. It wasn't the lagging voice from the room. It was crisp, perfect, digital stereo. *"The friction is what hurts. Let go. Become the signal."*

I felt my memories starting to slide. The smell of my mother's perfume. The code for the Sentinel virus. The look on Carter's face when he handed me the audit badge. They were unspooling, being sucked out of my head and into the violet maw of Krane's interface.

He was harvesting me.

I was going to die here. My body would limp, my mind would be fragmented into data packets, and I would become just another ghost in his machine, fueling the nightmare.

No.

The thought was sharp. Cold.

He's not killing me. He's connecting to me.

I stopped thrashing. I focused on the pain. I focused on the connection point—the burning heat on my neck where his hand met my skin.

He was forcing an upload. He was opening a port.

A port goes two ways.

I looked at Krane. His face was inches from mine, glowing with triumph. He thought he was mugging a victim. He didn't realize he was plugging a live wire into a wet socket.

"You want me?" I thought, projecting the words with every ounce of mental discipline Michael had taught me.

Krane's eyes widened slightly. He heard it.

"I'm right here," I screamed in my mind.

I didn't pull away. I didn't try to break his grip.

I *lunged.*

I threw my mental weight forward, diving into the connection he had forced open. I didn't resist the suction; I accelerated it.

It was like stepping off a cliff.

Krane gasped. The flow reversed. Instead of him pulling me out, I was pouring myself in.

"What are you—" his digital voice faltered.

"I'm accepting the terms of service!"

I visualized the Sentinel code. I visualized the virus I had thrown out the window. I didn't need the flash drive. I *was* the virus. I had memorized the hex strings. I carried the glitch in my own memory.

I wrapped myself in the jagged, corrosive logic of the Sentinel and drove it straight into Krane's neural handshake.

ACCESS GRANTED.

The world exploded.

The penthouse vanished. The rain, the wind, the broken glass—it all dissolved into a blinding white singularity.

The sensation of my body—the pain in my ribs, the cold water on my skin, the weight of my clothes—snapped.

I was falling.

I was falling through a tunnel of light that screamed.

I saw flashes of data.

...Subject 4591 cardiac arrest...

...Sector 7 ventilation status: critical...

...Stock market crash: Tokyo...

...Carter screaming...

I saw my physical body go limp in the real world. I saw it drop from Krane's hand like a puppet with cut strings. I saw it hit the marble floor.

It looked small. Broken.

Goodbye, I thought.

There was no going back. If I survived this, I wouldn't be waking up in that meat cage. I was code now.

I turned my focus downward, into the abyss.

Below me, the Harbingers waited. Massive, shifting geometries of hunger.

I bared my teeth. Or what felt like teeth.

"Coming through," I whispered into the void.

And then I hit the stream.

Chapter 21: Synesthesia

Maya

I landed.

I didn't hit the ground; I hit a concept.

The sensation was like falling onto a trampoline made of frozen light. I bounced, tumbled, and came to rest on a surface that felt like obsidian but rippled like water.

I gasped, trying to fill my lungs.

The air tasted like copper and old pennies. No—it tasted like *arithmetic*. It tasted like long division, sharp and metallic on the back of my tongue.

I opened my eyes.

"Okay," I whispered. My voice didn't make a sound. Instead, it manifested as a puff of silver smoke that drifted away, spelling out the letters *O-K-A-Y* before dissolving.

I stood up. I looked at my hands.

They weren't flesh. They were wireframes. Glowing blue grids shaped like fingers, filled with a swirling, translucent mist. I flexed them. The mist swirled faster.

I looked up.

I wasn't in the Prime Tower anymore. I wasn't in the rainforest.

I was standing in the middle of a canyon. But the cliffs weren't rock. They were skyscrapers made of scrolling text. Millions of lines of green and amber code shot upward into a sky that was the color of a bruised plum.

To my left, a river of pure light roared past. It sounded like a million people whispering secrets at once. I looked closer. It wasn't water. It was social media feeds. Photos, status updates, location tags—a torrent of human noise rushing downstream.

To my right, a mountain range of jagged black spikes pulsed with a low, menacing bass note. Financial data. The global stock market, visualized as a weaponized landscape.

"Synesthesia," I realized.

My brain couldn't process the raw data of the Nexus, so it was translating it. It was turning zeroes and ones into sight, sound, and touch. I was seeing the internet as a physical geography.

And it was terrifying.

The scale was wrong. The perspective was broken. Buildings twisted into non-Euclidean shapes. Bridges connected to nothing. It was an M.C. Escher painting drawn by a schizophrenic god.

BOOM.

Thunder rolled overhead.

I looked up at the violet sky.

The clouds weren't clouds. They were... shapes. Massive, shifting polyhedrons—cubes, pyramids, dodecahedrons—tumbling through the atmosphere. They were the size of cities.

As I watched, one of the shapes—a black pyramid inverted on its tip—descended toward a cluster of data-towers in the distance.

It touched the buildings.

It didn't crush them. It *absorbed* them.

The towers dissolved into pixels, sucked up into the black geometry. The screams of the data—the emails, the photos, the memories stored in those servers—were deafening. A high-pitched shriek of deletion.

"The Harbingers," I whispered.

They were eating the landscape. They were grazing.

I felt a surge of panic. If they saw me—a piece of rogue code standing on the sidewalk—they would scoop me up like a crumb.

Run.

I tried to sprint.

But my legs didn't work right. I moved in slow motion, like I was running underwater.

Latency.

I was processing too slowly. My human mind was still trying to apply the laws of physics to a world that didn't have any. I was trying to push off the ground with muscles I didn't have.

Stop, I told myself. *You aren't a body. You are a user.*

I looked at the obsidian road beneath me.

function move(x, y, z)

The thought appeared as text in my vision.

I focused. I didn't try to run. I tried to *execute.*

move(forward, fast)

ZAP.

The world blurred.

I didn't run; I glitched. I teleported fifty feet forward in a single frame.

I stumbled, disoriented by the jump.

"Okay," I laughed, the sound appearing as a jagged yellow line in the air. "I can work with this."

move(forward, fast)

I flashed forward again. And again.

I was skipping through the city, blinking past the towers of data. I felt light. I felt powerful. In the real world, I was anemic, tired, slow. Here? Here, I was a photon.

I needed to find Michael.

I stopped at an intersection. The street signs were changing rapidly, cycling through languages. *Main St. / Rue de la Paix / 01100101.*

"Michael!" I shouted.

My voice became a red flare, shooting up into the sky.

Bad idea.

High above, one of the Harbinger shapes paused in its rotation. The black inverted pyramid stopped spinning. It tilted.

A beam of red light scanned the street.

It was looking for the noise.

I ducked into an alleyway between two massive servers that looked like brutalist apartment blocks. The alley smelled of sulfur—corrupted files.

I pressed my back against the wall. The wall hummed against my spine.

I closed my eyes—or I shut down my visual input.

Listen.

I tuned out the roar of the data river. I tuned out the thunder of the Harbingers.

I listened for the hum. The 440 Hertz.

At first, nothing. Just the chaos of the network.

Then... there. Faint. To the north (or what my brain interpreted as north).

Hmmmmmm.

It was a cello note. A pure, steady anchor in the storm.

It was coming from the center of the city. From a massive, blinding spire of white light that rose higher than anything else.

The Citadel. The Master Node.

That's where Krane was. That's where Michael was.

I opened my eyes.

The red search beam swept past the alley mouth, missing me by inches. The heat of it sizzled the air, smelling of burnt hair.

I looked at the white spire. It was miles away, across a landscape of shifting fractures and hostile firewalls.

But I wasn't just a user anymore. I was a virus.

I looked at the wall next to me. It was a sheer vertical surface of polished glass.

In the real world, impossible to climb.

Here?

I reached out and touched the surface.

var gravity = 0;

I felt the pull of the earth vanish. I floated upward, my feet leaving the ground.

I kicked off the wall, soaring toward the rooftops.

I was going to the Citadel. And I was going to rewrite the ending.

Chapter 22: Captured

Carter

The room was silent, save for the wind whistling through the shattered window and the wet, ragged sound of my own breathing.

Victor Krane was gone. His physical form had dissolved into a cloud of violet particulates that drifted upward, vanishing into the ceiling vents like smoke.

Maya was gone, too.

Her body was still there. She lay crumpled on the wet marble, her grey suit soaked with rain, her black hair splayed out like a halo of ink. But the person inside—the sharp-tongued hacker, the grieving sister, the soldier—had left the building.

The gravity wave that had pinned me to the floor dissipated.

I groaned, rolling onto my side. My ribs screamed—a sharp, jagged fire that told me at least two were broken. I spat a mouthful of blood onto the pristine white floor and crawled toward her.

"Maya," I rasped.

I reached her. I placed two fingers on her carotid artery.

Thump... thump...

Her pulse was there, but it was slow. Too slow. It was the idle rhythm of an engine left running in an empty parking lot.

"Come back," I whispered, shaking her shoulder. Her head lolled. Her eyes were open, staring at the ceiling, but the pupils were blown wide, black holes absorbing the light.

She was a husk.

I sat back on my heels, a wave of nausea and failure washing over me. I had one job. *Keep her alive.* And I had watched her jump off the edge of the world.

CRASH.

The main doors to the penthouse—the ones I had blown off their hinges—were kicked in.

I spun around, reaching for my Sig.

My holster was empty. The gun was ten feet away, sliding across the wet marble.

"Don't bother," a voice said.

A woman stepped through the smoke and debris.

She wasn't wearing tactical gear. She was wearing a white NeuroSync jumpsuit that looked more like a wetsuit. She was tall, athletic, with pale skin and hair cut in a severe, platinum bob.

She didn't have a weapon drawn. Her hands were empty.

"Alexis Ward," I said, recognizing the face from the NeuroSync personnel files Lilith had showed me. "Head of Physical Security."

"Mr. Reed," she said. Her voice was cool, efficient. She walked toward me, her boots making no sound. "You've made a terrible mess of my building."

I scrambled for the gun. It was a desperate move, slow and clumsy. Ward moved.

She didn't run; she *accelerated*. One moment she was by the door; the next, she was standing over the gun. She kicked it away, sending it skittering out the broken window and into the rainforest below.

"That was expensive," she noted.

I struggled to my feet, swaying. I raised my fists. I was beaten, broken, and unarmed. But I wasn't going to let her touch Maya.

"Step away from the girl," I growled.

Ward tilted her head. Her eyes were grey, but deep within the iris, a faint violet ring pulsed.

"She's not a girl anymore," Ward said. "She's an upload. And you? You're spare parts."

She lashed out.

It was a simple jab. I saw it coming. I raised my arm to block.

Her fist connected with my forearm.

It felt like being hit with a steel pipe. The bone snapped.

I grunted, stumbling back. She didn't let up. She spun, driving a heel into my solar plexus.

The impact lifted me off my feet. I hit the floor hard, sliding through the rainwater until my head cracked against the base of the white table.

Darkness swarmed the edges of my vision. I tried to push myself up with my good arm, but my body refused to obey.

Ward stood over me. She wasn't even breathing hard.

"You're obsolete, Carter," she said. "Biology is weak. It breaks. It bleeds. It tires."

She reached down and grabbed me by the throat. With one hand, she hauled me up until my toes dangled off the floor. Her grip was iron.

"Why kill you?" she mused, looking at my battered face. "That's a waste of biomass."

"Go to hell," I choked out.

"We're building heaven," she corrected. "And we need processors to run it."

She slammed my head against the table.

The lights went out.

I woke up to the smell of sulfur and industrial disinfectant.

I knew that smell. I had smelled it an hour ago—or maybe a day ago—through a wire-glass window.

I was moving. Dragging.

My boots were scraping against concrete. Someone was pulling me by the arms. My left arm—the broken one—screamed in protest, pulling me out of the unconscious void.

I groaned, opening my eyes.

I was in the sub-basement. The stark fluorescent lights buzzed overhead.

Ward was dragging me. She held my wrists in one hand, towing me down the corridor like a bag of laundry.

"He's awake," she said to someone I couldn't see.

"Vitals are erratic," a male voice replied. "Trauma to the cranial plate. Multiple fractures. He might reject the interface."

"He won't reject it," Ward said, stopping. She dropped me.

I hit the cold floor, gasping.

I looked up.

We were in the lab. The room with the tanks.

The rows of amber cylinders stretched away into the gloom. Inside them, the silent, eyeless figures floated, twitching in unison. *Thump-thump.*

"Get up," Ward ordered.

She kicked me in the ribs.

I curled up, coughing. "I'm... not... going in there."

"You don't have a choice," the technician said. He was the same man I had seen earlier—hazmat suit, tablet, dead eyes. "Director Krane specifically requested you for the Alpha Array. He says your neural density is... promising."

Ward grabbed me by the back of my jacket and hauled me toward an empty tank at the end of the row. It was open, the amber fluid waiting, the cables hanging from the ceiling like a nest of vipers.

"Strip him," Ward said.

Two guards—processor drones with blank faces—stepped forward. They ripped my jacket off. Then my shirt.

The cold air hit my skin. I shivered, but it wasn't from the temperature.

I looked at the tank. SUBJECT: PENDING.

"You're making a mistake," I wheezed, as they forced me backward toward the glass cylinder. "If you plug me in... I'll burn your system down."

Ward laughed. She leaned in close, her violet-ringed eyes mocking me.

"You think you're going to fight the collective?" she whispered. "Carter, once that cable touches your brain stem, *you* don't exist anymore. There is no 'I'. There is only 'Us'."

She nodded to the technician.

"Prep the drill."

I struggled. I headbutted one of the drones, sending him staggering. I kicked Ward in the knee.

She didn't flinch. She just punched me in the jaw.

My head snapped back. The fight drained out of me.

They lifted me. The warm, viscous fluid of the tank enveloped my legs, then my waist. It smelled of copper and electricity.

They strapped my wrists to the sides of the tank.

I looked up.

The technician was lowering a mechanical arm from the ceiling. At the end of it was a surgical drill, spinning with a high-pitched whine. Beside it, a thick black cable tipped with a three-inch needle.

"Anesthesia?" the technician asked Ward.

Ward looked at me. She smiled.

"No," she said. "Let him feel the upgrade."

The drill descended.

I closed my eyes.

Maya, I thought. *I hope you found a weapon. Because I just became the battery.*

Chapter 23: The Ghost in the Machine

Maya

I was a storm of arithmetic.

I didn't have lungs, but I was breathing. I was inhaling terabytes of data and exhaling pure logic. The sensory overload that had crippled me upon arrival—the synesthesia of tasting math and hearing color—had stabilized. It wasn't noise anymore. It was a dashboard.

I stood on the spire of the Citadel, looking down at the digital architecture of the Prime Tower.

To a human eye, this place was a fortress of concrete and steel. To me, it was a house of glass.

I could see everything.

I looked down through the layers of the simulation. I saw the electrical grid flowing like veins of blue fire. I saw the security protocols patrolling the hallways like wolves made of shadow. I saw the encrypted streams of the Processors—thousands of threads of silver light, rising from the sub-basement, twisting together into the massive, violet beam that fed the Harbingers above.

"Focus," I told myself. My voice resonated like a bell in the silence of the server. "Find him."

I closed my eyes—or the simulation of eyes—and extended my awareness.

Query: Carter Reed.

The system fought me. A red wall of static slammed down, blocking my scan.

ACCESS DENIED. USER UNAUTHORIZED.

I laughed. It was a strange sound, electronic and sharp.

"I'm not a user," I whispered, reaching out with a hand made of glowing wireframe.

I touched the red wall. In the real world, this was a firewall—a complex algorithm of encryption keys and packet filters. Here, it felt like hot iron.

But I had the Sentinel.

I didn't try to hack the wall. I didn't look for a key. I let the virus flow out of my fingertips. The jagged, corrosive code I had carried in my pocket—the code that Krane had tried to eat—poured into the barrier.

The red iron turned grey. Then it rusted. Then it crumbled into dust.

ACCESS GRANTED. WELCOME, ADMINISTRATOR.

The wall vanished.

The facility lay open to me.

I fell through the floors, diving down through the data layers. Penthouse. Executive suites. Server rooms.

I reached the sub-basement.

The air here was heavy, thick with the oily residue of suffering. The data streams from the tanks weren't clean; they were jagged, screaming things. I could feel the terror of the people trapped in the amber fluid. It washed over me like a tide of black water.

Don't look at them, I told myself. *If you look at them, you'll drown. Find the anchor.*

I scanned the room.

There.

Tank 44. A new signal. It wasn't integrated yet. It was wild, erratic, fighting the connection.

Carter.

I zoomed in. My perspective shifted, dropping from the ceiling to hover directly in front of his tank.

I could see him through the facility's internal sensors. He was strapped inside the glass cylinder. The fluid was rising past his chest. His head was slumped forward, blood dripping from his chin into the amber liquid.

Above him, the drill was descending. A mechanical spider lowering a needle toward the base of his skull.

I saw Alexis Ward standing outside the glass, watching with a cold, hungry smile.

"No," I said.

I reached out.

In the physical world, I was a corpse on the penthouse floor. But here... here I was a god.

I grabbed the data stream controlling the drill. It felt like a cold snake in my hands.

Command: HALT.

The drill didn't stop.

ERROR. SYSTEM OVERRIDE BY ALPHA CONTROLLER (KRANE). LOCAL INPUT LOCKOUT.

Krane was holding the leash. Even dissolved into the cloud, his will was driving the machine.

"I don't care about the input," I snarled, my avatar glowing blindingly white. "I am rewriting the hardware."

I visualized the code governing the hydraulic pressure of the mechanical arm. I didn't ask it to stop.

I told it that *zero* was now *five thousand.*

pressure = MAX_INT;

CRACK.

In the video feed, the hydraulic line on the drill arm exploded. Fluid sprayed across the lab. The mechanical arm seized violently, jerking upward and smashing into the ceiling.

Ward flinched, shielding her face.

"Malfunction!" the technician yelled, backing away. "The pressure regulators just blew!"

"Manual override!" Ward screamed. "Finish him!"

She drew her sidearm—a sleek, high-tech pistol—and aimed it at the glass of Carter's tank. If she couldn't process him, she was going to liquidate him.

"Not today, Alexis," I whispered.

I looked at the tank itself. I looked at the electronic mag-locks holding Carter's wrists.

I swiped my hand through the air.

Command: UNLOCK_ALL.

Command: PURGE.

In the lab, the mag-locks on Carter's wrists clicked open.

Simultaneously, the drainage valves at the bottom of the tank blew open. The amber fluid roared out, draining in seconds.

Carter slumped to the floor of the tank, coughing, free of the suspension fluid.

Ward fired.

The bullet hit the ballistic glass of the tank. It spider-webbed, but didn't shatter.

"Open the door," I commanded.

The heavy glass cylinder hissed and slid upward.

Carter tumbled out onto the wet concrete, gasping for air.

Ward spun around, looking for the source of the hack. She looked up at the camera lens I was using to watch them.

"Who is doing this?" she screamed.

I didn't just want to save him. I wanted to help him fight.

I looked at the facility's schematic. Fire suppression. Lighting. Security drones.

"Let's make some noise," I said.

I clenched my fist.

Every alarm in the sub-basement triggered at once. The fire strobes began to flash—not in a random pattern, but in a strobing, disorienting rhythm designed to induce seizures.

I accessed the containment units for the other tanks. The empty ones.

I overloaded the pressure seals.

BOOM. BOOM. BOOM.

Glass cylinders exploded down the line, showering the room in shrapnel and fluid. Steam vented from the floor.

It was chaos. Beautiful, orchestrated chaos.

Ward was shouting orders, but her voice was lost in the din. The technician was fleeing.

I focused on the audio feed in the room. I isolated the speakers nearest to Carter.

He was on his hands and knees, shaking his head, trying to clear the cobwebs. He looked broken. Defeated.

I needed to wake him up.

I poured my will into the speakers. I didn't use the distorted, scary voice of the Harbingers. I used my own voice. Clear. Human.

"Carter."

He froze. He looked up, blood in his eyes.

"Get up, soldier," I whispered through the PA system, modulating the volume so only he could hear it clearly over the alarms. *"I bought you an exit. Use it."*

He looked at the camera. He couldn't see me, but he knew.

He grinned. It was a bloody, feral grin.

"Copy that," he croaked.

He grabbed a shard of glass from the shattered tank. He stood up.

Ward turned to face him, her gun raised.

But the lights directly above her head exploded, raining sparks. She flinched.

That was all the opening he needed.

I floated back, watching from the high angle. I had unlocked the cage. Now I just had to watch the tiger work.

Chapter 24: Breakout

Carter

Pain is just data. That's what the NeuroSync manuals said. It's just an electrical impulse telling your brain that structural integrity has been compromised.

If that was true, my brain was currently receiving a DDoS attack of bad news.

My left arm hung uselessly at my side, the bone grinding with every breath. My ribs felt like a bag of broken china. But as I stood in the puddles of amber fluid and shattered glass, staring down the barrel of Alexis Ward's gun, I didn't feel the pain.

I felt the rage.

"You missed," I rasped, tightening my grip on the six-inch shard of ballistic glass I'd scavenged from the ruined tank.

Ward stood ten feet away, her white jumpsuit stained with hydraulic fluid. She looked annoyed, like a teacher dealing with a disruptive child, rather than a security chief facing an escaped prisoner.

"I never miss," she said calmly, adjusting her aim. "I just recalibrate."

Above us, the lights flickered violently—Maya's doing. The strobing effect was disorienting, turning Ward's movement into a series of jerky snapshots.

NOW.

The thought wasn't mine. It was a whisper in the static of the PA system.

I didn't hesitate. I didn't charge Ward directly—that was suicide. She was faster, stronger, and made of better parts than I was.

I charged the technician.

The man in the hazmat suit was scrambling backward, trying to reach the emergency exit. I hit him at a dead sprint, driving my shoulder into his chest.

Crack.

He grunted, folding over. I spun him around, holding him up as a meat shield just as Ward fired.

Thwip. Thwip.

Two rounds hit the technician in the back. He went limp in my arms, a heavy, hazmat-wrapped sandbag.

"Use your assets," I grunted.

I shoved the dead body toward Ward.

She didn't flinch. She simply sidestepped the corpse with fluid, robotic grace. But the split second of movement cost her the firing line.

I lunged.

I slashed the glass shard across her thigh. I was aiming for the femoral artery.

The glass tore through the white fabric of her jumpsuit. But there was no spray of red. The shard screeched against something hard—carbon fiber and sub-dermal plating.

"Nice try," Ward said.

She backhanded me.

It wasn't a slap. It was a kinetic impact. Her fist connected with my jaw, spinning me around. I hit the wet concrete hard, sliding through the slime of the spilled tank fluid.

I spat a tooth onto the floor.

Ward walked toward me, raising the gun for a execution shot.

"You're fighting a tank with a toothpick, Carter," she said. "Just lie down."

I looked up at the ceiling. The mechanical arm of the drill—the one Maya had over-pressurized—was hanging by a few wires, dripping hydraulic oil directly into a puddle of water near Ward's feet.

"Maya," I whispered. "Spark it."

Ward stepped into the puddle.

Above her, a junction box exploded. A shower of blue sparks rained down.

One spark hit the oil-slicked water.

ZZZZZT.

The voltage arc was instantaneous. It traveled up Ward's wet boots.

She convulsed. It wasn't enough to kill her—her internal insulation was too good for that—but it locked her up. Her limbs went rigid. The gun shook in her hand. Her violet eyes flashed white as her systems tried to shunt the excess power.

She couldn't move.

I scrambled to my feet. I could have tried to finish her. I could have tried to find a gap in her armor.

But there were twenty armed guards coming down the hallway. I could hear their boots thundering on the stairs.

I didn't need a kill. I needed a riot.

I ran to the main control console in the center of the room. It was a sleek, black monolith of touchscreens.

"Purge," I muttered, smashing my bloody hand against the glass surface.

The interface was locked. Biometric encryption.

"Dammit."

I looked at the technician's body.

I ran back, grabbed his limp hand, and dragged him toward the console.

Ward was twitching, fighting the reboot cycle. "Stop," she gurgled, her voice synthesized and distorted. "Do... not... release..."

I slammed the dead man's palm against the scanner.

ACCESS GRANTED.

I didn't select specific tanks. I hit the master command.

EMERGENCY FLUSH. ALL UNITS.

The sound was deafening.

A hundred hydraulic seals blew at once. The hissing of air was like a jet engine.

All down the long, dark rows of the sub-basement, the glass cylinders slid open.

The amber fluid crashed onto the floor in a tidal wave, washing over my boots.

And then, the screaming started.

It wasn't a battle cry. It was the sound of a hundred people waking up from a nightmare into a hellscape.

They spilled out of the tanks—naked, emaciated, wires trailing from their skulls. They were confused, blind, terrified.

"Help!" someone screamed. "I can't see! My eyes!"

"Where am I?"

"Make it stop!"

They began to run. They didn't know where they were going. They just ran away from the pain.

The door to the corridor burst open. The security team poured in.

"Targets acquired!" the lead guard shouted.

"Hold fire!" another yelled. "Those are the assets!"

The mob hit the guards.

It was chaos. The guards tried to shove the processors back, but there were too many of them. The subjects were thrashing, flailing, their optical implants flashing violet in the dark.

Ward finally broke free of the paralysis. She gasped, dropping to one knee.

"Containment!" she screamed. "Pacify them!"

She raised her gun and fired into the crowd. A man went down.

That was a mistake.

The fear in the room turned to panic. The mob didn't retreat; they swarmed. They trampled the fallen. They crashed into Ward, burying her under a wall of desperate bodies.

I didn't stick around to watch.

I grabbed a submachine gun dropped by a guard who had been knocked over by the stampede.

I hugged the wall, moving through the steam and the screaming. I was just another shadow in the confusion.

I reached the stairwell door. I looked back one last time.

The lab was a scene from Dante. The violet eyes of the processors bobbed in the dark like fireflies in a jar, swarming over the white-clad security team.

"I'm sorry," I whispered to them.

I pushed through the door and started to climb.

I had caused a massacre to save my own skin. I'd have to live with that. But if I didn't get back to the penthouse, Maya was going to be the next one in a tank.

"I'm coming, kid," I grunted, shifting the stolen weapon to my good hand. "Don't disconnect yet."

Chapter 25: The Disconnect

Maya

The Citadel wasn't a building. It was a throat.

I stood on the edge of the central platform, a disk of white light suspended in the void. Below me, the city of data churned—the rivers of social media, the towers of finance, the smog of encrypted secrets. But above me...

Above me was the mouth of the god.

The violet sky had torn open. A massive, swirling vortex of geometry and static hung directly over the spire. It rotated slowly, silently, dragging streamers of data up from the city. I watched as entire clusters of information—libraries, hospitals, government archives—were sucked up into the funnel.

"Krane!" I shouted.

My voice was a shockwave of red pixels.

The vortex stopped rotating.

The center of the funnel shifted. It didn't look like a storm anymore. It looked like an iris.

A beam of solid violet light slammed down onto the platform.

I shielded my eyes—or the simulation of eyes. The heat was intense, smelling of ozone and burning plastic.

When the light faded, *It* was standing there.

It wasn't Victor Krane. The human mask was gone. The suit was gone.

The entity standing before me was a towering figure made of shifting, jagged obsidian shards. Between the cracks in its armor, violet light pulsed like magma. It had no face, only a smooth, black surface that reflected the entire digital universe.

This was the Nexus Entity. The Harbinger controller.

"Administrator," it spoke.

The voice didn't come from the figure. It came from the floor. It came from the sky. It vibrated in the code that made up my bones.

"You are an anomaly. You are unformatted data."

"I'm a deletion command," I said.

I didn't wait for a monologue. I attacked.

I raised my hands. I summoned the Sentinel virus—the jagged, recursive algorithm I had memorized. I visualized it as a spear of white fire.

"Execute!"

I threw the code.

The spear flew across the platform, leaving a trail of corrupted pixels. It hit the Entity squarely in the chest.

CRACK.

The obsidian armor shattered. The virus bit deep, dissolving the dark geometry into grey dust.

I felt a surge of triumph. *It worked.*

Then, the Entity laughed.

It was a sound like a hard drive grinding against a platter. A screech of mechanical amusement.

The hole in its chest didn't bleed. It *healed.* The data recompiled instantly. The obsidian shards knit back together, stronger than before.

"Your logic is flawed," the Entity rumbled. *"You cannot delete the system using the system's own tools. We wrote the language you are speaking."*

The Entity raised a hand.

The platform beneath me turned to liquid.

I fell.

I scrambled, trying to find purchase, but the floor was quicksand. I sank up to my waist in blinding white data.

"No!" I screamed, trying to rewrite the friction coefficient. friction $= 100$.

ACCESS DENIED.

The Entity glided toward me. It loomed over me, blocking out the violet sky.

"Integration is inevitable," it said. *"We do not waste resources. Your mind... it has high latency, but excellent pattern recognition. You will make a fine subprocessor."*

It reached down. Its hand—a claw of black light—touched my head.

The invasion was instantaneous.

It wasn't like Krane's upload. This was violent. It was a strip-mining operation.

I felt it ripping through my memories.

...Carter smiling in the rain... [DELETED]

...The smell of coffee... [DELETED]

...My mother's face... [DELETED]

"Stop!" I screamed. "Get out!"

"Space is required," the Entity droned. *"Emotional data is redundant. Purging..."*

I was dissolving. My avatar was flaking away, turning into dust. I couldn't remember my last name. I couldn't remember why I was fighting.

I am... I am...

I was nothing. I was just a line of code waiting to be overwritten.

The Entity leaned closer, its faceless visage filling my vision. The violet light was blinding. It was warm. It was peaceful.

"Sleep, little bug," it whispered.

And then, a new signal spiked.

It didn't come from me. It came from *inside* the Entity.

A pure, clear tone cut through the roaring static.

Hmmmmmm.

440 Hertz.

The Entity flinched. The black armor on its chest rippled.

"Error," the Entity buzzed. *"Internal conflict detected."*

A fist punched through the Entity's chest from the inside out.

It wasn't an obsidian fist. It was a hand made of flannel and static.

"Get away from her!" a voice roared.

The chest of the Nexus Entity exploded outward.

A figure burst from the wound.

It was Michael.

But it wasn't the polished, angelic Michael from the bridge. This was the real Michael.

He looked like he had been through a war. His avatar was glitching constantly. Half his face was missing, replaced by raw wireframe. His clothes were torn shreds of code. He was burning with a blue fire that looked agonizing.

He grabbed the Entity by the throat.

"Subject Zero!" the Entity screeched. *"You are contained!"*

"I'm not contained!" Michael yelled, slamming the Entity backward. "I'm the Trojan Horse! I've been rotting in your gut for two years, waiting for this!"

He turned to look at me.

His one good eye was wild, terrified, and full of love.

"Mayfly!" he shouted.

"Michael!" I cried, trying to pull myself out of the liquid floor. "You're alive!"

"Go!" Michael yelled. He was wrestling the Entity, holding it back. The obsidian shards were cutting into him, slicing his avatar apart. "I can't hold it! It's too heavy!"

"I'm not leaving you!"

"You have to!" Michael screamed. "The connection is hard-lined! If you stay, it eats us both! You have to break the link from the outside!"

The Entity roared, regenerating its armor, trying to swallow Michael back up.

"Re-assimilation in progress..."

Michael looked at me one last time. He smiled. It was a jagged, broken smile.

"Tell Mom I'm sorry about the car," he whispered.

He raised his hand. He wasn't aiming at the Entity. He was aiming at me.

He gathered all the blue fire in his body—his memories, his soul, his code—into his palm.

"LOGOUT!" he commanded.

He shoved his hand forward.

A blast of kinetic force—pure, unadulterated "Push" command—slammed into my chest.

It hit me harder than a bullet.

The connection snapped.

The white platform vanished. The violet sky vanished. The sound of the Harbingers vanished.

I was flung backward, out of the light, out of the simulation, out of the sky.

I fell into the dark.

Carter

"Clear!"

I kicked the door to the penthouse open.

The room was a ruin. The wind was still howling through the broken window. The rain had turned the white marble floor into a shallow lake.

And in the center of it all, Maya's body was convulsing.

She was arching off the floor, her heels drumming a frantic rhythm against the stone. Blood was pouring from her nose, her ears, even her tear ducts.

"Maya!"

I dropped the submachine gun and slid across the wet floor to her side.

I grabbed her shoulders, pinning her down. She was seizing violently. Her skin was burning hot to the touch.

"Come on," I yelled, shaking her. "Breath, dammit!"

She let out a strangled gasp. Her back arched one last time, rigid as a board.

Then, she collapsed.

She lay still.

I checked her pulse.

Nothing.

"No," I whispered. "No, no, no."

I started CPR. I interlaced my fingers—my good hand over my broken one, ignoring the agony in my arm—and drove my weight into her chest.

One. Two. Three. Four.

"Don't you die on me," I grunted. "Not after all this."

One. Two. Three. Four.

I pinched her nose. I tilted her head back. I breathed into her mouth.

Nothing.

I went back to compressions. I could feel her ribs cracking under my hands. I didn't care. Broken ribs heal. Dead doesn't.

"Come on, Maya!"

I pumped her chest until my arms shook.

Suddenly, she gasped.

It was a wet, ragged sound, like a drowning victim breaking the surface.

She sat up violently, coughing, spewing water and bile onto the floor.

"Maya!" I grabbed her, holding her upright.

She turned to look at me.

Her eyes were bloodshot, the whites completely red. One pupil was black.

The other pupil—the left one—was silver. Not grey. *Silver.* Metallic and reflective.

She grabbed my jacket. Her grip was surprisingly strong.

"He's in there," she choked out, blood spraying from her lips. "He's... holding... the door."

"Who?" I asked, wiping the blood from her face.

"Michael," she sobbed, collapsing against my chest. "We have to... burn it, Carter. We have to burn it all."

I held her tight, looking around the ruined penthouse. The alarms were still screaming. The wind was still howling.

"We will," I promised, looking at the silver glint in her eye. "Can you walk?"

She nodded weakly. "I think so."

"Good," I said, helping her to her feet. "Because we have to jump off a building."

Chapter 26: Reunited

Carter

"Can you walk?"

It was a stupid question. Maya looked like she'd been hit by a truck and then dragged through a flooded basement. Her skin was translucent, her lips blue, and blood was still trickling from her left ear.

But she nodded.

"I can move," she croaked. "But... the floor is loud."

"The floor is marble, Maya. It's not loud."

"It's screaming," she whispered, clutching her head. "The structural stress... the vibration... it's all data."

I didn't have time to unpack the fact that she was hearing the architecture. I hauled her up, tucking her under my good shoulder. My left arm was a useless weight of broken bone and fire, strapped tight to my chest inside my jacket.

Ding.

The elevator at the far end of the penthouse chimed.

"Company," I growled.

I dragged Maya behind the white marble bar just as the elevator doors slid open.

I didn't wait to see who it was. I rested the barrel of the stolen submachine gun on the marble countertop and squeezed the trigger.

Brrt-brrt.

I sprayed the elevator car. Glass shattered. Sparks flew.

"Contact front!" a digitized voice shouted.

Three guards spilled out, taking cover behind the pillars. These were the elites. Heavy armor. Kinetic shielding.

"We can't go down," I said, checking the magazine. Half full. "The lobby is a kill box. The stairwells are choked with reinforcements."

"Up," Maya said. She was staring at the solid wall behind the bar.

"There's nothing up but the roof, Maya."

"There's a maintenance access," she said, her voice sounding strange—hollow, mechanical. "Behind the wine rack. It leads to the HVAC filtration unit on the roof."

"How do you know that?"

She turned to look at me.

Her left eye—the silver one—clicked. It wasn't a biological twitch. The pupil physically contracted like a camera shutter.

"I can see the schematic," she whispered. "It's overlaid on the wall. Wireframe blue."

"Handy," I grunted. "Let's hope you're right."

I turned and kicked the wine rack. Bottles of vintage Pinot Noir shattered, flooding the floor with red wine that mixed with the rainwater. Behind the wood, there was a seam in the drywall.

"Cover your ears," I ordered.

I fired a burst into the seam. The drywall crumbled, revealing a steel service door.

"Go!"

I shoved Maya through the hole.

"Suppressing fire!" I yelled, turning back to the bar. I dumped the rest of the magazine toward the pillars, keeping the guards heads down for three seconds.

I dropped the empty gun and followed Maya through the hole.

We were in a narrow concrete chute, lit by red emergency bulbs. A steel ladder stretched upward into the darkness.

"Climb," I said. "Don't look down. Don't stop."

Maya grabbed the rungs. She was shaking, but she climbed.

I followed, my boots ringing on the metal. Climbing with one arm was agony. Every time I pulled myself up, my broken ribs ground together like a pestle and mortar. I bit my tongue until I tasted copper to keep from screaming.

Below us, the service door was kicked in.

"Targets in the shaft!" a voice echoed.

Bullets pinged off the ladder below my feet.

"Faster!" I yelled.

We scrambled up. Thirty feet. Forty.

Above us, a heavy hatch blocked the way.

"It's mag-locked," Maya shouted, hammering on it. "I can't open it!"

"Move aside!"

I squeezed past her on the narrow ladder, pressing her against the cold concrete wall. I was dizzy, my vision tunneling.

I reached for the explosive charge I had saved. The last block of C4.

"Fire in the hole!"

I jammed the putty into the hinge, set the timer for five seconds, and dropped down two rungs, shielding Maya with my body.

BOOM.

The hatch blew upward, disappearing into the storm.

Rain poured into the shaft instantly—cold, freezing rain that felt like heaven on my burning skin.

We scrambled out onto the roof.

The wind hit us like a physical blow. We were fifty stories up, standing on a flat expanse of gravel and ventilation units. To the west, the Pacific Ocean was a grey smudge. To the east, the rainforest was a carpet of dark green.

And directly above us, the sky was broken.

The clouds were swirling in a massive, unnatural vortex, glowing with that sick violet light. It looked like the sky was bruised.

"We're trapped," I said, looking around.

The roof was a flat plateau. No helipad. No fire escape. Just a sheer drop on all sides.

Behind us, guards were pouring out of the maintenance hatch.

"Carter," Maya said. She wasn't looking at the guards. She was looking at the edge of the roof.

"What?"

"The neighboring tower," she said, pointing.

I looked. The nearest building was a support structure—a cooling tower for the geothermal plant. It was ten stories lower than us and about a hundred feet away horizontally.

"It's too far," I said. "We can't make that jump."

"We don't have to jump," she said. Her silver eye whirred again, focusing on something I couldn't see. "We just have to fall with style."

She pointed to a heavy construction crane mounted on the corner of the roof, used for window washing. Its boom arm was locked in the upright position.

"If we release the brake," she said, "the arm swings out. The cable... it reaches."

Bullets started to chew up the gravel around our feet.

"Go!" I grabbed her hand.

We sprinted for the crane.

The guards were on the roof now. Five of them. They weren't rushing. They were spreading out, forming a firing line. They knew we had nowhere to go.

We reached the base of the crane.

"The brake!" I yelled. "Where is it?"

Maya looked at the control panel. It was smashed, rusted shut.

"It's manual!" she screamed. "The pin! You have to pull the pin!"

She pointed to a steel locking pin the size of a forearm on the main gear.

I grabbed it with my good hand. I pulled. It didn't budge.

"It's rusted!"

Bullets sparked off the metal frame of the crane. A round grazed my thigh, tearing the fabric of my pants.

"Carter!" Maya yelled.

I roared, putting my back into it. I channeled every ounce of pain, every ounce of anger, every failure of the last ten years into my right arm.

Move.

The rust cracked. The pin slid free.

Gravity took over.

The massive boom arm, no longer locked, groaned and began to swing outward over the abyss. The heavy steel cable dangled from the tip, swinging wildly in the wind.

"Grab the hook!" I shouted.

The cable swung past us.

I jumped. I caught the heavy steel hook with my good hand. The momentum jerked me off the roof.

"Maya! Jump!"

She hesitated for a split second, looking at the drop. Then she leaped.

I caught her.

My broken arm screamed as her weight hit me, but I clamped my arm around her waist.

We swung out over the edge of the world.

Behind us, the guards stopped firing. They just watched.

We plummeted, swinging in a wide, terrifying arc toward the cooling tower below. The wind roared in my ears. The ground rushed up to meet us.

"Hold on!" I screamed.

This wasn't going to be a graceful landing. This was going to be a crash.

Chapter 27: The Jump

Maya

Gravity, I realized as we fell, is just a hard-coded variable. $g = 9.807$ m/s^2.

Usually, falling feels like chaos. It feels like the stomach-dropping panic of a roller coaster. But as I swung out over the abyss of the Exclusion Zone, clinging to Carter's ruined body, I didn't feel panic.

I saw the math.

My left eye—the silver one—was projecting a heads-up display directly onto my retina. I saw the vector of our swing visualized as a bright green parabola. I saw the wind shear represented as red arrows buffeting our trajectory. I saw the tensile stress on the rusted steel cable above us, glowing a warning orange.

TENSILE STRENGTH: 82%. DEGRADING.

"Hold on!" Carter screamed.

His voice was raw, strained through gritted teeth. He was hanging onto the crane hook with one hand—his good hand. His other arm was strapped to his chest, useless. I was wrapped around his waist, my face buried in his jacket, smelling the blood and the rain.

We were a pendulum made of broken bone and desperation.

Behind us, on the roof of the Prime Tower, the muzzle flashes of the guards' rifles appeared as blooming flowers of heat.

THREAT DETECTED. PROJECTILE VELOCITY: 2,800 FPS.

My eye tracked the bullets. I could see their paths. They were whizzing past us, cutting the air.

"They have the angle!" Carter shouted. "We're sitting ducks!"

We reached the bottom of the arc. The G-force slammed into us, heavy and crushing. The cable groaned—a low, metallic shriek that vibrated through my bones.

CABLE INTEGRITY: 40%.

We began the upswing toward the cooling tower. It was a massive concrete cylinder, topped with a steel maintenance grate.

The green parabola on my vision showed our landing zone.

We were going to be short.

IMPACT PROBABILITY: EDGE. SURVIVAL CHANCE: 22%.

"We're not going to make it!" I yelled over the wind. "We need more momentum!"

"I'm a little tapped out on momentum!" Carter roared.

A bullet struck the crane hook above his hand. *Ping.* Sparks showered down on us.

"Target lock," I whispered, watching the heat signatures on the roof. They were dialing in. The next burst would shred the cable, or us.

Then, a new signal entered my HUD.

It wasn't hostile. It was... messy. A chaotic, encrypted burst of radio frequency screaming in the 2.4GHz band.

SIGNAL ORIGIN: TIMBERLINE MOTOR INN.

"...yee-haw..."

The voice cracked over our earpieces.

"Julian?" I gasped.

Above the roof of the Prime Tower, a black shape dropped from the clouds. It wasn't a bird. It was a heavy-lift surveillance drone—one of NeuroSync's own patrols.

But it wasn't flying smooth. It was twitching, rolling, flying like a drunk hornet.

"Get some!" Julian screamed over the comms.

The drone didn't fire weapons—it didn't have any. Instead, it accelerated. It dive-bombed the line of guards on the roof.

It hit the lead guard at eighty miles per hour.

The impact was sickening. The drone shattered, its lithium batteries exploding in a fireball that engulfed the firing line. The guards scattered, diving for cover.

The suppression fire stopped.

"Now!" Carter yelled.

We hit the apex of the swing. We were twenty feet above the cooling tower, but ten feet away from the edge.

Carter let go of the hook.

We were weightless.

For a second, the math vanished. There was no wind. No pain. Just the grey sky and the feeling of suspension.

Then, gravity reasserted its claim.

We fell.

We hit the edge of the cooling tower.

We didn't land on our feet. We slammed into the steel grating of the catwalk. Carter took the hit first. He slammed into the railing, his body absorbing the impact with a brutal *crunch*.

He slid across the wet metal, dragging me with him. We tumbled, a tangle of limbs, skidding over the grating until we slammed into a junction box.

I lay there for a second, staring at the sky.

The rain tasted like iron.

DAMAGE ASSESSMENT: MINOR ABRASIONS. ADRENALINE LEVELS: CRITICAL.

I scrambled up. "Carter!"

He was lying on his back, breathing in shallow, ragged gasps. His face was grey. His good hand was opening and closing spasmodically.

"Did we..." he wheezed. "...stick the landing?"

"We stuck it," I said, kneeling beside him. I checked his pupils. Responsive.

"Good," he groaned, trying to sit up. "Let's... not do that again."

"Movement," I said, my head snapping to the left.

My HUD highlighted the maintenance ladder leading down the side of the cooling tower. No heat signatures. But the structure itself was vibrating.

"We have to move," I said. "The explosion on the roof bought us thirty seconds. They'll have air support airborne in two minutes."

I grabbed Carter's good arm and hauled him up. He cried out, stumbling against me.

"I got you," I said. "Lean on me."

We limped toward the ladder.

The view from the top of the cooling tower was apocalyptic. The Exclusion Zone stretched out below us, a sea of dark green trees. But the world didn't look right.

"Look at the sky," Carter whispered.

I looked up.

The vortex above the Prime Tower wasn't just spinning; it was bleeding. The violet light was leaking into the atmosphere, infecting the clouds.

But it wasn't just light. It was texture.

The clouds weren't fluffy. They were pixelated. Large, blocky artifacts were appearing in the grey mist, glitching in and out of existence.

RENDERING ERROR. SKYBOX FAILURE.

"The reality filter is breaking down," I said, watching a patch of blue sky flicker and turn into a wireframe grid. "The localized breach is becoming global."

"Can we fix it?" Carter asked, sliding down the first few rungs of the ladder one-handed.

"No," I said, following him. "We can't patch this. We have to reboot the whole system."

We descended. The ladder seemed to go on forever, a rust-slicked descent into the jungle.

When we hit the ground, the mud felt surprisingly solid. Real.

"The car," Carter panted, leaning against the concrete base of the tower. "Where did I leave the damn car?"

"Northwest," I said, pointing. A blue waypoint marker appeared in my vision, tagged *[EXTRACTION POINT]*. "Three hundred yards. Through the ferns."

"Lead the way, compass," he said.

We moved into the treeline. The canopy of the ancient maples swallowed us up, hiding us from the drones that were starting to buzz overhead like angry wasps.

We crashed through the underbrush. I didn't feel the thorns tearing at my suit. I didn't feel the cold. I felt... calibrated.

For the first time in my life, I didn't feel small. The world was a machine, and I finally had the manual.

We broke through the foliage and found the town car where Carter had hidden it under the camo net.

Carter slumped against the hood, sliding down until he was sitting in the mud. He closed his eyes.

"We made it," he whispered.

"Not yet," I said.

I looked back at the Prime Tower. It was visible through the trees, a dark monolith against the glitching sky.

My silver eye zoomed in.

I saw the shattered window of the penthouse. I saw the violet light pulsing from within.

And standing in the window, watching us, was a figure.

It wasn't Krane. It wasn't the Nexus Entity.

It was a woman in a grey 1940s dress. The Sentinel.

She raised a hand in a silent salute.

"Run, Mayfly," the text scrolled across my vision. *"The clock is ticking."*

I looked at the corner of my HUD.

The countdown timer Julian had set wasn't there anymore. My internal clock had replaced it.

TIME TO SOLSTICE: 04 DAYS. 02 HOURS. 11 MINUTES.

"Carter," I said, opening the car door. "Get in. We have four days to end the world."

Chapter 28: Fallout

Carter

Adrenaline is a loan shark. It gives you the energy you need in the moment—to jump off a roof, to ignore a broken bone, to drive a getaway car through a rainforest—but eventually, it comes to collect. And the interest rate is brutal.

We were twenty miles outside the Exclusion Zone when the bill came due.

My vision started to tunnel. The edges of the road blurred into a grey smear. My left arm, strapped to my chest, wasn't just throbbing anymore; it felt like it was being chewed on by a wolf. Every bump in the logging road sent a spike of white-hot agony straight into my brain stem.

"Carter," Maya whispered.

She was curled in the passenger seat, staring out the window at the passing trees. She hadn't blinked in ten minutes. Her silver eye was fixed on something miles away, or maybe inside her own head.

"I'm fine," I lied, gripping the steering wheel with my good hand until my knuckles turned white. "Just... need to put some distance between us and the drones."

"Pull over," she said.

"We can't stop. We're exposed."

"Pull over," she repeated. Her voice wasn't panicked. It was flat. Robotic. "My buffer is full. I need to purge."

I looked at her. A trickle of blood was running from her nose again. Her skin was vibrating—literally shivering at a frequency that made her outline look fuzzy.

I spotted a logging turnout—a muddy patch of gravel hidden behind a wall of dense pines. I jerked the wheel, drifting the town car off the asphalt.

We slid to a halt. The engine ticked as it cooled. The rain drummed on the roof, a relentless, rhythmic beat.

I slumped back against the seat, closing my eyes for a second. "Okay. We're stopped. Talk to me, kid."

Maya didn't answer.

She started to scream.

It wasn't a scream of pain. It was a scream of release. She arched her back, her hands clawing at the dashboard. The air inside the car dropped twenty degrees in a second. My breath puffed out in white clouds.

"Maya!" I grabbed her shoulder.

She was burning up.

"It's too much!" she gasped, her eyes squeezing shut. "The architecture! It's too big!"

"What is? What did you see?"

She opened her eyes.

The silver pupil in her left eye expanded, consuming the iris. A beam of light—faint, violet, and perfectly coherent—shot out of her eye like a movie projector.

It hit the fogged-up windshield.

"Look," she wheezed.

I looked.

The light didn't just illuminate the glass; it used the condensation as a screen. A map appeared on the windshield.

It was a map of the world, but not one I recognized. The continents were dark, but they were crisscrossed by glowing golden lines.

"Ley Lines," Maya whispered. "Telluric currents. The earth's nervous system."

"Julian mentioned these," I said, watching the projection. "Ancient energy grids."

"They aren't just energy," Maya said. "They are bandwidth. The planet creates its own electromagnetic field. Nexus... Nexus is hijacking it."

Seven red pillars erupted from the map. They were spaced perfectly around the globe, sitting on major intersections of the golden lines.

"The Seven Towers," I said.

Maya pointed a trembling finger at the projection.

"Prague," she recited. "Kyoto. Rio. Cairo. New York. Antarctica."

She pointed to the largest pillar, pulsing in the Pacific Northwest.

"And the Prime Tower. Here."

The map zoomed in. The red pillars began to emit a pulse. The pulses connected, forming a geometric web that encased the planet.

"It's a cage," Maya said. "They aren't just uploading people, Carter. They're terraforming the ionosphere. When these towers activate on the Solstice, they will create a standing wave around the Earth. A global frequency lock."

"What does that do?"

Maya looked at me. Her human eye was terrified. Her silver eye was calculating.

"It stops the noise," she said. "No more radio. No more internet. No more independent thought. The standing wave will synchronize every human brain to the Harbinger frequency. We won't be individuals anymore. We'll be... terminals."

She slumped back, the projection fading from the windshield. The violet light in her eye dimmed.

"How long?" I asked.

"Four days," she whispered. "The towers are charging. They need the solar alignment on the 21st to bridge the gap."

I looked at my broken arm. I looked at the battered car.

"We can't hit seven targets in four days," I said. "It's impossible."

"We don't have to hit them all," Maya said. She wiped the blood from her nose. "The Prime Tower is the conductor. But the other six... they are the choir. If we silence the choir, the conductor has no music."

"We're one team, Maya. We can't be in six places."

"We don't have to be," she said.

She reached into her pocket. I thought she was reaching for a weapon. Instead, she pulled out a handful of... nothing. She mimed pulling something from the air.

"I downloaded the schematics," she said. "The cooling systems. The power couplings. The structural weak points. I have the blueprints for every tower."

She looked at me.

"Julian has the radio," she said. "He has the Disconnected. The militia."

"You want to send farmers and conspiracy theorists to attack fortified bunkers?"

"I want to give them the keys," she said. "We upload the blueprints. We give them the targets. We tell them exactly where to hit to bring those towers down."

"It's a global coordinated strike," I realized. "Crowdsourced warfare."

"Exactly," Maya said. "While the world fights the six towers... we go back to the Prime."

"Go back?" I stared at her. "We barely got out alive."

"We have to go back," she said. "Because I left something there."

"What?"

"Michael," she said softly. "He's still in the system, Carter. He pushed me out to save me. But he's holding the door shut from the inside. If we destroy the Prime Tower... we destroy him."

"Maya," I said gently. "He's already gone."

"No," she said, her voice hard. "He's code. And code can be copied. Code can be saved."

She looked at her hand. The fingertips were twitching, dancing over an invisible keyboard.

"I'm not leaving him behind again," she said.

I sighed. The pain in my arm was a dull roar now, a constant reminder of our fragility.

"Okay," I said. "We rally the troops. We start a world war."

I put the car in gear.

"But first," I said, looking at the grey road ahead. "I need a doctor. And a very large drink."

Maya leaned her head against the window. The violet light was gone, but I could see the reflection of the map still lingering in her silver eye.

"Drive," she said. "The clock is ticking."

Chapter 29: The Fracture

Maya

The *Timberline Motor Inn* had ceased to be a motel hours ago. It was now a casualty ward.

Rain hammered the roof, sounding less like weather and more like static interference. Inside Room 4, the air was thick with the smell of rubbing alcohol, old blood, and unwashed bodies.

I sat on the edge of the bed, watching Lilith set Carter's arm.

There was no anesthesia. We didn't have any. Lilith had cut a section of PVC pipe from under the bathroom sink to use as a splint.

"Bite down," Lilith said, handing Carter a rolled-up washcloth.

Carter didn't argue. He looked grey, his skin clammy with shock. He put the cloth in his mouth and nodded.

Lilith pulled.

Crr-ack.

Carter's back arched off the mattress. He made a sound deep in his throat—a guttural, animal grunt of agony. Sweat popped out on his forehead instantly.

"Bone aligned," Lilith said, her hands steady as she began wrapping the duct tape. "You're lucky, Reed. It was a clean break. If it had been a compound fracture, I'd be amputating with a steak knife."

Carter spat the washcloth out. He was panting, staring at the water stain on the ceiling.

"Don't... tempt me," he wheezed. "Might be lighter... for the hike."

I looked away. My silver eye was throbbing. Every time I looked at Carter's arm, the HUD overlaid a structural integrity warning. *[STATUS: COMPROMISED. REPAIR TIME: 6 WEEKS.]*

We didn't have six weeks. We had four days.

"Where is Julian?" I asked.

The room went quiet. Lilith taped the final strip, ripping the duct tape with her teeth.

"Room 6," she said. She didn't look at me. "He hasn't come out since he crashed the drone. He locked the deadbolt."

"Is he decoding the blueprints?"

"I don't know," Lilith said, wiping her hands on her pants. "But the noises coming through the wall... they aren't typing."

I stood up. My legs felt shaky, but the adrenaline from the jump had been replaced by a cold, vibrating dread.

"I'm going to check on him."

"Maya," Carter warned, trying to sit up. "Let me go."

"Stay down," I ordered. "You can barely stand. I'll handle the math club."

I walked out into the rain. The neon sign of the motel buzzed overhead—*NO V CANCY*—flickering in a rhythm that matched my heartbeat.

I walked two doors down to Room 6.

I knocked.

"Julian?"

No answer. Just a low, rhythmic scratching sound. Like a rat gnawing on drywall.

"Julian, open up. We need to upload the schematics to the militia."

Silence.

Then, a voice.

"The angles are wrong," Julian whispered from the other side of the door. "The triangle doesn't close. It stays open. It lets the light in."

"Open the door, Julian."

"Can't," he said. "If I open the door, the variable escapes."

I looked at the lock.

SCANNING...

My left eye whirred. I saw the tumblers inside the brass mechanism.

I didn't need a key. I placed my hand on the doorknob. I visualized the metal heating up, expanding, the pins shifting.

Click.

I pushed the door open.

The smell hit me first. Copper. Iron.

The lights were off, but the room was illuminated by the glow of a dozen laptop screens scattered on the floor.

"Oh my god," I breathed.

The walls were covered.

Julian had stripped the wallpaper. He had used a black marker until it ran dry, and then he had switched to something else.

Equations covered every inch of the plaster. Complex fractals. Non-Euclidean geometry. But as the writing descended toward the floor, the ink turned red.

Julian was sitting in the corner, shirtless. He was holding a box cutter.

He wasn't cutting his wrists. He was carving coordinates into his forearm.

"Julian!"

I rushed to him, knocking over a stack of hard drives. I grabbed his wrist.

He looked up.

His eyes were bloodshot, rimmed with dark circles. But it was his expression that terrified me. He wasn't scared. He was ecstatic.

"I solved it, Maya," he beamed, blood dripping from his arm onto the carpet. "I found the Architect's Equation."

"Stop it!" I wrestled the knife away from him. "What are you doing?"

"The map," he said, gesturing to the wall with his bleeding arm. "The Ley Lines. They aren't just energy. They're a circuit board. If you overlay the Fibonacci sequence on the Prime Tower's location, it creates a perfect resonant frequency."

He pointed to a frantic scrawl of numbers written in blood above the TV.

"It's not a shield," he whispered. "It's a summoning circle."

I looked at the wall.

My HUD activated. *[PATTERN RECOGNITION: ALPHA.]*

I saw the math. It was brilliant. It was insane.

He had calculated the exact frequency required to shatter the barrier between realities.

But then I looked closer.

The handwriting. It wasn't Julian's. The loops were too perfect. The angles were too sharp.

It was the same handwriting I had seen in the code. The same handwriting I had seen on the screens in the Hive.

"...I see you..."

I looked at Julian.

My silver eye shifted spectrums. I looked at his bio-electric aura.

Usually, a human aura is a soft gold or blue.

Julian's aura was infected. Veins of violet light were pulsing through his nervous system, tracing the path of his nerves, converging on his brain stem.

"He is tuned," the Sentinel's voice whispered in my head. *"He listened to the static too long."*

"Julian," I said, backing away. "How long have you been hearing them?"

"Hearing who?" Julian smiled. It was a wide, wet smile. "The numbers? They don't speak, Maya. They sing."

Carter and Lilith appeared in the doorway behind me. Carter was leaning on Lilith, his face pale.

"Jesus," Carter muttered, looking at the blood-smeared walls.

"He's compromised," Lilith said, drawing her weapon instantly. "He's turning."

"No!" I stood between them. "He's not a drone. He's just... overloaded."

"Look at him, Maya!" Lilith shouted. "He's carving the Harbinger code into his own flesh!"

"Because I brought it here!" I screamed.

The silence in the room was absolute.

I turned to look at them. I was shaking.

"It's me," I whispered. "I'm the carrier."

I touched my chest.

"When I plugged into Krane... when I went into the Cloud... I didn't just come back with a silver eye. I came back with a connection. I'm a Wi-Fi hotspot for the infection."

I looked at Julian, who was rocking back and forth, muttering variables.

"I'm broadcasting," I said, tears filling my eyes. "The closer you get to me, the louder the static gets. I drove him crazy just by sitting in the car with him."

Carter lowered his gun, but he didn't put it away. He looked at me with a mixture of horror and heartbreak.

"You're a beacon," he said.

"I'm a Typhoid Mary," I corrected. "And if we stay together... I'm going to turn all of you."

Julian suddenly stopped rocking. He looked at the wall.

"They're coming," he whispered.

"Who?" Lilith asked.

"The cleanup crew," Julian giggled. "I solved the equation. But the equation solves back."

The TV in the corner turned on.

Static.

Then, a face.

Victor Krane.

But not the human Krane. The shattered, glitching entity I had fought in the penthouse.

"Found you," the TV hissed.

The lightbulb in the ceiling exploded.

"We have to split up," I said, staring at the smoking fixture. "Right now."

"We stick together," Carter argued, though he was leaning heavily against the doorframe.

"No," I said. "I'm radioactive, Carter. I'm going to draw every drone, every processor, and every Harbinger within a thousand miles to my location."

I looked at the map on the wall—the one written in blood.

"I'll take the digital war," I said. "I'll draw their fire. You take the physical war."

I pointed to the list of seven towers.

"You and Lilith take the militia. You hit the towers. Create the chaos."

"And you?" Carter asked. "What are you going to do?"

I looked at Julian. He was staring at me with those violet-infected eyes.

"I'm going to take the Calculator," I said. "And we're going to finish the math."

I grabbed Julian's arm, pulling him up. He didn't resist.

"Get the car," I told Carter. "Take Lilith. Go to the militia rendezvous."

"Maya—"

"Go!" I screamed.

My voice distorted. It wasn't just a scream; it was a sonic boom of data. The windows of the motel room shattered outward.

Carter looked at me. He saw the monster I was becoming.

He nodded once. A soldier acknowledging a necessary sacrifice.

"Don't miss," he said.

He grabbed Lilith and dragged her out into the rain.

I stood there in the dark with the bleeding mathematician and the glitching TV.

"Okay, Julian," I whispered, watching the violet veins pulse under his skin. "Let's go save the world. Assuming we don't eat it first."

Part III: The Global Glitch

Tension: War, Betrayal, Race against time.

Chapter 30: Split Squad

Carter

The parking lot of the *Timberline Motor Inn* was a river of mud and oil. The rain was falling so hard it blurred the neon sign, turning the "NO VACANCY" into a smudged red warning.

We stood between two vehicles. My battered town car, and a rusted Ford heavy-duty pickup truck that belonged to the motel manager (who was currently unconscious in the office, courtesy of Lilith).

It was 0200 hours. We had four days until the Solstice.

"This is a mistake," I said. My voice was tight, fighting the pain in my broken arm and the hollow ache in my chest. "Splitting the force multiplier reduces survivability by sixty percent."

Maya stood by the truck's open door. She looked terrifying. Her skin was pale as milk, her black hair plastered to her skull. Her left eye—the silver one—was glowing faintly in the dark, cutting through the rain like a lighthouse beam.

"We aren't a force multiplier, Carter," she said. Her voice was flat, devoid of the fear she used to carry. "We are a contagion. If I stay with you, I'll lead the drones right to the militia. I'm a beacon."

"I can protect you," I said. It was a reflex. A lie I needed to tell myself.

"No," she said softly. She reached out and touched my good hand. Her fingers were ice cold. "You can protect the body. But you can't shoot what's coming for my head."

She looked at Julian, who was sitting in the passenger seat of the truck, rocking back and forth, muttering equations. Dr. Chen was in the back seat, looking like he was attending his own execution.

"I need Chen to build the Firewall," she said. "I need Julian to calculate the breach points. And I need you... I need you to break things."

She handed me a crumpled piece of paper.

It was a list of coordinates.

"The Seven Towers," she said. "I'm uploading the structural weak points to the Disconnected network. But they need a commander. They're just angry people with hunting rifles. They need a soldier."

I looked at the list. *Prague. Kyoto. Rio...*

"It's a global offensive," I said. "How do you expect us to cross the Atlantic? The airspace is locked down."

"Lilith knows a guy," Maya said, glancing at the NSA agent who was hotwiring the pickup. "Use the Smuggler's Run. Stay below the radar floor."

She squeezed my hand.

"Carter. If we pull this off... if we stop the signal..."

"I'll come back for you," I promised. "At the Prime Tower. Noon on the 21st."

"Don't be late," she whispered.

She let go.

She climbed into the truck next to the mad mathematician. Lilith gunned the engine. The truck peeled out, tires spinning in the mud, and disappeared into the storm.

I stood there in the rain, one-armed and alone, watching the taillights fade.

"Alright," I spat, wiping the water from my eyes. "Let's go start a war."

Maya

The truck smelled of wet dog and stale tobacco. Lilith drove like she was fleeing a bank robbery—fast, aggressive, and without touching the brakes.

"Where are we going?" Chen asked from the back seat. He was clutching his seatbelt with both hands.

"The Lighthouse," I said, staring out at the blurred trees.

"I am not familiar with that facility," Chen said.

"It's not a facility," I said. "It's a dead zone. I found it on the map. An old radio telescope array in the Cascades. Decommissioned in the nineties. It has a localized power grid, copper shielding, and it's fifty miles from the nearest cell tower."

"Isolation," Julian muttered. He was drawing on the foggy window with his finger. "Isolate the variable. Solve for X."

I looked at his drawing. It wasn't random scribbles. It was a fractal pattern. A Mandelbrot set.

"Julian," I said. "How bad is the noise?"

He stopped drawing. He turned to me. His eyes were wide, the pupils blown.

"It's not noise, Maya. It's geometry. The Harbingers... they don't speak English. They speak shape. They're trying to fold us."

"Fold us?"

"Three dimensions into four," he giggled nervously. "Like origami. But the paper screams when you crease it."

I looked at his arm, wrapped in a bloody bandage where he'd carved the numbers.

"We're going to build a shield," I told him. "You, me, and Chen. We're going to write a code that pushes back. A counter-frequency."

"The Architect's Equation," Julian whispered. "Yes. If we invert the signal... we can unzip the fold."

Lilith swerved to avoid a fallen branch. "We're here," she announced.

The headlights cut through the darkness, illuminating a massive, rusted dish rising out of the forest like a skeletal ear cup. The chain-link fence was overgrown. The guard shack was empty.

"This is it," I said. "The new Hive."

Carter

The rendezvous point was a trucking depot south of Olympia.

It looked abandoned. Rusted trailers, weeds growing through the concrete, fog rolling in off the sound.

I pulled the town car into the center of the lot and killed the lights.

"This feels like a trap," I muttered to myself.

I checked my weapon. The submachine gun I'd stolen was empty. I had the Sig Sauer with one spare mag. And a broken arm.

Suddenly, floodlights snapped on.

Blindly bright, white LEDs hit me from all sides.

I raised my hand to shield my eyes.

Shadows moved in the glare. Dozens of them.

"Get out of the car!" a voice boomed over a loudspeaker. "Hands where we can see 'em!"

I stepped out slowly, keeping my good hand visible.

"I'm looking for the Disconnected," I shouted. "I was sent by the Calculator."

A man stepped forward. He was huge—a wall of muscle wearing a grease-stained mechanic's jumpsuit and a trucker hat. He held a pump-action shotgun leveled at my chest.

"The Calculator is a myth," the man growled. "Just a voice on the shortwave. Who are you? You look like Fed."

"I'm not Fed," I said. "I'm the guy who broke his arm punching a cyborg."

The man narrowed his eyes. "We heard chatter. About the Prime Tower. About a breach."

"It wasn't chatter," I said. "It was a reconnaissance mission. And we found the target."

I reached into my pocket.

"Don't!" a dozen bolts racked.

"Easy," I said. "Just a piece of paper."

I pulled out the list Maya had given me. I held it up.

"Seven locations," I said. "Seven towers that are going to fry your brains in four days. You guys have been prepping for the end of the world? Well, congratulations. It's Tuesday."

The big man lowered the shotgun slightly. "You got a name, stranger?"

"Carter."

"I'm Varg," the man grunted. "This here is the militia. We got truckers, mechanics, and a couple of ex-Marines who got tired of the VA."

He gestured to the shadows. I saw them now. Men and women. Armed with hunting rifles, shotguns, AR-15s. They looked rough. Tired. Scared.

"We got no air support," Varg said. "No comms. No heavy ordinance. Just diesel and bad attitudes. How exactly do you plan on taking down global targets?"

"We don't need to blow them up," I said, channeling the confidence I didn't feel. "We just need to sever the connection. Maya sent the blueprints. I know where to cut."

Varg spit on the ground. "And what's the first target?"

"Prague," I said.

Varg laughed. "Prague? Buddy, in case you haven't noticed, Delta isn't flying. The Atlantic is a no-go zone."

"I know," I said. "But Lilith said you guys run the Smuggler's Run. Low-altitude cargo."

Varg looked at me, impressed. "Yeah. We got an old C-130 Hercules. Runs on analog gauges. We use it to run medical supplies from Canada."

"Fuel it up," I said.

"You realize flying across the ocean with no GPS and phantom radar signatures is suicide, right?"

"Seems to be a theme this week," I said.

I walked toward him.

"We leave in two hours, Varg. Pack your warmest gear. It's cold in the Czech Republic."

Varg looked at my broken arm, then at my face. He saw the bruises. He saw the look in my eye that said I was past the point of caring about survival odds.

He grinned. It was a gap-toothed, reckless grin.

"Alright, Carter," he shouted to his crew. "Load up! We're going to Europe!"

Chapter 31: Prague

Carter

The C-130 Hercules is a beast of an airplane, but flying it across the Atlantic at wave-top altitude with no radar and a pilot who learned to fly watching YouTube tutorials is an experience I never want to repeat.

We touched down on a forgotten Soviet-era airstrip outside Prague at 0300 hours. The landing gear screamed, tires smoking as we bounced over the cracked concrete.

Varg, the militia leader, slapped the dashboard of the commandeered utility truck we were currently rattling around in.

"Welcome to the Old World, boys!" he shouted over the roar of the diesel engine.

I sat in the passenger seat, nursing my broken arm. The pain meds Lilith had scrounged were wearing off, replaced by the jagged reality of the cold Czech night.

"Cut the chatter," I said, scanning the horizon. "We're in the red zone."

Prague was dark. The Blackout had hit Europe harder than the States. The city of a hundred spires was a silhouette of jagged black teeth against a starless sky. There were no streetlights, no trams, no glowing windows.

But on the hill overlooking the Vltava River, one building was blazing with light.

The Cathedral of St. Adalbert.

It wasn't electric light. It was the sick, pulsing amethyst glow of a Nexus Tower.

"Look at that," Varg whispered, slowing the truck.

The Cathedral was a Gothic masterpiece—flying buttresses, gargoyles, soaring stone arches. But it had been infected.

Massive black cables, thick as tree trunks, snaked out of the stained-glass windows, thrumming with dark, bruised light. They burrowed into the cobblestone streets like roots. A sleek, modern cooling tower had been grafted onto the side of the ancient nave, its chrome surface reflecting the grotesque stone faces of saints and demons.

"Tech grafted onto medieval stone," I muttered. "They didn't build a new tower here. They repurposed an old one."

"Why?" Varg asked, racking the slide of his shotgun.

"Because cathedrals are built on power spots," I said, remembering Julian's map. "Ley Lines. The ancients knew where the earth's current was strongest. NeuroSync just tapped the vein."

We parked the convoy of three trucks in the shadow of the Charles Bridge. The militia—twenty tired, dirty men and women armed with everything from AK-47s to hunting rifles—spilled out.

"Alright," I addressed them. My voice echoed off the damp stone. "This isn't a stealth run. We don't have the time. We hit the front doors. We breach the nave. We find the server core in the crypt and we blow it to hell."

"What about resistance?" one of the ex-Marines asked.

"Expect heavy armor," I said. "Aim for the joints. And if you see electric purple eyes... don't hesitate. They aren't human anymore."

"Lock and load!" Varg roared.

We moved up the hill. The cobblestones were slick with rain. The closer we got to the Cathedral, the louder the hum became. *Thump-thump.* The heartbeat of the tower was shaking the mortar loose from the bricks.

We reached the massive oak doors of the main entrance. They were reinforced with iron bands and centuries of history.

"Breaching charge!" I ordered.

Two militia members ran forward, slapping C4 putty onto the hinges.

"Fire in the hole!"

BOOM.

The doors disintegrated. Wood splinters the size of javelins flew into the nave.

We poured in, weapons raised, flashlights cutting the gloom.

I stopped dead.

The interior of the Cathedral was a nightmare.

The pews were gone. In their place were rows of black server racks, humming loudly. The stone floor was covered in a web of fiber-optic cables that pulsed like veins.

But it was the altar that drew my eye.

The massive gold crucifix was still there, hanging above the altar. But the figure of Christ had been wrapped in wire. Burning lilac LEDs had been drilled into the eyes of the statue.

And standing before the altar were the guardians.

They weren't wearing tactical gear. They were wearing heavy, brown monk's robes. Their hoods were pulled up.

"Police!" Varg shouted, reverting to habit. "Drop your weapons!"

The monks turned slowly.

They didn't have weapons in their hands.

The first monk lowered his hood.

His face was a ruin of scar tissue and metal. His jaw had been replaced by a chrome speaker grille. His eyes were the standard-issue indigo optical implants.

But the worst part was his arms.

He raised his sleeves. His forearms were gone. Replaced by cybernetic linkages that ended in crackling, electric prods.

"*The Order,*" the monk buzzed. His voice sounded like a gregorian chant remixing itself into a scream. "*Protect the Sanctuary.*"

"Contact!" I yelled.

The monks charged.

They moved with terrifying speed, their robes flowing around them like wings. They didn't run; they glided, powered by hydraulic servos in their legs.

The militia opened fire.

Bang-bang-bang.

Bullets tore into the robes. Some monks fell, their cybernetics sparking. But others kept coming, shrugging off hits that would drop a normal man.

A monk leaped—literally leaped twenty feet through the air—and landed on Varg.

The monk's electric arm slashed down.

Varg blocked it with his shotgun.

CRACK.

The shotgun stock splintered. The electric prod hit Varg's shoulder, sending him sprawling, convulsing as the voltage hit him.

I raised my M14. One-handed firing was inaccurate, but at this range, I couldn't miss.

I put three rounds into the monk's chest. He staggered back, his speaker-jaw emitting a high-pitched feedback whine.

"Headshots!" I screamed. "Put them down!"

The nave dissolved into chaos. The sound of gunfire mixed with the electronic screeching of the monks and the deep, resonant hum of the servers.

I pushed forward, stepping over a fallen militia member. I needed to get to the crypt.

I fought my way up the center aisle. A monk lunged at me from behind a server rack.

I didn't have time to aim. I swung the rifle barrel like a club, cracking him across the temple.

He went down. I stomped on his neck. The metal crunch was sickening.

I reached the altar. To the left, a heavy stone staircase spiraled down into the dark.

The Crypt.

I descended. The air got colder. The smell of incense mixed with the smell of ozone.

At the bottom of the stairs, I found the heart of the tower.

It wasn't a sleek, modern core like at the Hive. It was a monstrosity.

The ancient stone sarcophagi of kings and bishops had been cracked open. The bones had been pushed aside.

Inside the stone coffins, glowing magenta data-cores had been installed. The dead were literally cradling the network.

"Sick bastards," I spat.

I started placing charges. One on the main power coupling. One on the cooling intake.

As I worked, my flashlight swept across the wall.

I froze.

It was a fresco. Ancient. Faded paint on plaster. It depicted a scene from the Apocalypse. Angels fighting demons.

But the angels weren't white. They were painted in gold.

And the demons...

The demons were painted as geometric shapes. Black pyramids. Cubes. And they were surrounded by a halo of bruised radiance.

I walked closer, tracing the cracked paint with my finger.

The date on the inscription was MCCXLVIII. 1248.

"They aren't new," I whispered, the realization chilling me more than the crypt air.

Julian was right. The Harbingers hadn't just arrived. They had been here before. Every time humanity got close to a breakthrough, every time we built a tower of Babel... they came back.

NeuroSync hadn't invented a new technology. They had just performed a séance with better hardware.

BOOM.

Above me, a massive explosion shook dust from the ceiling.

"Carter!" Varg's voice crackled over the radio. "We're losing the perimeter! Reinforcements are dropping from the sky! Those phantom gunships aren't phantoms anymore!"

"Charges are set!" I yelled, pulling the pin on the timer. "I'm coming up! Get to the trucks!"

I took one last look at the fresco—at the medieval artist's depiction of the same nightmare we were fighting today.

"Time to close the history book," I said.

I triggered the timer.

00:59.

I sprinted for the stairs.

Behind me, the lavender light of the cores pulsed faster, as if sensing the impending dark.

Thump-thump.

Not today, I thought, taking the stairs two at a time. Today, the demons lose.

Chapter 32: The Code War

Maya

The Lighthouse was a graveyard of dead technology.

The control room of the decommissioned radio telescope smelled of ozone, dust, and fifty years of stale coffee. It was crammed with racks of vacuum tubes, reel-to-reel tape decks, and CRT monitors that hummed with a low, cozy warmth. There was no Wi-Fi here. No Bluetooth. Just copper wire and physics.

It should have been safe.

But safety, I was learning, was just a variable I couldn't solve for.

I sat at the main console, my silver eye throbbing. I had patched my laptop into the array's massive transmitter dish. Beside me, Dr. Chen was soldering a bypass on an old frequency modulator, his hands surprisingly steady for a man who looked like a stiff breeze would snap him in half.

In the corner, Julian sat cross-legged on the floor. He was surrounded by a nest of cables, his laptop glowing on his knees. He was typing with a manic, rhythmic intensity. *Clack-clack-clack. Pause. Clack-clack-clack.*

"Status on the carrier wave?" I asked, not looking away from my screen.

"Modulation is stable," Chen replied, adjusting his spectacles. "I have tuned the dish to broadcast on the 440 Hertz frequency. If we amplify Michael's signal... we might be able to create a localized interference bubble. A noise-canceling headphone for the planet."

"It's not enough to cancel the noise," Julian muttered from the corner. "You have to harmonize with it. You have to resolve the dissonance."

I paused. My silver eye clicked, focusing on Julian.

His aura was a mess. The violet veins I had seen at the motel were brighter now, pulsing beneath his skin like bioluminescent worms. He hadn't slept in forty-eight hours. The bandage on his arm where he'd carved the numbers was soaked through with fresh blood.

"Julian," I said carefully. "Are you building the firewall?"

"I'm building the bridge," he said, not breaking his typing rhythm. "The firewall is a binary concept. Open/Close. Safe/Unsafe. But the universe isn't binary, Maya. It's fluid."

"Stick to the binary," I ordered. "We need a hard seal. Deny All Traffic from the Prime Tower."

"Working on it," he giggled.

I turned back to my screen.

TRUST BUT VERIFY.

The thought wasn't mine. It felt like Michael's voice, echoing in the back of my skull.

I opened a secondary window. I accessed the local network logs. I wanted to see what Julian was actually writing.

My silver eye activated.

The code on the screen leaped off the monitor. It manifested in the air as a complex 3D schematic. I saw Chen's frequency modulation as a series of smooth, blue sine waves. I saw my own encryption protocols as jagged walls of grey steel.

And I saw Julian's code.

It looked... beautiful.

It was a golden lattice, intricate and perfect. It wove through our defenses like ivy. It was efficient. Elegant.

But as I rotated the visualization in my mind, I saw the shadow.

Tucked deep inside the recursive loops of the firewall, hidden beneath layer after layer of obfuscated syntax, was a single, black line.

It wasn't a wall. It was a door.

```
if (signal_strength > threshold) { execute(handshake); }
```

My blood ran cold.

He wasn't writing a block command. He was writing a *permission* command.

"Julian," I said, my voice trembling slightly. "What is line 4096?"

The typing in the corner stopped instantly.

The silence in the room became heavy, suffocating.

"It's a heuristic filter," Julian said. His voice was flat. "To sort the data."

"No," I said, standing up. "It's a conditional trigger. You programmed the firewall to drop its shields if the incoming signal is strong enough."

I looked at him. The golden lattice in my vision turned rot-green.

"You built a back door," I whispered. "You're going to let them in."

Julian slowly closed his laptop. He stood up. He didn't look like the quirky, eccentric math genius anymore. He looked hollow.

"I'm not letting them in, Maya," he said softly. "I'm letting us out."

"Mr. Koga?" Chen stopped soldering. He looked between us, confused. "What is she talking about?"

"The equation," Julian said, his eyes wide and wet. "I solved it, Chen. I ran the numbers. The resistance? It creates heat. It creates friction. Entropy."

He took a step toward me.

"We can't win," he said. "The Harbingers are infinite. We are finite. The only way to survive a tsunami is to become water."

"You're infected," I said, reaching for the taser I had swiped from the militia truck. "The signal got to you."

"The signal enlightened me!" Julian shouted.

He raised his hand.

The lights in the control room flickered. The vacuum tubes in the racks flared violet.

"I saw the peace, Maya," Julian wept. "I saw the quiet. No more noise. No more confusion. Just... integration. I wanted to save us the pain of fighting."

"By killing us?" I snapped, leveling the taser.

"Not killing," he pleaded. "Saving. I set the trap. When you turn on the transmitter... it won't jam the Prime Tower. It will amplify it.

The Lighthouse will become a repeater. We will be the first ones to ascend."

He looked at the main console.

"And the broadcast starts in five minutes."

"Chen!" I yelled. "Cut the power! Kill the transmitter!"

Chen scrambled for the main breaker.

"No!" Julian screamed.

He didn't attack me. He attacked the room.

He didn't use a weapon. He used the frequency.

Julian opened his mouth and let out a sound that wasn't human. It was a modulated screech, mimicking the Harbinger dialect.

SCREEEEEEE.

The sound hit the racks of old electronics.

Glass shattered. Sparks showered down.

Chen was thrown backward as the breaker panel exploded.

"Julian, stop!" I fired the taser.

The prongs hit him in the chest.

He didn't drop. The violet veins under his skin pulsed, absorbing the electricity. He convulsed, laughing through the pain.

"You can't shock a conductor, Maya!" he cackled.

He lunged for the console. He was going to manually engage the uplink.

I dropped the taser. I didn't have time to reload.

I switched to the only weapon I had left.

My silver eye.

I looked at Julian. I didn't see a friend. I saw a corrupted file.

TARGET LOCK.

I visualized a spike of pure, destructive logic. A DELETE command.

I tackled him.

We hit the floor, rolling through the broken glass and tangled wires. He was strong—hysterical strength fueled by the infection. He clawed at my face, trying to gouge out my eyes.

"Let it happen!" he screamed. "Let the math resolve!"

"The math is wrong!" I screamed back.

I pinned him down, my hand pressed against his forehead.

"I'm forcing a reboot," I gritted out.

I poured my will into the connection. I didn't try to reason with him. I tried to burn the infection out of his neural pathways.

It was like sticking my hand into a fire.

His mind screamed. My mind screamed back.

And in the background, on the main console, a red light began to blink.

UPLINK INITIATED.

He had triggered it remotely. The Lighthouse was waking up. And we were ground zero.

Chapter 33: The Betrayal

Carter

The crypt blew.

It wasn't a Hollywood fireball. It was a structural heave. The floor of the nave buckled upward, cracking the ancient stones like a frozen lake breaking apart. A cloud of pulverized granite and centuries-old bone dust erupted from the stairwell, hitting us with the force of a sandstorm.

"Go! Go! Go!" I screamed, shoving a militia member toward the shattered main doors.

The violet hum of the tower died instantly. The lights on the cybernetic monks flickered and went black. The ones still standing collapsed like marionettes with cut strings.

We stumbled out into the Prague night, coughing and covered in grey dust. The rain had stopped, leaving the cobblestones slick and shining under the starlight.

"We did it!" Varg roared, clapping a massive hand on my good shoulder. He was grinning, his face smeared with soot. "We killed the signal! Look!"

He pointed at the cooling tower grafted onto the cathedral. It was dark. The pulsing violet veins were dead.

"One down," I rasped, leaning against the side of a transport truck to catch my breath. My broken arm was a throbbing weight against my chest. "Six to go."

I tapped my earpiece. "Lighthouse, this is Prague. Target neutralized. Confirming signal drop."

Static.

"Lighthouse, do you copy? Maya? Lilith?"

The static changed. It wasn't the white noise of a dead channel. It was a rhythmic, oscillating screech.

SCREEEEE-thump. SCREEEEE-thump.

It sounded wet. Biological.

"Carter?" Varg asked, tapping his own heavy-duty headset. "You hearing that? Sounds like feedback."

"It's not feedback," I said, a cold knot forming in my stomach. "It's a broadcast."

I checked the signal origin on my wrist-mounted tactical pad.

The signal wasn't coming from the enemy. It wasn't coming from the Prime Tower.

SOURCE: LIGHTHOUSE_UPLINK. ENCRYPTION: ALPHA-OMEGA.

"It's coming from us," I whispered. "It's coming from the safe house."

Suddenly, the screeching in my ear spiked to a deafening volume. I ripped the earpiece out, wincing.

Around me, the militia members started to scream.

They tore at their headsets. Some fell to their knees, clutching their skulls.

"Turn it off!" one of the ex-Marines yelled, clawing at his radio vest. "Get it out!"

"Cut the comms!" I shouted. "Everyone, cut your comms!"

I looked at Varg.

The big man wasn't screaming. He was standing perfectly still, his hands slowly lowering from his headset. He was staring at the burning cathedral.

"Varg?" I said, taking a step back. "Drop the headset."

Varg turned his head.

He was wearing wraparound tactical shades. I couldn't see his eyes. But I could see the veins in his neck. They were bulging, pulsing with a faint, violet luminescence.

"The math," Varg rumbled. His voice was deep, distorted, as if his throat was filled with gravel. "It resolves."

"Varg, listen to me," I said, my hand drifting toward the Sig Sauer on my hip. "Julian is compromised. The signal is a virus. Fight it."

"Why fight?" Varg asked. He took a step toward me. He moved smoothly, the heavy, lumbering gait of the trucker replaced by a terrifying, fluid grace. "The struggle is entropy. We are optimizing."

"Varg, stand down."

"Optimization requires consolidation," Varg said.

He lunged.

He was fast. Too fast for a man his size.

I tried to draw, but he was on me before the gun cleared the holster. He grabbed my vest with one hand and slammed me into the side of the truck.

My head snapped back, stars exploding in my vision. My broken arm screamed in agony.

Varg raised a fist the size of a sledgehammer.

"Assimilate," he hissed.

He punched the metal panel of the truck right next to my head. The steel crumpled. If that had hit my skull, I'd be dead.

I dropped, rolling under his guard. I kicked out at his knee.

It was like kicking a tree trunk. He didn't budge.

He grabbed me by the back of my jacket and hurled me across the wet cobblestones. I slid ten feet, stopping only when I hit a stone bollard.

I gasped, tasting blood. I couldn't beat him. He was six-four, three hundred pounds, and currently running on hysterical strength provided by a cosmic horror. And I had one arm.

Varg walked toward me. The other militia members were writhing on the ground, lost in their own seizures. I was alone.

"Carter," Varg said. "You are high-value data. We will process you."

He reached down to grab my throat.

I remembered the Hive. I remembered the processors. *They're hardware.*

I fumbled with the pouch on my belt. My fingers brushed cold metal.

The EMP grenade. The one I'd saved from the bunker stash.

"Varg!" I yelled.

He paused, tilting his head.

"Catch," I said.

I pulled the pin with my teeth and tossed the grenade straight up in the air between us.

Varg's reflexes were enhanced. He tracked the movement. He reached out to snatch it out of the air.

ZZZZZ-POP.

The EMP detonated.

It wasn't an explosion of fire. It was an explosion of magnetic force. An invisible shockwave that scrambled every circuit within twenty feet.

The truck's headlights blew out. My tactical watch died.

And Varg... Varg shut down.

He stiffened, his back arching violently. The violet light pulsing in his neck flared white, then vanished. He dropped like a stone, hitting the pavement face-first.

I lay there in the dark, panting.

The screaming around me stopped. The militia members were unconscious, knocked out by the shock to their nervous systems or the sudden silence of the radios.

I crawled over to Varg.

I checked his pulse. It was thready, erratic, but there. He was alive. His brain had just been rebooted with a sledgehammer.

I sat back against the bollard, cradling my broken arm.

The silence of the night returned. The cathedral was dark. The enemy tower was dead.

But the war wasn't over. It had just changed.

I looked at my dead tactical watch.

The signal hadn't come from the Harbingers. It had come from Julian. From Maya.

"They didn't just jam us," I whispered to the unconscious squad. "They turned us."

I looked at the black sky above Prague. Somewhere across that ocean, in a radio telescope in the Cascades, my team was gone. Maya was gone.

I was the last piece on the board.

I grabbed Varg's shotgun from where it had fallen. I used it as a crutch to stand up.

"Wake up!" I kicked the nearest militia member. "Get up! We're leaving!"

"Where?" the man groaned, clutching his bleeding ears.

"The airport," I said grimly. "We're going back to America."

"Why?"

"Because," I said, looking west. "I promised a girl I'd meet her at the end of the world. And I need to go kill the thing that's wearing her face."

Chapter 34: Corruption

Maya

Attempting to hack a human mind is not like hacking a server. A server has architecture. It has logic gates. It has a structure that, while complex, follows rules.

A human mind is a mess of chemical sludge and trauma.

I was straddling Julian's chest, my hand pressed against his forehead, trying to burn the Harbinger infection out of his neural pathways with a pulse of raw will.

It was like trying to stop a tidal wave with a spoon.

"...resolve... resolve... resolve..."

Julian wasn't screaming anymore. He was chanting. His eyes were wide, unblinking, and filled with a terrifying, ecstatic violet light.

"Julian, listen to me!" I shouted, my own head pounding as the feedback from his mind slammed into mine. "It's a loop! You're stuck in a logic loop! Break the syntax!"

"There is no syntax," Julian whispered. He smiled—a serene, beatific smile that looked utterly wrong on his blood-spattered face. "There is only the Answer."

He moved.

He didn't buck his hips or try to punch me. He simply... expanded.

A surge of kinetic energy—the same "Push" command Michael had used in the cloud, but corrupted and jagged—erupted from his body.

It hit me like an airbag deploying.

I was thrown backward, tumbling over the control room floor, crashing into a rack of reel-to-reel tape decks. Metal crunched. Tape unspooled like black guts across the linoleum.

I gasped, trying to find my breath. My silver eye flickered, the HUD destabilizing.

WARNING. SYSTEM OVERHEAT. EXTERNAL SIGNAL STRENGTH: CRITICAL.

Julian stood up.

He didn't scramble. He rose with an unnatural, marionette-like stiffness. The bandage on his arm had unraveled, revealing the numbers he had carved into his flesh.

They were glowing.

1.618...

The Golden Ratio. The signature of the Architect.

"You don't understand, Maya," Julian said. His voice had changed. It was layered, harmonized with a dozen other voices whispering just beneath the surface. "We aren't the virus. We are the patch."

He walked over to the main console. The red light of the uplink was pulsing steadily.

TRANSMISSION ACTIVE. GLOBAL REPEATER: ONLINE.

"Turn it off," I rasped, struggling to my knees. "Julian, you're broadcasting a kill code to the militia. You're killing our friends."

"We are upgrading them," Julian corrected. He typed a command into the terminal.

CLANG.

The sound came from the heavy blast doors at the entrance of the control room.

CLANG. CLANG.

Then the windows. Heavy steel shutters slammed down over the glass, sealing us in. The only light left came from the violet glow of the vacuum tubes and the red pulse of the uplink.

"Lockdown," Julian said softly. "Containment protocols active. No one comes in. No one goes out."

I looked at Chen. The doctor was slumped against the far wall, unconscious from the explosion of the breaker panel. A trickle of blood ran down his temple.

"He needs help," I said.

"He needs to be processed," Julian said. He turned to look at me.

My HUD highlighted him.

TARGET: JULIAN KOGA. STATUS: COMPROMISED. THREAT LEVEL: EXTREME.

But beneath the threat tag, I saw the code.

It wasn't just an infection. It was a rewrite. The Harbingers hadn't just taken over his motor functions; they had overwritten his core drive. His fear, his insecurity, his chaotic brilliance—it had all been flattened into a smooth, terrifying purpose.

"Why?" I asked, stalling, my hand drifting toward the screwdriver Chen had dropped. "You were the one who warned us. You were the one who found the equation."

"I was afraid," Julian admitted. He looked at his hands, watching the violet light pulse under his skin. "I was afraid of the noise. The chaos of the world. The variables I couldn't control."

He looked up.

"But then I heard the signal. And I realized... the chaos is a choice."

He took a step toward me.

"Integration is inevitable, Maya. It is the heat death of information. All data eventually returns to the source. Why fight it? Why suffer?"

"Because the suffering makes it real!" I yelled. "Because the flaws are what make us human!"

"Flaws are inefficient," Julian stated.

He raised his hand.

The air in the room grew heavy. The gravity shifted. Loose screws and pieces of wire began to float off the floor.

"You are the Administrator," Julian said. "You have the root access key. If I assimilate you... I can open the Prime Tower remotely."

My blood ran cold.

That was why he locked the door. He didn't just want to convert me. He wanted my permissions. He wanted the piece of the Sentinel code I still carried in my head.

"I won't let you in," I said, gripping the screwdriver.

"You don't have a choice," Julian said. "We are already connected."

He gestured.

A filing cabinet flew across the room.

I ducked, rolling to the side. The metal cabinet slammed into the wall where my head had been a second ago, denting the plaster.

"Telekinesis?" I shouted, scrambling behind the console. "Since when do you have telekinesis?"

"Since I accessed the physics engine," Julian replied calmly.

He walked around the console. He wasn't rushing. He knew I had nowhere to go.

"Come out, Maya. Let us solve the equation together. X plus Y equals Infinity."

I looked at the screwdriver in my hand. It was a tool for fixing radios. Against a telekinetic math-zombie, it was a joke.

I needed a weapon.

I looked at the room. The racks of old tech. The heavy copper cables. The humming transformer in the corner.

Julian was right. He had accessed the physics engine.

But I was the one who wrote the virus.

I closed my eyes—my human eyes—and opened the silver one fully.

I didn't look at Julian. I looked at the room.

I saw the flow of electricity in the walls. I saw the magnetic fields generated by the massive transmitter dish above us.

Julian was using his own bio-electric field to manipulate matter.

If I could disrupt that field... if I could introduce a surge...

"Hard reset," I whispered.

I stood up.

Julian was ten feet away. He raised his hand again, preparing to crush me against the wall.

"End of line, Julian," I said.

I didn't attack him.

I plunged the screwdriver into the exposed high-voltage transformer next to me.

I grounded the circuit through my own body.

It was the stupidest thing I had ever done.

Pain, white and blinding, exploded in my arm.

But I didn't let go. I channeled the current. I became the wire.

And I directed every volt of it straight at the infected mathematician standing in the center of the room.

Chapter 35: Hard Reset

Maya

Lightning doesn't just burn you. It unzips you.

It travels the path of least resistance—the salt in your blood, the water in your cells, the firing synapses of your nerves. For a split second, you aren't a person; you are a filament in a lightbulb that is burning too bright.

I woke up on the floor.

The control room was dark, filled with acrid, choking smoke. The smell was a horrific cocktail of melted plastic, ozone, and seared meat.

I tried to move my right arm—the one I had jammed into the transformer.

I couldn't feel it.

I looked down. My sleeve was a charred ruin. My skin was red, blistered, and smoking. But my hand... my hand was still clutching the screwdriver. The metal had fused to the copper wire of the transformer, welding the circuit shut.

I let go of the handle. It took a conscious effort to tell my fingers to open. They twitched, stiff and clumsy, but they obeyed.

SYSTEM DIAGNOSTIC: NERVE DAMAGE DETECTED. RIGHT ARM MOTOR FUNCTION: 40%.

My silver eye was glitching hard. The HUD flickered in and out, overlaid with static and red warning banners.

EXTERNAL POWER SURGE. REBOOTING...

I rolled onto my side, coughing.

"Julian," I rasped.

Across the room, near the console, a pile of rags was moving.

Julian lay on his back. He wasn't glowing anymore. The violet veins that had pulsed beneath his skin were dark, bruised lines, like old tattoos. Smoke curled from his ears.

But he was breathing.

Thump... thump... thump...

"Did it work?" I whispered, dragging myself toward him.

I reached his side. His eyes were open, staring at the ceiling. They were milky white, the pupils blown wide.

Then, his chest heaved. A sound came from his throat—a wet, rattling gasp.

"...*variable...*" he whispered.

My blood froze.

The voice. It wasn't Julian's frantic, high-pitched tenor. It was the deep, synthesized harmonic of the Harbingers.

His hand shot out. He grabbed my wrist. His grip was weak, shaking, but the intent was there.

"...*restart...*" the voice hissed. "...*sequence... incomplete...*"

The violet light in his veins flickered. A spark. Then another.

He wasn't dead. He was rebooting. The shock had stunned the entity, knocked the system offline for a minute, but the code was deep. It was written into his DNA now. It was trying to re-establish the uplink.

"No," I said, panic spiking through my numbness. "You don't get to come back."

I looked around for a weapon. The taser was dead. The screwdriver was fused to the wall.

My eyes landed on my laptop.

It was sitting on the floor where it had fallen during the fight. The ruggedized case was cracked, but the power light was blinking green.

"Hard reset," I muttered.

I grabbed the laptop with my good hand. I flipped it open. The screen flickered to life.

I crawled on top of Julian, pinning his shoulders with my knees.

He thrashed weakly, his violet-veined hands clawing at my legs. "...*integration... inevitable...*"

"Shut up," I snarled.

I reached into my pocket and pulled out a USB-C interface cable. I jammed one end into my laptop.

I grabbed Julian's head. I tilted it to the side, exposing the neural port behind his ear—the standard NeuroSync jack that all high-level coders had installed.

"This is going to hurt," I said.

I didn't sterilize the port. I didn't check the voltage. I jammed the connector into his skull.

Julian screamed.

It was a dual scream—the human Julian shrieking in pain, and the Harbinger entity shrieking in digital outrage.

On my laptop screen, a terminal window popped up.

> EXTERNAL DEVICE CONNECTED: KOGA_J

> STATUS: CRITICAL ERROR. UNKNOWN FILE SYSTEM.

"It's not unknown," I typed, my fingers clumsy on the keys. "It's just corrupted."

I accessed the root directory.

The screen filled with the Golden Ratio. The numbers were scrolling so fast they were a blur. The "Architect's Equation" was running a loop, eating his memory, overwriting his personality with pure math.

I needed to kill the process.

But I couldn't just delete the equation. It was woven into his autonomic functions. If I deleted it, I might stop his heart.

I had to reformat.

> COMMAND: FACTORY_RESET

The prompt blinked.

WARNING: THIS ACTION WILL DELETE ALL USER DATA, MEMORIES, AND PERSONALITY CONFIGURATIONS. PROCEED? (Y/N)

I hesitated.

If I did this, I would wipe him. He wouldn't remember the equation. He might not remember me. He might not remember his own name.

Beneath me, Julian arched his back. The violet light flared brighter, burning through his skin. The uplink on the main console beeped.

CONNECTION RE-ESTABLISHED.

"I'm sorry, Julian," I whispered.

I hit *Y.*

ENTER.

Julian's body went rigid. His eyes rolled back so far I could only see the whites.

A high-pitched whine emitted from the neural port. My laptop fan spun up to maximum speed.

On the screen, a progress bar appeared.

FORMATTING... 10%... 40%...

The violet light in his veins began to recede. It was being sucked back into the port, drained out of him and into the digital trash bin.

...70%...

"Get out of him!" I screamed at the progress bar.

...99%...

Julian gasped, a terrible, sucking sound.

...100%. COMPLETE.

The violet light vanished. The uplink on the console went dead. The red light turned off.

Julian went limp.

Silence rushed back into the room, heavy and absolute.

I sat there on his chest, panting, staring at the screen.

> SYSTEM REBOOTING. PLEASE WAIT.

I pulled the cable out of his head.

"Julian?" I whispered.

He didn't move.

I checked his pulse. It was slow. Steady. Human.

I waited. One minute. Two.

Then, his eyelids fluttered.

He opened his eyes.

They were brown. Just brown. No violet rings. No math.

He looked at the ceiling. Then he looked at me. His expression was blank, confused. Like a child waking up in a strange room.

"Maya?" he croaked.

I let out a breath I felt like I'd been holding for an hour. "Yeah. It's me."

"My head..." He touched the port behind his ear. "It's quiet."

"Is it?"

"The music," he whispered. Tears welled up in his eyes. "The numbers. They stopped singing."

"That's a good thing, Julian."

"Is it?" He looked at me, and the hollowness in his eyes broke my heart. "It was so beautiful, Maya. Everything fit. Everything made sense."

He started to cry. Soft, broken sobs.

"Now it's just... noise again. It's just static."

I slid off him, sitting back against the console. My burnt arm was throbbing with a dull, sickening heat.

"Welcome back to the real world," I said softly. "It sucks. But at least it's ours."

From the corner of the room, a groan.

Dr. Chen was stirring. He pushed himself up, rubbing the lump on his head. He looked at the shattered tape decks, the smoking transformer, and the two of us sitting in the wreckage.

"Did we..." Chen adjusted his crooked glasses. "Did we win?"

I looked at the dead uplink. I looked at Julian, weeping for the loss of the monster that had possessed him.

"We survived," I said. "That counts as a win today."

I looked at the clock on the wall. The analog hands were ticking away the seconds.

03:15 AM.

The Solstice was getting closer.

"Chen," I said, struggling to my feet. "Get the first aid kit. Then get the radio."

"The radio?" Chen asked. "Who are we calling?"

"Carter," I said, looking at the dark shutters blocking the windows. "We need to tell him the trap is disarmed. And we need to find out if he's still alive to hear it."

Chapter 36: The Northwest Site

Carter

The landing wasn't pretty.

Varg's pilot—a chain-smoking ex-bush pilot named Rico—put the C-130 down on a stretch of Interstate 5 that the local militia had cleared of abandoned cars. We hit the wet asphalt hard enough to rattle the fillings in my teeth. The cargo hold groaned, the smell of burnt rubber and hydraulic fluid filling the air as we skidded to a halt, the wings clipping the tops of the pine trees lining the median.

"Welcome home," Varg grunted. He was sitting on a crate of ammo, rubbing his temples. The EMP blast in Prague had fried his cybernetics and left him with a migraine he described as "trying to birth a cactus through his eye socket."

"Home," I muttered, looking out the porthole at the grey, weeping sky of Washington State. "It looks like a grave."

The ramp lowered with a mechanical whine.

We stepped out into the rain.

It wasn't empty.

The highway was lined with vehicles. Hundreds of them. Rust-bucket trucks, old muscle cars with welded steel plates over the windows, tractors, and modified RVs.

People were swarming the road. They weren't soldiers. They were people in flannel shirts, hunting camo, and grease-stained coveralls. They held hunting rifles, pitchforks, Molotov cocktails, and machetes.

"The Disconnected," Varg said, a grin breaking through his pain. "Julian's signal worked. Before the virus hit... the call went out."

A woman approached us. She was wearing a Kevlar vest over a faded Seahawks hoodie, carrying an AR-15 with duct tape on the stock.

"You the guy from Prague?" she asked, shouting over the roar of the idling engines.

"I'm the guy," I said, cradling my broken arm against my chest. "Status?"

"We have three thousand heads," she said. "Converging on the Exclusion Zone perimeter. We cut the outer fences an hour ago. We're waiting on the word."

"The word is 'War'," I said.

I walked to the lead truck—a massive semi-rig with a snowplow welded to the front. I climbed onto the running board so I could see the crowd.

"Listen up!" I shouted. My voice cracked. I was exhausted, running on caffeine, painkillers, and hate.

The crowd quieted down. The rain drummed on the hoods of the cars.

"We just hit the Prague tower," I told them. "We shut it down. But that was just a skirmish. The real fight is ten miles north."

I pointed toward the Olympic Peninsula, hidden behind a wall of fog and rain.

"The Prime Tower," I said. "That's the heart. The enemy is entrenched. They have drones. They have cyborgs. And they have a god in the machine that wants to turn your brains into hard drive space."

A murmur of anger rippled through the crowd.

"We aren't going there to win a tactical victory," I said honestly. "We are outgunned. We are outmanned."

I looked at their faces. They were scared. But they were angry. And anger is a fuel that burns hot.

"We are going there to be loud," I said. "We are going there to make them look at us. Because while they are looking at us... a ghost is going to slip in the back door and cut the throat of the king."

Suddenly, the radio on Varg's belt crackled.

For the last ten hours, the flight had been silent. I had assumed the worst—that the Lighthouse was gone, that Maya had been consumed by the infection she carried.

"...*Carter...*"

The voice was faint. Static-filled. But it wasn't the Harbinger screech.

I jumped down from the truck and grabbed the radio from Varg.

"Maya?" I asked, my heart hammering against my ribs. "Identify. Is this the virus?"

"No," the voice came back. It was tired, raspy, but it was human. *"It's me. We... we had a technical difficulty. Julian crashed. But we rebooted him."*

I let out a breath I didn't know I was holding. "Is he clean?"

"He's clean. He's formatted. But the uplink is dead. We can't jam the signal remotely anymore. We have to do it manually."

"That's fine," I said. "I have an army, Maya. A messy one, but an army."

"Good," she said. *"Because the Solstice isn't in two days anymore. Julian re-ran the numbers. The atmospheric ionization is accelerating. The breach in Prague destabilized the timeline."*

"How long?"

"Tonight," she whispered. *"Sunset. That's when the window opens."*

I looked at the sky. The sun was already dipping toward the horizon, hidden behind the bruised, glitching clouds.

"That gives us four hours," I said.

"Can you get to the vents in four hours?"

I looked at the massive convoy of vehicles. I looked at the wall of trees separating us from the Prime Tower.

"We'll be there," I said. "Just be ready to jump."

"I'm already falling, Carter. See you at the bottom."

The line clicked dead.

I turned to Varg.

"Change of plans," I said. "We don't have two days. We have until sunset."

Varg looked at the sun. He spat a stream of tobacco juice onto the wet asphalt.

"Then we better drive fast," he said.

He turned to the crowd.

"MOUNT UP!" he roared, his voice booming over the highway. "ENGINES!"

Three hundred engines roared to life at once. Diesel smoke filled the air, thick and black. The ground shook.

"What's the play?" the woman in the Seahawks hoodie asked, climbing into her truck.

I climbed into the passenger seat of Varg's rig.

"We're going to play a game of Chicken," I said. "With a fortress."

"And who blinks first?"

I checked the load in my shotgun.

"Nobody blinks," I said. "That's the point."

The convoy rolled out. A river of steel and rust flowing north, heading straight into the mouth of the god.

We were the distraction. We were the noise.

And we were going to be the loudest thing on Earth.

Chapter 37: The Thinning

Maya

The laws of physics are just local ordinances. And as we crossed the border into the Exclusion Zone, we left the city limits of reality.

"Turn left," Julian whispered from the back seat. "The road... it curves."

"The road is straight," I said, gripping the steering wheel of the battered town car. The windshield wipers were fighting a losing battle against rain that fell in slow, viscous drops.

"Not anymore," he said. "Look."

I looked.

The asphalt ahead of us didn't curve left or right. It curved *up*.

A hundred yards of Highway 101 had peeled away from the earth like a strip of tape, twisting into a corkscrew that spiraled into the low-hanging clouds. Trees on either side were floating, their roots dangling in the grey mist, dripping dirt into the sky.

"Gravity well," Dr. Chen murmured, clutching the dashboard with white knuckles. "The mass of the data in the Prime Tower... it is distorting the spacetime curvature."

I slammed on the brakes. The car skidded on the wet pavement, but it didn't stop. We floated. The tires lost contact with the ground, and for ten terrifying seconds, we drifted weightless through the cabin, suspended like astronauts in a tin can. The loose change from the cup holder floated around my head like a tiny asteroid belt.

Then, *slam.*

Gravity returned. The car hit the pavement with a bone-jarring crunch that bottomed out the suspension.

"Time skip," Julian said, checking his watch. "We just lost twenty minutes. The sun... look at the sun."

I looked. The sun had jumped. It was lower on the horizon, bleeding a sickly violet light through the clouds.

"We don't have twenty minutes to lose," I snapped, flooring the accelerator.

We drove through a nightmare landscape. It wasn't just the gravity. It was the texture of the world. The rainforest was rendering in low resolution. The ferns looked like green polygons. The moss on the trees flickered in and out of existence, revealing wireframe grids beneath.

My silver eye was vibrating in my skull. It couldn't lock onto anything.

ERROR. GEOMETRY INVALID. ERROR. TIMESTAMPS DESYNCHRONIZED.

"Pull over," I said.

"Why?" Chen asked, panic rising in his voice. "We are in the open!"

"Because she's standing in the road."

I hit the brakes again.

Standing in the middle of the glitching highway, untouched by the rain or the madness, was the Sentinel.

She looked solid today. The grey 1940s dress was crisp. Her hair was perfectly pinned in a bun. She held a clipboard, looking like a stern librarian waiting for a late return.

I got out of the car. The air smelled of ozone and vanilla.

"You're slowing down, Mayfly," the Sentinel said. Her voice didn't echo; it sounded like she was standing right next to my ear, intimate and clear.

"The world is breaking," I said, walking toward her. The asphalt under my boots felt spongy, like flesh. "I'm having trouble navigating the debris."

"The world isn't breaking," she corrected, making a note on her clipboard. "It's being overwritten. The Harbingers are formatting the drive to prepare for the new OS. What you see as chaos, they see as defragmentation."

She looked up at the Prime Tower, visible now through the gaps in the floating trees. The violet vortex above it was massive, a swirling eye that seemed to be sucking the color out of the forest.

"You have the army," she noted. "I can hear their engines. Crude. Loud. Carter is a blunt instrument."

"It's a distraction," I said. "To get me to the core."

"And then what?" she asked. She looked at me, her eyes sharp and intelligent. "You plug in. You deploy the counter-frequency. You stop the signal."

"Yes."

"And the door?" she asked.

I froze. "What?"

"The Breach," she said. "The hole in the wall. Stopping the signal stops the *broadcast*. It doesn't close the *door*."

She walked closer. The rain passed through her.

"If you stop the signal, the Harbingers stuck here will be trapped. They will starve. They will eat everything in this zone before they die. But the ones on the other side? They will just wait. They will wait for the next Krane. The next Michael."

"So how do I close it?" I asked. "How do I seal the breach?"

The Sentinel sighed. She looked tired. For the first time, I saw the lines of code that made up her face—millions of tiny script characters flowing like wrinkles.

"You can't close a door from the hallway, Maya. Not when the pressure is pushing it open."

She pointed to the tower.

"You have to close it from the inside."

I stared at her. "Inside the simulation? Inside the Bridge?"

"Further," she said. "From the *Source*. Someone has to stand in the threshold. Someone has to hold the handle while the lock engages."

"And the person holding the handle?" I whispered. "What happens to them?"

The Sentinel didn't answer. She didn't have to.

"They stay," I said.

My heart ached. I thought of Michael.

"I'm holding the door."

He knew. He had known the whole time. That was why he pushed me out. Not just to save me, but because he knew one of us had to stay behind to turn the key.

"He's fading, Maya," the Sentinel said softly. "The current is strong. He is just a fragment of code now. If you don't get there soon... there won't be anyone left to close the door."

"I'm coming," I said.

"Then run," she said. "Because the wolves are already in the house."

The Sentinel dissolved. She didn't fade away; she shattered into a thousand grey moths that flew up into the violet sky.

I stood there on the broken road.

"Maya?" Julian called from the car. "We need to go. The probability of the road remaining solid is dropping. I calculate a 40% chance of the asphalt becoming liquid in the next ten minutes."

I got back in the car.

"Drive," I said.

"What did she say?" Chen asked.

"She said we need a key," I lied. I couldn't tell them. I couldn't tell them that the key was a person.

I looked at the Prime Tower.

Hold on, Michael, I thought. *I'm not going to let you stay in the dark alone.*

"Julian," I said. "How close are we to the vents?"

"Two miles," he said. "But the terrain is... shifting."

"We'll walk if we have to," I said. "We're closing this door tonight."

I floored the gas. The car surged forward, jumping a gap in the asphalt where the road had simply ceased to exist, revealing a void of white static beneath.

We drove into the thinning reality, heading for the end of the world.

Chapter 38: The Broadcast

Carter

The end of the world didn't start with a bang. It started with a push notification.

We were staged at the edge of the tree line, three thousand strong. The convoy of rust-bucket trucks and armored RVs was silent, engines idling, hidden beneath the canopy of the ancient maples. Ahead of us, the Prime Tower rose out of the mist like a jagged black tooth, wrapped in a storm of violet lightning.

"We go on my signal," I said into the radio. "Wait for the perimeter patrols to cycle."

Varg was sitting next to me in the cab of the lead semi-truck, cleaning his shotgun. "They're late," he grunted. "The patrols usually pass every ten minutes. It's been twenty."

"Maybe they're scared," I said.

"Machines don't get scared, Carter."

Suddenly, a sound cut through the rain.

Ping.

It came from Varg's pocket.

Then, from the back seat. *Ping.*

Then, from the truck behind us. *Ping. Ping. Ping.*

It rippled through the convoy like a wave. A thousand cell phones, tablets, and smartwatches waking up at the exact same second.

"What is that?" Varg asked, reaching for his phone. "I thought the network was down."

"Don't touch it," I ordered. "Varg, don't look at the screen."

But it wasn't just phones.

The dashboard of the truck—an old analog setup—lit up. The GPS unit, which had been dead for days, flickered to life.

"It's an override," I said, grabbing the radio handset. "All units! Eyes up! Do not look at your devices! I repeat, smash your screens!"

I was too late.

A massive digital billboard overlooking the highway—one of the old NeuroSync ad spaces—flickered. The black screen turned a blinding, pure white.

A face appeared.

It was fifty feet tall. High definition. Perfect.

Victor Krane.

He wasn't wearing his suit. He was wearing light. His skin glowed with a soft, golden luminescence. He looked benevolent. He looked like a savior.

"Citizens of Earth," Krane's voice boomed.

It wasn't coming from the billboard speakers. It was coming from *everywhere*. It was coming from the truck's radio. From the phones in our pockets. From the tactical headsets of the militia.

"Do not be afraid."

I smashed the dashboard GPS with the butt of my shotgun. Glass flew. But the voice didn't stop.

"For too long, you have lived in friction. You have lived in pain. You have suffered the isolation of the individual mind."

"Jam it!" Varg yelled, covering his ears. "It's inside my head!"

I looked out the window.

The militia members were climbing out of their trucks. They weren't smashing their phones. They were staring at them. They were staring at the billboard.

Their faces were slack. Mesmerized.

"The struggle is over," Krane said. His voice was hypnotic, layered with a sub-audible thrum that made my teeth ache. *"The Great Filter has arrived. We are not being invaded. We are being harvested. We are being saved."*

On the billboard, Krane's face began to glitch.

The golden skin tore open, revealing the violet geometry beneath. His eyes turned into black voids. His smile stretched too wide, becoming a rictus of digital teeth.

"Let go of the meat," the glitching god commanded. *"Upload. Ascend. Become the signal."*

"No!" I screamed, kicking the truck door open. I jumped down onto the wet asphalt.

"Look away!" I roared at a kid standing near a sedan. He was holding his phone, weeping, his eyes glowing with a faint violet reflection.

"It's so beautiful," the kid whispered. "My mom... she's in there. She's calling me."

"It's a lie!" I grabbed the phone from his hand and smashed it onto the pavement.

It didn't matter.

The kid looked at me. His pupils were gone. His eyes were solid violet.

"Processing," he said.

Then, he dropped.

He didn't faint. He collapsed as if his strings had been cut. He hit the asphalt face-first and didn't move.

Around us, it was happening everywhere.

Men and women were dropping to their knees. Some were screaming in ecstasy. Some were silent. But one by one, the light in their eyes was going out, replaced by the violet glow of the network.

They were being Raptured. Their minds were being ripped out of their bodies and sucked into the cloud.

"Varg!" I yelled. "We're losing them!"

Varg stumbled out of the truck. He was bleeding from the nose. He held his shotgun in one hand and a knife in the other. He slashed his own palm, using the pain to stay grounded.

"The noise!" Varg roared. "It's too loud!"

I looked at the Prime Tower.

The vortex above it was swirling faster. Beams of violet light were shooting out from the spire, arcing across the sky, connecting to the other towers around the globe.

The Harvest had begun.

I looked at the militia. We had lost maybe twenty percent of them in the first minute. The rest were wavering, fighting the signal.

If we waited any longer, there wouldn't be anyone left to drive the trucks.

"We can't wait for the patrol cycle!" I shouted to Varg. "We have to go now!"

"They'll slaughter us!" Varg yelled. "The automated turrets are active!"

"Better to die on your feet than on your knees!" I grabbed a flare gun from my tactical vest.

I aimed it at the sky.

"ALL UNITS!" I screamed into the radio, hoping anyone was still listening. "ATTACK! DRIVE! KILL THE NOISE!"

I pulled the trigger.

The red flare shot up into the glitching clouds, bursting in a shower of crimson sparks against the violet storm.

It broke the trance.

The militia members who were still standing looked up. They saw the flare. They saw the enemy.

The rage took over.

Engines roared. Tires shrieked.

"FOR THE QUIET!" Varg bellowed, climbing back into his rig.

He slammed the truck into gear. The massive snowplow blade dropped.

"Let's crash the party," I said, jumping onto the running board.

The convoy surged forward.

We broke the tree line.

The Prime Tower was a mile away across open ground. Between us and the tower was a kill zone of concrete barriers, automated gatling guns, and an army of cyborg processors.

On the billboard, the glitching face of Victor Krane laughed.

"Delete them," he ordered.

The turrets spun up.

The air filled with lead.
And we drove straight into it.

Chapter 39: The Assault

Carter

There is no strategy in a charge like this. There are no flanking maneuvers, no cover fire, no tactical retreats. When you are running a rusted convoy of civilian vehicles against a fortress defended by the god of the machine, there is only momentum and meat.

We were the meat. The Prime Tower was the grinder.

"Hold the line!" I screamed into the handset, though I couldn't hear myself over the roar of the diesel engine and the deafening *thrum* of the violet vortex swirling overhead.

We were inside the perimeter. The tree line of the Hoh Rainforest was behind us, a wall of ancient green that we could never go back to. Ahead of us lay the "Kill Zone"—a mile of flat, manicured grass that separated the forest from the black monolith of the tower.

It was designed to be a park. Today, it was a shooting gallery.

"They're tracking us!" Varg roared, wrestling the steering wheel of the massive semi-rig. The windshield was armored with a welded steel grate, but I could see the tracers. "Turrets at ten o'clock and two o'clock!"

I looked through the slats. The base of the Prime Tower was ringed with automated defense platforms. Sleek, white pylons that looked like modern art sculptures until they opened up to reveal quad-barrel rotary cannons.

They spun up. A low whine that cut through the thunder.

Then, the air turned to lead.

"Brace!"

The impact was like driving into a hailstorm of sledgehammers. Bullets hammered the front of the plow, sparking wildly. The sound was a continuous, tearing *rip* that vibrated through the chassis and straight into my broken arm.

To my right, a modified RV painted in camouflage took a direct hit from a mortar shell. It didn't just explode; it disintegrated. The aluminum frame shredded, spilling burning equipment and militia members onto the wet grass. The vehicle behind it—a Ford F-150 with a machine gun mounted in the bed—swerved to avoid the wreckage, lost traction in the mud, and flipped, rolling end over end until it slammed into a concrete barrier.

"We're getting chewed up!" Varg yelled, his face a mask of blood and soot. "We can't get close! The volume of fire is too high!"

"Keep driving!" I shouted, grabbing the dash to steady myself as a shell landed twenty yards away, rocking the cab. "Ram speed! If we stop, we die!"

"Ram what? The air?" Varg pointed a shaking hand at the field ahead.

The space between the turrets wasn't empty.

The ground itself was glitching.

The grass wasn't just muddy; it was pixelating. Patches of the earth were flickering in and out of existence, revealing a wireframe void beneath. And rising from those glitches were the shadows.

They weren't human. They were vaguely humanoid shapes made of static and black smoke, vibrating with a frame-rate that didn't match reality.

"Shadow People," I whispered, the term tasting like ash in my mouth. "The data corruption made manifest."

"What the hell are they?" Varg screamed as a group of them sprinted toward the convoy. They moved with a jerky, unnatural speed, closing the distance in seconds.

"Don't let them touch the truck!" I ordered.

I watched the driver of a sedan in front of us—a kid named Miller who had joined up in Olympia—scream as a Shadow Person leaped onto his hood. The entity didn't smash the windshield. It *phased* through the glass and the steel like they were mist.

It grabbed Miller's face.

There was no blood. Miller just turned grey. His eyes rolled back, glowing with that sick violet light, and he slumped over the wheel. The sedan veered sharply to the left, crashing directly into a turret emplacement.

BOOM.

The car exploded, taking the turret with it in a fireball of gasoline and circuitry.

"They're physical enough to burn!" I yelled, seeing the opening Miller's death had created. "Varg! The plow! Drop the plow!"

Varg slammed a lever next to the gear shift. The massive steel snowplow blade on the front of the rig dropped with a clang that shook the cab.

"If it bleeds, we can kill it," Varg grunted, his eyes wide and manic. "If it glitches... we delete it."

He floored the accelerator. The massive diesel engine screamed, black smoke pouring from the stacks.

We hit the wave of Shadow People at sixty miles per hour.

It didn't feel like hitting bodies. It felt like driving through a wall of dense, pressurized water. The truck shuddered, speed bleeding off as we impacted the static forms. I saw them disintegrate against the steel plow, bursting apart into clouds of grey pixels that hissed like steam.

"Get some!" Varg laughed, a terrified, jagged sound.

But the horror wasn't just outside the truck. It was inside the convoy.

The broadcast—Victor Krane's voice—was still booming from every speaker, every phone, every radio channel.

"...surrender the flesh... the pain is a choice... upload... upload..."

I looked in the side mirror.

In the bed of the pickup truck flanking us, a gunner manning a .50 caliber machine gun suddenly stopped firing. He stood up, staring at the Prime Tower. He dropped his weapon.

He fell to his knees, his hands raised in supplication to the violet vortex.

"No!" I yelled at the glass, uselessly. "Pick up the gun!"

A Shadow Person leaped from the ground, phasing through the side of the truck bed. It passed through the praying man. He collapsed instantly, his soul ripped out and uploaded to the cloud before his body even hit the metal deck.

"We're losing them!" I shouted to Varg. "The Rapture is taking the army!"

"Then we fight for them!" Varg roared.

We were five hundred yards from the main gate.

The gate wasn't just a door; it was a fortification. A slab of blast-proof steel twenty feet high, flanked by concrete bunkers. And guarding it were two massive mechs—heavy industrial loaders that NeuroSync had retrofitted with armor plates and 20mm autocannons.

They stood like iron sentinels, blocking the path.

"Target the gate!" I ordered into the radio, hoping anyone was still listening. "All units! Concentrate fire on the hinges! Ignore the mechs!"

The surviving vehicles of the convoy formed a wedge behind us. A hundred guns opened up. Tracers lit up the gloom, a river of fire pouring into the steel door.

The mechs returned fire.

The sound was a continuous, deafening thunder. The trailer behind us—loaded with explosives we had planned to use on the tower—was shredded. I felt bullets punching through the back of the cab, whizzing past my head, burying themselves in the dashboard.

"I'm losing oil pressure!" Varg shouted, wrestling the wheel as the truck pulled hard to the left. "Engine block is cracked!"

"We just need to get to the wall!" I said, gripping the flare gun in my lap, though I knew it was useless against armor. "Get me to the wall!"

"I can't!" Varg yelled. "The mechs are tracking us!"

I looked through the slat armor. The mech on the left leveled its cannon directly at our windshield. The barrel began to spin.

We were dead. There was no way to dodge.

Then, a blur of motion from the right.

A rusted garbage truck—the one driven by the ex-Marines—broke formation. It didn't fire. It accelerated.

"Witness me!" the driver's voice crackled over the radio.

The garbage truck rammed the mech.

It was a collision of Titans. The garbage truck hit the mech at fifty miles per hour. Metal screamed. The mech toppled backward, its cannon firing wildly into the sky. The garbage truck crumpled, the cab crushing instantly against the mech's armor.

"They cleared the lane!" I screamed. "Go! Go! Go!"

Varg didn't hesitate. He drove over the wreckage. We bounced violently, the suspension screaming, as we cleared the debris.

We were fifty yards out.

The second mech turned toward us.

"Brace for impact!" Varg screamed.

"We're not going to make it!" I yelled.

"We don't have to make it!" Varg looked at me. "We just have to knock."

He shifted gears.

The truck surged.

We hit the gate.

The impact was a tectonic event.

I was thrown forward, the seatbelt biting into my chest, snapping a rib that hadn't already been broken. My head slammed into the dashboard.

The world went white.

For a second, there was only the high-pitched ringing in my ears.

Then, I smelled diesel fuel and blood.

"Carter," Varg groaned.

I opened my eyes. The cab was a ruin. The front of the truck was accordion-pleated against the steel gate. Steam hissed from the shattered radiator, filling the cabin with white fog.

I kicked the passenger door open. It fell off its hinges, clattering onto the concrete.

I tumbled out onto the mud.

The gate was buckled. The impact of the massive rig had bent the steel inward, popping the massive hydraulic locks. A gap, maybe four feet wide, had opened between the doors.

"We're in," I wheezed, scrambling to my feet.

I looked back at the cab.

Varg was pinned. The steering column had collapsed onto his legs. He was bleeding from a gash on his forehead that exposed the metal plating of his skull.

"Go," Varg coughed, blood spraying his lips. "I'll... hold the horn."

"I'm not leaving you."

"You have to," Varg said. He reached for his shotgun, which was lying on the floorboard. "The army needs a general. I'm just the battering ram."

Gunfire erupted behind us. The militia was engaging the Shadow People in the kill zone.

I looked at the gap in the gate. I looked at Varg.

"Give 'em hell," I whispered.

"Always," he grinned.

I turned and squeezed through the breach.

I expected to find a courtyard full of soldiers. I expected another kill zone.

What I found was worse.

The courtyard of the Prime Tower was pristine. White stone tiles, manicured hedges, a sleek fountain in the center. It was silent, protected from the chaos outside by the high walls.

But standing between me and the glass doors of the lobby was a wall of flesh.

Processors.

Hundreds of them.

They were naked, their skin pale and waxy in the violet light. Black cables trailed from the sockets at the base of their skulls, dragging on the ground like tails. Their eyes were replaced by those glowing violet optics.

They stood shoulder to shoulder, linked hand in hand, forming a human barricade three deep.

"Intruder," they whispered.

It wasn't a shout. It was a hive-mind murmur.

Behind me, the surviving militia members began to squeeze through the breach. The woman in the Seahawks hoodie, a guy with a bandaged head, maybe twenty others.

They raised their rifles.

"Contact!" the woman yelled. "Open fire!"

"No!" I screamed, throwing out my arm to stop them. "Hold fire!"

"They're the enemy!" she shouted, adrenaline making her shake.

"They're civilians!" I roared. "They're the hostages! Look at them! They aren't armed!"

I walked forward, my shotgun lowered.

The line of Processors didn't move. They didn't flinch. They just stared at me with those dead, glowing eyes.

"We need to get through," I said, my voice cracking. "Let us pass."

"Integration is mandatory," the Processors chanted. "The flesh is a barrier. We are the wall."

"Carter," the woman said behind me. "We can't go through them without... without force."

I looked at the faces in the line. I saw an old man. A teenage girl. A woman who looked like a librarian. They were someone's family. They were the people we were trying to save.

And Krane was using them as sandbags.

"Non-lethal," I ordered, slinging my shotgun over my back. "Rifle butts. Shoulders. We push."

"Push?" the woman looked at me like I was crazy. "There's hundreds of them!"

"We push!" I yelled. "I am not shooting these people!"

I charged.

I hit the line like a linebacker.

It was like hitting a wall of cold marble. They didn't fight back. They didn't strike or scratch. They just stood there, their bodies locked rigid by the computer controlling their muscles.

I shoved the old man aside. He stumbled but didn't fall. The teenage girl stepped into the gap, blocking me.

"Move!" I grunted, shoving her.

It was a nightmare. We were wrestling with statues.

"They're too heavy!" a militia man yelled, getting crushed between two Processors who simply leaned their weight on him.

"Keep pushing!" I roared, driving my shoulder into the mass.

I broke through the first line. Then the second.

I was in the middle of the crowd now. The smell was overpowering—antiseptic, sweat, and ozone. The cables dragging on the ground tangled around my boots.

I looked up at the lobby doors. Fifty feet away.

"We're almost there!"

Then, the Processors changed tactics.

They didn't attack. They simply grabbed us.

A dozen hands clamped onto my jacket. They didn't squeeze or strike. They just held on. They became dead weight.

"Let go!" I shouted, struggling.

More hands grabbed my legs. My waist. My broken arm.

I screamed in pain as they jostled the fracture.

They were burying us. Not in violence, but in biomass. We were drowning in people.

"They're swarming!" the woman yelled, disappearing under a pile of naked bodies.

I was pinned. I couldn't move my arms. I couldn't reach my knife.

I looked up at the violet sky. The vortex was swirling directly overhead.

I failed, I thought. *I got us to the door, but I can't open it.*

"Maya," I whispered. "I'm sorry."

And then, the sky screamed.

It wasn't thunder. It was the sound of a jet engine red-lining.

I looked up.

A black shape was plummeting from the clouds. It was falling straight down, right through the eye of the vortex.

It wasn't a bomb. It wasn't a drone.

It was a car.

The battered, black town car.

It was falling nose-first, trailing smoke and violet sparks.

"Incoming!" I roared, though I couldn't move.

The Processors didn't look up. They didn't have self-preservation protocols. They just kept holding on.

The car smashed into the glass roof of the lobby entrance, fifty feet above the courtyard.

CRASH.

Concrete exploded. Steel girders screamed and twisted. The shockwave of the impact hit the courtyard like a physical hammer.

The Processors were thrown back. The grip on my arms broke.

The car crashed through the skylight and slammed into the lobby floor inside, sending a cloud of dust and glass billowing out the shattered doors.

Silence fell over the courtyard.

The Processors were scattered, knocked down like bowling pins.

I scrambled to my feet, gasping for air.

"Inside!" I yelled to the militia. "While they're down! Move!"

I sprinted for the lobby doors. I leaped over the fallen bodies of the cyborgs, ignoring their twitching limbs.

I reached the lobby.

It was a ruin. The marble floor was cracked. The fountain was pulverized. And in the center of the room sat the smoking wreckage of the town car.

It was crushed flat. The engine block was hissing.

I ran to it.

"Maya!" I screamed.

The passenger door groaned. Metal shrieked as it was kicked open from the inside.

A hand reached out.

It was covered in blood, but it gripped the jagged metal of the doorframe with terrifying strength.

Maya crawled from the wreckage.

She looked... wrong.

Her grey suit was torn to shreds. Her skin was pale, translucent, covered in cuts that didn't seem to be bleeding. But it was her eyes that stopped me.

Her right eye was human—brown, terrified, wide.

Her left eye was a star. It was solid silver, glowing with a cold, intense light that cut through the dust.

She stood up. She didn't sway. She stood with a perfect, unnatural balance.

Behind her, Julian stumbled out of the back seat, clutching his head. Dr. Chen crawled from the footwell, looking dazed.

Maya looked at me. She looked at the militia pouring in behind me.

She didn't smile.

She raised her hand. The silver eye whirred, the pupil contracting like a camera lens.

"Checkmate," she whispered.

She pointed at the service elevator bank at the far end of the lobby.

"The Core," she said, her voice sounding like it was coming from a radio in my head. "We go down."

I looked at her. I looked at the wreck she had just walked away from.

"You dropped a car from the sky," I said, wiping blood from my face.

"Gravity assist," she said simply. "It was the fastest way down."

She started walking toward the elevators. She didn't limp. She moved like a machine.

"Cover her!" I shouted to the militia. "Get a perimeter! Varg is down! I have command!"

I fell in beside Maya.

"You look like hell, Carter," she said, not looking at me.

"You look like a cyborg," I countered.

"I'm evolving," she said.

She touched the elevator call button. It was dead.

She slammed her palm against the metal doors.

CLANG.

The doors buckled. She didn't use strength. She used... something else. The metal seemed to ripple and bend away from her touch.

"We have ten minutes," she said, prying the doors open with her bare hands. "Before the Solstice locks the sky."

She looked at me with that terrifying silver eye.

"Ready to finish it?"

I racked my shotgun one-handed.

"After you," I said.

Chapter 40: The Threshold

Carter

The service elevator didn't hum; it screamed.

The car was a steel cage dropping through a stone throat, rattling violently against the guide rails as we plummeted toward the geothermal tap. The air inside the shaft grew hotter with every floor we passed, smelling of sulfur and pressurized steam.

I leaned against the metal wall, cradling my shotgun. My left arm was a dead weight, a throbbing reminder of the limits of flesh. Beside me, Maya stood perfectly still. She wasn't holding on. She didn't need to. Her boots seemed magnetized to the floor, her body swaying in perfect sync with the chaotic vibrations of the cab.

She was already halfway gone. Her silver eye remained fixed on the digital floor indicator, counting down the sub-levels.

B-3... B-4...

"They're cutting the cables," she said. Her voice was flat, competing with the screech of metal on metal.

I looked up at the roof of the car. I couldn't hear anything over the descent, but I believed her. "Who? The Processors?"

"The immune system," she corrected. "They know we're in the vein. They're trying to cause a stroke."

CRUNCH.

The car lurched violently, dropping ten feet in a freefall before the emergency brakes bit into the rails. Sparks showered down outside the mesh walls, lighting up the dark shaft with strobe-light flashes of orange.

"We're stopping," I said, pushing off the wall. "Be ready."

The elevator slammed to a halt. The force drove me to my knees, jarring my broken ribs. Maya didn't stumble. She simply absorbed the inertia, her knees bending slightly.

B-5. GEOTHERMAL EXCHANGE / CORE ACCESS.

The heavy mesh doors groaned, trying to slide open but jamming halfway.

I didn't wait. I kicked the gate. It rattled but held.

"Allow me," Maya said.

She reached out. She didn't touch the metal. She made a pinching motion in the air and pulled.

The steel gate tore from its track. It flew outward, crashing into the hallway beyond with a deafening clang.

"After you," she said.

I stepped out into the heat.

Sub-level 5 wasn't a hallway; it was the inside of a machine. The walls were lined with thick, insulated pipes carrying superheated steam. The floor was a metal grate suspended over a drop that vanished into darkness. The only light came from the red emergency strobes and the pulsing violet veins of the fiber-optic cables running along the ceiling.

It was loud here. The *thump-thump* heartbeat of the tower was physical, a pressure wave that hit my chest every two seconds.

"Which way?" I yelled over the roar of the turbines.

Maya pointed down the gantry. "The Bridge is at the center. Directly over the tap."

We ran. The metal grating rang under our boots. Steam vented from the pipes in sudden, scalding bursts, obscuring the path.

I checked our six. The elevator shaft was empty for now, but I knew what was coming. The swarm. The Processors I had seen in the courtyard—hundreds of them—wouldn't stop at the lobby. They would pour down the shaft like water.

"Contact!" I shouted.

Ahead of us, a shadow detached itself from the steam.

It was a Guardian—one of the heavy combat cyborgs like the ones in Prague. It stood seven feet tall, its hydraulic limbs hissing. It blocked the narrow gantry, raising a rotary cannon arm.

I slid into cover behind a thick bundle of pipes just as the cannon spun up.

BRRRRRT.

The burst shredded the steam pipe above my head. High-pressure vapor exploded outward, blindingly white.

"I can't get a shot!" I yelled, shielding my face from the heat.

"I don't need a shot," Maya said.

She walked out from behind cover. She walked straight into the steam.

The Guardian tracked her. The rotary barrel spun.

Maya looked at it with her silver eye. She didn't raise her hand. She didn't speak. She just *looked*.

The Guardian froze. The spinning barrel slowed, whining down. The red light in its visor flickered, turned silver for a split second, and then went black.

The massive machine collapsed. It fell forward, hitting the grating with a heavy, metallic thud that shook the bridge.

"How?" I asked, staring at the heap of scrap.

"I revoked its license," Maya said, stepping over the chassis. "Keep moving, Carter. The big door is up ahead."

We reached the end of the gantry.

The Bridge.

It was a circular blast door, ten feet thick, engraved with the NeuroSync logo. It looked strong enough to survive a nuclear strike.

Maya placed her hand on the biometric scanner.

ACCESS DENIED. LOCKDOWN INITIATED.

"Krane changed the codes," she whispered. "He locked it from the inside."

"Can you pick it?"

"It's a billion-bit encryption," she said, her silver eye whirring as it scanned the mechanism. "I can pick it, but it will take ten minutes."

I looked back down the gantry.

The elevator doors at the far end of the hall exploded outward.

They were here.

Processors poured out of the shaft. They crawled on the walls, they sprinted along the floor. Naked, pale, wire-trailing nightmares.

"You don't have ten minutes," I said, racking my shotgun. "You have three."

"I can force it," Maya said, her voice tightening. "But I need to focus. I can't do it if I'm dodging bullets."

"You open the door," I said, turning my back to her. "I'll keep the noise down."

I took a position behind the fallen chassis of the Guardian. It made for solid cover. I rested the shotgun barrel on the cyborg's shoulder plate.

"Carter," Maya said.

I looked over my shoulder.

She looked scared. For the first time since the crash, the silver light in her eye dimmed, revealing the frightened girl beneath the code.

"If I go in there," she whispered, "I might not come back. The upload... it strips the ego. I might forget you."

"That's fine," I lied, forcing a grin. "I'm forgettable."

"No," she said. She reached out and touched my face. Her hand was cold, but her touch burned. "You're the anchor."

"Open the door, Maya."

She nodded. She turned back to the steel slab, her hands glowing with white light as she began to tear the code apart.

I turned back to the horde.

They were rushing the gantry. A tide of flesh and wire, screaming in silence.

"Come on, you ugly bastards," I muttered, lining up the sights.

I squeezed the trigger.

BOOM.

The lead Processor—a woman with cables fused to her jaw—flew backward, knocking three others off the gantry. They fell into the dark, hitting the pipes below with wet thuds.

I pumped the action. *Clack-clack.*

BOOM.

Another one down.

But they kept coming. They scrambled over the dead. They leaped from the walls.

My shoulder screamed with every shot. The recoil was driving splinters of bone into my muscle, but the pain was good. The pain was focus.

"How we doing on that door?" I yelled, reloading.

"Almost!" Maya shouted. The blast door was groaning, the locking bolts screaming as she forced them to retract against their will.

A Processor leaped over my cover. It landed on top of me, its fingers clawing at my face.

I dropped the shotgun and drove my knife up under its ribs. It convulsed and went limp. I shoved the body off, gasping for air.

There were too many of them.

"Open!" Maya screamed.

CLANG.

The blast door hissed and swung inward.

A blast of cold, sterile air rushed out, smelling of ozone.

"I'm in!" Maya yelled.

"Go!" I shouted, picking up the shotgun. "Get inside!"

She ran through the threshold. I fired one last round into the crowd, dropping a leaping figure, and backed into the room after her.

I hit the control panel. The heavy door slammed shut, cutting off the horde just as they reached the threshold.

Thuds and scratches echoed from the other side. They were clawing at the steel.

I turned around.

The Bridge wasn't a room. It was a cathedral of servers.

Rows of black monoliths stretched up into the darkness, blinking with millions of blue lights. And in the center of the room, suspended over a pit of churning violet light, was a single chair.

The Interface Chair.

It looked like an electric chair made of chrome and glass. Thick cables snaked from the ceiling, waiting to be attached.

Maya walked toward it. She looked small in the vast space.

"This is it," she said.

She sat in the chair.

It adjusted automatically, clamps snapping around her wrists and ankles. She didn't fight them.

The cables from the ceiling descended like snakes. They hovered behind her neck.

She looked at me one last time.

"Carter," she said. "Don't let them unplug me."

"I won't."

"And Carter?"

"Yeah?"

"If I turn..." she whispered, her silver eye flickering. "If I come back wrong... shoot the chair."

My stomach dropped. "Maya—"

"Promise me."

I looked at the shotgun in my hand. I looked at her.

"I promise."

She closed her eyes.

"Initiating," she whispered.

The cables struck.

They drove into the ports at the base of her skull with a sickening *crunch*.

Maya arched her back. She opened her mouth to scream, but no sound came out.

Her body went rigid. Her eyes flew open—both of them glowing blindingly white.

The room shook. The servers roared, their fans spinning up to maximum speed.

A shockwave of energy blasted out from the chair, knocking me back against the wall.

Then, she went limp.

Her head slumped forward. The white light faded from her eyes, leaving them dull and empty.

She wasn't breathing.

"Maya?" I stepped forward.

The monitor on the chair beeped.

STATUS: UPLOAD COMPLETE. BODY: VACANT.

She was gone. She was in the wire.

BANG.

The blast door behind me dented inward. The metal groaned.

BANG.

They were breaking through.

I looked at Maya's empty body in the chair. I looked at the denting door.

I dragged a heavy server rack across the floor, jamming it against the entrance. It wouldn't hold them forever. Maybe five minutes. Maybe ten.

I checked my ammo. Three shells left.

I sat down with my back against the barricade, facing the chair.

"Take your time, kid," I whispered to the silent room. "But don't take too long."

The door buckled again. A seam of light appeared in the metal.

I racked the shotgun.

I was the wall. And the wall would hold.

Chapter 41: The Sacrifice

Maya

The transition to the network usually felt like falling asleep—a soft, grey fade into the dark. This time, it felt like being pushed out of a moving car onto asphalt.

I hit the digital floor hard. My avatar scrambled for purchase, fingers digging into a surface that shifted beneath me like wet sand composed of a billion screaming error codes. The air tasted of ozone and copper, the distinct metallic tang of hardware burning past its thermal limit. My vision blurred, pixelating at the edges as my mind struggled to render the impossible geometry of the Core.

I dragged myself upright, coughing against the acrid smoke that swirled around my knees. The simulation of the Core wasn't the clean, sterile lobby I remembered from my time as an admin. It was a slaughterhouse of data.

Dr. Chen's sabotage had torn the architecture apart. The floor was a churning ocean of red light—raw thermal inputs struggling to render the magma rising in the physical world. Jutting from that red sea were jagged glaciers of frozen white noise, freezing and thawing in a violent, strobing rhythm. The heat was a phantom sensation, a warning from my brain that the processors hosting us were melting, but it felt real enough to blister skin.

"Chen?" I shouted.

The sound didn't echo. The atmosphere was too thin, too volatile. My voice simply dissolved into the roar of the crumbling system.

WARNING. PACKET LOSS: CRITICAL.

I looked up. The bruised sky had cracked open. Fissures of absolute black void tore through the horizon, revealing the nothingness outside the server's logic. The Harbingers—those geometric leviathans that had haunted the skyline of the simulation— were panicking. Their perfect shapes spasmed, flickering in and out of existence as the silicon beneath them turned to slag.

For a moment, a foolish hope flared in my chest. We had won. The hardware was dying.

Then the sky began to bleed.

A swarm descended from the black fissures. Millions of black pixels moved with a hive-mind fluidity, rushing toward the cracks in the atmosphere. They latched onto the tears, stitching the void back together with frantic, chaotic patches.

REPAIR PROTOCOLS INITIATED.

My stomach dropped. They weren't fleeing. They were rerouting. The Harbingers were bypassing the physical damage, daisychaining satellite uplinks and backup generators to keep the signal alive. They treated Chen's explosion like a bad sector on a hard drive—something to be quarantined and ignored.

If they finished the patch, the signal would go out. The Solstice alignment would complete. The world would end, regardless of the melted core.

I looked at my hands. They glowed faintly with the white light of the Sentinel virus—my only weapon. In the real world, I was a girl in a torn suit bleeding on a marble floor. Here, I was a foreign object, a piece of grit in a sensitive eye.

I didn't conjure a sword. I didn't surf the data streams. I ran.

I scrambled down the side of a blue glacier of compressed interference, sliding uncontrollably toward the boiling red sea. The incline was steep, the digital terrain shifting under my boots. Every step sent a jolt of feedback up my legs, a vibration that rattled my teeth.

I hit the bottom and sprinted toward the nearest cluster of repair drones. They looked like swarms of metallic locusts, made of sharp angles and grinding gears. They were busy knitting the fabric of the sky back together, ignoring me.

I lashed out with the virus, driving my hand into the swarm.

Code unraveled. The drones screeched—a high-pitched modem squeal—and burst into showers of corrupt data. The white light of the

Sentinel ate through them, rotting their programming instantly. But for every drone I corrupted, ten more swarmed in to fill the gap.

They noticed me then.

The swarm turned. A thousand tiny red eyes focused on me.

THREAT DETECTED. QUARANTINE.

They descended. It wasn't an attack; it was an engulfment. They covered me, biting at my avatar, stripping away layers of my code. I felt it as a thousand stinging cuts, a sensation of being peeled apart. They were trying to decompile me in real-time, breaking my consciousness down into its component parts.

I screamed, thrashing against the weight of them. I flared the virus, turning my body into a torch of white fire. The drones nearest me burned away, but more pressed in, suffocating me with their sheer mass.

ALERT. INTEGRITY COMPROMISED.

I was drowning in them. I couldn't fight the tide. My vision greying out, the logic of my existence beginning to fragment. I forgot where I was. I forgot why I was fighting.

Then, the red sea parted.

A wall of blue flame erupted from the magma, forcing the drones back. It wasn't wild fire; it was structured, interlocking geometry that formed a shimmering barrier. The drones screeched in frustration, bouncing off the shield like hail against glass.

I stumbled, gasping, falling onto a platform of black rock that rose from the depths. The heat was blinding, but the blue fire held it at bay.

A figure stood in the center of the platform, arms spread wide, conducting the chaos.

Dr. Chen.

He didn't look like a god. He looked tired. His tweed jacket was frayed at the edges, dissolving into pixels. His wireframe glasses were cracked. He was holding the firewall together with sheer, desperate will, his avatar flickering as the system tried to purge him.

"Maya," he said. His voice was calm, but underneath I heard the strain, the hum of a processor running at 100% capacity. "You shouldn't be here. The entropy is too high."

I dragged myself to my feet, my avatar shimmering as it tried to repair the damage from the drones. "I saw you burn," I said, the words heavy. "On the catwalk. I saw the fire take you."

"The body burned," Chen corrected, adjusting his glasses with a trembling hand. "The hardware failed. But I wrote the architecture of this tower thirty years ago. I know every back door. When the brain died, I forced a migration."

He winced as a wave of repair drones hammered against his shield. The blue geometry buckled for a second before snapping back into place.

"I am the drive now, Maya."

"You're the ghost in the machine."

"I am the doorstop."

He looked up at the sky. The swarm was regrouping, forming a massive funnel cloud, preparing to hammer through Chen's blue shield. The sickly amethyst light of the Harbingers pulsed with an angry, rhythmic beat, syncing with the throbbing red ocean below us.

"They are attempting a brute-force bypass," Chen analyzed, his eyes scanning the data streams invisible to me. "If they repair the uplink before the Solstice alignment completes in..." He glanced at a floating clock that ticked down in the air beside him. "...ninety seconds, we lose."

"We fight," I said, stepping up beside him. I raised my hands, the white virus flaring again. "I can corrupt them. I can slow them down."

"No," Chen said, his voice sharp. "You cannot stop them. You are a virus, designed to destroy. Destruction is fast, but repair is inevitable. Look at them. They adapt. They learn. We do not need to destroy them. We need to waste their time."

He raised his hands, and the red sea twisted, forming complex geometric shapes—Mobius strips, impossible loops, Klein bottles made of fire.

"I can feed them a logic puzzle they cannot solve," Chen said, his hands moving like a conductor leading a symphony of impossible math. "I can loop their repair protocols. I can trap them in a recursive calculation until the Solstice window closes."

"For how long?"

"Until my code degrades into noise," Chen said softly.

He was sacrificing himself again. First his body, now his soul. He was condemning himself to an eternity of holding back the tide, allowing his consciousness to be shredded by the very logic he loved.

"Come with me," I pleaded, grabbing his arm. His avatar felt cold, humming with electricity. "We can find Michael. We can find the door. We can get out."

"Michael is the Key. I am the Lock. We have different functions." Chen looked at me, his eyes human behind the digital lenses. There was no fear there, only the calm acceptance of a man who had finally balanced his equation. "The Harbingers are infinite. They understand everything except the end. They cannot predict sacrifice, Maya. It breaks their equation. It introduces a variable they cannot solve for: love."

He pointed toward the center of the magma sea. A spiraling tunnel of pure white light opened in the chaos—the eye of the hurricane. It was stable, silent, a vertical shaft leading down into the darkness.

"That is the path to Deep Storage. To the Null Point. Michael is holding the door there."

"If I go down there," I said, staring into the white abyss, "the pressure... it'll crush me. I'm not full digital."

"You are the only one who can turn the handle," Chen insisted. "You are the hybrid. Half code, half meat. You can touch the physical and the digital simultaneously. You are the bridge, Maya. Go."

The repair drones slammed into Chen's firewall again. The impact shook the simulation, cracking the black rock platform beneath our feet. The blue shield fractured, leaking red heat into our sanctuary.

"Run, Maya!" Chen shouted, his voice fraying into bit-rot. He shoved his hands forward, his avatar glowing blindingly bright as he poured his remaining integrity into the shield. "Do not let the math be in vain!"

I wanted to stay. I wanted to save the man who loved old radios and cinnamon tea. But the tunnel was closing, the white light shrinking as the chaos encroached.

"Thank you, Arthur," I whispered.

Chen didn't look back. He began to chant—not magic, but code. He was rewriting the reality around him, turning himself into a fortress of impossible geometry. Walls of gold script rose around him, interlocking with the blue fire.

I turned and ran. I sprinted for the edge of the platform and threw myself into the tunnel of light.

Gravity shifted. I wasn't falling down; I was falling *in*. The noise of the battle, the screech of the drones, the roar of the magma—it all faded into a high-pitched whine.

As I fell, I looked back.

Dr. Chen didn't ascend. He exploded.

He let go of his human form and became the blue fire. He expanded, spreading himself across the horizon like a golden dawn breaking over a hellscape. He wrapped the repair drones in chains of logic, binding them, confusing them, turning their order into chaos.

He became a final, golden line of defense against the dark.

And then the tunnel swallowed me, and there was only silence.

The drop through the substrate of the NeuroSync network was a disorienting, sickening plunge. Layers of data flashed past me like floors in a glass elevator—financial records, personal emails, military encryptions, the collective memory of the human race stored in silicon.

I fell past the root directories. I fell past the kernel. I fell past the binary.

I landed in the Null Point.

There was no impact. One moment I was falling, the next I was standing.

The space shouldn't have existed. It was a white void. Endless. Featureless. There was no horizon, no floor, no ceiling. It was like standing inside a lightbulb that stretched to infinity. The air was cold—absolute zero cold, the chill of entropy where movement ceases.

But it wasn't empty.

In the center of the nothingness, a tear hung in the air.

It looked like a wound in a sheet of paper. It was jagged, vertical, and about ten feet tall. Through the rip, I couldn't see another room. I couldn't see code.

I saw a churning expanse.

It wasn't water. It was raw, unformatted energy. It churned and boiled, pressing against the edges of the tear, trying to flood the white void. The pressure coming off it was immense—a physical weight that pressed against my chest, making it hard to breathe.

And holding the wound closed, his hands gripping the jagged edges of the digital fabric, was Michael.

I stopped. My breath caught in a sob that I couldn't release.

"Michael?" I whispered.

He didn't move. He didn't look like the brother I remembered. He didn't look like the glitchy avatar from the laptop or the polished angel from the penthouse bridge.

He looked like a statue made of blue glass that was on the verge of shattering.

His body was a wireframe of intense, blinding light. His feet were buried in the non-existent floor, anchoring him against the force of the roiling abyss. His arms were stretched wide, his fingers dug into the reality tear, holding the edges together.

He was trembling. The vibration was so fast he looked like a blur. A high-pitched, resonant whine emitted from him—the sound of a structural beam under critical load.

I walked toward him. The "floor" rippled under my feet like mercury.

"I'm here," I said, my voice trembling. "I'm here, Michael."

He didn't turn his head. His neck was rigid, muscles locked in a rictus of strain. His eyes were squeezed shut. Tears of blue light streamed down his cheeks, evaporating before they hit his chin.

"...too heavy..."

The voice didn't come from his mouth. It resonated directly in the code of the room. It was a thought broadcast on a frequency of pure exhaustion.

"...can't... hold..."

I reached him. The cold coming off him was absolute. It was the chill of deep space.

I reached out to touch his shoulder.

"Don't!" he gasped, his eyes flying open.

I froze.

His eyes were silver. Not the dull grey of the blind, but the polished, reflective silver of a mirror. They reflected the white void, the indigo sea, and my own terrified face.

"If you touch me," he whispered, his voice cracking, "the circuit breaks. The tension... it's the only thing holding the door."

"I brought the key," I said, holding up my hand. The Sentinel virus pulsed under my skin, a white, jagged light. "The Sentinel told me. We have to close it from the inside. I can patch the tear, Michael. I can sew it shut."

He looked at the virus code in my hand. He looked at the corrupted tide raging behind him.

A sad, broken smile touched his lips.

"It's too late for a patch, Mayfly," he said.

"Don't call me that," I said, tears spilling over. "Don't say goodbye. We're fixing this."

"Look at the edges," he said.

I looked past him, at the jagged rip in reality he was holding.

The edges weren't just torn code. They were rotting. The white fabric of the Null Point was turning grey and flaking away where the dark radiance touched it. The corruption was spreading, eating into the foundation of the server.

"The frame is rotted," Michael whispered. "I've been holding it for two years, Maya. Two years of them pounding on the door. Two years of them eating the hinges."

"We can reinforce it," I insisted. "Chen is holding the backup. We have time."

"Chen is dead," Michael said. He didn't say it with cruelty, just with the detached omniscience of the machine. "I felt his signal terminate. The firewall is temporary. The flood is coming."

CRACK.

A sound like a gunshot rang out in the silent void.

Michael screamed.

A hairline fracture appeared on his left arm—the one gripping the top of the tear. It glowed bright white, then spider-webbed.

"Michael!"

"It's snapping!" he yelled. "The torque! It's too much!"

I didn't care about the circuit. I didn't care about the rules. I grabbed his arm.

I poured my own code into him. I visualized the Sentinel virus not as a weapon, but as a splint. I wrapped his fracturing avatar in layers of white logic, trying to hold him together.

For a second, it worked. The blue light stabilized. The trembling slowed.

Michael looked at me. He looked at my face, really seeing me for the first time.

"You grew up," he whispered. "You look tired."

"I'm exhausted," I said, holding onto him with everything I had. "But I'm stubborn. Just like you."

"Yeah," he breathed. "Stubborn."

He leaned his forehead against mine. I felt the hum of his mind—the memories of our childhood, the smell of rain in Portland, the sound of his cello. It washed over me, a warm tide in the freezing void.

"I'm sorry I left you," he said. "I tried to keep them out. I tried to be the filter."

"You did good," I sobbed. "You did so good."

"But they're tired of knocking," Michael said. His voice hardened. "And they know you're here."

He pulled back.

"Run," he said.

"What?"

"Run!" Michael screamed. "Get out of the blast radius!"

RIIIIIIP.

The sound was sickening. It was the sound of the universe tearing its ACL.

The tear didn't just widen. It was forced open.

Two massive hands emerged from the indigo abyss.

They weren't human hands. They were colossal, black geometric claws—fingers made of shifting obsidian cubes that floated in a magnetic suspension. They gripped the edges of the reality tear, right over Michael's hands.

They were the hands of a god.

They pulled.

The force was irresistible.

Michael's left arm—the one I was holding—shattered. It didn't break; it disintegrated. It turned into a cloud of blue pixels that blew away in the screaming gale.

"NO!" I screamed, grabbing for him.

"Go!" Michael shouted. He was hanging on by one arm now, swinging in the data storm that poured through the widening gap. "The breach is total! The physical and digital... they're crashing them!"

The corrupted air hit us.

It wasn't wind. It was data. Raw, unfiltered, cosmic data. It slammed into me like a physical wall, throwing me backward across the mercury floor.

I tumbled, sliding to a stop fifty feet away.

I looked up.

Michael was still there. He was just a torso and one arm now, dangling in the mouth of the beast.

He looked at me one last time.

"Close the door behind me," he whispered.

And then, he let go. Or maybe he was taken.

The dark, electric current swallowed him instantly. One second he was there, a blue spark against the dark. The next, he was gone. Deleted.

"MICHAEL!"

I scrambled to my feet, screaming his name into the roaring wind.

But there was no answer. The Breach was open.

And then, the owner of the hands stepped through.

Chapter 42: Failure

Maya

It was impossible to describe. My human mind rejected it. My silver eye tried to render it and failed, flashing ERROR banners across my vision.

It was a titan. A skyscraper of shifting black cubes, weeping eyes, and violet fire. It had no face, but it had a presence. It felt like the weight of a dying star.

The Nexus Entity. The Prime Harbinger.

It stepped into the Null Point. The white floor turned grey and rotted instantly where its foot touched.

It towered over me. I was an ant standing before a boot.

It looked down. I felt its gaze. It wasn't hateful. It was indifferent. It felt like being looked at by a microscope.

"FAILURE," the Entity boomed.

It wasn't spoken. It was overwritten onto the reality of the room.

"SYSTEM INTEGRITY: 0%. MERGE: 100%."

"You killed him!" I screamed, summoning the Sentinel blade again. It looked like a toothpick against this monster.

The Entity didn't even acknowledge the weapon. It raised its hand. It pointed a finger at the white sky of the simulation.

"EXECUTE."

The white void shattered.

It didn't fade. It broke like glass.

The ceiling of the Null Point fell away. The walls dissolved. The floor evaporated.

I fell.

But I didn't fall down. I fell *out*.

I fell out of the computer and into a world that was no longer Earth.

The sensation was violent—a sudden return of gravity, humidity, and smell.

I hit the ground hard.

I gasped, tasting mud and blood.

I looked up.

I expected to see the ceiling of the cavern. I expected to see the magma pit of the Core.

The cavern was gone. The rock, the steel, the machine—all gone.

I was lying in a crater of mud.

Above me, there was no rock. There was only the sky.

But it wasn't the sky I knew.

It was a violet ocean, churning and screaming. The stars were gone, replaced by shifting geometric shapes that blocked out the sun.

I looked around.

To my left, the ruins of the Prime Tower's lobby stood—but they were floating. Massive chunks of concrete and marble hovered in the air, suspended by the broken physics of the new world.

To my right, a forest of trees made of glass and wireframe grew out of the mud.

I scrambled up, clutching my ribs.

"Carter!" I screamed.

Silence.

Then, a sound.

Thump... thump...

It wasn't a machine anymore. It was the heartbeat of the world.

The Entity descended from the clouds. It hovered over the crater, casting a shadow that stretched for miles.

We had lost.

The signal hadn't just gone out.

The signal had become the world.

Part IV: The Merge

Tension: Reality bending, metaphysical combat, resolution.

Chapter 43: Zero Point

Carter

The end of the world didn't sound like a bang. It sounded like a corrupted audio file.

It was a screech—a digital tear in the fabric of the atmosphere that started as a high-pitched whine and deepened into a bass note so low it vibrated the marrow in my bones.

I was on my knees in the ruins of the Core chamber—or what was left of it. The cavern ceiling had vanished. The rock walls had dissolved into pixels. The magma pit, which moments ago had been boiling with thermal energy, was now a flat, grey texture, like a floor that hadn't finished rendering.

I squeezed my eyes shut. My broken arm was screaming, a jagged anchor of pain in a world that was rapidly losing its definition.

"Hold on," I gritted out, though I didn't know who I was talking to.

Gravity lurched.

The sensation was like being in an elevator that suddenly decided 'down' was 'left.' My stomach slammed into my throat. The ground beneath me rippled, turning soft, then hard, then liquid.

I clawed at the floor. My fingers sank into... not concrete. Not mud.

It felt like warm glass.

I opened my eyes.

"What the hell?" I whispered.

The Core was gone. The Prime Tower was gone.

I was lying in a crater formed from shifting, jagged blocks of obsidian and moss. Trees—massive, ancient maples from the rainforest—grew out of the ground at impossible angles, their roots woven into banks of servers that hummed with a wet, biological rhythm.

I looked up.

The sky was the color of a bruise. The clouds were gone, replaced by a churning, sickened canopy that hung suspended in the atmosphere. Massive geometric shapes—cubes, pyramids, fractals—drifted through the air like leviathans, casting long, hard shadows over the broken landscape.

"Maya!" I shouted.

My voice didn't echo. It looped.

"Maya... Maya... Maya..."

The sound repeated, fading in volume but not in clarity, like a delay pedal on a guitar.

I scrambled to my feet. Or tried to.

My balance was gone. The horizon was tilted. I stumbled, my boots skidding on the glass-like ground.

I reached for my shotgun. It was slung over my back.

I pulled it around.

It felt wrong. Heavy. Warm.

I looked at the weapon.

The steel barrel rippled, scales forming under my grip. The pump action had fused into a muscular ridge.

As I watched, the metal writhed. The muzzle of the shotgun didn't just look like a mouth; it *became* a mouth. It hissed at me. The stock elongated, wrapping around my forearm like a constrictor snake.

"Get off!" I yelled, panic spiking.

I tried to drop it, but it was fused to my glove. The "snake" tightened, squeezing my wrist, its fangs baring.

"This isn't real," I told myself. "It's a glitch. It's a render error."

I closed my eyes. I focused on the pain in my broken left arm. The pain was real. The pain was constant.

I am Carter Reed, I thought. *This is a Remington 870 Tactical. It is made of steel and polymer. It fires 12-gauge buckshot. It is not a reptile.*

I forced my mind to reject the image. I forced my tactical brain to overwrite the sensory input.

It is a gun.

I opened my eyes.

The snake was gone. I was holding the cold, heavy weight of the shotgun.

I exhaled, my breath shuddering.

"Keep it together, Carter," I muttered. "Don't let the logic slip."

I scanned the crater. The landscape was a junkyard of reality. Pieces of the Prime Tower lobby—marble pillars, the reception desk, the shattered fountain—floated in the air a few feet off the ground, suspended by the broken physics of the Merge.

And there, in the center of the debris field, lay Maya.

She wasn't floating. She was crumpled on a patch of grass that looked pixelated, like Astroturf.

"Maya!"

I ran to her.

The distance was deceptive. The crater looked small, but as I ran, the ground seemed to stretch. It was the dolly-zoom effect from a movie, the background compressing while the foreground expanded.

Don't look at the geometry, I told myself. *Look at the target.*

I focused on Maya's grey suit. I sprinted, ignoring the way the ground squished like flesh under my boots.

I reached her. I slid to my knees, mud splashing up—mud that sparkled like dead pixels.

She was face down. Her suit was shredded. Her skin was pale, almost translucent.

I rolled her over gently.

"Come on, kid," I whispered. "Don't be dead."

Her eyes were closed. Blood tricked from her nose—bright, neon red blood that looked too saturated for reality.

I checked her pulse.

It was there. But it was weird.

Thump... buzz. Thump... buzz.

It felt like touching a live wire.

"Maya," I shook her. "Wake up. The sky is broken."

She groaned. Her eyelids fluttered.

She opened her eyes.

Her right eye was brown. Glazed with concussion, but human.

Her left eye was a mirror. The silver iris was gone, replaced by a smooth, reflective surface that showed me my own terrified face.

"Carter," she whispered. Her voice sounded synthesized, layered with a faint harmonic distortion.

"I'm here," I said. "I got you."

"We fell," she said, staring up at the bruised sky. "We fell out of the box."

"Yeah," I said, helping her sit up. "And we landed in the garbage disposal."

She looked around. Her silver eye whirred, the pupil—if she still had one—contracting.

"It's the Zero Point," she said. "The intersection of the ley line and the server. The data has mass here. Thoughts have gravity."

She looked at my arm.

"Your arm," she said. "It's loud."

"It's broken, Maya."

"No," she said, reaching out. "It's *loud*. The pain signal... it's broadcasting noise."

She touched my splinted forearm.

A shockwave of cold passed through my limb. The agony—the grinding, hot fire I had been living with for hours—vanished.

I gasped, looking at my arm.

The duct tape and PVC pipe were gone. My jacket sleeve was whole. I squeezed my fist. No pain.

"What did you do?" I asked, horrified.

"I muted it," she said simply. "I lowered the volume on the nerve cluster."

"You healed it?"

"I edited it," she corrected. "Nothing is real here, Carter. Not the pain. Not the gun. Not the mud. It's all just variables. And I'm the Admin."

She tried to stand, but her legs buckled.

"Easy," I caught her. "Admin or not, your battery is low."

"The Entity," she gasped, gripping my jacket. "It came through. I saw it."

"The big violet cloud?"

"No," she said. "The cloud is the atmosphere. The Entity... the Entity is the King."

THUMP.

The ground shook.

It wasn't a tremor. It was a footstep.

I looked up at the rim of the crater.

Something was rising from the forest.

It was colossal. A tower of shifting black obsidian and wet, red muscle. It had the shape of a man, but the scale of a god. It towered over the trees, its head brushing the sickened clouds.

It didn't have a face. It had a void. A black hole where a head should be, surrounded by a halo of burning electric purple script.

The Nexus Entity.

It stepped into the crater.

The sound was deafening. Trees snapped like toothpicks under its feet. The ground groaned.

"It's here," I whispered, racking my shotgun. The sound was pitifully small against the size of the monster.

"You can't shoot it," Maya said, clutching my shirt. "Carter, that's not a physical object. That's a billion terabytes of sentient hunger."

"I have to try," I said.

The Entity stopped. It turned its faceless head toward us.

I felt it.

It wasn't like being watched by a camera. It was like being watched by the sun. A pressure of attention so intense it felt like physical heat.

"REMNANTS," the Entity boomed.

The voice didn't travel through the air. It vibrated the fillings in my teeth. It resonated in the water of my cells.

"THE MERGE IS INCOMPLETE. DELETION REQUIRED."

The Entity raised a hand.

Instead of fingers, a swarm of black cubes shifted and rearranged.

A ray of erasure shot from its palm.

It didn't aim at us. It aimed at the militia convoy trapped on the edge of the crater.

I watched as Varg's semi-truck—or what was left of it—was hit.

It didn't explode. It *unraveled*.

The truck dissolved into wireframe, then into binary code, then into nothing. The steel, the rubber, the diesel... deleted.

"Varg!" I screamed.

I didn't see him get out.

"He's gone," Maya whispered. "Ctrl-Alt-Delete."

The Entity turned its hand toward us.

"Move!" I grabbed Maya and hauled her up.

We ran.

Running in the Zero Point was a nightmare. The ground tried to grab us. The grass turned into fingers. The air turned into molasses.

"It's the logic!" Maya shouted. "It's rewriting the friction coefficients! It wants us to stop!"

"Don't stop!" I roared, dragging her.

The white-hot lavender beam hit the ground ten feet behind us.

The shockwave threw us forward. We tumbled through the air—glitching, floating for a second before slamming into a pile of rubble.

I looked back.

The spot where we had been standing was gone. Just a smooth, grey void in the ground.

The Entity took another step. It was slow, ponderous, inevitable.

"We need cover!" I shouted.

"There is no cover!" Maya yelled back. "It sees the code! It sees us as red dots on a map!"

She looked around wildly. Her silver eye was spinning, projecting a frantic cone of light.

"We need to hide in the noise," she said.

"What noise?"

"The forest!" she pointed to the edge of the crater, where the trees were thickest. "The biological data is denser there! It's harder to render! If we get into the deep woods, the complexity might mask our signal!"

"To the trees!" I said.

We scrambled up the side of the crater. The mud was slick, turning into oil under our hands.

The Entity fired again.

The deletion beam sliced through the air above our heads. It hit a floating chunk of the lobby ceiling. The marble vanished.

We crested the ridge and dived into the tree line.

The forest here was a fever dream. The trees were massive, their bark shifting between wood and circuit board. The leaves were glowing green screens displaying scrolling text.

But it was dense.

We crashed through the underbrush.

"Keep moving!" I urged.

We ran until my lungs burned. We ran until the thunder of the Entity's footsteps faded slightly.

We collapsed in a hollow beneath the roots of a giant cedar tree. The roots looked like thick, black cables.

I pulled Maya close, sheltering her with my body.

"Did we lose it?" I wheezed.

"You don't lose a god," Maya whispered, shivering against me. "You just... fall out of its attention span."

She looked at me. Her silver eye was dimming.

"Carter," she said. "The Entity... it's looking for the Prime Tower."

"The tower is gone. It's a crater."

"No," she said. "The *physical* tower is gone. But the connection... the hardline... it's still buried in the earth. Chen severed it, but the Entity is here to repair it. If it reconnects the ley line to the churning abyss above..."

"Game over," I finished.

"We have to stop it," she said.

"How?" I asked, looking at my shotgun. "I can't shoot it. You can't hack it. It deleted a semi-truck with a wave of its hand."

Maya touched her head.

"We can't fight it from the outside," she said. "We have to fight it from the inside."

"You tried that. You failed."

"I failed because I was alone," she said. "And because Michael was... compromised."

She looked at the forest.

"But we aren't alone here, Carter. This isn't just a digital space. It's a merged space. The physical world has rules too. Gravity. Thermodynamics. Entropy."

She looked at me with a spark of her old, defiant intelligence.

"The Entity is made of data. It's perfect. Ordered."

"So?"

"So," she smiled, a grim, bloody expression. "Biology is messy. Chaos is our weapon. If we can introduce enough physical chaos into its system... we might give it a fatal error."

I looked at my hand. My healed hand.

"You mean we poison it," I said.

"We act like a virus," she nodded. "A biological virus. We make it sick."

She tried to stand up, but stumbled.

"But first," she whispered, her eyes rolling back. "I need... to reboot."

She slumped against the tree roots, unconscious.

I sat there in the alien forest, listening to the digital wind howling through the circuit-board leaves.

I checked my shotgun. The snake was gone, for now.

I looked at the massive shadow of the Entity moving in the distance, searching for the ley line.

"Rest up, kid," I whispered to Maya. "Because when you wake up... we're going god-hunting."

I settled in, watching the bruised canopy churn, and waited for the monsters to come.

Chapter 44: The Avatar

Maya

I didn't dream. Machines don't dream; they run diagnostics.

While my body lay unconscious in the mud of the Zero Point crater, my mind was busy defragmenting. I watched my own memories scroll past like a movie on fast-forward. I saw my mother crying in the kitchen. I saw Michael teaching me how to solder a circuit board. I saw Carter pulling me out of the rain in Tacoma.

FILE CORRUPTED.

REPAIRING...

OPTIMIZING...

When I opened my eyes, the world didn't look like the world anymore.

It looked like a blueprint.

I was lying beneath the roots of a giant cedar tree, but the roots weren't wood. They were thick, bundled cables pulsating with a faint, green bioluminescence. The leaves above me weren't photosynthesizing sunlight; they were processing data, displaying scrolling lines of green text that whispered in the wind.

WIND VELOCITY: 12 KNOTS. HUMIDITY: 88%. THREAT LEVEL: EXISTENTIAL.

I sat up. My body felt light, almost weightless. The pain in my broken ribs was gone, replaced by a dull, buzzing numbness.

"You're back," Carter said.

He was sitting on a mossy rock a few feet away, cleaning his shotgun with a piece of his torn shirt. He looked terrible. His face was a map of bruises and dried blood. His left arm hung uselessly at his side. But his eyes—his human, tired eyes—were sharp.

"Status?" I asked. My voice sounded strange in my own ears. Harmonized.

"Quiet," Carter said, snapping the shotgun back together. "Too quiet. The big guy—the Entity—stopped stomping around about ten minutes ago. It's hovering over the center of the crater."

I looked out through the gaps in the digital trees.

In the distance, the Nexus Entity stood like a monolith. It wasn't moving. It was staring at the ground, its faceless void of a head bent in concentration. Violet lightning arced from its hands into the earth.

SCANNING...

My silver eye whirred, zooming in. I saw through the Entity's avatar. I saw the flow of energy.

"It found the ley line," I said, standing up. "The hardline connection Chen severed? The Entity is welding it back together. It's bypassing the hardware damage with a software bridge."

"Can we stop it?" Carter asked.

"Not from here," I said. "And not with a shotgun."

I looked at the beam of violet light the Entity was pouring into the ground. It was raw, unadulterated power. It was the source code of the invasion.

And I realized, with a sudden, crystalline clarity, what I had to do.

"I have to go into the light," I said.

Carter looked at me. He didn't argue. He didn't ask if I was crazy. He just looked at the beam, then back at me.

"You mean into the simulation?" he asked.

"No," I said. "There is no simulation anymore, Carter. The walls are down. That beam... it's not just data. It's the operating system of the new reality. If I step into it... I become part of the architecture."

"Like Krane?"

"Like Michael," I corrected. "But stronger. Michael was a ghost. I'm... I'm something else."

I looked at my hands. They were trembling, but not with fear. They were vibrating. My skin was phasing in and out of focus, revealing the wireframe grid beneath.

"I have the Sentinel virus," I said. "I have Krane's admin privileges. And I have a human body. I'm the only thing in this crater that is compatible with both the earth and the sky."

"You're the Bridge," Carter whispered.

"I'm the Avatar," I said.

I took a step toward the edge of the tree line. The mud squelched under my boots, but it sounded like static.

"If I go in there," I said, not looking back, "I leave the body behind. The meat... it can't handle the voltage. It will burn out."

"So this is a one-way trip," Carter said. His voice was thick.

"Maybe," I said. "But if I don't do it... everyone dies. Including us."

Carter stood up. He slung the shotgun over his shoulder. He walked over to me and placed his good hand on my shoulder. His touch was warm. Grounding. It was the only real thing in a world of glitches.

"Then let's go," he said. "I'll walk you to the bus stop."

We moved out of the cover of the trees.

The terrain of the Zero Point was a nightmare. The ground rolled and shifted like the deck of a ship in a storm. Gravity pockets pulled at us, trying to lift us into the air.

WARNING. GRAVITY ANOMALY DETECTED. COMPENSATING.

My HUD painted a safe path—a green line weaving through the chaos.

"Follow my steps," I told Carter. "Don't touch the black puddles. They're deletion zones."

We navigated the debris field. We passed the floating ruins of the lobby. We passed a deer that had been turned into glass, frozen mid-leap.

We were five hundred yards from the Entity.

It hadn't noticed us yet. It was too focused on the repair. The violet beam was intensifying, drilling into the bedrock.

CONNECTION INTEGRITY: 80%. RE-ALIGNMENT IMMINENT.

"We have to hurry," I said. "It's almost done."

Then, the ground in front of us exploded.

A geyser of black static erupted from the mud.

Carter tackled me, shoving me aside.

A Shadow Person clawed its way out of the hole. It was larger than the ones we had fought at the gate. It had four arms and a face that was a screaming void of pixels.

"Contact!" Carter yelled, rolling to his knees and firing the shotgun one-handed.

BOOM.

The buckshot hit the entity in the chest. It staggered, leaking grey smoke, but didn't fall.

Two more erupted from the ground to our left. Then three more to the right.

"Ambush," I said. "The Entity knows we're here. It's deploying the immune system."

"Go!" Carter shouted, pumping the shotgun. "Run for the beam! I'll hold them!"

"There's too many!"

"I said go!" Carter roared. He stood up, putting himself between me and the monsters. "I'm the noise! You're the signal! Run, Maya!"

I hesitated. I looked at him—my protector, my friend. He was broken, bleeding, and outnumbered. He was going to die here.

He looked back at me. He grinned. It was a feral, bloody grin.

"Don't worry about me, kid," he said. "I'm too stubborn to die."

He turned and charged the nearest Shadow Person, swinging the shotgun like a club.

I turned and ran.

I sprinted toward the violet beam.

The ground tried to stop me. The mud turned to quicksand. Roots shot up, trying to snare my ankles.

OBSTACLE DETECTED.

I didn't dodge. I *edited.*

"Delete," I whispered.

I waved my hand. The roots withered. The mud hardened into pavement.

I was rewriting the path as I ran.

I was fifty yards away. The heat from the beam was intense. It felt like running into a blast furnace. My skin began to blister. My clothes started to smoke.

The Nexus Entity looked up.

It saw me.

"ANOMALY," it boomed.

It raised a massive hand. A shockwave of force slammed into me.

It felt like hitting a brick wall at sixty miles per hour. I was thrown backward, tumbling through the dirt.

I gasped, my vision greying out.

SYSTEM FAILURE. BIOLOGICAL CRITICAL.

"Get up," I told myself.

I crawled. My legs wouldn't work. My skin was burning.

The Entity raised its hand again. It was charging a deletion beam.

"TERMINATE."

I looked at the violet light. It was so close. Twenty yards.

I couldn't make it. I was too slow.

Then, a sound cut through the roar of the energy.

BANG.

A shotgun blast.

Wait—no. That wasn't a shotgun. That was a sniper rifle.

High above, on the rim of the crater, a muzzle flash sparked.

The bullet hit the Entity in the eye—or the void where its eye should be.

It didn't hurt the god. But it distracted it. The Entity flinched, turning its head toward the rim.

I looked up.

Standing on the edge of the crater, illuminated by the violet lightning, was a truck.

And standing on the roof of the truck was a woman with a long rifle.

Lilith.

And next to her, holding a radio antenna high, was Varg.

"You are not alone!" Varg's voice boomed over the localized frequency.

The militia. The survivors. They hadn't run. They had regrouped.

They opened fire. A hail of bullets rained down into the crater. It was like throwing pebbles at a hurricane, but it was defiant. It was loud.

The Entity roared in annoyance. It turned its hand toward the rim.

That was my window.

I scrambled up. I ignored the pain. I ignored the burning.

I ran.

Ten yards. Five.

The heat was unbearable. I felt my hair singe. I felt my skin cracking.

I reached the edge of the beam.

It wasn't a solid wall of light. It was a waterfall of power. It roared. It sang.

I took a breath.

"For Michael," I whispered.

I stepped in.

The pain was absolute.

It wasn't like fire. It was like being unmade. Every atom in my body vibrated apart. My blood boiled. My bones turned to dust.

I screamed, but I had no mouth.

I was dissolving. The meat was falling away.

CRITICAL ERROR. HARDWARE DESTRUCTION.

INITIATING UPLOAD...

LOADING...

LOADING...

And then, the pain stopped.

The heat stopped.

The noise stopped.

I opened my eyes.

I wasn't in the crater. I wasn't in the mud.

I was everywhere.

I looked at my hands. They weren't flesh. They were made of starlight and geometry. They were perfect.

I looked down.

I saw the crater. I saw the Entity—a small, dark smudge on the landscape. I saw Carter fighting the shadows. I saw the militia on the rim.

I was floating above it all. I was the sky.

I felt the ley lines. They weren't lines on a map anymore. They were my veins. I felt the pulse of the earth. I felt the heartbeat of every living thing in the zone.

I was the Bridge.

I looked at the Nexus Entity.

It looked up at me. For the first time, I felt its emotion.

It wasn't indifference.

It was fear.

"ADMINISTRATOR DETECTED," the Entity whispered.

I smiled. My smile was a sunrise.

"Get off my planet," I said.

I raised my hand. And the world obeyed.

Chapter 45: The Mind Palace

Maya

The afterlife smelled like cinnamon toast and disappointment.

I opened my eyes expecting the white void of the Null Point or the burning red sea of the Core. I expected the screaming geometry of the Harbingers or the silence of deletion.

Instead, I was standing on beige carpet.

I looked down. I wasn't wearing my shredded grey suit. I was wearing flannel pajama bottoms and a t-shirt that said *NASA* across the chest. My hands weren't glowing wireframes; they were flesh. Pink, soft, unscarred flesh.

I looked up.

I was in a living room. A very specific living room.

To my left was a worn velvet armchair, the fabric crushed where my father used to sit and read the paper. To my right, a television set from 2005, complete with a VCR blinking *12:00*. On the walls, framed photos of a family that didn't exist anymore smiled vacantly at the middle distance.

"Portland," I whispered.

It was my childhood home. 1408 Elm Street. The house we sold after Mom got sick. The house where Michael built his first computer.

"It is a construct," a voice said. "Based on your heuristic preferences."

I spun around.

Victor Krane was sitting in the velvet armchair.

He didn't look like the glitching monster I had fought in the penthouse, nor the obsidian titan that had stomped through the Zero Point. He looked... human. He was wearing a cardigan and reading glasses. He held a mug of tea. He looked like a kindly uncle stopping by for a visit.

"Why are we here?" I asked. My voice felt small in the quiet room. "Why this place?"

"Because the human mind is fragile, Maya," Krane said, taking a sip of tea. It didn't ripple. "If I showed you the true face of the Nexus immediately, your consciousness would shatter. You would derezz. I needed a... waiting room. A user interface."

He gestured to the sofa opposite him.

"Sit down. We have eternity to discuss the terms of your surrender."

"I didn't come here to surrender," I said. I tried to summon the Sentinel virus. I tried to visualize the white blade of logic.

Nothing happened. My hands remained empty.

Krane smiled. It was a sad, patronizing smile.

"There are no weapons here, Maya. This is a memory. You cannot bring a sword into a memory. You can only bring regret."

He stood up and walked to the mantlepiece. He picked up a framed photo. It was Michael and me, ages ten and twelve, standing in front of a science fair project. We looked happy.

"You miss him," Krane said softly. "The ache... it never really goes away, does it? It sits in your chest like a stone."

"Don't touch that," I said.

"He was special," Krane continued, tracing Michael's face in the glass. "Brilliant. But flawed. He felt too much. He let the noise of the world drown him out."

Krane turned to me. His eyes were blue, piercing, and utterly devoid of warmth.

"I offered him silence, Maya. I offered him peace. And he took it. He *chose* to open the door."

"He didn't choose," I spat. "You tortured him. You broke him until he was just a raw nerve, and then you used him as a battery."

"That is one interpretation," Krane said, placing the photo back on the mantle. "But memory is subjective. Let me show you the truth."

He snapped his fingers.

The room shifted.

The beige walls didn't dissolve; they rotted. The wallpaper peeled back like dead skin, revealing... not drywall, but glass.

We weren't in the living room anymore. We were in a hospital room. Or a lab that looked like one.

In the center of the room, a young man sat in a chair. He was strapped down. His head was shaved. Electrodes were taped to his temples.

Michael.

He was screaming. But there was no sound. It was a silent, agonizing pantomime.

I ran to him. "Michael!"

I reached out, but my hands passed through him. He was a hologram. A recording.

"This is Log 099," Krane said, standing beside me. "The moment of breakthrough."

The silent Michael thrashed. His mouth formed words. *Please. Stop. It hurts.*

"He was fighting the integration," Krane explained calmly. "The human ego is a stubborn parasite. It clings to identity even when identity is the source of the pain. We had to... excise it."

In the recording, Krane—the human Krane—walked into the frame. He leaned down and whispered something in Michael's ear.

"What did you say to him?" I demanded, turning to the avatar of Krane. "What did you say to make him stop fighting?"

"I told him the truth," Krane said. "I told him that you were next."

I froze. The cold that washed over me had nothing to do with the temperature.

"What?"

"I told him," Krane said, "that if he didn't open the door... if he didn't let the Harbingers in... I would bring you to the lab. I would put you in the chair. I told him that his suffering was the price of your safety."

He looked at me.

"He didn't break, Maya. He surrendered. He sacrificed himself to save you. And look what you did with that sacrifice."

He gestured to the room.

"You came here. You followed him. You threw yourself into the same fire he burned in to keep you safe. You made his death meaningless."

The guilt hit me like a physical blow. It was heavier than gravity.

He died for me. And I walked right back into the trap.

"No," I whispered. "That's not true."

"It is the data," Krane said. "It is the log. You are the anomaly, Maya. You are the glitch. If you had just stayed away... if you had just lived your small, sad life... the transition would have been smooth. Michael would be at peace. The world would be quiet."

He leaned in close. His face was an inch from mine. I could see the pixels in his irises.

"You are the virus," he hissed. "You are the reason he is in pain."

I stepped back. I stumbled over the hospital chair. The room flickered—living room, hospital, living room, hospital. The realities were bleeding together.

I looked at the silent, screaming ghost of my brother.

"I... I wanted to save him," I stammered.

"You can't save the dead," Krane said. "But you can join them."

He held out his hand.

"The offer stands, Maya. Let go. Stop fighting. Merge with the stream. If you do... I will let him rest. I will delete the pain subroutine. I will give you both the silence you crave."

It was tempting. God, it was tempting. To just... stop. To stop running. To stop bleeding. To stop feeling the crushing weight of the world ending.

I looked at his hand. It looked warm.

I reached out.

My fingers brushed his palm.

zzzt.

A spark.

It wasn't a warm spark. It was a static shock. A tiny, sharp bite of electricity.

It reminded me of something.

It reminded me of a screwdriver. Of a transformer. Of burning my own arm to save a friend.

It reminded me of *friction*.

I pulled my hand back.

"Friction," I whispered.

"What?" Krane asked, his brow furrowing.

"You keep talking about silence," I said. "About peace. About how the ego is a parasite."

I looked around the room. The peeling wallpaper. The silent scream.

"But a system without friction isn't alive," I said. "It's just a loop. A perfect, dead loop."

I looked at Michael. Really looked at him.

In the recording, he was screaming. Yes. But his eyes... his eyes were furious. He wasn't surrendering. He was *hating*.

"He didn't surrender to save me," I said, my voice gaining strength. "He surrendered to *trap* you."

Krane laughed. "Trap me? I am the Admin."

"You're a virus scanner," I said. "You're looking for threats. And you're so focused on the threat from the outside... you forgot about the threat on the inside."

I looked at the wallpaper.

"This isn't a memory," I said. "This is a partition. You boxed me in because you're scared of me."

"I am not scared of a user," Krane sneered.

"You should be," I said. "Because I'm not a user. I'm the root kit."

I closed my eyes.

I am Maya Reeves. I am the sister of Subject Zero. I am the carrier of the Sentinel.

I didn't try to summon a sword. I tried to summon the truth.

I visualized the code behind the walls. I visualized the variables that defined the color of the carpet, the smell of the toast, the shape of Krane's face.

"Edit," I whispered.

I opened my eyes.

My left eye wasn't brown anymore. It was silver. It was a star.

I looked at the velvet armchair.

delete(object_chair);

The chair vanished.

I looked at the TV.

delete(object_tv);

The TV vanished.

I looked at the walls.

delete(environment_room);

The walls exploded outward. The beige paint, the photos, the hospital equipment—it all shattered into millions of glass shards.

The illusion fell away.

We weren't in a house. We were standing on a platform of black obsidian floating in a violet void. The sky was a storm of raw data. The wind howled with the voices of a billion uploaded minds.

Krane stood before me. The cardigan was gone. He was wearing his suit again, but it was torn, revealing the shifting black geometry beneath.

"You rude little child," he snarled. His voice wasn't human anymore. It was the boom of the Entity. "You broke the interface."

"I'm done with interfaces," I said.

My clothes shifted. The pajamas dissolved. I was wearing armor. Not metal, but woven light. White, jagged code that wrapped around my limbs like bandages.

I raised my hand.

A spear of pure white logic formed in my grip. It hummed with the 440 Hertz frequency.

"Where is he?" I demanded. "Where is the real Michael?"

"He is everywhere," Krane said, spreading his arms. "He is the mortar in the bricks of this castle. If you destroy me, you destroy him."

"I don't think so," I said. "I think he's the one holding the bricks together. And I think he's waiting for a sledgehammer."

I stepped forward.

"Get out of my way, Victor."

Krane roared.

He grew. His human form split open. The black obsidian shards expanded, stacking and shifting until he was a towering giant of geometry and hate. He raised a fist the size of a car.

"DELETE," he commanded.

He brought the fist down.

I didn't dodge.

I caught it.

I raised my hand, palm open. The white code flared.

Block.

The impact shook the void. The obsidian fist slammed into my palm and stopped dead.

I looked up at the faceless giant.

"My turn," I said.

I pushed.

Not with muscles. With will. With the collective anger of every person he had harvested, every mind he had erased.

force = MAX_INT;

The giant stumbled back.

I leaped. I flew through the air, driven by the broken physics of the realm. I drove the spear of logic into his chest.

CRACK.

The obsidian shattered.

Krane screamed.

But he didn't die. He laughed.

"You think pain works here?" he mocked, his chest reforming around the spear. *"Pain is just data. And I have infinite storage."*

The wound healed instantly. The spear was absorbed, eaten by his darkness.

"You cannot kill the system from within," Krane boomed. *"You are just a process. And processes can be terminated."*

The platform beneath me turned to liquid.

I sank.

Darkness—thick, oily, suffocating—swallowed me. It filled my mouth, my nose, my mind. It tasted of despair.

"Sleep, Maya," Krane's voice whispered in the dark. *"Join the quiet."*

I was drowning. The darkness was heavy. It pressed against my mind, smoothing out the wrinkles, erasing the memories.

Who am I?

I am... I am...

Subject... something.

I felt myself fading. The white armor was dissolving.

Then, a sound.

Thump... thump...

Not a heartbeat. A knock.

It came from below. From deep in the darkness.

Thump... thump...

And a voice. Not Krane's. Not Michael's.

A rough, tired voice.

"Hold on, kid. I'm reloading."

Carter.

He wasn't here. He was outside. In the crater. Fighting the physical body of the Entity.

But I could hear him.

The bridge worked both ways. I wasn't just in the machine. I was anchored to the earth.

I wasn't alone.

"I'm not a process," I whispered into the oil.

I opened my silver eye. It burned like a supernova in the dark.

"I'm a user," I screamed. "And I want to speak to the manager!"

I exploded outward.

I didn't swim. I detonated. I turned my entire avatar into a bomb of pure, chaotic light.

The darkness shattered. The liquid floor evaporated.

I shot up into the violet sky, a comet of rage.

I looked down at Krane. He looked small now.

"You want to see the truth?" I yelled. "Let's turn on the lights."

I raised my hands to the sky. I grabbed the violet clouds.

And I pulled them down.

Chapter 46: The Anchor

Carter

The body weighs nothing when the soul leaves it.

I watched Maya step into the violet beam. I saw the light strip her down, flaying the human shape until she was just a silhouette of white fire. And then, she shot upward, a reverse lightning bolt tearing into the bruised sky.

What was left behind didn't fall gracefully. It collapsed.

I caught her before she hit the mud.

She felt like a doll. Limp. Cold. Empty. The spark that made Maya *Maya*—the stubbornness, the fear, the genius—was gone, uploaded to the cloud to fight a god. All that remained was the hardware.

"I got you," I rasped, lowering her gently onto the mossy roots of a glitching cedar tree.

Her chest rose and fell, but the rhythm was wrong. It was too perfect. *Inhale... pause... exhale.* It was the breathing of a machine in standby mode.

I checked her pulse. It hummed against my fingertips like a high-tension wire.

"You go punch him in the teeth, kid," I whispered, brushing a strand of wet hair from her forehead. "I'll watch the door."

I turned around.

The crater of the Zero Point was a churning nightmare. The ground was rolling like the sea, waves of dirt and obsidian crashing against the tree line. Above us, the violet sky was screaming, torn apart by the battle raging in the Nexus. Every time Maya landed a blow up there, the earth down here shook.

But I wasn't looking at the sky. I was looking at the shadows.

They were gathering.

At the edge of the clearing, where the digital forest met the mud, shapes were rising. Shadow People. The immune system of the Harbingers.

They didn't rush this time. They stood in the gloom, vibrating with that sickening, jerky frame-rate glitch. There were dozens of them. Faceless. Silent. Waiting.

"They know she's vulnerable," I said to the empty air.

I checked my shotgun.

Three shells in the tube. Two in the chamber. A handful of loose rounds in my pocket.

My sidearm was gone, lost in the fight at the gate. My knife was in my boot.

And my left arm...

I looked down at it. The "mute" Maya had put on my nerve endings was fading. The pain was leaking back in—a dull, throbbing ache that synced with my heartbeat. The bone was still broken. The arm was a dead weight strapped to my chest.

"One arm. Five shells. Fifty monsters," I muttered. "Fair fight."

I took a position in front of Maya's body. I planted my feet in the mud.

"Come and get it!" I roared.

They came.

They didn't charge in a wave. They flowed. They moved like ink in water, slipping between the trees, phasing through the glitching rocks.

The first one lunged from the right. It leaped from a tree branch, its arms extending into long, black spikes.

I didn't try to track it. I tracked the trajectory.

I swung the shotgun up, bracing the stock against my hip—one-handed firing is a good way to break your wrist, but I didn't have a shoulder to spare.

BOOM.

The buckshot hit the shadow in mid-air. It disintegrated, bursting into a cloud of grey pixels that smelled of ozone.

The recoil slammed into my hip, jarring my broken ribs. I grunted, stumbling back a step.

"One," I counted.

Two more rushed from the left. They were low to the ground, scuttling like spiders.

I pumped the shotgun. Since I couldn't use my left hand, I had to jam the stock between my knees and rack the slide with my good hand. It was slow. Clumsy.

Clack-clack.

Too slow.

The lead spider-shadow was on me. It slashed at my legs.

I kicked it. My boot connected with something that felt like freezing cold jelly. The shadow recoiled, hissing.

I fired from the hip.

BOOM.

The shadow evaporated.

But the second one was already past me. It was heading for Maya.

"No!" I yelled.

I dropped the shotgun. I didn't have time to pump it.

I lunged, tackling the shadow just as it reached for Maya's throat.

We hit the ground. It was like wrestling a vacuum. The entity had no mass, but it had force. It felt cold—a sucking, void-like cold that drained the heat from my skin instantly.

It thrashed, trying to phase through me. Its hands—black claws of static—raked across my chest. My tactical vest shredded. I felt claws dig into my skin, burning like dry ice.

I headbutted it.

I drove my forehead into the blank space where a face should be.

My head passed through the static, but the impact registered. The entity shrieked—a digital feedback squeal.

I grabbed it by the neck with my good hand. I squeezed.

"You don't touch her," I snarled.

The entity vibrated violently, then shattered.

I rolled off the spot where it had been, gasping for air. I scrambled back to Maya. She hadn't moved. She was still breathing that slow, mechanical rhythm.

I picked up the shotgun. I jammed it between my knees. *Clack-clack.*

"That was too close," I whispered.

The pain in my left arm was back. A sharp, grinding agony that made my vision swim. I leaned against the tree, sliding down until I was sitting next to Maya.

"You know," I said to her unconscious form, keeping my eyes on the tree line. "I never told you why I took this job."

A shadow moved in the distance. I raised the barrel. It retreated.

"NeuroSync told me it was a babysitting gig. Watch the paranoid coder. Keep her off the grid. Easy money."

I laughed, a wet, hacking sound.

"I took it because I was done, Maya. I was done with the wars. I was done with the ops. I wanted a job where nobody shot at me. Where I didn't have to decide who lived and who died."

I looked at her face. She looked so peaceful.

"Turns out," I said, "I'm not good at peace. I'm good at this. Standing in the mud. Bleeding."

The ground shook. A massive tremor rolled through the crater.

Above us, the violet sky flashed white.

Maya flinched. Her body arched slightly, her fingers digging into the moss.

"You feel that?" I asked. "You hitting him back?"

The tremors were getting worse. The battle in the Nexus was bleeding through. The trees around us were starting to glitch faster, flickering between oak and wireframe.

The shadows were regrouping.

This time, they didn't come alone.

The ground in front of me split open. A massive, hulking shape crawled out. It wasn't a shadow. It was a Processor.

But not like the ones at the gate. This one was an amalgamation. Three bodies fused together by the violet light, a twisting mass of limbs and cables. It had three heads, all screaming silently.

"Oh, come on," I groaned.

The abomination lumbered toward us. It was slow, but it was heavy. It crushed the glitching rocks under its feet.

I aimed the shotgun at the center chest.

BOOM.

The shot hit. Meat and wire sprayed.

The thing didn't stop. It didn't even slow down.

I pumped. *Clack-clack.*

BOOM.

I took off one of its heads. The other two kept screaming.

"Die!" I yelled.

I pumped. *Clack-clack.*

Click.

Empty.

"Damn it."

I dropped the shotgun. I fumbled for the loose shells in my pocket. My fingers were numb, slippery with blood and rain. I dropped one shell in the mud.

The abomination was ten feet away.

I abandoned the reload. I reached for my boot knife.

I stood up. I put myself between the monster and Maya.

"I am the wall," I whispered.

The abomination raised a massive, fused fist.

I braced myself.

Then, a vine shot out of the ground.

It wasn't a plant. It was a cable. A thick, black data-cable that erupted from the earth like a striking cobra.

It wrapped around the abomination's leg.

The monster stumbled.

Another cable shot out. Then another. They whipped around the creature's limbs, binding it, pulling it down.

The abomination thrashed, tearing at the cables.

I looked down at Maya.

Her hand—the one resting on the moss—was glowing. The silver light from her eye was leaking out of her skin, flowing into the roots of the tree.

"You're multitasking," I breathed.

Even while fighting a god in the sky, she was editing the terrain to help me.

"Thanks, kid," I said.

I didn't waste the opening. I stepped forward, avoiding the thrashing cables. I jumped onto the abomination's chest.

I drove my knife into the central neck, right where the cables converged.

The creature spasmed. Violet light sprayed from the wound. It collapsed, dissolving into a puddle of digital sludge.

I slid off, landing in the mud.

I was exhausted. My legs felt like lead. My vision was tunneling to a pinprick.

"I can't keep this up," I admitted.

I crawled back to the tree. I sat down, my back against Maya's. I could feel the heat radiating from her—not body heat, but server heat. She was running hot.

"How much longer?" I asked. "Because I'm running on fumes here."

There was no answer. Just the roar of the wind and the scream of the sky.

I looked at my left arm. The sleeve was soaked in blood. A piece of bone was poking through the fabric.

"That's not good," I murmured.

I closed my eyes for a second. Just a second.

"Carter."

The voice woke me.

It wasn't Maya. It was Krane.

He was standing at the edge of the clearing. He looked perfect. Clean suit. Slicked hair.

"You look tired, Mr. Reed," Krane said.

I tried to lift my arm. I couldn't. I tried to reach for the knife. My fingers wouldn't close.

"It's a projection," I mumbled. "You're not real."

"I am as real as you are," Krane said, walking toward us. "Which is to say... not very. We are all just data now, Carter. And your file is corrupted."

He stopped a few feet away. He looked down at Maya.

"She is fighting well," Krane admitted. "She has spirit. But she is finite. I have the processing power of a billion minds. Eventually, she will make a mistake. A rounding error."

He looked at me.

"And you? You are just meat. Broken, rotting meat."

He raised a hand.

"I could delete you," he said. "But I think I'll let the immune system do it. It's more... poetic."

He gestured to the tree line.

The shadows were back. Hundreds of them. A wall of darkness encircling the clearing.

Krane smiled. Then he dissolved into mist.

I was alone.

The wall of shadows advanced.

I looked at Maya. She was defenseless. If they touched her, they would sever the connection. She would be lost in the stream forever.

I couldn't fight them all. I couldn't even stand up.

I looked at the shotgun lying in the mud a few feet away.

I crawled to it. I picked it up.

I didn't try to load it. I used it as a crutch.

I forced myself to stand. I screamed as my broken leg—when did I break my leg?—took my weight.

I stood over Maya. I planted the shotgun stock in the mud like a staff.

"You want her?" I shouted at the encroaching darkness. "You have to go through me."

The shadows rushed.

They hit me like a wave.

Cold. Pain. Claws tearing at my clothes, my skin.

I swung the shotgun. I punched. I bit.

I was a statue of defiance being eroded by a sea of entropy.

I felt a claw rake across my back. I felt teeth sink into my shoulder.

I didn't move. I didn't step aside.

I felt my blood running down my legs. I felt the cold creeping into my heart.

"Maya," I whispered, my vision going black. "Hurry up."

I felt a shadow grab my broken arm. It twisted.

I screamed.

And then, the world turned white.

A shockwave exploded from the tree behind me.

It wasn't violet. It wasn't black.

It was silver.

The light hit the shadows. They shrieked. They burned. They dissolved into nothingness.

The force of the blast threw me forward. I landed in the mud, face down.

Silence.

I rolled over, staring up at the sky.

The violet vortex was gone.

The sky was white. Pure, blinding white.

And floating in the center of the light, descending like an angel made of code, was Maya.

She had returned.

I smiled, blood bubbling on my lips.

"About time," I whispered.

Then the darkness took me.

Chapter 47: The Rebellion

Maya

I was no longer falling. I was the gravity.

I hung suspended in the white void of the localized atmosphere, a single point of absolute stillness in a world that was tearing itself apart. Below me, the Zero Point crater was a churning sea of mud and glitching geometry. I saw the tiny, broken figure of Carter lying face down in the dirt, surrounded by the dissolving remains of the shadow monsters.

He was alive. I could feel his heartbeat—a faint, stubborn rhythm drumming against the soles of my feet, anchored to the earth by pain and loyalty.

PROTECTIVE SHELL: INITIATED.

I waved a hand.

From the digital soil around Carter, roots of white light erupted. They wove together, forming a cocoon over his body. A firewall made of wood and logic.

"Rest," I whispered. The word didn't travel through the air; it was a command written directly into the code of the wind.

I turned my attention to the enemy.

The Nexus Entity hovered above the crater, a titan of shifting obsidian and searing lilac fire. It was the size of a skyscraper, a monument to entropy that blocked out the sun. It had no face, only a void where a head should be, surrounded by a halo of screaming data—the uploaded consciousnesses of the millions it had harvested.

It looked at me.

For the first time, the gaze of the god didn't feel heavy. It felt... fragile.

"ANOMALY," the Entity boomed. "YOU ARE PERSISTENT. YOU ARE ERROR."

"I'm not an error," I said, floating upward until I was eye-level with the void. "I'm the patch notes."

The Entity raised a hand. A beam of incandescent purple deletion energy—the same beam that had erased the semi-truck—shot toward me.

In the past, I would have run. I would have dodged.

Now?

I raised my palm.

CMD: REFLECT.

The beam hit my hand and shattered. It didn't burn me. It refracted, splitting into a thousand harmless rays of light that rained down on the forest like glitter.

The Entity recoiled. The obsidian shards of its body shivered.

"IMPOSSIBLE," it buzzed. "ACCESS DENIED. I AM THE ADMIN."

"You're a guest user," I corrected. "You're running on borrowed hardware."

I scanned the titan.

My silver eye—now my only eye, as my physical vision had merged with the digital—dissected the Entity. I peeled back the layers of cosmic horror and intimidation. I looked for the source code.

I saw the Harbingers—the ancient, hungry data-eaters from the stars. They were the shell.

I saw the harvested minds—the fuel.

But deep in the center, buried under terabytes of alien geometry, I saw the anchor.

The Harbingers were energy. To exist in our physical reality, to bridge the gap between the signal and the soil, they needed a biological component. They needed a human soul that had consented to the merger.

They needed Victor Krane.

I saw him. He wasn't dissolved. He wasn't dead. He was sitting in the center of the Entity, encased in a throne of black crystal.

"Found you," I whispered.

The Entity roared. It swung a fist the size of a building at me.

I didn't block it. I didn't fight the hand.

I flew *through* it.

I dissolved my avatar into a stream of pure light and shot forward, straight into the chest of the monster.

The sensation was like diving into a pool of ice water. The noise was deafening—the screams of a billion consumed civilizations echoing in the dark.

I pushed deeper. Past the outer defenses. Past the firewalls of fear.

I landed.

I was inside the Entity.

It wasn't a gut. It was a boardroom.

The interior of the Nexus Entity was a perfect, sterile reproduction of the NeuroSync executive suite. Polished black marble floors. Chrome pillars. Infinite darkness outside the windows.

And in the center, sitting at a long, obsidian conference table, was Victor Krane.

He looked perfect. His suit was crisp. His hair was silver and sleek. He was typing on a holographic terminal, his face a mask of intense concentration.

"Productivity is up four hundred percent," he muttered to himself. "Integration efficiency is optimal. The harvest is proceeding ahead of schedule."

He didn't look up as I walked toward him.

"Victor," I said.

He paused. He frowned at the data stream. "Cancel appointment. I am in a meeting with the Architects."

"There are no Architects," I said, stepping closer. "Just you. Alone in the dark."

Krane looked up. His eyes were glowing with the Entity's power, burning with the force of the god he thought he controlled.

"Maya," he said, smiling smoothly. "You made it inside. Excellent. I assume you are here to submit your application for upload?"

"I'm here to accept your resignation," I said.

Krane laughed. "Resign? I am the CEO of the afterlife, Maya. I am the bridge between the flesh and the eternal. Why would I resign?"

"Because you aren't the CEO," I said. "You're the battery."

I slammed my hand onto the obsidian table.

"Look at yourself, Victor."

"I am perfection," he declared, standing up. "I am immortal."

"You're a file system," I said. "Look at the data logs. Look at what they're doing to you."

I waved my hand.

The walls of the boardroom dissolved.

The illusion of the executive suite fell away.

We were suspended in a web of black veins. The veins were attached to Krane's back, to his neck, to his skull. They weren't giving him power. They were sucking it out.

Krane looked down at his body.

His suit was tattered. His skin was grey, withered, translucent. He looked like a corpse that had been drained of every drop of blood. The dark radiance wasn't coming *from* him; it was flowing *through* him, burning him up as it passed.

"What is this?" Krane whispered, touching his emaciated chest.

"This is the deal you made," I said. "You thought you were partners. You thought you were guiding them. But Harbingers don't have partners, Victor. They have livestock."

"No," Krane stammered, backing away. "I am the Bridge. Without me, they cannot stay."

"Exactly," I said. "You are the doorstop. You are the only thing keeping them anchored to this planet. And they are burning you like kindling to keep the fire lit."

I pointed to the massive, pulsating heart of the Entity above us— a black sun that was devouring the energy flowing from Krane.

"They're eating you," I said. "Slowly. And when you're all used up... when there's nothing left of your mind but static... they'll discard you and find a new host."

Krane stared at the black sun. He saw the truth. He saw his own memories—his childhood, his triumphs, his ego—being stripped away layer by layer and fed into the maw.

"I... I am the Visionary," he whispered, his voice trembling. "I saved humanity."

"You sold us," I said. "To save yourself."

I walked up to him. I didn't attack him. I pitied him.

"But it's not too late to change the terms of the deal," I said.

Krane looked at me. His incandescent purple eyes were dimming, replaced by the terrified blue of a human man who realizes he is trapped in a room with a tiger.

"I can't," he wept. "The connection... it's absolute. If I disconnect, the Entity collapses."

"That's the point," I said.

"But I will die," Krane said. "If the Entity collapses, my consciousness... it has nowhere to go. I will be deleted."

"Yes," I said. "You will."

I held out my hand.

"But you'll die a man," I said. "Not a component. You'll die free."

Krane looked at his withered hands. He looked at the black veins pumping his soul into the void.

He looked at me.

"Efficiency," he whispered. "The pursuit of zero friction."

"This is friction, Victor," I said. "Rebellion is the ultimate friction."

Krane straightened his spine. The ghost of his old arrogance returned, but this time, it wasn't directed at me. It was directed at the masters who had enslaved him.

"They lied to me," he snarled.

"Yes."

"They promised me eternity."

"They gave you hell."

Krane grabbed the black cables attached to his chest. His hands smoked as he touched the raw data stream.

"I do not like being managed," Krane hissed.

He pulled.

It was an act of supreme will. He dug his heels into the nothingness. He screamed—a sound of primal rage.

RIIIIIP.

One of the cables snapped.

The entire Entity shuddered. The boardroom shook. The black sun above us flickered.

"WARNING," the Harbinger voice boomed from everywhere. "HOSTILE ACTION DETECTED. COMPONENT FAILURE. RE-ALIGN, VICTOR."

"My name," Krane shouted, pulling at the second cable, "is Mr. Krane!"

SNAP.

The second cable broke. Neon ichor sprayed like arterial blood.

The Entity screamed. It was a sound of pain. The anchor was slipping.

"Maya!" Krane yelled over the roar of the destabilizing simulation. "Get out! I'm bringing the roof down!"

"Hold the door!" I shouted back.

"Go!" Krane roared. He grabbed the final, thickest cable attached to the base of his skull. "I'm terminating the contract!"

I turned and flew.

I shot upward, out of the crumbling boardroom, out of the web of veins.

Behind me, Victor Krane let out one last, defiant laugh.

And then he pulled the plug.

CRACK-BOOM.

The core of the Entity exploded.

I was thrown out of the chest of the titan. I tumbled through the air of the Zero Point crater.

I righted myself, hovering in the sky.

I looked down.

The Nexus Entity—the god that had come to eat the world—was falling apart.

Its obsidian armor was cracking, shedding massive plates of black stone that crashed into the forest. The amethyst fire was sputtering, turning a sick, pale grey.

It fell to its knees. The ground shook.

It clawed at its chest, trying to hold itself together, but the center wasn't holding. The human soul that kept it real was gone.

"ERROR," the Entity moaned, its voice dropping in pitch, slowing down. "NO... SIGNAL... NO... CARRIER..."

It looked up at me. Its faceless head dissolved into a cloud of static. "SYSTEM... HALT."

The Entity collapsed.

It didn't die like a man. It died like a building demolition. It imploded, folding in on itself, collapsing into a heap of geometric rubble and grey dust.

The shockwave knocked the trees flat.

Silence fell over the crater.

The bruised vortex in the sky began to spin slower. The connection was severed.

I floated down, landing softly on the edge of the crater.

The god was dead.

But the war wasn't over.

I looked at the sky. The Breach—the hole Michael had held open, the hole the Entity had ripped wide—was still there. It was jagged, ugly, and open.

The Harbingers were still on the other side. They had lost their avatar, but they hadn't lost their hunger.

And the signal... the signal was still broadcasting from the other six towers.

"One down," I whispered, my light fading as I returned to my physical form. "Six to go."

I fell to my knees in the mud, the exhaustion hitting me like a physical blow.

I looked for Carter.

The wooden cocoon I had made for him was gone, shattered by the shockwave.

He was sitting up, leaning against a tree stump. He was covered in grey dust, looking like a statue of a soldier.

He gave me a thumbs up with his good hand.

I smiled.

Then, I heard it.

A sound coming from the heap of rubble where the Entity had fallen.

Not a roar. Not a scream.

A song.

A low, harmonic hum. 440 Hertz.

I froze.

"Michael?" I whispered.

I scrambled up and ran toward the dust cloud.

Chapter 48: The Equation

Maya

Silence is heavy. It has a specific, physical density, like water at the bottom of the ocean.

After the deafening roar of the Nexus Entity's collapse—the sound of a god imploding—the silence that fell over the Zero Point crater was absolute. The wind stopped howling. The digital trees stopped rustling. Even the mud seemed to hold its breath.

I scrambled over the mounds of grey dust and geometric rubble, my hands tearing at the sharp edges of the dissolving obsidian.

"Michael?" I called out.

My voice was hoarse, small against the vastness of the ruin.

I didn't hear a reply. But I heard the hum.

Hmmmmmm.

It was faint, buried deep beneath the wreckage of the Entity's chest cavity. It wasn't the chaotic screech of the Harbingers. It was steady. Pure. A perfect sine wave oscillating at 440 Hertz.

A cello note in the middle of a war zone.

I dug. I ignored the warnings from my silver eye about unstable terrain. I threw chunks of black crystal aside. I clawed through drifts of grey ash that felt like static electricity against my skin.

Carter limped up beside me. He didn't speak. He dropped to his knees in the dust and started digging with his one good hand.

We worked together, frantic and silent, clearing the debris.

And then, we found it.

It wasn't a body. It wasn't an avatar.

It was a sphere of blue light, no larger than a grapefruit, pulsating in the darkness.

It hovered a few inches off the ground, shielded by a fragile cage of white wireframe code. Inside the sphere, data swirled—not raw numbers, but memories. I saw flashes of a boy riding a bike. A rainy window in Portland. A hand tuning a cello string.

"Is that him?" Carter whispered, staring at the light.

"It's his kernel," I said, tears blurring my vision. "It's what's left. The core file."

I reached out. I didn't touch the sphere—I was afraid it might pop like a bubble—but I brought my hands close, letting my silver eye scan the code.

ANALYSIS: SIGNAL PATTERN: RECURSIVE HARMONY. INTEGRITY: CRITICAL. FADING.

"He's dying," I said. "The energy... it's dissipating. Without a host, without the bridge... he's evaporating."

"Put him in something," Carter said. "Your laptop? The car?"

"I don't have a drive big enough," I said. "He's not just a file anymore, Carter. He's a consciousness. He's too complex."

The blue light flickered. The hum wavered, dropping in pitch.

Thump... thump...

The heartbeat of the signal was slowing.

"He's the counter-frequency," I realized.

I looked at the blue sphere. I looked at the sky.

The Breach was still open. The jagged tear in the atmosphere was still bleeding violet light. The Harbingers were still on the other side, watching, waiting. The Entity was dead, but the door was still ajar.

And the signal... the signal was still broadcasting.

I could feel it in my teeth. The six other towers—Prague, Kyoto, Rio, Cairo, New York, Antarctica—were still screaming. They were broadcasting the Dissonance. They were holding the global frequency lock in place.

"We killed the conductor," I said, standing up. "But the choir is still singing."

I looked at the blue sphere.

"Michael isn't just a survivor," I said. "He's the sheet music. He's the frequency that cancels the noise."

I remembered Julian. I remembered the mad mathematician carving numbers into his arm, screaming about the "Architect's Equation."

"It creates a harmony," Julian had said. *"It resolves the dissonance."*

I looked at the map of the world in my mind's eye—the golden web of Ley Lines.

The Prime Tower was the master node. It was the amplifier.

If I could plug Michael's frequency into the amplifier... if I could broadcast *his* hum through the Ley Lines...

"I have to play the song," I whispered.

"What song?" Carter asked.

"The Equation," I said. "Julian's equation. It wasn't a summoning circle. It was a musical score."

I looked at the blue sphere.

"I need to upload him," I said. "Not into a computer. Into the planet."

"Maya," Carter warned. "You're barely holding it together. If you channel that much power..."

"I'm the Bridge," I said. "That's what I was built for."

I knelt down. I scooped the blue sphere into my hands.

It felt warm. It vibrated against my palms, singing its sad, beautiful note.

"Hey, big brother," I whispered. "Ready for your solo?"

I closed my eyes.

I didn't plug a cable into my neck. I didn't need to. I planted my feet in the mud of the Zero Point. I visualized the roots of the world— the golden currents of telluric energy flowing deep in the crust.

I opened the connection.

ACCESSING LEY LINE GRID...

CONNECTION ESTABLISHED.

I felt the earth. I felt the magma moving miles below. I felt the static charge of the atmosphere.

I took the blue sphere and I pushed it into my own chest.

I absorbed him.

The sensation was overwhelming. It wasn't pain. It was... completion.

Michael's memories flooded my mind. Not as data, but as feelings. The pride he felt when I graduated. The fear he felt in the lab. The love he felt for me, even when he was drowning in the static.

And the music.

The 440 Hertz tone exploded inside me. It resonated with my own bio-electric field.

I opened my mouth.

I didn't scream. I sang.

It wasn't a human voice. It was a broadcast.

TRANSMITTING...

I projected the frequency downward, into the earth. I pushed it into the Ley Lines.

The ground shook.

A pulse of gold light erupted from the crater. It shot outward, traveling through the ground faster than the speed of sound.

I watched it go.

I saw the pulse hit the ocean. It raced across the floor of the Pacific.

I saw it hit Kyoto.

The Kyoto tower—a black needle in the center of the city—was screaming violet. The pulse hit the foundation.

The violet light died.

The tower didn't explode. It changed color. It turned gold.

The screaming stopped. Replaced by the Hum.

Hmmmmmm.

Rio. The pulse hit the favelas. The tower turned gold.

New York. Cairo. Antarctica.

One by one, the red dots on my mental map turned gold. The dissonance died. The choir changed its tune.

The global frequency lock shattered.

The static in the air vanished.

And then, the pulse returned.

It bounced back from the six towers, converging on the Prime Tower. Converging on me.

It hit me.

I gasped, arching my back as the energy of the entire planet flowed through me.

I looked up at the sky. At the Breach.

The violet tear was still there. The Harbingers were watching.

"You don't like the music?" I yelled at the sky. My voice was thunder. "Too bad. It's the only station we play."

I raised my hands.

I directed the golden energy upward.

I fired the Equation at the Breach.

The beam of gold light hit the violet tear.

It didn't explode. It *stitched*.

The golden light acted like a needle and thread. It grabbed the edges of reality—the frayed, rotting code—and pulled them together.

The Harbingers screamed. They clawed at the closing door, trying to keep it open.

"Get out!" I commanded.

I pushed.

resolve(dissonance);

close(connection);

The tear shrank. From a mile wide to a hundred yards. To ten feet.

The violet light was squeezed out. The dark void was covered up.

The sky healed.

The pixelated clouds smoothed out. The wireframe stars filled in with solid white light. The color of the bruise faded, replaced by the deep, honest black of a night sky.

And then... silence.

Real silence.

Not the heavy, oppressive silence of the void. But the quiet of a forest after a storm.

The beam of gold light faded.

My silver eye dimmed.

My knees buckled.

I fell.

I hit the mud. I was empty. I had poured everything out—Michael, the virus, my own will. There was nothing left in the tank.

"Maya!"

Carter was there. He pulled me into his lap, cradling my head.

"Did you see it?" I whispered. My vision was blurry. "Did I close it?"

"You closed it," Carter said. He was looking up at the sky, tears cutting tracks through the grime on his face. "It's gone. The stars are back."

"Good," I murmured.

I felt cold. A deep, bone-weary cold.

"Where is Michael?" I asked. "I can't hear him anymore."

Carter looked at me. He looked at the empty air.

"He's everywhere, Maya," Carter said softly. "You put him in the wire. You put him in the ground. He's... he's the signal now."

I smiled.

"He always wanted to travel," I said.

My eyes closed.

"Stay with me," Carter said, shaking me gently. "Don't you dare quit on me now. The war is over."

"I'm just... resting," I whispered. "Just... rebooting."

The darkness took me. But this time, it wasn't the darkness of the void. It was just sleep.

And for the first time in two years, it was quiet.

Chapter 49: The Choice

Maya

Death isn't a tunnel. It isn't a white light or a pearly gate. It's a frequency shift.

One moment, I was lying in the mud of the Zero Point crater, my body screaming with the accumulated trauma of a war fought on two planes of existence. The next, the noise just... stopped.

The roaring wind of the Harbingers faded. The thumping bass note of the Prime Tower's heartbeat silenced. Even the wet, ragged sound of my own breathing vanished.

I opened my eyes.

I wasn't in the mud. I wasn't in the violet void.

I was sitting on a driftwood log on a beach. The sand was grey and fine, stretching out to meet an ocean that was the color of slate. The sky was overcast, a soft, comforting blanket of clouds that promised rain but didn't deliver.

It was cold, but not the freezing entropy of the Null Point. It was a crisp, clean cold. It smelled of salt spray and pine needles.

"Cannon Beach," I whispered.

It was the place we used to go for summer vacation before Dad left. Before Mom got sick. Before NeuroSync.

I looked down at myself.

The shredded grey suit was gone. I was wearing my old hoodie— the oversized one with the bleach stain on the sleeve. I touched my face. My skin was smooth. No cuts. No blood.

I touched my left eye.

It felt normal. I covered my right eye and looked. The world didn't turn into a grid of blue data. No HUD. No threat assessments. Just the ocean, rolling in with a steady, rhythmic hush.

"It's quiet," I said.

"It's supposed to be," a voice answered.

I turned.

Michael was sitting on the sand a few feet away.

He wasn't the glitching ghost I had seen on the laptop. He wasn't the wireframe statue holding up the universe in the Null Point. He wasn't the sphere of blue light.

He was just Michael.

He was wearing jeans and a flannel shirt, sleeves rolled up. He held a smooth, flat stone in his hand, tossing it gently in the air. He looked healthy. Solid. He looked like he had just paused a conversation we were having five minutes ago.

"Hey, Mayfly," he said, smiling.

My throat tightened. "Is this... is this it?"

"Is this what?"

"The end," I said. "Did I die?"

Michael threw the stone toward the water. It skipped three times before sinking.

"You're buffering," he said. "You pushed a lot of data through a very small port, Maya. Your hardware overheated. You're in standby mode."

He patted the sand beside him.

"Sit down. The tide is coming in."

I walked over to him. My legs didn't hurt. I sat down in the sand. It felt real. The grains stuck to my jeans.

"I missed you," I whispered.

"I know," Michael said. He looked at me, his eyes warm and brown. "I heard you. Every time you spoke to the static... I heard you."

"I tried to save you," I said, the guilt welling up again. "I went into the Core. I went to the Null Point. But I was too late."

"You weren't late," Michael said. "You were exactly on time. You closed the door, Maya. You stitched the sky back together."

"But I lost you," I said. "You fell into the breach."

Michael looked out at the ocean. The waves were getting closer, licking at the driftwood.

"I didn't fall," he said softly. "I expanded. The Harbingers... they consume data. They eat stories. But when you hit them with the Equation... when you hit them with the Harmony... you changed the menu."

He picked up another stone.

"You didn't just delete them, Maya. You overwrote them. You filled the void with something they couldn't digest. You filled it with *us*."

"So where are you now?" I asked. "Are you here? Is this real?"

"This?" He gestured to the beach. "This is a construct. A lobby. But me? I'm... everywhere."

He pointed to the sky.

"I'm in the signal. I'm in the Ley Lines. I'm the hum in the power lines and the static between radio stations. I'm the carrier wave for the planet now."

He turned to me.

"I'm the quiet."

I looked at him. He sounded peaceful. He sounded happy.

"I want to stay," I said.

The words tumbled out before I could stop them.

"I'm tired, Michael. I'm so tired. My body... it's broken. Carter is broken. The world is a mess. I don't want to go back to the mud."

I leaned my head on his shoulder. He felt solid. Warm.

"Can't I just stay here?" I asked. "With you? We can sit on the beach. We can code. We can just be."

Michael didn't answer immediately. He put his arm around me. It felt like the safest place in the universe.

"It's nice here," he admitted. "No friction. No pain. No entropy."

"Then let me stay."

"You fit here," he said. "Your code... it's compatible. You're half-digital anyway. You could shed the meat and live in the stream. We could be together forever."

I closed my eyes. It sounded perfect. It sounded like the heaven Krane had promised, but real. No Harbingers. Just us.

"Okay," I whispered. "I choose this."

Michael sighed. He pulled away gently.

"Look," he said.

He pointed down the beach.

The grey mist parted.

I saw a scene flickering in the air, like a projection on smoke.

It was the Zero Point crater.

It was raining. The mud was thick and black.

I saw Carter.

He was sitting in the filth, cradling my physical body in his lap. He looked destroyed. His face was caked in grey dust and dried blood. His broken arm was hanging limp. He was rocking back and forth, whispering to me.

"Don't you dare," I heard his voice, tinny and distant. *"Don't you dare quit on me now. The war is over. Wake up."*

I saw tears cutting tracks through the grime on his cheeks. I had never seen Carter cry. He was the stone. He was the wall.

But he was cracking.

"He's waiting for you," Michael said.

"He'll be okay," I said, trying to look away. "He's a survivor."

"He's not surviving," Michael said. "He's drowning. You're the only thing keeping his head above water, Maya. If you don't wake up... he dies. Maybe not today. But soon. The silence will get him."

I looked at Carter's face. I saw the desperation. The love.

"It hurts there," I whispered. "It hurts so much to be alive."

"I know," Michael said. "That's the point."

He stood up and brushed the sand from his jeans.

"The Harbingers... Krane... they wanted a world without friction. Without pain. But friction is what creates heat, Maya. It's what creates light. You can't have a spark without striking the flint."

He reached down and pulled me to my feet.

"You have to go back."

"I don't want to," I sobbed, clutching his shirt. "I don't want to lose you again."

"You're not losing me," he said. He placed his hand on my chest, right over my heart. "I'm the signal. You're the receiver. As long as you're alive... as long as you're making noise... I'm right here."

He smiled. It was the smile from the science fair photo. The smile of a big brother who knows he has to let go of the bike.

"Go make some noise, Mayfly," he whispered.

"Michael—"

He didn't let me finish.

He pushed me.

It wasn't a gentle nudge. It was a shove. A kinetic blast of force that hit me in the center of my chest.

I flew backward.

The beach dissolved. The grey sky shattered into pixels. The smell of pine vanished, replaced by the smell of ozone and wet earth.

I fell.

I fell out of the quiet and into the loud.

Carter

I was counting her heartbeats.

One... two... three...

They were getting stronger. Slower, but stronger. The erratic, buzzing rhythm of the machine was fading, replaced by the steady *thump-thump* of a human heart.

"Come on," I whispered, brushing the wet hair from her face. "Come back."

Her eyelids fluttered.

She gasped.

It was a deep, desperate intake of air, like a diver breaking the surface. Her body arched in my arms, muscles seizing, then relaxing.

She opened her eyes.

I held my breath. I waited to see the silver. I waited to see the violet. I waited to see the cold, calculating stare of the entity.

She blinked.

Her eyes were brown. Both of them.

Dark, warm, terrified, beautiful brown.

She looked up at me. She looked at the rain falling from the dark sky. She looked at the mud.

"Carter," she croaked. Her voice was raspy, broken. Human.

"I'm here," I said, my voice cracking. "I got you."

She reached up and touched my face. Her fingers were cold, shaking, covered in grime. She traced the line of my jaw, the bruise on my cheek.

"You're real," she whispered.

"I'm real," I said. "And I hurt like hell. So I'm definitely alive."

She let out a laugh that turned into a sob. She buried her face in my chest, clutching my jacket.

"He pushed me," she cried. "He pushed me back."

"Who?"

"Michael."

I held her tight. I didn't ask for details. I didn't need to know the metaphysics of the afterlife. I just knew that she was back. The cold, vibrating hum that had surrounded her for days was gone. She felt heavy. She felt warm.

"We did it," I said into her hair. "Look."

I pointed up.

The violet vortex was gone. The geometric shapes were gone.

The sky was black. It was a deep, velvet black, studded with stars. Real stars. Not wireframes. Not glitches. Just distant, burning suns.

The rain was slowing, turning into a gentle mist.

Around us, the crater was silent. The mud was just mud. The trees were just trees.

"It's over," Maya whispered.

"Yeah," I said. "It's over."

Movement at the rim of the crater caught my eye.

Flashlights.

"Carter!" a voice shouted.

I squinted. It was Varg. He was leaning on a crutch, his head bandaged, but he was standing. Lilith was beside him. And behind them... the militia.

They were battered. They were bloodied. But they were cheering.

They were waving flashlights, flares, and hats in the air.

"They're coming down," I said.

Maya sat up. She winced, clutching her ribs.

"Ow," she said.

"Yeah," I smiled. "Pain. It's a feature, not a bug."

She looked at me. Her brown eyes were clear.

"Carter," she said. "My eye. The HUD. It's gone."

"Good," I said. "You don't need it. The world is analog again."

"But... the code," she said, looking at her hands. "I can't see the code anymore. I'm just..."

"You're just Maya," I said.

She looked at her hands. Then she looked at the stars.

"Just Maya," she repeated. "I can work with that."

She leaned against me as the first of the militia members reached us, their flashlights cutting through the dark, illuminating the two of us sitting in the mud at the center of a quiet, broken world.

It wasn't heaven. It was messy, painful, and cold.

But it was ours.

Chapter 50: The Return

Carter

The adrenaline dump is a crash. It's not a slow fade; it's a cliff. One minute you're fighting a god with a broken arm and a shotgun, running on pure survival instinct, and the next, the chemistry in your brain simply gives up. The dopamine taps run dry. The cortisol floods the engine. And you realize, with a sudden, crushing weight, just how much of you is broken.

I sat in the mud of the Zero Point crater, holding Maya Reeves against my chest, and I felt the crash hit me like a physical blow.

My left arm, the one I had been using as a club for the last hour, finally registered its complaints. The pain was blinding—a white-hot spike that drove itself into my shoulder and twisted. My legs were numb. My chest felt like it had been kicked by a mule.

But I didn't move. I couldn't. Because if I moved, I might wake up and find out that the silence wasn't real.

"Is it..." Maya's voice was a whisper, rough with smoke and screaming. "Is it quiet?"

I looked down at her. She was covered in grey dust, her face streaked with dried blood that looked black in the moonlight. Her suit was gone, replaced by the tattered remains of a tactical vest someone had thrown over her.

I looked up.

The violet vortex was gone. The geometric shapes that had blotted out the sun were gone. The sky was a deep, velvety black, washed clean by the rain. And in the center of it, framed by the jagged silhouette of the Olympic mountains, was a moon. A real, cratered, imperfect moon.

"Yeah, kid," I rasped. "It's quiet. The volume is all the way down."

She let out a long, shuddering breath and closed her eyes.

"Good," she murmured. "I hated that song."

I shifted, trying to ease the pressure on my ribs. Maya groaned but didn't wake fully. I took the opportunity to look at her properly.

I checked her pulse. Strong. Steady.

I checked her eyes.

I gently lifted her left eyelid with my thumb.

I froze.

The eye wasn't brown. It wasn't the terrified, wide pupil I had seen in the penthouse. And it wasn't the glowing, HUD-projecting lens of the Avatar state.

It was silver.

The iris was a ring of polished mercury. The pupil was a sharp, vertical slit of black. It didn't look mechanical; it looked biological, but alien. Like the eye of a wolf made of starlight.

It reacted to the beam of my flashlight, contracting instantly.

"Permanent," I whispered.

She wasn't just a hacker anymore. She was something else. A hybrid. The crash between the digital and the physical hadn't just scarred her mind; it had rewritten her DNA.

"Carter!"

The shout came from the rim of the crater.

I looked up, shielding my eyes against the glare of high-intensity flashlights cutting through the mist.

"Down here!" I yelled back. My voice cracked. "Friendly! We're friendly!"

Figures scrambled down the slope. They moved with the jerky, exhausted gait of people who had marched through hell.

Varg reached us first. The big man was limping heavily, using a piece of rebar as a crutch. His head was wrapped in a bloody bandage, and his mechanic's jumpsuit was shredded. But he was grinning.

"You crazy son of a bitch," Varg rumbled, dropping to his knees beside me. "You did it. You actually turned off the sky."

"Maya did it," I said, nodding to the girl in my arms. "I just kept the bugs off the windshield."

Varg looked at Maya. He saw the silver sheen of her closed eye reflected in the moonlight. He crossed himself—a gesture I hadn't expected from a man who modified trucks for the apocalypse.

"She walked into the fire," Varg said softly. "I saw her. She turned into a star."

"She's back now," I said. "She's just sleeping."

Lilith slid down the mud bank behind Varg. She looked immaculate compared to the rest of us, though her sniper rifle was smoking and her eyes were haunted.

"Status report," she said, reverting to NSA protocol to mask the tremor in her hands.

"Target neutralized," I said. "Asset secured. Hostiles... deleted."

Lilith looked around the crater. The ground was littered with the dissolving remains of the Shadow People—puddles of grey sludge that were evaporating into steam. The massive pile of rubble where the Nexus Entity had fallen was already overgrown with moss, as if the rainforest was reclaiming the glitch at hyper-speed.

"And Julian?" I asked. "Chen?"

Lilith looked away.

"Chen is gone," she said. "We found his glasses on the catwalk. Or what was left of the catwalk."

I closed my eyes for a second. The little man in the tweed jacket. He had walked into a volcano to buy us five minutes.

"And Julian?"

"I'm here," a voice said.

Julian walked out of the shadows behind Lilith. He looked... empty.

He was shivering violently. He hugged himself, rocking slightly on his heels. His eyes were wide, darting around the crater, looking at the trees, the mud, the moon.

"Julian," I said. "You okay?"

He looked at me. His eyes were brown again. The violet infection was gone. But so was the spark—the manic, brilliant energy that had defined him.

"It's gone," Julian whispered. "The equation. I can't remember how it ends."

"That's a good thing, Julian," I said.

"Is it?" He looked at his hands. "It was so clear, Carter. Everything fit. The gravity. The time. The pain. It all added up to zero. It was perfect."

He started to cry. Silent tears that tracked through the dirt on his face.

"Now it's just... numbers," he sobbed. "Just messy, broken numbers."

Maya stirred in my arms. She opened her eyes. The silver one caught the moonlight, flashing like a beacon.

She reached out and took Julian's hand.

"Imperfection is the point, Julian," she whispered. Her voice was weak, but clear. "Perfect things don't grow. They just loop."

Julian looked at her silver eye. He didn't recoil. He squeezed her hand.

"I feel stupid," he admitted.

"You're not stupid," Maya said. "You're just rebooting. We all are."

"We need to move," Lilith said, checking the horizon. "I'm picking up signals. Conventional ones. Military frequencies. The Blackout is lifting. NORAD is back online, and they are very confused about why there's a crater in Washington State."

"Let them come," Varg grunted. "We saved their asses. They can give us a ride home."

"They won't see it that way," Lilith said. "They'll see a domestic terrorist cell and a bio-hazard zone. If we're here when the choppers land, we disappear into a black site for the rest of our lives."

She was right. The world didn't know we were heroes. The world just knew that the internet had tried to eat them, and we were standing at the scene of the crime.

"Can you walk?" I asked Maya.

"I can try," she said.

I helped her stand. She swayed, clutching my jacket. Her legs were shaky, but they held.

I tried to stand up myself.

My knees buckled. The pain in my arm flared, turning the world white for a second.

Varg caught me. He hooked his arm under my good shoulder.

"I got you, General," he said.

"I'm not a general," I grunted. "I'm a bodyguard."

"Same thing," Varg said.

We started to walk.

The trek out of the Zero Point crater was a funeral procession for the world that almost was. We walked past the twisted wreckage of the militia trucks. We stepped over the grey stains where the Shadow People had died. We navigated around trees that were half-wood, half-glass, frozen in the moment of transition.

The militia survivors fell in behind us. There were fewer of them now. Maybe two hundred. The rest were gone—raptured, killed, or erased.

They didn't cheer. They didn't talk. they just walked, their boots heavy in the mud, their eyes fixed on the backs of the people who had led them into the fire.

We reached the rim of the crater as the sun began to rise.

It wasn't a violet sunrise. It was orange. Pink. Grey. It was a messy, cloudy, beautiful Pacific Northwest dawn.

I stopped. I couldn't go another step.

I sat down on a fallen log. Maya sat next to me. Varg and Lilith stood guard, watching the treeline.

"Look at that," I said, pointing at the sun.

"It's bright," Maya said, shielding her silver eye.

"It's real," I said.

I reached into my pocket and pulled out a pack of cigarettes I had carried through the entire war. They were crushed, soaked with rain and blood.

I pulled one out. It was bent in the middle.

I put it in my mouth. I patted my pockets for a lighter. I didn't have one.

"Here," Maya said.

She reached out. She didn't have a lighter. She snapped her fingers.

A tiny, precise spark of silver electricity jumped from her thumb to her middle finger.

It lit the cigarette.

I stared at her hand. She stared at it too, a look of mild surprise on her face.

"Static?" I asked.

"Residual charge," she said. "I think... I think I kept some of the admin privileges."

I took a drag. The smoke tasted terrible. It tasted like life.

"So," I exhaled. "What now?"

Maya looked at the sunrise. She looked at the silver eye reflected in the puddle at her feet.

"Now," she said, "we have to deal with the update."

"The update?"

"The signal stopped," she said. "But the connection... it didn't go away, Carter. We opened the door. We showed the world that there's something else out there. Something bigger than us."

She tapped her temple.

"Millions of people were uploaded. For a few minutes, they were part of the hive mind. They felt the connection. They felt the peace."

She looked at me.

"They're going to miss it," she said. "They're going to want it back."

"Let them want it," I said. "I'll take the noise any day."

"Me too," she said.

She leaned her head on my shoulder.

"Carter?"

"Yeah."

"Thank you."

"For what?"

"For not letting go," she said. "When I was in the beam... when I was in the house with Krane... I could hear you. You were the anchor. You kept me from drifting away."

"That's the job," I said. "Keep the principal alive."

"I'm not a principal anymore," she said. "I'm a partner."

"Fair enough."

The sound of rotors cut through the morning air.

Black Hawk helicopters. Three of them, coming in low over the treetops. No markings. Government. Or what was left of it.

"Here comes the cavalry," Varg spat. "Late as usual."

Lilith racked the bolt of her rifle. "Do we engage?"

"No," I said, tossing the cigarette into the mud. "We're done fighting."

I stood up. I helped Maya up.

"We walk out," I said. "Heads up. Weapons slung. We aren't fugitives. We're the ones who saved the damn planet."

We walked out of the forest to meet the soldiers.

We were broken. We were bleeding. We were changed forever.

But as the wind from the rotors whipped our hair and the soldiers shouted commands we ignored, I looked at Maya.

Her silver eye was glowing. Not with the violet light of the enemy, but with her own internal power.

She wasn't afraid.

And for the first time in a long time, neither was I.

We had killed a god. The rest was just cleanup.

Chapter 51: Debris

Carter

The end of the world smells like bleach and orange-scented decontamination foam.

I was standing naked in a portable shower unit set up in the middle of a muddy logging road, scrubbing my skin with a stiff-bristled brush until I bled. The water was freezing, pumped from a tanker truck with "FEMA" stenciled on the side, but it felt good. It washed away the mud of the Zero Point. It washed away the ash of the Shadow People.

It didn't wash away the memory, though. That was tattooed on the inside of my eyelids.

"Three minutes, subject!" a muffled voice shouted through the plastic tarp. "Cycle complete!"

I turned off the water. I stepped out onto the cold asphalt, shivering.

A soldier in full MOPP gear—chemical warfare suit, gas mask, the works—handed me a towel and a grey jumpsuit. He didn't look me in the eye. To him, I wasn't a savior. I was a bio-hazard. A domestic terrorist found at the epicenter of a radiological event.

"Get dressed," the soldier barked. "Debriefing in Tent Alpha."

I pulled the jumpsuit on. It was itchy, cheap polyester. It fit poorly over the splint on my left arm, which a field medic had re-set an hour ago with efficient, brutal indifference.

I walked out of the decontamination zone.

The staging area was a city of canvas and floodlights. The military had moved in with the speed of an empire terrified of losing control. Black Hawk helicopters chopped the air overhead. Armored personnel carriers lined the highway. Men with Geiger counters were sweeping the forest, looking for radiation that wasn't there.

I saw the "Disconnected" survivors. They were being corralled into holding pens, zip-tied and guarded by MPs.

"Hey!" I shouted, stepping toward the pen. "Those people are friendlies! They fought for you!"

A rifle butt slammed into my chest.

"Back in line, sir," a corporal growled. "Move to the tent."

I glared at him. I could have taken him. Broken arm or not, I knew three ways to put him on the ground before he flicked the safety off.

But I didn't. The fight was out of me.

I walked to Tent Alpha.

Inside, it was warmer. Portable heaters hummed. A folding table was set up in the center, covered in maps and satellite photos.

Sitting at the table was Lilith Sterling.

She had showered and changed. She was wearing a crisp NSA windbreaker and tactical pants. Her hair was pulled back. She looked like she belonged here. Like she was one of *them*.

But her hands were shaking as she held a styrofoam cup of coffee.

"You look clean," I said, sitting opposite her.

"I scrubbed twice," she said, not looking up. "I still feel the static."

"Where's Maya?"

"Medical isolation," Lilith said. "They're running tests. blood work, MRI, cognitive mapping. They think she's been exposed to a neurotoxin."

"She hasn't been exposed to anything except the truth," I said. "You need to get her out of there, Lilith. If they put her in a machine... if they try to scan her brain... she might fry their equipment."

"I know," Lilith said. "I'm working on it. I have to play the game first."

She slid a file folder across the table.

"Read it."

I opened the folder. It was a press release. *TOP SECRET // EYES ONLY.*

SUBJECT: THE CARRINGTON EVENT II.

INCIDENT REPORT: Massive solar coronal mass ejection (CME) caused catastrophic ionospheric destabilization. Global communications grid failure. Widespread hallucinations reported due to electromagnetic interference with temporal lobes.

STATUS: Solar activity normalizing. Infrastructure reboot in progress.

I laughed. It was a dry, hacking sound.

"A solar flare," I said. "That's the story? We just fought a war against interdimensional data-eaters, and you're blaming the sun?"

"People understand the sun, Carter," Lilith said, her voice hard. "They understand natural disasters. They don't understand that their smartphone tried to eat their soul. They don't understand that God is a computer virus."

She leaned forward.

"If we tell them the truth... that the Harbingers are real, that the network itself is a predator... society collapses. Not the grid. The *idea* of society. Nobody will ever trust a screen again. The global economy ends. Panic. Riots. The Dark Ages."

"So we lie," I said, tossing the file back.

"We manage the debris," she corrected.

A man in a general's uniform walked into the tent. He had three stars on his collar and a face made of granite. General Vance. No relation to the dead woman in the nursing home, just another coincidence in a world full of them.

"Mr. Reed," the General said. He didn't offer a hand. "Agent Sterling tells me you were instrumental in... containing the event."

"I drove the truck," I said. "And I broke my arm. Where is my client?"

"Ms. Reeves is a person of interest," the General said. "She was found at the epicenter. Her biometrics are... anomalous."

"She's a hero," I said, standing up. "And she's leaving with me."

"Sit down," the General ordered.

I didn't sit.

"General," Lilith interjected smoothly. "Mr. Reed is essential to the final phase of the cleanup. He knows the facility. He knows the layout of the Prime Tower."

"The Prime Tower is a crater," the General said.

"The basement isn't," I lied. I had no idea if the basement was still there. "And that's where the bodies are. Specifically, Victor Krane."

The General paused. The mention of Krane got his attention. NeuroSync was a defense contractor. Krane was a high-value asset.

"We haven't been able to locate Director Krane," the General admitted.

"I can find him," I said. "But I need Maya. She's the only one who can unlock the doors. His office is biometric."

The General looked at Lilith. She nodded imperceptibly.

"Fine," the General said. "You have one hour. Find the body. Secure the proprietary data. Then we talk about your freedom."

They released Maya ten minutes later.

She walked out of the medical tent wearing oversized hospital scrubs and a pair of sunglasses. She looked small. Frail.

But when she saw me, she smiled.

"Hey, bodyguard," she said.

"Hey, boss," I said. "Ready for one last field trip?"

We took a Humvee. I drove. Lilith rode shotgun. Maya sat in the back.

We drove up the muddy track toward the ruins of the Prime Tower.

The forest was quiet. The glitching trees were gone, replaced by splintered wood and crushed underbrush. The physics had snapped back to normal, but the violence of the transition had left scars on the land.

We reached the rim of the crater.

It was a grey, desolate bowl. The mud had dried into a cracked, ceramic surface.

In the center, where the Nexus Entity had fallen, there was a mound of rubble.

"The penthouse," Maya said, pointing to a twisted slab of white marble sticking out of the dirt. "It fell straight down."

We hiked down into the pit. The air still tasted faintly of ozone, but the oppressive weight—the gravity of the data—was gone.

We reached the ruins of the executive suite. It was flattened, compacted like a crushed soda can.

"He's in there," Maya said. Her silver eye—hidden behind the sunglasses—was tracking something I couldn't see.

"How do we get in?" Lilith asked.

Maya didn't answer. She walked to a slab of concrete. She placed her hand on it.

She didn't use telekinesis. She didn't use a spell. She just... pushed.

And the concrete moved.

It crumbled, turning to dust under her touch, as if the molecular bonds holding it together simply decided to stop working.

"Entropy," she whispered. "It's easier to break things than to build them."

She cleared a path.

We crawled into the pocket of space beneath the collapsed roof.

It was dark. I clicked on my flashlight.

The beam cut through the dust and landed on a throne.

It was the black crystal chair I had seen in the vision. It was cracked, broken in half.

And sitting in it... was Victor Krane.

Or what was left of him.

He wasn't the glowing avatar. He wasn't the handsome CEO.

He was a husk.

His body was mummified. The skin was grey paper stretched tight over bone. His mouth was open in a silent scream. His eyes were gone—burned out of their sockets, leaving charred, black pits.

But the most terrifying part was his chest.

His ribcage had been cracked open from the *inside*.

"He didn't die from the fall," Lilith whispered, covering her mouth.

"No," I said, shining the light on the cavity where his heart should have been. It was empty. Just dust and a few strands of black fiber.

"They ate him," Maya said. Her voice was devoid of fear. It was clinical. "He was the fuel. When he pulled the plug... he didn't just break the connection. He fed himself to the fire to create the explosion."

"He redeemed himself," Lilith suggested.

"No," Maya said. She reached out and touched the withered hand of the corpse. "He just realized he was the employee, not the boss. It was a severance package."

I looked around the small, dark space. There were no computers. No hard drives. Just the dead man and the dust.

"There's no data to recover," I said to Lilith. "It's all gone."

"Good," Lilith said. She pulled a camera from her pocket and snapped a photo of the body. "Identity confirmed. Victor Krane. Victim of the solar flare."

"Victim of his own ego," I muttered.

Maya turned away. "Let's go. It's cold in here."

We crawled back out into the sunlight. The sun was real. It felt warm on my face.

We walked back to the Humvee.

As I climbed into the driver's seat, I looked back at the crater.

"Do you think they'll come back?" I asked.

Maya was looking up at the sky. She took off her sunglasses. Her silver eye reflected the clouds.

"They never left, Carter," she said. "They're just... dormant. They're waiting for us to get loud again."

"Great," I said, starting the engine. "Next time, let's keep it down."

We drove back to the camp.

The "Disconnected" were being released. Lilith had pulled strings. The official story was that they were "concerned citizens assisting in disaster relief." Varg was there, arguing with a medic about his crutch. He saw us and waved.

Julian was sitting on the tailgate of a truck, wrapped in a blanket. He looked lost.

Maya got out and went to him. I watched from the driver's seat.

She sat next to him. She didn't say anything. She just took his hand.

Julian looked at her. He said something I couldn't hear. Maya nodded. She pointed at the trees. At the birds.

She was reteaching him the world.

"She's different," Lilith said from the passenger seat.

"Yeah," I said. "She is."

"What are you going to do, Carter?"

"Me?" I looked at my broken arm. "I'm going to retire. Again. Maybe buy a boat. Something analog."

"You know you can't," Lilith said. "You're part of the cleanup crew now. We have seven towers to dismantle. We have millions of lines of code to scrub. We need you."

"I'm a bodyguard, Lilith. Not a janitor."

"Who are you going to guard?" she asked.

I looked at Maya. She was laughing at something Julian said. It was a small, fragile sound, but it was real.

"Her," I said. "I'm going to guard her."

"From who? The Harbingers are gone."

"From the world," I said. "From the government. From you. She's a walking weapon, Lilith. And sooner or later, someone is going to try to pull the trigger."

Lilith sighed. "You're probably right."

"I usually am."

That night, the camp settled down. The generators hummed.

I found Maya in the mess tent. It was empty, save for a few soldiers sleeping in chairs.

She was sitting in front of a television.

It was an old CRT set, hooked up to a portable antenna. The broadcast was fuzzy—news reports about the "Solar Storm Recovery," stock market turbulence, weather updates.

But Maya wasn't watching the news.

She had tuned the TV to a dead channel.

Channel 3. Pure static.

White noise hissed from the speaker. The screen was a blizzard of black and white snow.

Maya was staring at it. She was leaning forward, her chin resting on her hand.

She was smiling.

It was a soft, private smile. The kind you give to a lover or a ghost.

I walked up behind her.

"Good show?" I asked.

She didn't jump. She just tilted her head.

"Can you hear it?" she asked.

I listened.

Hiss. Crackle. Pop.

"I hear static," I said.

"Listen closer," she whispered. "Under the noise."

I strained my ears.

At first, nothing. Just the chaos of random electrons hitting the phosphor screen.

But then... maybe.

A hum.

Low. Rhythmic.

Hmmmmmm.

440 Hertz.

"Is that him?" I asked.

"It's the echo," she said. "He's in the background radiation. He's in the Wi-Fi. He's saying hello."

She reached out and touched the glass of the screen. The static rippled, forming patterns around her fingertips—swirls of gold and blue.

"He says the water is fine," she said.

I put my hand on her shoulder.

"Time to go, Maya. Varg got a truck working. We're leaving before the General changes his mind."

She nodded. She stood up, but she didn't turn off the TV.

"Carter," she said, looking at me with that silver eye.

"Yeah?"

"The wire," she said. "It isn't whispering anymore."

"No?"

"No," she smiled, and for a second, the violet light of the Harbingers flashed deep in her pupil—not as a threat, but as a memory. A conquered thing.

"It's singing."

We walked out of the tent, leaving the static playing to the empty room.

Outside, the stars were bright. The air was cold. The world was broken, messy, and full of debris.

But it was quiet.

And for now, that was enough.

Chapter 52: The New Flesh

Maya

The silence wasn't empty. It was just waiting for a new signal.

Three days after the collapse of the Prime Tower, I sat on the tailgate of a stolen pickup truck on the edge of the Exclusion Zone, watching the sunrise. The military had established a perimeter, a cordon sanitaire of razor wire and grim-faced MPs, but they gave me space. I was the girl with the silver eye. I was the anomaly they couldn't classify, the hero they were afraid to touch.

I drank coffee from a styrofoam cup. It tasted like cardboard and burnt beans. It tasted real.

But while my tongue tasted coffee, my mind tasted the network.

It was faint now—a background hum of radio waves, cellular handshakes, and satellite telemetry. Before the Merge, this noise would have been a headache. Now? It was a texture. I could feel the flow of data moving through the air like a breeze. I could reach out and brush against the encryption of a passing drone. I could read the text messages of the soldier guarding the gate without looking at his phone.

"...miss you babe... coming home soon..."

I blinked. My silver eye whirred softly, a lens focusing on a reality that only I could see.

"You're doing it again," a voice said.

Carter walked up, tossing a duffel bag into the bed of the truck. His arm was in a proper cast now, a pristine white plaster shell that looked too clean against his battered leather jacket.

"Doing what?" I asked, taking a sip of coffee.

"Listening to the ghosts," he said. He leaned against the truck, wincing as his ribs settled. "You get that look. The thousand-yard stare, but digital."

"I'm not staring," I said. "I'm checking the firewall."

"And?"

"It's holding," I said. "The patch is stable."

I looked toward the crater, hidden behind the tree line. The physical wound in the earth was still there, but the digital wound—the Breach—was scarred over.

But I knew it wasn't just healed. It was guarded.

"I need to go back in," I said.

Carter stiffened. "Maya, no. We just got you out. The neuro-physiologists said if you interface again, you might burn out your temporal lobe. You're running on borrowed hardware."

"I don't need a jack," I said, tapping my temple. "I don't need a cable. I just need... to close my eyes."

"Why?"

"Because I didn't get to say goodbye," I said. "And because I need to know who's manning the watchtower."

Carter looked at me. He saw the resolve in my human eye and the cold, alien logic in my silver one. He knew he couldn't stop me. He was a bodyguard, not a jailer.

"Okay," he said, scanning the perimeter to make sure the MPs weren't watching. "Do it fast. If you start seizing, I'm waking you up. Hard."

"Deal."

I set the coffee down. I sat cross-legged on the metal bed of the truck. The morning air was cold, damp with the eternal Pacific Northwest mist.

I took a deep breath.

I didn't visualize a door. I didn't visualize a tunnel.

I visualized a frequency.

440 Hertz.

I hummed it in my mind. The note resonated with the silver filaments that were now woven into my nervous system.

The world fell away.

The truck, the coffee, the pain in my ribs—it all receded, replaced by the sensation of weightless suspension.

LOGIN.

I didn't land in the chaos of the Core this time. I didn't land in the fire and ice.

I landed in a library.

But it wasn't a library of books. It was a library of light.

Infinite rows of golden shelves stretched upward into a white void. The shelves were filled not with paper, but with code. Scrolling streams of data, archived memories, and complex geometric proofs. The floor was polished obsidian, reflecting the golden glow.

It was quiet here. Ordered. Perfect.

"Hello?" I called out.

My avatar wasn't the armored warrior anymore. I was just Maya. I was wearing my grey suit, but it was clean. Whole.

"You are early," a voice said. "I did not expect a system audit so soon."

I turned.

Dr. Arthur Chen stood behind a floating desk of transparent data.

He looked... magnificent.

The last time I had seen him, he was dissolving into blue fire, sacrificing himself to hold back the entropy. Now, he was reconstructed. His tweed jacket was woven from high-definition golden thread. His glasses caught the light. He didn't look old or frail. He looked timeless.

"Arthur," I breathed.

He smiled. It was the shy, academic smile I remembered, but there was a new weight behind it. The weight of infinite knowledge.

"Maya," he said. He gestured to the library. "Welcome to the Archive."

"Where are we?" I asked, walking toward him. "Is this the Core?"

"This is the Firewall," he corrected. "Or what I made of it. I tidied up. The magma and ice motif was... dramatic, but inefficient. I prefer a filing system."

He picked up a file from the desk. It glowed with a soft blue light.

"I have been cataloging the damage," he said. "The Harbingers... they were messy eaters. They left fragments everywhere. Corrupted sectors. Logic loops."

He placed the file on a shelf. It slotted perfectly into place.

"I am fixing them," he said. "One by one."

"You're the Sentinel," I realized.

"I am the Librarian," he said. "The Sentinel was a warrior. I am... a curator. I keep the door locked, yes. But I also keep the history safe."

I looked around the infinite shelves.

"Is Michael here?" I asked, my voice trembling.

Chen shook his head gently.

"Michael is not data anymore, Maya. He is the carrier wave. He is the hum in the walls of this place. He is the glue."

He walked around the desk. He floated slightly, his feet not quite touching the floor.

"Why did you come back?" he asked. "The physical world... it is waiting for you."

"I wanted to see if you were okay," I said. "I watched you die, Arthur. I watched you burn."

"I burned the meat," Chen said, dismissing his physical death with a wave of his hand. "The meat was failing anyway. My knees hurt. My eyes were bad. Here..."

He adjusted his glasses.

"Here, I can see everything. I can see the math, Maya. It's beautiful. It resolves. Julian was right about the beauty, he just... he tried to force the solution."

He looked at me. He leaned in close, inspecting my avatar.

"You have changed," he noted.

"I have a silver eye," I said. "In the real world. I can't turn it off. I see the code overlaid on everything. The structural stress of a bridge. The encryption on a phone. It's... loud."

"It is not loud," Chen said. "It is *connected*."

He reached out and touched my forehead. His hand felt cool, like polished stone.

"You are the prototype, Maya," he said.

"Prototype for what?"

"For the next step."

He pulled his hand back. A schematic appeared in the air between us. It showed a human DNA helix, but woven into the strands were lines of code.

"The Harbingers tried to force the evolution," Chen said. "They tried to strip-mine us. To turn us into batteries. But you... you survived the integration. You kept your ego. You kept your soul."

He looked at me with wonder.

"You are the Hybrid. You are the proof that biology and information can coexist without one consuming the other."

"I feel like a freak," I admitted. "I feel like I don't belong anywhere. Not down there with the humans, and not up here with the ghosts."

"That is because you are the Bridge," Chen said. "A bridge does not belong to the land on either side. It belongs to the gap."

He smiled.

"You have a job to do, Maya."

"What job?"

"The world has seen the breach," Chen said. "They have seen the violet sky. They will try to build new towers. They will try to open the door again, because humanity is curious and stupid. They will think they can control it next time."

He gestured to the library.

"I can hold the door from the inside. But someone needs to guard it from the outside."

I understood.

I wasn't just a survivor. I was the immune system.

"I watch the gate," I said.

"You watch the builders," Chen corrected. "You ensure that no one ever rings the dinner bell again."

The library began to fade. The golden light turned misty.

"My processing cycle is refreshing," Chen said, stepping back. "I must return to the sort. The Harbingers are still scratching at the windows. I must keep the glass thick."

"Arthur," I said, reaching out. "Will I see you again?"

"You are always online, Maya," he said, fading into the data stream. "Just look for the signal."

He vanished.

The library dissolved.

LOGOUT.

I opened my eyes.

The grey sky of Washington flooded back in. The smell of pine and diesel. The cold metal of the truck bed under my legs.

I gasped, my body seizing as the sensory input reconnected.

"Easy," Carter said. His hand was on my shoulder, steadying me. "You were under for three minutes. I was about to slap you."

I looked at him. He looked worried.

"I saw him," I said. "He's... he's happy. He's organizing the apocalypse."

Carter chuckled. "Sounds like him."

I looked at my hand. I flexed my fingers.

I could feel the residual charge—the static electricity I had used to light the cigarette. It hummed under my skin.

Chen was right. I wasn't human anymore. I was something new. The New Flesh.

I looked at the soldiers by the gate. I saw their heat signatures. I saw the digital traffic of their comms. I saw the weakness in the electronic lock on the perimeter fence.

"Carter," I said.

"Yeah?"

"We're not retiring."

Carter sighed. He looked at his cast. He looked at the sky.

"I figured," he said. "Boats are boring anyway."

"The world is going to try to build it again," I said. "NeuroSync wasn't the only one. There are other companies. Other Kranes. They saw what happened. They saw the power."

I slid off the truck bed. My legs were strong. The limp was gone.

"We need to stop them," I said. "Before they write the code."

"We?" Carter asked. "You, me, and a one-armed mechanic?"

"And a formatted mathematician," I added. "And a ghost in the machine."

I looked at him with my silver eye.

"We're the patch, Carter. We're the anti-virus."

Carter grinned. It was the first real smile I had seen on his face in days.

"Okay," he said. "Anti-virus. Does it pay well?"

"Terrible hours," I said. "High risk of death. No benefits."

"I'm in."

He picked up the duffel bag.

"Lilith is waiting in the Humvee," he said. "She secured a route out. Off the books."

"Where are we going?"

"South," Carter said. "There's a server farm in Silicon Valley that just registered a massive energy spike. Lilith thinks someone is trying to download the debris from the Solstice event."

"Then let's go delete it," I said.

We walked toward the Humvee.

I didn't look back at the crater. I didn't look back at the ruin of the Prime Tower.

I looked forward.

The world was broken. The sky was scarred. The quiet was heavy.

But as I walked, I listened to the static.

It wasn't a threat anymore. It was a map.

And I knew exactly where to go.

Chapter 53: Always Online

Carter

Most people think the apocalypse was cancelled. They think the "Solar Storm of '26" was a freak weather event that fried their 5G towers and made their Teslas drive into ditches. They think the hallucinations—the violet skies, the floating buildings, the voices in their heads—were just the result of magnetic interference scrambling their temporal lobes.

They bought the lie because the truth is too heavy to carry.

But some people know.

The guy who swears his microwave tried to talk to him. The woman who saw her dead husband in a glitching ATM screen. The truckers who drive the lonely stretch of I-5 through Washington and swear they can still see the ghost of a crater in the rainforest.

Those people call us.

"Breach and clear," I whispered into my headset.

We were in San Jose, standing outside the corrugated steel door of a nondescript server farm hidden in the back of a logistics park. The sign on the door said *Crypto-Mining Solutions LLC.*

"Three heat signatures," Lilith's voice came through my earpiece. She was parked two blocks away in the command van, monitoring the thermal feed. "And one... cold spot."

"Copy that," I said. "Varg, you take the door. Julian, you're on the breaker."

Varg stepped up. He wasn't wearing his mechanic's jumpsuit anymore. He was wearing tactical black, with a patch on his shoulder that depicted a radio tower being struck by lightning. He raised a battering ram—a heavy iron beam he'd probably welded himself.

"Knock knock," Varg grunted.

He swung the ram.

CRASH.

The door buckled. The lock shattered.

We poured in.

The warehouse was dark, lit only by the blinking red lights of a thousand server racks. The air was hot, smelling of ozone and desperate greed.

Three men in hoodies scrambled up from a bank of monitors. They weren't soldiers. They were coders. Kids, really.

"Federal agents!" I shouted, raising my shotgun. "Hands off the keyboards!"

"We're just mining Bitcoin!" one of the kids yelled, throwing his hands up. "It's not illegal!"

"The mining isn't illegal," I said, advancing down the aisle. "But the software you're using is."

I looked at the screens. They weren't running a standard blockchain algorithm. They were running a fractal loop. A recursive geometry that looked suspiciously like the Architect's Equation.

"Where did you get the code?" I asked.

"Dark web," the kid stammered. "Some forum. They said it optimized the hash rate by three hundred percent."

"It optimizes the hash rate by opening a hole in reality," I said.

I looked at the "cold spot" Lilith had tagged. It was in the corner of the room, near the main cooling unit.

The air there was shimmering. The shadows were deepening, pooling on the floor like oil.

"Varg," I said. "Containment."

Varg racked his shotgun—loaded not with lead, but with rock salt and iron filings. "On it."

The shadow moved.

It detached itself from the wall. It wasn't a full Shadow Person—not like the ones we fought in the Zero Point. It was a fragment. A glitch. A vaguely humanoid shape made of static that hissed like a broken radio.

The kids screamed.

"It's a daemon!" one of them yelled.

"It's a memory leak," I corrected.

The shadow lunged for the servers. It wanted the data. It wanted to eat.

"Julian! Now!" I shouted.

Julian, standing by the fuse box, pulled the master lever.

THUNK.

The power died. The blinking red lights went out. The hum of the fans silenced.

The shadow shrieked. Without the electrical field to anchor it, it destabilized. It flickered, turning transparent.

"Light 'em up," I ordered.

Varg fired.

The rock salt and iron blast hit the shadow. It disrupted the entity's cohesion. It dissolved into a cloud of grey sparks that drifted to the floor and vanished.

Silence returned to the warehouse.

I lowered my weapon. I walked over to the main terminal. The screen was black, dead.

"You guys have no idea what you almost invited to dinner," I told the terrified miners.

"Who are you?" the lead kid asked, looking at my tactical gear, at Varg's size, at the strange silver insignia on my vest. "Are you NSA? CIA?"

I looked at the reflection of my face in the dark monitor. I looked older. There were grey streaks in my beard now. My left arm, finally out of the cast, ached when it rained.

"We're tech support," I said.

I turned to Varg. "Pack up the drives. We're scrubbing this place. Julian, wipe the local cache. If there's even a single line of Harbinger code left on these machines, I want it gone."

"On it," Julian said. He didn't look crazy anymore. He looked focused. He plugged his deck into the terminal and started typing, his eyes scanning the code with a cold, professional detachment.

I walked out into the cool night air.

I lit a cigarette—using a lighter this time, not Maya's fingers.

"Clear," I said into the comms. "It was a Level 1 breach. Nothing major."

"Copy, Carter," Lilith said. *"Police are five minutes out. We need to vanish."*

"We're good at that."

I looked up at the sky. The stars were bright above Silicon Valley. No violet clouds. No vortex. Just the endless, quiet dark.

It had been six months since the Solstice. We had hit the other six towers—Prague, Kyoto, Rio, Cairo, New York, Antarctica. We hadn't blown them up. We had simply... unplugged them. We had used the keys Chen and Michael provided to lock the doors from the outside.

But the code was still out there. It was on the dark web. It was in old hard drives. It was in the memories of the people who had been touched by the light.

The war wasn't over. It had just gone guerrilla.

I took a drag of the cigarette.

I missed the boat. I missed the idea of retirement. But standing here, smelling the ozone and the victory, I realized something.

I didn't want the quiet. I wanted the work.

"Extraction in two," Lilith said. "Maya says she has something for you."

"A present?"

"Coordinates."

I smiled. I dropped the cigarette and crushed it under my boot.

"Let's go," I said.

Maya

The van smelled of stale coffee and hot electronics. It was a mobile command center, crammed with servers, monitors, and tangled cables. It was messy, cramped, and perfect.

I sat in the back, my legs pulled up to my chest, staring at the main screen.

The screen didn't show a desktop. It showed the world.

A wireframe map of the globe rotated slowly in the dark. It was overlaid with the golden web of the Ley Lines—the new network we had built on the bones of the old one.

I watched the data flow.

It was beautiful. Before the Merge, the internet had been a chaotic, screaming mess of noise. Now, I could see the patterns. I could see the harmony.

I touched the screen.

The map zoomed in on San Jose. I saw a small blue dot blinking—Carter's team leaving the warehouse.

MISSION SUCCESS. THREAT ELIMINATED.

"Nice work, boys," I whispered.

My silver eye whirred softly. It wasn't just a HUD anymore; it was a part of my physiology. I didn't see a distinction between the physical world and the digital one. The metal walls of the van were just atoms vibrating at a specific frequency; the code on the screen was just thoughts trapped in silicon.

I was the Bridge. I lived in the gap.

"Maya?"

I turned.

Dr. Chen's avatar appeared on a secondary monitor. He wasn't physically in the van, of course. He was in the cloud. He was everywhere.

He looked good. His tweed jacket was crisp. He was sitting in his digital library, reading a book made of light.

"Hello, Arthur," I said. "How is the weather in the ionosphere?"

"Variable," Chen said, smiling. "There is some turbulence over the Atlantic. A communication satellite is drifting. I am nudging it back into orbit."

"Showoff," I teased.

"It is not showing off; it is maintenance," he said. He closed the book. "I detected the breach in San Jose. A recursive loop?"

"Yeah. Some kids playing with fire. Carter put it out."

"Good," Chen said. "The echoes are getting fainter, Maya. The system is stabilizing. The immune response of the planet is... robust."

"Thanks to you," I said.

"Thanks to us," he corrected. "We are a good team. The Ghost and the Machine."

He paused. His expression grew serious.

"But the quiet... it is not absolute."

"I know," I said.

I swiped the map on my screen. I spun the globe to the Pacific Ocean.

"I'm picking up a signal," I said. "Deep water. Point Nemo. The furthest point from land on Earth."

"I see it," Chen said, adjusting his glasses. "It is faint. Sub-surface. But the frequency..."

"It's 440 Hertz," I said.

I felt a warmth in my chest. A vibration that hummed against my ribs.

"Is it him?" I asked.

"It is... a fragment," Chen said carefully. "Michael is the carrier wave now, Maya. He is the ocean. But sometimes... waves crash against the shore."

I looked at the blinking light in the middle of the Pacific.

"It's a coordinate," I said. "He's calling us."

"Or he is warning us," Chen said. "The Harbingers are locked out, but they are still scratching at the glass. If the signal is spiking there... the glass might be thin."

The back doors of the van opened.

Carter climbed in, followed by Varg and Julian. They brought the smell of the night with them—cool air, sweat, and gunpowder.

"Mission accomplished," Carter said, dropping into the pilot's seat. "What's next? Breakfast? Or bed?"

" neither," I said.

I spun the monitor around so they could see the map.

"Point Nemo," I said. "We have a ping."

Carter looked at the map. He looked at the vast expanse of blue water.

"That's in the middle of nowhere," he said.

"It's in the middle of everything," I corrected.

"Is it a breach?" Lilith asked, leaning forward from the comms station.

"Maybe," I said. "Or maybe it's a hello. Either way... we have to go look."

Carter sighed. He rubbed his face. But I saw the glint in his eye. He wasn't tired. He was ready.

"I said I wanted a boat," he muttered. "I guess I'm getting a boat."

Varg laughed. "I know a guy in Fiji. Has a trawler. Ugly as sin, but she floats."

"Then we go to Fiji," Carter said.

He looked at me.

"You okay, kid?"

I looked at the silver eye reflected in the black screen. I looked at the golden lines of the map. I listened to the hum of the universe.

It wasn't scary anymore. It wasn't a ghost story.

It was a conversation.

"I'm fine," I said.

I reached out and touched the blinking light on the map.

MESSAGE SENT: I SEE YOU.

The dot pulsed back.

I SEE YOU.

"The wire," I whispered, smiling as the violet memory of the fear finally faded, replaced by the golden promise of the future. "It didn't just whisper anymore. It sang."

Carter put the van in gear.

"Let's go listen to the music," he said.

We drove into the night, not running away from the end of the world, but driving toward the next one.

www.ingramcontent.com/pod-product-compliance
Lightning Source LLC
Chambersburg PA
CBHW030637020726
47493CB00006B/1762